VISITING HER NEXT-DOOR NEIGHBOR

Holding the pants up, she liked what she saw. They were even better than the shorts she had made. A nice silhouette. Slim through the hips and tight enough through the seat to showcase a fabulous backside. Excited, she grabbed the pants, went downstairs, dashed outside, and crossed over to Colt's house.

It took a while but he finally opened the door in his boxer shorts and a heavy dose of sleep in his voice. That's when it hit her that all his lights had been out.

"Everything okay?" he asked.

No shirt, just his Gerard Butler chest staring her in the face. And his hair sticking up on end should've been the opposite of hot. But somehow it worked for him and the temperature rose twenty degrees.

She took one look at his sexy, sleepy self, then at her watch, and flushed with embarrassment. Here she was on his doorstep at two a.m. in the same dress she wore to dinner. This could only look like one thing.

"Sorry," she stammered, and started to go.

"Delaney."

She turned around to face him and that's when he kissed her. Soft and slow at first, then exploring her mouth. Delaney leaned in, reveling in the taste and feel of him—so good— realizing that if she let this go any further, they'd wind up doing a whole lot more than kissing. But as he took the kiss further, tangling his hands in her hair and holding her head so he could go deeper, she let him. . . .

Books by Stacy Finz

The Nugget Series
GOING HOME
FINDING HOPE
SECOND CHANCES
STARTING OVER
GETTING LUCKY
BORROWING TROUBLE
HEATING UP
RIDING HIGH
FALLING HARD

The Garner Brothers
NEED YOU

Collections
THE MOST WONDERFUL TIME
(with Fern Michaels, Shirlee McCoy, and Sarah Title)

Published by Kensington Publishing Corporation

Need You

STACY FINZ

ZEBRA BOOKS
KENSINGTON PUBLISHING CORP.
http://www.kensingtonbooks.com

ZEBRA BOOKS are published by

Kensington Publishing Corp.
119 West 40th Street
New York, NY 10018

Copyright © 2017 by Stacy Finz

All Kensington titles, imprints, and distributed lines are available at special quantity discounts for bulk purchases for sales promotion, premiums, fund-raising, educational, or institutional use.

Special book excerpts or customized printings can also be created to fit specific needs. For details, write or phone the office of the Kensington Sales Manager: Attn.: Sales Department. Kensington Publishing Corp., 119 West 40th Street, New York, NY 10018. Phone: 1-800-221-2647.

Zebra and the Z logo Reg. U.S. Pat. & TM Off.

First Printing: August 2017
ISBN-13: 978-1-4201-4190-0
ISBN-10: 1-4201-4190-2

eISBN-13: 978-1-4201-4191-7
eISBN-10: 1-4201-4191-0

10 9 8 7 6 5 4 3 2 1

Printed in the United States of America

To my wonderful family

ACKNOWLEDGMENTS

It takes a village to write a book and I am truly blessed to have an amazing one. A huge thanks to Kristi Yanta, the Picky Editor, for your mad skills and impeccable editorial guidance. I am so thankful to have you in my life. A special shout out to Carolyne Zinko and Tony Bravo for advising me on all things fashion. Any mistakes, technical, or otherwise, are mine. And Tricia Linden thanks for saving my behind. You are a wonderful friend and supporter and I'm thrilled to have you onboard.

To my editor, John Scognamiglio: wow! Eleven books and two novellas together and we're still going strong. You are the best and I love working with you. Thanks for everything you do. An enormous thank you to my agent, Melissa Jeglinski of the Knight Agency, who's my biggest cheerleader and my greatest asset. Boy did I hit the agent lottery. And to all the folks at Kensington Publishing, including Alexandra Nicolajsen, Michelle Forde, Lauren Jernigan, Kimberly Richardson, and Jane Nutter: You guys rock!

Chapter One

Colt Garner wacked his hand over the clock radio, searching for the button to make Lisa Laredo's voice stop. At first, in his foggy state, he'd thought they were back on stage, doing a duet. But the infernal song had actually awakened him from a deep sleep.

He turned on his side, took one look at the time, and muttered, "Shit." In his slightly inebriated state, he must've set the alarm wrong the night before and was now running late for a meeting with the mayor, who more than likely wanted to fire him.

Warm sunlight streamed through his window, making him shield his eyes with the back of his hand. Another hot August day in Glory Junction, California. Which meant record numbers of people would flood the town over the weekend to raft on the Glory River, waterski on Lake Paiute, and hike the Sierra mountains. In the winter, the tourists came for the snow. The town boasted five ski resorts, and from Main Street you could see chairlifts and gondolas going up and down the mountainsides. St. Moritz of the West is what some people called it, but the town hadn't always been this affluent. When Colt's parents had settled here it had been home to ranchers and ski bums and a haven for back-to-the-land hippies.

But it hadn't taken long for the rest of the world to discover the hamlet, only three and a half hours northeast of San Francisco and seven hours from Los Angeles. Professional athletes came for the world-class skiing, rock climbing, and river rapids. Tech moguls and celebrities for the cachet and property values of a picturesque ski town in the Mother Lode. It even had a private airport so part-timers could fly in for quick stays at their lake houses or ski-in condos.

The growth was great for his family, who owned and operated Garner Adventure, an extreme-sport and tour company. But as chief of the Glory Junction Police Department, not so much. Most days he was understaffed for the barrage of tourists and weekenders. Still, he wouldn't trade the job for anything.

Colt finally found the radio knob and shut the music off. Every time he heard the song it reopened old wounds. Wounds he wanted permanently scabbed over. The phone rang, further reminding him that he needed to get out of bed, pronto. He checked the caller ID and answered.

"I'm running late," he said by way of greeting. "What's up?"

"Good show last night." His usually workaholic brother, TJ, along with the rest of his family, had sat through three sets. It meant a lot to Colt, especially TJ, who had his hands full running Garner Adventure.

"Not bad, considering how rusty I am." It was the first time he'd had a gig in months. Between getting called out on police emergencies and being asked to pick up the slack at his family's company, Colt was lucky if he got a full night's sleep, let alone have the time to play music.

"You didn't sound rusty to me," TJ said. "What are you doing Sunday?"

It was Colt's only day off. "Sleeping."

"We had a last minute guide cancellation and I was wondering if you had a couple of hours to lead a river-rafting tour. Before you say no, it's a bachelorette party. Bikinis."

Colt didn't care if the women were naked, he wanted his day off. "I thought you were hiring more guides."

TJ let out a breath. "We did. We're still having trouble keeping up with the amount of business we're getting."

"Try harder."

"Working on it. So, can you do it? Come on, I went to your show. That's three hours I'll never get back."

Colt swung his feet off the bed and scrubbed his hand through his hair. "Yeah, all right." He'd fit it in somehow. "I hope you can afford the three hours for my funeral when I die of sleep deprivation. Maybe do a eulogy, if it's not too much trouble for you. I've got a meeting with Pond, so gotta go." Colt hung up before his younger brother could rope him into something else.

In the kitchen, he started a pot of coffee and headed for a quick shower. His uniform, the only clean one left in the closet, could've used a good pressing, but he put it on anyway, along with his gun belt and badge. Colt filled a mug with caffeine. If he could've mainlined it, he would've.

His cell vibrated in his pocket, making him jump, and he sloshed the coffee over the rim of his cup and all over his shirt.

"Shit!" Hot.

He grabbed a dish towel and futilely tried to clean himself. Giving up, he stuck his chest over the sink and turned on the sprayer. As he dripped onto the kitchen floor, he checked the missed call. Win, the youngest of his three brothers. He thought about changing his shirt, caught sight of the clock, and grabbed another towel from the drawer to blot himself dry the best he could. A fresh shirt and Win would have to wait. As it was, he was cutting it too close for comfort.

On the way out the door, Colt snagged his keys, put on his aviators, and jogged down his back porch stairs. If he avoided Main Street, he might be able to get to city hall on time.

"Dammit." His neighbor's car blocked his cruiser. Again.

The two of them shared an easement road that forked off onto their respective driveways and garages. Like most of the homes in Glory Junction, his was on a hillside with a driveway so steep it should've been illegal. And because his house was on a small lot, there was no place to turn around. Street parking didn't exist on account of there being no curbs, just an occasional dirt shoulder barely wide enough for a Smart car. So Colt liked to park on the shoulder of the easement for quick access to his vehicle. There wasn't room for two cars, yet she continually parked there anyway.

He crossed over to her ostentatious mini mansion, climbed the front porch, and knocked on the door. Colt knew she was home. Yet it took her so long to answer, he considered going inside, justifying it as a welfare check.

She finally came out in exercise clothes that looked too nice to work out in. The top was some kind of wraparound thing that dipped low, giving him a nice view of her cleavage. He tried really hard not to look, but failed miserably. He chalked it up to being a degenerate and not to the fact that she had a spectacular rack. She was doing some leering of her own, her eyes roving over his chest.

"What happened to your shirt?" she asked.

He glanced down to see what she was talking about. Oh yeah, the coffee.

Colt cocked his head at her Tesla. "I thought we talked about the parking situation . . . how a lot of times I need to get out of here in a hurry."

"And I thought I explained to you that I need to be close to the outlet to plug in my car."

"Don't you have one in your garage or near your garage?" The house had a security system that rivaled most banks'. Colt figured the builder hadn't skimped on electrical outlets.

"I told you this already. Clearly you weren't listening. It's the only two-hundred-forty-volt outlet. It was installed on a fifty-amp circuit breaker. They're not like your run-of-the-mill house outlets."

Thanks for the lesson on electrical capacity, he wanted to say, but didn't have time to argue with her. "Delaney, work with me here, okay? I've got to be somewhere."

"What, are they having a special on donuts at Tart Me Up?"

He rolled his eyes. "Clever. Because I never heard that one before."

She glanced at her watch and sighed. "Fine. But you do realize that you only have the easement because I allow it. It's my land."

"The easement has been on the books longer than either of us has lived here." Before she and her husband bought the property and tore down the perfectly fine house that occupied it to build the Palace of Versailles.

"I can change that." She squinted her blue eyes at him, then turned and went inside, giving him a good look at her spandex ass.

This time, he forced himself not to stare, raising his gaze to take in her black hair, which made him think of the song "Galway Girl" and laugh to himself. He was in no danger of losing his heart to Delaney Scott, not like the guy in the song. She might be beautiful but she was a royal pain in the butt. Besides, the last time he'd fallen for one of Glory Junction's resident celebrities . . . Well, let's just say he wouldn't be doing it again. Ever. Not if he wanted to survive. Because while some men drank their blues away, he binged on BASE jumping, parachute skiing, cave diving, and other death-defying sports.

A few minutes later, she returned with keys. He followed

Delaney and waited while she unplugged her car. At this rate, Colt was in danger of missing his meeting altogether. The mayor would assume that he was being insubordinate. Ordinarily, he couldn't care less what the mayor thought. Colt's job had always been nonpolitical. He'd served under two different mayors and had been largely left alone to run the department as he'd seen fit. But the Honorable Carter Pond had a thing for micromanaging—and promptness.

Maybe Colt was being paranoid—his brothers certainly thought so—but Pond seemed to be gunning for him. So strolling in twenty minutes after their scheduled meeting wasn't going to help his cause. Not one bit.

"I'm probably missing a conference call right now," she said, her voice clipped.

"I'm sorry." He probably should've left it at that, but couldn't help adding, "You wouldn't have, if you hadn't blocked me in."

"You shouldn't have parked so close to my house and outlet."

"You have a driveway. Just use it."

"So do you."

They sounded like two little kids bickering in the sandbox. Most days, Colt was an easygoing guy. Sometimes, downright congenial. But the day had gotten off to a bad beginning—starting with the damned song—and he figured it was only going downhill from here. "We need to figure this out," he said, not wanting to fight with her anymore. "But I don't have time to do it now."

Colt got in his cruiser and watched through his rearview mirror as she pulled the Tesla up her drive. Difficult woman. Why she'd moved to the mountains full time was beyond him. She was a big-deal fashion designer from LA. His sister-in-law, Hannah, carried some of her stuff at Glorious Gifts on Main Street. Delaney's husband, according to town gossip, was no longer in the picture. Which was too bad because when he was, they rarely, if ever, came up, just letting that big house of theirs sit empty. And quiet.

Colt pulled out and drove to city hall. By the time he parked he was fifteen minutes late. By the time he made it to the mayor's office, Pond was good and pissed off.

"Glad you could show up, Chief," he said with derision.

"Sorry I'm late . . . small emergency." It wasn't exactly a lie.

"With your family's business?" Pond motioned for Colt to take a seat. "You seem to spend a lot of time there."

Colt did, but never on the city's dime. "It had nothing to do with Garner Adventure."

Pond got up and came around his desk. He was tan and fit and Hannah said he had hair plugs. Colt wouldn't know, but could tell the mayor put a lot of time into his appearance. Unlike the past two mayors, who wore khakis or jeans and boots, Pond opted for Italian suits and loafers. They probably went better with his Porsche. He turned a lot of heads in town, that was for sure.

To Colt, the mayor reeked of midlife crisis.

"You want a drink?" Pond reached into a mini fridge against the wall where old photographs of the town hung.

Colt was surprised he hadn't taken them down. Carter Pond was a relative newcomer. He'd moved to Glory Junction from Silicon Valley seven years ago. Word on the street was he'd made a mint selling his start-up before the dot-com bust. He certainly lived like a fat cat with his sprawling estate and a membership at Glory Junction's only country club. Though Colt was always suspicious of people who flashed their money a little too loudly. In any event, the mayor tended to ignore anything in Glory Junction that was BC—Before Carter.

"No thanks," Colt said, and pointedly gazed at his watch, wanting the mayor to get to the point of this meeting. Colt had things to do.

Pond pulled out a bottle of designer water. That's what Colt called it. Fancy bottle, hefty price tag, same damn water as the tap. He hoped the city wasn't footing the bill for it. The mayor sat back down—Colt suspected he wanted the big, mahogany desk between them—and took a drag of the water.

"What happened to your uniform?"

Colt's shirt had dried, but the coffee had left a noticeable stain. "I collided with a cup of coffee."

The mayor laughed. "Was that the emergency?"

Nope. His black-haired, blue-eyed, curvy-as-sin neighbor had been his emergency. She and her Tesla. "It was a busy morning."

"Hmm," the mayor muttered, then took another swig of his expensive water. "I wanted to talk job performance."

"Yours or mine?" Colt asked, unable to help himself.

The mayor feigned a belly laugh. Colt knew Carter thought his comment was anything but funny.

"I want good things for this town, Colt. I want to take Glory Junction into the future . . . reinvent our reputation as a small, quaint town to something more relevant. I want us to have a place at the table."

Colt nodded, thinking to himself: *What the hell does that even mean? A place at the table. What table?* He supposed it was a euphemism for making Glory Junction a top tourism attraction, even though it already was. Pond wanted to pretend that commerce in the town was failing so he could take credit for turning it around.

"For far too long, Glory Junction has operated like a back-road campground when what it should be is an international destination resort. I want to make that happen."

It had been happening long before Pond became mayor. The Four Seasons and Glory Junction's other luxury hotels had been doing fine for years. During ski season they were booked solid. And going by Garner Adventure's stats—and its overworked guides—summers here were quickly becoming just as popular.

"The problem, Colt," the mayor continued, "is you're stuck in the past."

"How's that?" Colt asked, trying to read what the mayor was working up to. No question Pond had an endgame. Colt just didn't know what it was yet.

The mayor drained the rest of his water and squeezed the bottle until it made a crinkling noise. "You're too close to the residents, which is understandable since you grew up here. But to build a brighter future we need to make the town more tourist friendly . . . more welcoming."

Colt assumed that was code for loosening the rules for anyone with a reservation. "Why don't you cut to the chase here, Carter? I've got a town to patrol."

"Do you know how many traffic tickets you issued last year?"

Colt didn't know the number off the top of his head, but for a town this size with as many visitors as it got, it wasn't unprecedented. "What's your point?" he asked, even though he knew damned well what the mayor's point was.

"My point is a tourist charged with a hefty fine for violating the speed limit isn't a happy tourist."

"You do know that the city benefits financially from these fines, right?" It's not why Colt's officers gave tickets, but if the mayor was worried about losing revenue . . .

"Not as much as the city benefits from the tax base of its businesses."

"Are you asking me to look the other way when an out-of-towner drives sixty in a twenty-five-mile-an-hour zone or when a drunken tourist up from the city causes a fight at Old Glory?" Because it had been known to happen. "What about the locals? Is it business as usual for them? I figure since we're not going to protect them, we may as well look the other way when they speed or steal or trespass, too. Does that work for you?"

"Cut the sarcasm, Colt. You're on thin ice as it is. All I'm saying is we all need to do our part, be on the same page."

Colt didn't want any part of Pond's page, but he held his tongue. Managing up had never been his strongpoint, but he loved this town and continuing to pop off to the mayor wouldn't serve anyone. People here needed someone to watch their backs and that definitely wasn't Carter. The mayor wanted to turn Glory Junction into goddamned Disneyland. Even Colt's family, who profited from the town's tourism trade, didn't want to see that. And Colt's job was to keep everyone safe, not just the people with the biggest wallets.

"We through here?" Colt started to get up.

"Yep, we sure are."

Colt found his way out of Pond's office, through the long corridor of city hall, to the exit, barely able to corral his temper. The mayor was actually asking him to obstruct justice so Glory Junction could have a place at the "table." Translation: Carter Pond wanted the world to think he'd taken Glory Junction from a modest, dusty town to a thriving ski village at the safety expense of Colt's family, friends, and neighbors—the people he'd known his whole life.

"Someone die?"

Jolted from his thoughts, Colt looked up from the sidewalk to see his brother Josh. "What are you doing here?"

"Last I looked, I lived here," Josh said.

"I meant city hall." Josh, like the rest of the family, worked at Garner Adventure on Main Street, a few blocks away. And his and Hannah's Victorian was on the other side of town.

Josh pointed at a four-story office building that used to be a kitschy western motel. "My new physical therapist."

"How's the leg?" His brother's limp had become less pronounced since Christmas, when he'd returned from Afghanistan.

An IED explosion had killed three and injured seven soldiers in his squad. Josh and another army ranger had managed to carry the survivors to safety. But his brother's leg had been torn and mangled so badly that doctors had wanted to amputate. One of the surgeons had stitched together enough of Josh's blood vessels to save the leg long enough to get him to Germany. There, they'd reconnected his bones with plates and rods and mended his wounds with muscle and skin from other parts of his body.

His little brother was a walking miracle of science, which none of them took for granted. Colt credited a lot of Josh's recovery to Hannah. She'd kicked his ass when he'd first returned, angry at the world. They'd gotten married in June and Colt had never seen his brother happier.

"Good," Josh answered. "The goal is to be rock climbing by next summer." In the meantime, Josh was leading the inner-tube cave tours and had taken a few groups down the Glory River. "What's going on in city hall?" he asked.

"I had a meeting with Pond. The guy's a douche bag . . . put me in a foul mood."

"What happened?"

Colt did a quick scan of the street. There were big ears in Glory Junction. As if on cue, Rita Tucker, one of the town's biggest busybodies and a member of the city council, waved from across the street. "We'll talk later; I've got to get to the office."

"You up for a beer tonight with the brothers?"

"I don't know how late I'll be." Friday nights in Glory Junction could get busy and he'd been out late the night before.

"Text if you can make it. If not, no worries."

"I'll see what I can do." Colt bit back a yawn.

"I better get going." Josh started to walk away, then called over his shoulder, "Hey, Colt, wash your shirt."

At the police station, he found a spare uniform top in his

coat closet, stripped the stained shirt, and shrugged into the fresh one.

Carrie Jo, his receptionist, barged in without knocking. "You want me to drop that off at the cleaners?"

Colt had been in the same graduating class with her in high school. Back then she'd been head cheerleader, homecoming queen, and whatever other crap the popular girls did. Instead of going to college, she'd married an investment banker. Last year, she'd caught him cheating on her and had left him. She had zero job skills but Colt hired her anyway. Best thing he ever did because as his gatekeeper, Carrie Jo had turned out to be adept at keeping the crazies away.

"Sure." He sat down at his desk to check his messages. Unlike Pond's desk, it was your standard city-issued L-shaped metal number. "While you're there, if you wouldn't mind picking up my clean uniforms I'd greatly appreciate it. And if you grab me one of those breakfast sandwiches at Tart Me Up I'll love you forever. Get one for you too. You fly, I'll buy."

"No sandwiches for me, I'm back on Paleo." She'd packed on fifty pounds since high school.

"Just exercise and you'll be fine. You look great, Carrie Jo."

"If I look so great why don't you ever set me up with anyone?" She balled up his stained shirt and sank into his sofa, waiting for an answer.

"I would if I knew any single guys."

"Uh . . . you have two single brothers. Both gorgeous. Both employed."

"Uh-uh. Win nails anything in a skirt and TJ's a workaholic. You deserve better."

"What about you?" she challenged.

Wouldn't Pond love that, Colt thought. Dating a subordinate. "One of us would have to quit. But yeah, I'm good with that." He winked at her.

"You're such a liar, but I love you anyway. I want to have a baby, Colt."

He held up his hands. "Don't look at me."

"Denny wouldn't have cheated on me if I'd still been a size four and I'd have a child by now."

"That's bullshit, Carrie Jo, and you know it. Denny was an insecure prick. His cheating had nothing to do with you. Why don't you try online dating? I hear people have good luck with it."

"Why don't you?"

"I wasn't the one complaining about the state of my love life."

"You should be. Lisa was a bitch and every single woman in Glory Junction hopes you'll finally get over her and pick one of them."

As much as he liked to shoot the shit with Carrie Jo, that particular topic was off limits. Being the police chief required discretion where women were concerned. And now with the mayor breathing down his neck—*"You're too close to the residents"*—Colt couldn't afford to be gossiped about.

"I need to get some work done, Carrie Jo."

"What about your neighbor . . . Delaney Scott? She's beautiful, talented, and rich."

"She's also annoying as hell."

"Is she still blocking your access road?"

"Yep. Work, Carrie Jo, I've gotta work."

"Can we make out first?"

"Bye, Carrie Jo."

"You're no fun."

Nope. He sure the hell wasn't. Who had time for fun?

Chapter Two

Delaney sat on the phone fuming. "How can that be? How can he get to keep my name? It's mine. It's on my birth certificate, for God's sake."

"The judge was firm," her lawyer said. "Robert gets the name and the clothing company. You get the shoe and handbag business, the homes, and the warehouse."

"I don't care about the homes or the warehouse, I want my name back. Besides the fact that it's the name my parents gave me, it's my brand, Liz. It's the name I built the lines on."

"I know, Delaney, and if you want me to appeal the decision, I will. But I'm not going to lie to you; Robert's got you over a barrel. Everything was in his name. The company, the licenses, the studio, and the contracts. On paper, you're nothing more than a fashion designer who worked for Delaney Scott. You got bad legal advice."

"I got *no* legal advice." Just Robert's. "I was a starry-eyed kid when we started Delaney Scott. I ran the creative side and Robert ran the business end. I didn't pay attention to whose name was on what. I never thought Robert and I would break up." *Stupid me thought love was forever.*

"I'm sorry, Delaney. I did everything I could do. My

advice: move on, rebuild in a big way, and remember that success is the best revenge."

After the call, Delaney went into the kitchen to make a cup of tea. What she really needed was a shot or two (or three) of tequila. The last year had been like a surreal dream, watching everything in her life disintegrate. First her marriage and then her company. Maybe she hadn't worked hard enough on the former, but the business had taken everything she had and then some. All a labor of love. From the moment she'd been accepted to Parsons School of Design, Delaney had plotted her career trajectory, never veering from her goal of being a top designer. An internship at Marc Jacobs led to a design position at Donna Karan and her future seemed to write itself.

She'd met Robert, a bright and rising content marketing manager, at Donna Karan. At their first meeting she spilled red wine on his four-thousand-dollar suit and proceeded to tell him why his campaign for Donna's new lingerie line was all wrong. The next day he sent her a dozen red Ecuadorian roses, claiming to find pushy women hot, and she fell a little bit in love. They got married a year later and it was Robert who convinced her to leave her six-figure job at Donna Karan and go out on her own. He supported her while she worked on her designs and created her first eponymous couture line, which the trades reviewed glowingly. That's when Robert quit his job to run the burgeoning Delaney Scott fashion company.

Two years later, they launched a ready-to-wear line, Delaney Scott Every Day. Then came the handbags and the shoes, which turned out to be a significant business on its own. And now, her only business, which came with a small team of designers and salespeople and a warehouse supervisor, who was temporarily overseeing the order shipments until Delaney could hire a fashion house manager to maintain the operation. Right now, she had to develop a new line of clothing from scratch. Unfortunately, in the last year, she hadn't been able to focus. Her designs were flat and uninspired. Just a lot of the same old, same old.

She'd moved into the Glory Junction house full time nine months ago to take cover after the divorce and ensuing court battle and to get her joo joo back. Too many people in LA wanted to gloat over her failed marriage or use it to their advantage. The fashion industry could be very opportunistic, which was a nice way of putting it. And Glory Junction was such a pretty, happy place with its surrounding mountains, rivers, lakes, and charming downtown, a combination of the old West and an Aspen-style ski town. The area attracted some of the world's most famous skiers, avid rock climbers, and mountain bikers. For Delaney, who wasn't much of a sports enthusiast, the town offered unrivaled peacefulness.

Except for her immediate neighbor, who drove her nuts. Colt Garner's family was an institution in Glory Junction. Everyone loved them. The parents had founded the family's adventure company in the late 1970s. While Gray and Mary Garner were still a big part of the operation, for all intents and purposes their sons ran it. They were some of the nicest people—Colt being the exception—in town, so she tried to be civil to him. But the man busted on her last nerve. He treated the easement part of their driveway as if it was his alone, even though she owned it. He was rude, condescending, and sour. Oddly enough, the women around here actually swooned over him. Maybe it was the uniform, or, if she were being perfectly honest, the chiseled face, the square jawline, and the mile-wide shoulders.

Anyway, she'd taken to calling him Chief Hottie from Hell and did her best to avoid him.

Delaney sipped her tea and thought about food. Since the divorce, she'd lost six pounds and her clothes were beginning to hang off her. Maybe she'd go to the grocery store later and fill her cupboards and freezer with cookies and ice cream. When had she ever been able to do that before?

What she really needed to do was plant her ass at the drafting table and come up with a clothing design that wasn't crap. Channel the old Delaney Scott, who had so many ideas swimming in her head she couldn't get them on paper fast enough. And at some point—sooner rather than later—she had to hire that manager to run the handbag and shoe lines, which from now on would be her bread and butter.

It was no secret that Robert had approached some of the luminaries in the fashion world to take over as head designer of Delaney Scott. It would be interesting to see what direction the company would go in. The vindictive part of Delaney wanted to see Robert and the business bomb. The part of her that had built the company from nothing, though, didn't want to see it damaged. It was a weird predicament having someone else control a brand with her name on it that she no longer owned.

She got up, put the cup and saucer in the dishwasher, and went upstairs to her studio, a converted bedroom with spectacular lighting and a view to die for. From the south-facing windows she could see Misty Summit, the lake, and tree-dotted hillsides. Unfortunately, her cork board lacked the same great wonders. Delaney examined yesterday's sketches, hoping that they weren't as bad as she'd thought.

Ugh. They were worse.

Dull evening gowns that looked like they walked down last year's runway. Her designs had always been fresh and cutting edge. Now they looked like everything else. She sat at the table and began to sketch. Two hours later, her trash can was full.

Wandering back to the kitchen, she made herself a tuna sandwich and wound up dumping half of it down the garbage disposal. She returned to her studio and spent the rest of the day trying to conjure some magic. The best she came up with was an ugly tuxedo dress. The next time she looked outside it was nearly dark and Colt had parked his police cruiser in her spot.

For now, it didn't matter with the Tesla charged. It was his sense of entitlement that irked her. She got that he was the police chief and had to respond quickly to accidents and crime scenes, but that didn't give him the right to use her property as his personal parking lot. He had his own driveway and a garage.

And she was in a bad mood . . . a really bad mood.

Slipping on a pair of tennis shoes, she dashed down the stairs and outside into the balmy August evening. There was a light on in Colt's kitchen, so she made a beeline for the back door and banged on it. He came out shirtless in a pair of shorts, his brown hair slicked back, wet. Her eyes met him midchest and she immediately dropped them to stare at his bare feet. Crazy, but she found them incredibly sexy. Big, tan, and sprinkled with a dusting of dark hair.

"What can I do for you?" he asked, not all that friendly.

She jerked her gaze upward and cleared her throat. Right. This wasn't a social call. "You parked your car in my spot."

"It's Friday night, Delaney. You know how many times I get called out on a Friday night? Look, I'll pay to have an outlet installed at the top of your driveway if it means that much to you."

She snorted. "I can afford my own damn outlet. That's not the point."

"Then what is the point?"

"Your presumptuousness. First you take the easement for yourself. Next, you'll be coming for my name."

He stood there, looking confounded. "What the hell are you talking about?"

"You just seem to take for granted that because of your job you have the right to park wherever you want. My driveway is just as steep and inconvenient as yours. Why should I have to cede the convenient space to you? Especially when technically it's my land."

"How about for the sake of the town? Five extra minutes to get down a driveway in police time is an eternity."

"Or maybe you're just lazy," she said.

He glared at her, then blew out a long breath. "Delaney, it's been a crappy day. If you need to charge your car, I'll move my cruiser. If not, you think we can table this for another time?"

That's when she noticed the tightness around his eyes and his stiff jaw. Maybe he'd had to respond to a gruesome crime scene. As much as she hated to admit it, being police chief had to be a difficult job.

"Fine, you can stay where you are for now. But I don't want this to become a habit. And for the record, my day was lousy too." She turned to walk away.

"What happened, you lose your thread and needle?"

"Nope, I lost Delaney Scott." She kept walking without giving him a backward glance.

Not wanting to go back to her studio, where the walls seemed to be closing in on her, Delaney decided to go to the market. She got her bag from inside the house, nosed her car down the driveway, and drove less than a mile to Glory Junction's only strip mall, which consisted of a big chain supermarket, a Wells Fargo, and a Starbucks. Last she counted there were three in town.

Delaney grabbed a cart and was starting down the produce aisle when she bumped into Hannah Garner, who carried Delaney Scott designs in her gift shop and just so happened to be married to one of Colt's brothers. They didn't know each other well, but were friendly. Hannah had made it a point to make her feel welcome in the town as opposed to treating her like one of the celebrity newcomers.

"Hey, I sold one of your handbags today," Hannah said. "I could use more inventory. This is our best summer yet."

"That's great. I'll have my people send a shipment out tomorrow. You want the same merchandise as last time?" It would make it easier for her warehouse supervisor to follow the existing order, which only reminded her how badly she needed a fashion house manager who could deal directly with retailers. Sometimes she wondered if being stretched too thin contributed to her designer's block.

"Sure. Or you can mix it up a little. Whatever you think." Hannah gave her an assessing once-over. "You have a long day? You look tired." She was perceptive, that was for sure.

Delaney self-consciously fluffed her hair. "It was long, but nonproductive and frustrating. You come straight from the store?"

"Yeah. I've got book club at my house on Monday night. I figured now would be a good time to pick up a few things since my weekends are crazy. You should come." She gazed at Delaney expectantly.

"Uh, I doubt I've read the book." Delaney liked to read but never had time anymore.

"It doesn't matter. We mostly drink wine and talk about people," she said, then added, "I'm joking."

Delaney wouldn't mind getting to know more of the residents. She'd been so caught up in her problems and trying to rebuild that she hadn't circulated much. Even though it wouldn't be her full-time town forever, she'd continue to use the house on weekends, and it would be nice to have a group of friends here who weren't part of her life with Robert.

"If you're sure it'd be okay with everyone else, I'd love to come."

"Great. I'll text you my address, or if Colt comes you can hop a ride with him."

"Colt's in your book club?" Delaney had just assumed it was all women.

"No, but he sometimes comes over to hang with Josh while we're in the other room. How's things going with you two?"

Delaney could feel her face heat. In the nine months she'd lived in Glory Junction, word of their ongoing battle over the easement had gotten around. The work of a small-town grapevine, she supposed. "You know about that, huh?"

"Colt mentioned something about it," Hannah said sheepishly. "Not in a disparaging way. He just said that you two had a conflict over the road. Easements, fences, property lines, they tend to be battlegrounds in rural areas."

"Big cities too."

"Colt's a good guy. He can come across as gruff, probably because he's a cop, but he's a big teddy bear."

More like a mean old grizzly bear, Delaney thought to herself. "We're sort of at an impasse. To be honest, I don't think he likes me much right now." Or ever. He appeared to have a stick up his ass where she was concerned.

"Eh, don't worry. He'll get over it." Hannah waved her hand in the air, dismissing the thought as if it was no big deal.

"Still, it would be nice if we could get along better, since we're stuck living next door to each other."

"Maybe a small gesture would help. Colt sometimes plays at Old Glory . . . just did the other night. You could come with us and watch him. We usually go in a big group and that might break the ice between you two."

"Colt plays at Old Glory?" she repeated, making sure she heard Hannah right. The local watering hole and gastropub featured live music, but she had no idea that Colt performed there.

"Uh-huh. He's really good."

"What kind of music?" Somehow Delaney couldn't visualize Chief Hottie from Hell crooning.

"A little bit of everything, I guess. But mostly folky, country stuff."

"Really?" She'd have to see it to believe it. To her, Colt seemed about as creative as a white lamp shade. Of course, she hardly knew him. They only talked when they were fighting over the easement road. One time she'd watched him change the oil in his truck from her upstairs window. He seemed to know what he was doing, so perhaps there were other hidden talents.

"Yep. He plays guitar and sings. I'll find out when he's performing next and keep you in the loop," Hannah said.

"Okay. So, what should I bring to book club?" It was lovely of Hannah to include her. And the timing couldn't be better; Delaney was tired of hiding from the world and ready to socialize again.

"Just yourself," Hannah said. "I've got everything else covered."

They said good-bye and pushed their carts in opposite directions. Delaney intentionally bypassed the cookie aisle, but got two kinds of ice cream. On her way to the cash register she tossed a trashy magazine and a romance novel on top of her groceries. She could at least experience sex vicariously. At this rate, she didn't know when she'd get back in the saddle again. Robert's peculiar remedy to fixing their marriage had put her off being intimate with anyone. The truth was she hadn't even dated since their breakup a year ago.

She paid at the cash register and unloaded her bags when she got home. Colt's cruiser was still parked on the shoulder pad of their shared road. He must've not gotten called out. There were a few lights on in his house and she wondered if he was practicing his music. That had certainly been a revelation. Colt Garner, a troubadour.

She went up to her studio and doodled, hoping something would come to her. Nothing did. Around eleven o'clock she took a soak in the tub and went to bed with her romance novel. Sometime in the wee hours of the morning she was awakened by a siren fading in the distance. Delaney padded to the studio, peeked outside, and noted that Colt's car was gone.

The next day passed much like the previous one. As hard as Delaney tried, she couldn't seem to sketch anything original. She decided to walk downtown and peer inside the shop windows for inspiration. In LA, a stroll down Rodeo Drive often triggered her imagination. She'd see something— even a sculpture in a gallery—go running home and ideas would pour out of her brain like a rainstorm. Granted, Glory Junction wasn't quite on par with Rodeo Drive as far as eye candy, but who knew what might spark something.

She changed into a pair of Delaney Scott jeans and a sleeveless lace top she'd designed for her Every Day line, and it suddenly struck her she was now a walking advertisement for someone else's company. Weird.

Although it was hot, she decided to walk rather than drive. The town had changed a lot since she and Robert had first discovered it eight years ago. Back then, neighborhoods consisted of a hodgepodge of modest Victorians and ski-chalet style homes. Now, those homes had either been super-sized or torn down and replaced by contemporary mountain houses with lots of steel and stone and glass to take advantage of the breathtaking views.

On their first trip here—a weekend getaway so Robert could go skiing—they'd instantly adored the area. Robert, who'd always been gifted at detecting a good investment, convinced her that they should buy right away, the hope being that they would fly up on weekends and use the house as a retreat from their bustling lives in LA.

Delaney preferred the original homes with their quirky front porches and manageable square footage. But for Robert, size mattered. So they'd torn down the existing bungalow on their property and built a modern version of a Frank Lloyd Wright prairie-style home. Very large and what Robert liked to call "architecturally significant." Delaney hadn't thought she'd like the house with its cold, metal staircase and stark design. She was born and raised in the

Midwest, in a home that was cluttered with keepsakes and clothed in hand-made braided rugs and quilted blankets. To her that's what a house should be.

But surprisingly, when the Glory Junction home was finished she fell in love with its clean lines and the way it let the outdoors in. Larger than one person needed, the house was open and airy, yet unexpectedly cozy.

And Robert had been right about Glory Junction being a sound investment. Shortly after they'd rebuilt, the market got red hot. They hadn't used the house as much as they had planned. Work seemed to always get in the way. But she was here now, at least for the time being.

The walk to Main Street was short, just six blocks. Tourists in shorts and bathing suits thronged the streets, filling the restaurants and shops. She watched as a family posed for a picture in a gazebo on the river walk. The place that rented inner tubes, bicycles, and surreys had a line. But not as long as the one at Oh Fudge!

She started her stroll at the east end of the street and slowly made her way up, figuring she'd make her return on the west side where the river was. Even in summer the gondolas and chairlifts ran full time with cyclists brave enough to plow down the mountains at breakneck speed. Crazy, if you asked her. The most adventurous she got was wearing a swimsuit from last season. But Glory Junction was all about taking advantage of the roaring rapids, steep mountains, and black-diamond slopes. That's why a company like Garner Adventure did so well here.

Rita Tucker came out of the Morning Glory diner with another woman and flagged Delaney down. "I was just thinking about you today and was wondering if you'd be interested in designing the costumes for the junior theater's production of *Grease*. It's a fund-raiser for the new stage we're building."

Delaney didn't know Rita well, but according to Hannah,

she had her hand in just about everything in Glory Junction. That included organizing the production of an annual calendar, featuring local hunks, to raise money for the volunteer fire department.

"Uh . . . sure." Delaney was busy building a new company, but how could she say no to helping a children's theater?

"Great." Rita handed Delaney a flier. "That's got all the information about the next meeting. We'll see you there." And with that she walked away.

Delaney could hear the other woman saying, "You just asked Delaney Scott to sew costumes for a rinky-dink children's play. Do you know who she is? That's like asking Emeril Lagasse if he'd cook at the school cafeteria."

As their voices drifted off, Delaney laughed to herself, buoyed by being considered the Emeril of fashion. She stuffed the flier in her purse and continued up the street, gazing into the windows of the hardware store, the housewares shop, and the sporting goods place. A handsome man who looked a lot like Colt came out of Glorious Gifts. Delaney assumed he was Josh Garner, Hannah's husband, whom she hadn't yet met. The family resemblance was uncanny, though Josh walked with a pronounced limp. She'd heard Josh, a former army ranger, nearly lost his leg in a bombing in Afghanistan.

She popped in to find Hannah busy with a customer and explored the store, which carried everything from candles and clothing to pillows and furniture. Hannah hadn't been kidding about her inventory. Delaney's handbags were almost gone. It said a lot about the clientele in Glory Junction. The same purses sold in Neiman Marcus, Bloomingdale's, and Barneys New York. She'd already sent an e-mail to her warehouse people to deliver another shipment.

"See?" Hannah said, watching Delaney scope out the near

empty shelf as she rang up someone buying a cheese board made from an old wine barrel.

"Yeah. Wow. I figured the winter sales were an anomaly."

"Nope. People go nuts for them. Your clothes too."

Delaney waited for the customer to leave and said, "They're no longer mine, they're Robert's."

She didn't talk much about the divorce or the bitter court battle. But she didn't want to mislead Hannah, who got a lot of sales mileage out of telling patrons that Delaney lived locally. Soon Delaney Scott couture and ready-to-wear would be designed by someone else, who most assuredly wouldn't be living in Glory Junction.

"Oh," Hannah said, clearly at a loss as to how to react. "Was that in the plans?"

Delaney gave a mirthless laugh. "No. Given that California is a community-property state, I knew Robert would get half. I just didn't think he'd get the clothing business. He also got the name, Delaney Scott."

Hannah gasped. "How can that be? *You're* Delaney Scott."

Yes, one would think it would be equitable to let a person keep her own name. "Apparently, I'm a brilliant designer but unsavvy in the ways of business. On paper Robert ran the company, so he gets to keep the name."

"Oh, Delaney, I'm so sorry. What are you going to do?"

"Start a new clothing line and get a new name."

"That hardly seems fair. And it's bizarre."

Bizarre indeed. Delaney just shrugged. A year ago, Robert had thrown her such a curveball that nothing surprised her anymore. As far as the business, her lawyers had warned her that the judge would likely side with Robert. But losing the Delaney Scott brand . . . Well, that she hadn't seen coming.

"I'm sorry, Delaney. I can't imagine how upsetting this must be for you."

"Success is the best revenge," she said with a tight smile. At least according to her attorney.

"Was he . . . Robert . . . awful?" Hannah asked.

No one knew the real reason for her and Robert's breakup. Most assumed he'd been cheating on her. She let them believe it because it was less humiliating than the truth.

"We just had different values." Delaney took a pair of hand-tooled cowboy boots off the shelf, hoping to change the subject. "These are beautiful."

"Aren't they? A woman I grew up with makes them. She has a studio in Nugget, a town about thirty minutes away. She's designed boots for rock stars, professional baseball players, and rodeo cowboys. In fact, you guys would love each other. One of these days, I'll take you over there to meet her. Or do a trunk show in the store."

Delaney examined the boots with a discerning eye. They were gorgeous, the leather supple to the touch and the tooling an intricate design that must've taken hours to execute. The boots were giving her all kinds of ideas and that's exactly why she'd walked downtown in the first place. "Would you mind if I took a picture of them?"

"Not at all. My guess is Tawny would be tickled pink to know Delaney Scott shot a photograph of her boots."

Delaney retrieved her phone from her bag, snapped a few shots, and left Hannah's store feeling a little more optimistic. That was until she ran into Colt outside Old Glory. He bobbed his chin at her in greeting, reminding her of the jocks she went to high school with and their overinflated egos. Just for kicks she mimicked the gesture and saw one corner of his mouth kick up. He took off his aviator sunglasses, hooked them in his shirt pocket, leaned against the exterior wall of the bar, and assessed the street as if he were Lord of Glory Junction.

"Looking for criminals?" she asked, slowing down in front of him.

He just made that arrogant *you're-bothering-me* expression he nearly always wore. "Shopping?"

She could've sworn that he sneered. "Window shopping. I needed a little exercise and it's too nice of a Saturday to waste it indoors."

"It is that." He gave her a quick, efficient once-over and she wondered what he saw. A confident, put-together woman of the world or the mess that she'd become?

"I guess you're on duty." She motioned at his uniform.

"Yep."

And not much of a conversationalist, she thought.

His gaze snapped past her and she saw him squint at something on the river walk as he pushed off the wall. She turned to see what had captured his attention. A man and woman were fighting. Delaney couldn't hear them over the din of the cars and the crowds, but from their body language she could tell they were engaged in a heated argument. The woman started to walk away and the man grabbed and shoved her against the beach wall. Then he backhanded her across the face.

Colt briskly moved around Delaney, stopped traffic, and crossed the road, jogging toward the couple. The man didn't welcome his interference, though, and what she saw next made her shout out a warning.

Chapter Three

Colt caught a fist in his gut. It didn't hurt as much as it pissed him off. He twisted away from his attacker, grabbed his arm in a wristlock, and turned his hand. Colt didn't want to break the man's wrist or elbow, so he forced him to the ground.

"What the hell are you doing?" the man yelped.

"You're under arrest for assaulting an officer." Colt wrestled a pair of cuffs from his duty belt.

"I didn't know you were a cop."

"You think I wear this uniform because I like to sweat in the hot sun?"

The woman got in Colt's face. "Let him go. This is police brutality."

"Are you all right, ma'am?" Both she and the man stank of alcohol.

"Of course I am. Why wouldn't I be?"

He shot her a look but didn't respond, cuffed the man, and called for backup because he'd walked to Old Glory and had left his patrol car at the station.

"I don't know what you think you saw, but you're wrong. We'll sue you and the department."

Colt pulled the guy up off the ground and told him to sit

on the river wall. A small crowd had formed; some in the group had their phones out and appeared to be taking video.

"Nothing to see here, folks."

A few people dispersed but most loitered on the sidewalk. It was public property; they could stay if they wanted to. The woman kept screeching about constitutional rights and abuse of power. A short time later one of his officers pulled up in a patrol car and loaded the man into the backseat. She tried to get in the car with him, but Colt told her she'd have to get to the jail in Nevada City, the county seat, on her own. There, she could bail the man—presumably her boyfriend or husband—out of jail.

"Don't drive until you've sobered up or I'll have to arrest you," Colt told her.

She cussed him out, stringing obscenities together in ways Colt had never heard before. He gave her credit for creativity. A few shopkeepers came out, watched for a little while, then went back inside. He was getting ready to leave when she delivered her parting shot by vomiting on his boots.

Great! He'd just had the boots polished.

Colt walked back to the station gagging on the stench and took them off before he went inside.

Carrie Jo gaped at his stocking feet and the bits of barf that clung to the bottom of his pant legs. "Oh my God, you smell awful."

"What are you doing here on a Saturday?"

She shrugged. "I don't have anything else to do, so I thought I'd work on updating the filing system. And I suppose I'll be taking another trip to the cleaners." She gestured at his lower half. "Off with the pants."

He shook his head, went inside his office and found a pair of basketball shorts, a T-shirt, and tennis shoes in his closet, and headed to the locker room for a shower. When he got out he wrapped his dirty uniform pants and the boots in a couple

of evidence bags. He'd drop them off at the cleaners himself
after work.

Back in his office, he started writing the report for the
incident when he heard noise coming from the bull pen. It
sounded like a small aircraft was taking off from inside the
police station. He went out to see what the racket was and
found Carrie Jo in the small efficiency kitchen making
something green in an industrial-looking blender.

"What the hell is that?" he shouted over the whir.

She turned it off. "It's for my cleanse. Kale, mango, celery,
tangerine juice, parsley, and mint. Want some?"

He scrunched up his nose. "God, no. I thought you were
doing that other thing . . . Paleo."

"I decided to do this instead. My friend Rona lost ten
pounds in three weeks."

He sat at the small table and watched her pour the slop
into a tall glass. Win drank similar crap, said it made him feel
healthier. He shook his head. "Going from trend to trend is
not the way to lose weight."

"Easy for you to say." She eyed him up and down. "When
was the last time you needed to be on a diet?"

"Exactly. I exercise and eat sensibly. It has to be a lifestyle.
Fad diets don't work."

"How would you know? You ever think that you were just
blessed with good genes?"

"It's just common sense. Let's start running together."

"As if I could keep up with you." She took the seat across
from him, held her nose, and drank. "It's . . . not that bad."

He didn't say anything, just raised his brows.

"All right, it's disgusting." She forced down a few more
sips. "Do you know what it's like to have once been the hot
chick—the one all the guys ogled—and to now look like
this?" She waved her hand over her body.

"You and I don't see the same thing. Because I still see a
hot chick."

She put down her drink and reached over the table to hug him. "Aw, you're the best guy ever, and Lisa is such a bitch."

"We're not talking about her, Carrie Jo."

"Fine. But I hope that she who shall not be named trips, falls, and cracks her head open on the next red carpet she walks down."

Colt got to his feet. "You have a good pair of running shoes?"

"No."

"Get a pair. I'm picking you up tomorrow morning. We'll use the track over at Glory Junction High for your first time out. Then it's trails."

"I have a bad knee," she said. "And it's supposed to be really hot tomorrow."

He ignored her as she continued to sputter excuses. "See you at seven."

Colt put in a few hours doing paperwork and then dropped his uniform at the cleaners before going home. When he got there, Delaney's Tesla was parked in the contested spot. Too tired to fight with her, he drove up the driveway and spent several minutes doing a three-point turn to get the cruiser in position in case he was called out on an emergency.

He went in his back door and found Win eating cereal at his kitchen counter. "What's wrong with your cereal?"

"I ran out," he said around a mouthful.

"You ever hear of a store?"

"Why, when you've got perfectly good cereal here? And beer." Win pointed his spoon at Colt as he chewed.

Colt grabbed a stool next to Win at the bar. "Didn't Mom make dinner?" She usually did something like chili or stew on a Saturday night so her sons could stop by and load up for the week.

"Uh-uh. They went to San Francisco to check out new equipment. A couple of snowmobiles, kayaks, and inflatable boats. Dad knows a guy."

Colt laughed. As long as they were growing up Gray Garner had always "known a guy." A guy who could get you a good deal on a car, a guy who could fix a leaky roof cheaper than anyone else, a guy who could come up with tickets for the World Series when no one else could. Colt and his brothers had turned it into a joke. Whenever something needed to be done, one of them would say, "Dad knows a guy. . . ."

"You don't have a date tonight?" Colt used the term "date" loosely. Win was the womanizer in the family. His idea of a date was Colt's idea of a hookup.

"Nope. TJ's coming over to drink beer and watch TV."

"Why wasn't I invited?"

"You are, because we're doing it here. Thanks for having us, by the way." Win grinned as he stood up.

Colt shook his head but grinned back. Even though his two brothers would eat and drink him out of house and home, he enjoyed their company.

Win got the milk out of the refrigerator and added more to his cereal. "So, I heard someone hurled on you today."

"Yeah, right after I got sucker punched."

"Shit, no kidding? Dude, your job sucks."

"Sometimes." Like when he had Pond making his life miserable. Otherwise, Colt loved being the police chief. He loved the town, he loved the residents, and he wanted to keep them safe. Call it corny, but that's the way he rolled. "You invite Josh?"

"He and Hannah had something going on. What's the deal with the chick next door?"

Colt kicked off his tennis shoes. "What do you mean, what's the deal with her?"

"She's hot. What happened to her husband?"

"They're divorced . . . I think." That's what Carrie Jo had told him. But she'd probably heard it from someone else and people in Glory Junction tended to talk out of their asses.

"Really? She seeing anyone?"

"How the hell would I know?" Colt took the cereal box and poured himself a bowl.

"Maybe I should go over there and say hello."

He reached for the milk. "Do me a favor and don't."

"Why not? It's the neighborly thing to do." Win grinned and Colt had a sudden urge to wipe the smile off his brother's face.

"You're not her neighbor, I am. And she and I aren't exactly on amicable terms."

"See, that's the difference between you and me. If I lived next door to a beautiful woman we'd be on extremely amicable terms."

Colt snorted. "She's out of your league, bro."

Win looked affronted. "What makes you think that?"

"She's some big-name fashion designer, like Ralph Lauren or Calvin Klein. Her real home is in LA and she's probably not interested in a ski bum." Or anyone born and raised in Glory Junction for that matter.

"Hey, who are you calling a ski bum? I own a sixth interest in an excellent adventure company. I'm a businessman."

"Who's a businessman?" TJ walked in without bothering to knock, which was standard operating procedure for the Garner brothers.

"Win," Colt said, and he and TJ both cracked up. Seeing the look on Win's face, he added, "Oh, Winifred, we're laughing with you, not at you."

Of all of them, TJ was the businessman. Their brother Josh liked to say that he was Garner Adventure's chief bean counter, hiring director, and marketing guru rolled into one. He was eighteen months younger than Colt, but people always thought TJ was the eldest—and the smartest, which he probably was.

TJ took one look at their bowls of cereal and grimaced. "If

I knew that's what you were serving for dinner I would've gotten takeout at the Indian place." The name of the downtown restaurant was Zaika, but everyone just called it the Indian place.

"Blame Win. This is his party. I didn't even know you guys were coming over."

TJ picked up the box of cereal and shook it. "There's nothing left."

Colt went in his pantry, pulled out another box, and handed it to him with a bowl and spoon.

TJ reached for the milk and joined them at the breakfast bar. "I heard someone upchucked on you," he said between bites.

"Yeah. Long, boring story." Apparently enough people saw the incident that the whole town was talking about it. "What's going on at Garner Adventure? Win says Mom and Dad are buying new equipment."

"Yep. But I wish we could find more guides. The summer is killing us, though it's good for our bottom line. You're still doing the river-rafting trip tomorrow, right?"

"Yeah." Though Colt wished he could have the day to himself. He hadn't done laundry in a week, the lawn needed mowing, and after tonight he'd be out of groceries. And beer.

"You on call?" TJ asked.

"I am. Brewster isn't back from his fishing trip until tomorrow, and Saber's wife just had a baby."

"How come your patrol car is at the top of the hill?"

"Because Delaney parked in my spot."

"I didn't see her Tesla there when I came in."

Colt got up and peered outside the window. Sure enough, her car was gone. She'd either parked it at the top of her driveway or she went out for the night. He was tempted to move his to the easement road before she got back, but she'd probably need to charge the damn vehicle.

"What's her deal?" TJ asked.

"Dude, I've got dibs," Win called out.

Colt and TJ looked at each other and rolled their eyes.

"Her deal is that she's a pain in my ass," Colt said. "I liked it better when she and her husband never used the place."

"Ex-husband," TJ said. "According to Ross up at Winter Bowl where the ex buys his lift tickets, she got the houses and the shoe and handbag business and he got the clothing company. Sounds like she got rooked to me. I don't know a lot about the fashion industry, but the brand's a household name. Her clothes are in every department store in America. Supposedly when they split they were in the midst of negotiating a multimillion-dollar deal with Target to do some kind of housewares line."

"Why'd they break up?" Colt didn't have a lot of use for gossip, especially about someone he barely knew, but he was curious.

"Have no idea. But according to Ross, it was pretty sudden, because the ex was planning to spend the winter skiing at Winter Bowl and had to give away his tickets. Delaney doesn't ski."

Then why the hell live in Glory Junction? That's what Colt wanted to know. "When is she going back to LA?"

"Don't know. But she's still got a business in LA to run. Hannah says Delaney Scott shoes and handbags blow out of her store faster than she can stock them."

"My guess is she'll wind up selling," TJ continued. "Ross says it was the ex who wanted to live up here. Maybe he'll buy her out."

Colt didn't care who owned the house so long as he got his parking space back. As far as he was concerned the house was a monstrosity of epic proportions. Too big for the lot, too stark for the land, and too modern for an old western California town. Delaney, on the other hand, was gorgeous. No way he could deny it, despite their differences.

He could absolutely find her attractive without being attracted to her, Colt told himself. Because he wasn't in the least bit . . . attracted. Her situation was too much like Lisa's had been.

After their cereal Win and TJ grabbed a couple of beers out of the refrigerator and moved to the living room. Colt abstained in case he got called out. It was a rare night when he didn't. The department was small enough that he or the assistant chief, Jack Brewster, were required to respond to most of the big accidents, violent crimes, and to all of the fatalities.

Colt claimed the recliner while Win queued up *Mad Max: Fury Road* on Netflix.

"Josh says Pond's giving you shit," TJ said.

"I suspect if he could get away with canning me, he would."

"He's a moron. You're the best chief this town has ever had. I don't know what voters ever saw in him."

"He's slick . . . appeals to the new residents, the ones who think the rest of us are a bunch of hayseeds and hippies."

"What are you planning to do?"

Colt shrugged. "My job."

Win started the movie, then promptly fell asleep on the couch while TJ talked Colt's ear off about Garner Adventure, including his lofty plans to expand. At eleven-thirty they called it a night. It was the first time in weeks Colt got a full night's sleep.

The next morning, Colt picked up Carrie Jo and kicked her ass for eight laps around the track before heading to Garner Adventure to meet his river-rafting group. TJ wasn't kidding about it being a bachelorette party. Five women, including the bride-to-be, showed up in tiaras, minuscule shorts, and bikini tops.

Win, already committed to teaching a group of teenagers

how to wind sail, took it upon himself to give the ladies a tour of the company while Colt got their gear ready. During the recession their parents had purchased the building, an abandoned log lodge on the corner of Main Street, to replace the original location, which had been a few miles out of town. They'd gutted and renovated it, adding a gym, rock-climbing wall, locker rooms with showers, a reception area with a huge stone fireplace, and offices. It was not only roomier than what they'd had before, but also more visible to tourists. Now, a third of their business was walk-ins.

"You ladies ready to go?" Colt called to the group.

He'd loaded one of the shuttle vans with equipment and snacks and hoped to get a couple of hours on the river before lunchtime. The women had paid for a six-hour trip and he wanted to make sure they had plenty of time on the rapids.

"Can we wear our tiaras on the water?" one of the women asked.

"Nope. But you get to wear these." He held up a helmet. "And PFDs—personal floatation devices."

The women didn't complain, which instantly scored them points in Colt's book. They got situated in the van and Colt drove a short distance out of town to a launching spot on the river.

"Everyone wear tennis or water shoes and bring sunscreen?" Garner Adventure sent out a check list to anyone who made a reservation.

"Yes," came a chorus of female voices.

One of the women, a blonde with dimples, popped her head between the two bucket seats up front. "What's your name?"

"Colt," he said, and repeated it louder for the others. "And I'll be your guide today."

"Are you single, Colt?" the blonde asked, her smile wide and unmistakably flirtatious.

"Single but off limits." He winked.

"Why?" asked the bride, whose veil had become tangled in her tiara.

"Um, aren't you getting married?" he teased.

Her eyes twinkled. "I'm not asking for me, silly, but for my beautiful bridesmaids."

"Because we run a professional operation at Garner Adventure."

The women booed and Colt shrugged his shoulders. When they got to the river he told them to help themselves to the snacks while he unloaded the raft and paddles. In no time he had everything ready to go and assisted the women with putting on their PFDs and helmets, adjusting straps, making sure everything was on correctly. He gave them a safety talk and a quick lesson on paddling and what to do if one of them fell overboard. He was glad to find out a few of them had white-water rafted before and knew the drill.

"Let's go," he said, and they dutifully took their places on the raft while Colt launched them from the put-in and maneuvered a course for the best rapids.

They screamed every time they hit heavy water or a waterfall, giggled when they got hung up on a boulder—which was often because they couldn't paddle worth a shit—and flirted with him relentlessly. Fending off their advances quickly got tiresome, but he wanted them to have a good time. Lord knew that Garner Adventure trips didn't come cheap. For that reason, everyone at the company aimed to give the clients their money's worth. So he worked extra hard to find them the best rapids and flirt back. Just a little.

They broke for lunch and the girls slipped their shorts off to dry in the sun while they lay on the beach in their bikini bottoms. He wanted to take a picture and send it to Win with the message: "Eat your heart out, sucker." But he resisted. Barely.

"Hey, Colt, you should take off your rash guard," Dimples called to him, and flashed him a naughty smile.

In unison, the women began chanting, "Take it off, take it off."

If he did, he'd be looking at a lawsuit. "Not gonna happen, ladies," he said as charmingly as he knew how.

They got back in the water at one and he spent much of the afternoon fishing his boaters out of the drink. He was pretty sure they fell out on purpose just so he would rescue them. By four they were beat from the sun and asked to go back. He assigned Dimples the job of agile bow, meaning she had to jump out on shore with a line and hold the raft while everyone got out.

"Will you put lotion on my back, Colt?" the bride's maid of honor, a smoking hot brunette, asked. He rolled his eyes but took the proffered container and did what she asked.

"What about me, Colt?" One of the others batted her eyelashes.

He shook his head. "All right, ladies, enough. Let's pack up."

"Not before we get a group picture," the bride said.

"Everyone get next to the boat and I'll take it," he told them.

"No, we want you in the picture, too."

One of the girls got a selfie stick from her bag in the van. They gathered next to the boat, close enough so everyone would be in the photo.

"On the count of three," the bride said. "One . . . two . . ."

When they reached the magical number all five women lifted their bikini tops and flashed their tits. And there he was like a dumb-ass, standing in the middle of five topless babes.

"You want me to e-mail the picture to you?" the bride asked him.

He was sorely tempted. If nothing else he'd like to flaunt the photo in Win's face, but said, "No thanks."

By the time he got home he was ready for two fingers of Jack and a cold shower. As he turned up the easement road he saw Delaney watering her flowers. Her Tesla was parked on the pad and he silently cursed her. At least he wasn't on call tonight; Brewster had him covered. Still, she didn't know that.

He drove to the top of his driveway, parked the truck in the garage, and decided to have a few words with his pesky neighbor.

Chapter Four

Delaney watched Colt approach in board shorts and rash guard, looking better than any male model she'd ever had the privilege of dressing. But as her gaze landed on his face, her stomach sank. He wasn't coming over for a neighborly chat, that was for sure, and her sour mood from Robert's call came roaring back.

He pointed at her car. "We've got to work this out, Delaney."

"As far as I'm concerned, there is nothing to work out." She was tired of being pushed around. By Robert, by Colt, by anyone. "While the easement allows you to drive over the road, it doesn't give you the right to park on it. End of story."

"Actually, the easement doesn't distinguish what I can or cannot do. It simply says the road is to be shared by both of us." He folded his arms over his chest and waited for her to challenge him. There was a gleam in his eyes and she got the impression that he was enjoying this.

"I'll have my lawyer look at it," she said. "In fact, if I have to I'll go to court over it." She was bluffing, of course, and a small part of her knew she was taking out her frustration with Robert on Colt.

"No can do. It's grandfathered in. I honestly don't get why you're being so difficult about this."

"I'm tired of losing, that's why," she blurted. Crap. She hadn't meant to say that. It made her sound petulant and even a little hysterical, but it was the truth. In the last year she'd lost everything.

His demeanor suddenly changed, probably because her lips were quivering and he didn't want to deal with a sobbing female. "This isn't a competition, Delaney." His voice was softer now. Gentler. "I'm not trying to best you; I'm just trying to do right by the town I'm charged with keeping safe."

Okay, now she really was going to cry . . . for being a bitch and for everything else going wrong in her life. To preserve her dignity and to keep him from seeing the emotional wreck she'd become, Delaney marched off, went inside, and slammed the door shut.

Now he'd think she was crackers for sure. But it was better than falling apart in front of her arrogant neighbor.

Earlier, Robert had delivered the coup de grâce. He claimed the divorce decree required her to take the Delaney Scott name off her handbags and shoes—the ones already manufactured and in stores as opposed to just future products. It being Sunday, she couldn't get a hold of her attorney. But if there was any truth to what Robert said it would cost her a fortune to have her name removed, not to mention that the merchandise would be worthless without it. Consumers paid three times as much for a product with a designer label.

Work was the only thing that would take her mind off impending bankruptcy. She headed for the stairs, and halfway to her studio the doorbell rang. Crossing the front room to the foyer, she gazed through the peephole. Colt stood there, holding up a six-pack of beer. For a second, she considered ignoring him, turning off the lights, and pretending she wasn't home. Silly, because he knew she was. She took a deep breath, wiped her eyes, and opened the door.

"I come in peace," he said, and handed her the beer. "I don't know what just happened out there, but I have a feeling it has nothing to do with me or the easement road. But maybe I'm wrong."

"No, you're not wrong." She let out a sigh, opened the door wider, and moved aside so he could enter. "Come in."

He stepped over the threshold and swept his gaze around the room. "Big place you've got here." She wasn't sure if that was a compliment or not.

Leading him into the kitchen, she got down two pilsners from the cupboard and poured them each a glass. The beer was cold. Straight from his refrigerator, she presumed.

"It's a local microbrew," he said, watching her examine the label. "A couple of friends of mine make it."

She nodded, pushed the glass across the center island, and offered him a seat at the bar. "I'm sorry about before. I may have overreacted."

"May have?" He quirked an eyebrow, then immediately checked himself. "You know, I don't think we ever did the new-neighbor thing, like maybe I was supposed to bring you a cake or something when you moved in."

That was nearly a year ago, she thought to herself. "You bake?"

"No." He chuckled. "I meant it just seems like we by-passed 'hello' and went straight to fighting over parking. So, can we start over? I'm hoping beer is an acceptable substitute for cake."

"Okay." She flashed a small smile and held the glass up to him in a toast. "Today . . . was difficult. I shouldn't have taken it out on you."

She suspected he wanted to ask her about it but settled for "I get it," instead.

"It doesn't mean I'm ready to cede the parking space to you, but I'm usually less . . . emotional."

"Would you let me use it when you aren't charging your car, at least when I'm on call?"

"When's that?"

"Pretty much always. The assistant chief takes half the week and I take the other half. But if it's something big, I always go out."

"What counts as big?" It was a relatively small town and there didn't seem to be much crime, not like in LA.

"Anything that involves a fatality or in some circumstances a violent crime, big car accident, or a suspicious fire."

"Are there a lot of those?"

"There aren't a lot, but it happens, and when it does I have to get there quickly."

"We might be able to work something out." She just didn't want to argue with him anymore. It was exhausting. But she also didn't want to commit to giving him the parking space.

"Thank you," he said halfheartedly, as if he had expected her to completely surrender.

Colt obviously wasn't used to having to grovel to get what he wanted, so she gave him credit for doing it now. Okay, maybe not groveling, but he was definitely sucking up. Obnoxious, but she was quite enjoying it.

"You planning to live here full time?" he asked.

"For the time being, yes. My husband and I split up. I'm using this time to regroup." That was an understatement.

"I'm sorry to hear about your breakup."

"Thank you," she said. She could tell he meant it, even though he hadn't known them as a couple, not really. She and Robert had been in and out to oversee the building of their house and, after it was finished, visited occasionally. Colt had waved from his yard or as they passed each other driving, but that was about it.

Eager to change the subject, she noted that he was still in his swimwear. "Were you at the lake earlier?"

"The river. I took a group white-water rafting for Garner Adventure."

"You work there as well?" She'd known that his three

brothers did but figured he was too busy working at the police department.

"When they're shorthanded I fill in, which seems to be all the time now."

"You don't like it?"

"I do." He grinned. "But I already have a full-time job."

"I've always wanted to go white-water rafting." It had always looked fun to her and not too scary, nothing like bombing down a mountainside on skies.

"It's awesome. Garner Adventure offers trips all summer long."

"Good to know. I'll have to sign up for one." She got up to refill his glass.

"Did you design that?" When she looked at him, clueless, he said, "The outfit you're wearing."

"Oh." She glanced down at herself, not remembering what she had on. "Uh, I did. Several years ago." It was part of her summer 2013 Every Day collection, one of her favorites.

"It's nice."

"Thanks." She'd take "nice." The fact that he'd noticed at all was somewhat surprising. Colt struck her as one of those alpha guys who only noted what a woman was wearing if it was short, tight, and obscenely low cut. But she supposed she was stereotyping.

"My brother says your clothes are in every department store in America."

"I don't know about every store, but we have a lot of retailers. That company now belongs to my ex, though. He got it in the divorce."

He angled his head to look at her. Really look. "I'm guessing you're not happy about that."

"No, I'm not. But there's not much I can do about it. He also gets to keep the name, Delaney Scott." She didn't know why she was telling him this. But he was here and listening and she supposed she needed a shoulder to cry on and he had broad ones capable of absorbing a lot of tears.

"How the hell did that happen? It's your name. Why doesn't he use his own?"

"Because my name is an established brand."

"That you put on the map, right?"

"Well, to be fair, we both put it on the map. My designs, his business acumen."

He nodded understandingly. "That sucks."

That was putting it mildly. She poured more beer for herself. Usually a wine person, she found that the hoppy flavor of the microbrew was growing on her. And honestly, she could use a good buzz but never would've considered drinking alone. "How long have you been chief?"

"This is my sixth year. Before that I was a cop in San Francisco for a while."

"Why'd you leave?" It seemed like a great gig to her. San Francisco was one of the most cosmopolitan cities in the West.

"I'm not a city guy and frankly, I missed home. . . . Couldn't wait to come back. I hated Los Angeles when I went to UCLA." He stopped. "No offense."

"None taken. I'm from the Midwest so LA feels pretty exotic to me, but I realize it's not for everyone." Her parents couldn't stand it. But her whole life she'd wanted to live in a big, exciting city. Show that she'd made it.

"It must be the epicenter of the fashion world, huh?"

"London, Paris, Milan, New York, and to some extent LA. It's always been part of my brand . . . Hollywood, glitz, and glamour."

He listened to her as she yammered on about the industry and design. It occurred to her that he was actually paying attention to a topic that no doubt bored him. It also struck her that he was even better looking than she'd originally given him credit for. In the nine months she'd lived in Glory Junction, she hadn't paid too much attention to Colt's physical attributes, only to his crabby personality. No wonder the women all went gaga for him. Dark hair, thick brows, sharp cheekbones, and dreamy, deep brown eyes.

"What happened to the man who punched you yesterday?" She didn't want to monopolize the conversation by talking only about fashion design.

"Arrested and will presumably be charged with assaulting a peace officer."

"And the woman?"

"Unfortunately, there's no law against projectile vomiting on a peace officer."

She laughed, even though the incident had been beyond disgusting. Poor Colt. She supposed it was part of the job, though. Clearly, he had a lot of integrity to brush it off the way he did. If someone had intentionally thrown up on her, she didn't know if she could be so forgiving.

"And even though she was belligerent, her husband decked her." He shook his head. "She's a victim."

He finished his drink and got up from the island. "Thanks for the beer and conversation. It's getting late and I should get going."

"Hey, it was your beer. Thanks for bringing it over."

"We good on the parking?"

Of course that had been his main objective for coming over. Their visit had been so pleasant that she'd nearly forgotten that he had an agenda. She felt a pang of disappointment, but what had she expected? It wasn't like they were going to become bosom buddies. "I'll stick to the top of my driveway when I'm not charging my car," she said reluctantly.

"I appreciate that, Delaney. And like I said, I'd be happy to foot the bill for an outlet in your garage or wherever."

"Don't press your luck, Colt."

His lips curved up into a full-fledged smile and it took her breath away. Chief Hottie from Hell could melt ice with that smile. It would be wise for her to remember that.

She saw him out, cleaned up in the kitchen, and went up to her studio. After an hour or two of drawing she realized she'd come up with exactly the same outfit she was wearing. "Argh! How long is this dry spell gonna last?" she asked herself aloud, fearful that she'd never get her mojo back.

The next day it was more of the same. Around noon her attorney finally called.

"Sorry, I was in court," she told Delaney. "Robert's interpretation of the ruling is not mine at all. While it's true that your future bag and shoe designs cannot have the Delaney Scott label, the idea that the ruling was retroactive . . . I don't think so. I could ask the judge for a clarification, but why make it easy on Robert? Let him pay his attorneys to do it. If he calls again, tell him to go through his lawyers and hang up."

That worked for Delaney. She wanted to have as little to do with her ex as humanly possible. After the phone call, she made herself lunch and got on the Internet to take a look at the trades. Being away from Los Angeles, away from the industry, had left her out of the loop. As she scanned *The Business of Fashion*'s top stories of the day, she spotted a headline that made her stomach drop: OLIVIA LOWELL TO TAKE TOP DESIGNER POSITION AT DELANEY SCOTT. She jumped over to her Twitter feed, and sure enough, the news was everywhere, including another story in *Women's Wear Daily*.

Olivia was young, innovative, and seen as a rising star in the industry. She was also gorgeous, and according to rumors, had more in common with Robert than fashion. The staff must be buzzing and Delaney was tempted to call Karen, who made the trains run at Delaney Scott. But it wouldn't be appropriate. For all intents and purposes they were competitors now. Oh, but to be a fly on the wall.

She turned off the computer, more depressed than ever. Olivia Lowell had extraordinary talent and, harnessed right, could take the company to the next level. Not so long ago Delaney had been Olivia Lowell. But look at her now. If she didn't get her act together soon, her career in fashion would be over.

Her cell rang and she hesitated until she saw the caller's ID.

"I was just thinking about you," she told Karen.

"I'm guessing you saw the news."

"I did. Congratulations. She's a great hire. Robert must be paying her an arm and a leg."

"I'm sorry, Delaney. I was shocked when you guys broke up. But honestly, I was even more surprised when you left the company . . . your company." Under the circumstances she couldn't have stayed. "I know it's not any of my business, but isn't there a way you two can still work together?"

"I'm afraid not." Delaney was tempted to tell her why, but it was too personal . . . too mortifying. "Olivia will be good for the company; she'll infuse it with fresh ideas." Because Lord knew Delaney didn't have any.

"I don't know." There was a long pause. "She seems high maintenance, prone to tantrums if she doesn't get her way."

That was her reputation, but who knew if it was true?

"We're all like that," Delaney said, trying to stay objective. Her differences with Robert had nothing to do with Olivia.

"That's the thing—you never were. You were a dream to work with, even keeled and open to suggestions. And it was fun when you were here."

"It's not fun anymore?" Robert was a lot of things but he wasn't a tyrant. He believed in creating a good work environment as much as Delaney did.

"It's not that it isn't fun, it's just different," Karen said.

"Sometimes it feels a little too corporate. When you were here it never did."

"That's just because the design side was upended when I left. Robert's always been about the business part of the company, counting beans. It'll be better when Olivia is there, more balance." Delaney loved the employees—many who had been there from the beginning—and she would hate to see them unhappy.

"Hopefully . . ." Karen said, though something in her voice sounded doubtful. "So what are you working on? Or is it a big secret?"

If Karen only knew. "I'm still playing with some ideas . . . not exactly a secret, but nothing I'm ready to talk about yet."

"We're all waiting, knowing it'll blow us away."

It would certainly do that. Nothing like a blank sketch pad to set the fashion world on fire.

"Thanks," Delaney said. "I appreciate your vote of confidence. Don't be a stranger." She wished she could lure Karen away to run her company, but at the rate she was going, Delaney wouldn't have one.

As soon as she got off the phone with Karen, Delaney called her real estate agent in Los Angeles. She wanted to sell the Beverly Hills house. While the huge Mediterranean-style mansion was beautiful, Delaney didn't need that much square footage. She needed the money more, at least until she got investors, which would be extraordinarily difficult without a line of clothing to show them.

By the end of the day, she'd listed her house but still hadn't come up with any new designs worth keeping. She quit trying and got ready for book club at Hannah's house, slipping into a pair of white linen pants and a Delaney Scott navy tee. When the simple cotton shirts first hit the market people went nuts. They were the most slimming tees out there and came in every color of the rainbow. Tying a silk scarf around her neck, she decided to add some chunky jewelry and finished the outfit with a pair of strappy sandals from her summer collection.

She hoped she wasn't overdressed for the gathering. Shorts, tank tops, and yoga pants were typically the clothing of choice for summers in Glory Junction. In winter, jeans, fleeces, and snow boots. Not exactly Paris or Milan, yet perfectly suited for the recreational, outdoorsy feel of the town.

She applied mascara and lip gloss, grabbed her keys, purse, a bottle of rosé, and headed out. She noticed that Colt wasn't home yet, unless he'd parked his patrol car in the garage, which she doubted, given his hypervigilance to speedy response times. At least they'd sort of dealt with the parking situation, though Delaney had every intention of using the space when she wanted to. She wouldn't fool herself into thinking that having a beer with the guy had made them friends, but at least it had been a step toward civility.

Hannah's home, a charming Victorian that reminded Delaney of a dollhouse, turned out to be closer than she thought. Unlike her street, which had seen a lot of teardowns and rebuilds, Hannah's block harkened back to the town's Gold Rush roots with rows of colorful cottages, complete with gingerbread, front porches, and dormer windows.

Delaney parked, stuffed the wine in her purse, and took the brick walkway and stairs up to Hannah's front porch. Before she could knock, a brunette opened the door.

"Hi, I'm Deb. You must be Delaney."

Deb ushered her in, took the wine, and pointed Delaney to the living room where a group of five women sat around a coffee table, eating and drinking. Hannah got up to make the introductions and a chorus of voices welcomed Delaney. She found a place on the floor and sat cross legged next to someone named Carrie Jo, who was telling the group about how she was on the third day of a juice cleanse and hadn't lost a pound.

"I thought Colt talked you out of the cleanse and you two

were running together," Hannah said, and Delaney's ears perked up, wondering if Carrie Jo was Colt's girlfriend.

"I read somewhere that only twenty percent of losing weight is due to exercise. The rest is diet," Carrie Jo said, and sipped her wine, which Delaney doubted was part of the cleanse.

"Carrie Jo's right," said another woman. Delaney thought her name was Amanda. "After Leo was born I didn't lose the weight until I joined Weight Watchers, even working out two hours a day."

Deb came in, carrying two glasses of wine, and handed one to Delaney.

"You can't live on juice alone, Carrie Jo." Hannah refilled her glass from an icy pitcher filled with what looked like lemonade or Tom Collins mix.

"Well, it's either that or get my stomach stapled."

"Oh God, do they even do that anymore?" Deb asked as she gracefully got down on the floor without spilling a drop of her wine. Impressive.

"Could we talk about something other than weight loss?" Rita, one of the few people at the gathering Delaney recognized, stuffed a quarter of a sandwich in her mouth.

"Why?" Deb asked. "Then we'll have to talk about the book, which I still haven't read."

A man holding a gorgeous floral arrangement came into the room and in unison everyone shouted, "Foster!"

"Sorry I'm late. My last client discovered she was allergic to Asiatic lilies"—he held up the vase—"and had me do a completely new arrangement. So you get this one, Hannah."

"Yay!" She got up and took the vase from him and set it on an antique end table, taking a moment to admire the yellow and orange flowers.

Foster plopped down next to Deb, tugged her wineglass out of her hand, and drained it.

"Uh, you're welcome." She stood up, disappeared inside

the kitchen, and returned a few minutes later with a bottle of chardonnay, Delaney's rosé, and an extra glass for Foster. "Carrie Jo was just telling us about her cleanse."

"The Master Cleanse Lemonade Diet?" Foster asked. "I did that one and lost twenty pounds in ten days."

Carrie Jo's eyes grew big. "You did not!"

"I did. You want the diet?"

"Hell yes, I want it. E-mail it to me."

Rita growled something in annoyance and Hannah deftly changed the subject to the junior theater's production of *Grease*. Delaney reasoned that Rita had never had to diet in her life. She was thin as a rail.

"Rita said you're doing the costumes, Delaney."

Everyone turned to look at her. Like most artists, she preferred sitting on the sidelines, not being the center of attention.

She cleared her throat. "I am."

"Seriously?" Foster said, and made a face. "I wouldn't go to too much trouble if I were you."

Deb buried her face in Foster's shoulder and smothered a laugh.

"I'll have you know it's going to be an excellent production," Rita huffed. "Probably our best yet."

"That's not saying much," Foster mumbled under his breath.

"What did you say, Foster?"

"I asked if you brought in Lin-Manuel Miranda."

Rita narrowed her eyes. "I don't even know who that is."

"Uh . . . *Hamilton*? Won a Pulitzer Prize, not to mention a bazillion Tony Awards."

Rita waved her hand at Foster in dismissal. Both he and Hannah dissolved in hysterics, until even Rita laughed. Delaney was quickly getting the impression that Rita didn't know a thing about theater and had probably volunteered because no one else did.

"The kids try their best," Hannah said, and turned to Delaney. "It's so nice of you to do the costumes."

"I'm looking forward to it." Why not? It would be her small contribution.

Foster leaned into her and whispered, "Liar."

They'd never met before tonight, but she liked him already.

"Foster, are you posing for my calendar this year?" Rita wanted to know. "I got all four Garner brothers signed on."

"Yeah, I'll do it."

"You should have Delaney help you," Hannah suggested. "I bet she's done all kinds of model photo shoots."

"I'd be happy to help." She had seen last year's calendar and it was a hoot. A lot of beefcake in this small town, but Glory Junction attracted world-class athletes, so she wasn't surprised. "It's to raise money for the volunteer fire department, right?"

"Yes, ma'am," Rita said. "I shoot it myself."

The calendar definitely had an amateurish, goofy feel to it, but that was part of the charm.

"Are you planning to live here full time, Delaney?" Carrie Jo asked, and again all eyes turned to her.

"For a few months." As soon as she figured out what she was doing, she'd return to LA, buy a condo in Santa Monica or Venice, and find new office space. Her shoe and accessory designers were temporarily in the warehouse she'd won in the divorce in downtown LA's garment district. Since it was no longer filled with clothes, there was plenty of studio space.

"Are you and Colt still fighting over parking?" Deb asked.

It appeared that everyone in Glory Junction knew about her and Colt's disagreement, which was embarrassing, to say the least.

"We've worked it out," she said.

"Don't let him jerk you around," Carrie Jo said. "The man can be stubborn and pushy."

Delaney couldn't help herself, and asked, "Are you two a couple?"

"Colt and me?" Carrie Jo hooted. "Eww, no. That would be like incest."

Delaney felt herself breathe. She didn't know why she was relieved, but she was.

After book club she drove the short distance home, turned up the drive and, of course, Colt's stupid cruiser sat in her space. She could've sworn that the police car mocked her— *neener, neener, neener*—as she gingerly took the sharp grade up to the garage.

Chapter Five

"Pond is in your office and he doesn't look happy," Carrie Jo told Colt as he came through the door Tuesday morning.

It wasn't even nine yet. On Monday, the mayor had been in Sacramento for a meeting and Colt missed him as much as a bad case of food poisoning.

"What does he want?"

"Beats me."

Whatever it was it couldn't be good, otherwise he would've just used the phone. Colt went into the kitchen and poured himself a cup of coffee, Carrie Jo trailing after him.

"Go in there and get it over with," she said.

Colt pinned her with a look. "I'll go when I'm good and ready." He leaned against the counter, sipping his morning caffeine.

Carrie Jo shook her head. "Do you want to fight or do you want to win? Because taking your sweet-ass time is bound to piss him off."

"Do I look like I care?"

"You're an obstinate man."

He couldn't argue with that. All Garners were. You didn't make it up the mountain, ski the roughest courses, ride the biggest rapids, or jump off the tallest cliffs without being obstinate. Although he'd prefer to call it determination.

"What's your point?" he asked.

She rolled her eyes. "My point is, this"—she pointed at his languid position—"is childish. Go in there and meet him head on." She punctuated her pep talk with a jab to his shoulder and walked out of the kitchen.

He finished the rest of his coffee and ambled into his office like he didn't have a care in the world. Childish or not, Colt didn't want the mayor to think he could push him around. There had to be some autonomy as police chief, otherwise there'd be no checks and balances.

"It's about time," Carter Pond said, pointedly gazing at his watch.

"I didn't realize we had an appointment."

"I'm the mayor, I don't need one."

Colt moved around his desk and sank into his chair. "What can I do for you, Mr. Mayor?"

"Because of your little stunt on the river walk Saturday, we're getting sued."

"What stunt would that be?"

"The spectacle you made with the couple from Southern California."

"You mean the guy who socked me in the stomach after smacking his wife around?" Colt hadn't known where they were from.

"They claim that wasn't the case . . . that you rushed in like a cowboy, caused a scene, and used unnecessary force."

"And you're willing to take their word over mine?" Not that he was surprised, but it still stung to be second-guessed by Pond, again.

"What I'm not willing to do is cost this city money because you can't restrain yourself."

The SOB looked so self-satisfied that Colt wanted to

throw a fist in his face. *See? I can restrain myself*, he almost said. *Otherwise you'd be flat on your ass right now.*

"I want you to talk to Benjamin and work this out," the mayor continued. "I don't care if you have to apologize to the couple or offer them something complimentary from your family's company. Just make this go away."

Pond rose from his seat and stormed out of the office.

Colt shook his head, then picked up the phone and called the city attorney. "Hey, Ben."

"I tried to talk him off the ledge," Ben said, clearly anticipating the call. For the last fifteen years Benjamin Schuster had represented Glory Junction in everything from public sidewalk slip and falls to accusations of sexual harassment. Before that, he was the city attorney for Berkeley but decided that he wanted to raise his family in a small town, away from crime and smog. "He's adamant about making nice with these people."

"Do you know what kind of precedent that sets? The man sucker punched me after knocking his wife around. How do I explain to my officers that we now have to let tourists beat us up so we don't get sued?"

Benjamin let out an audible sigh. "Let me work on it, see what I can do."

"What the hell is wrong with him, Ben? I've dealt with some prickly council people in my time, but we've never had a mayor like this."

"He's different, that's for sure. But we both serve at his whim, so let's keep our cool. I'm talking with the couple's attorney later today and will call you."

"I didn't do anything wrong. You know me, I wouldn't ever use unnecessary force."

"I know," Ben said. "Hold tight."

"Thanks."

Not five minutes after hanging up, Colt got called out

on a six-car pileup on the outskirts of town. It was a mess.
Paramedics triaging at the scene because so many were injured. And firefighters using the Jaws of Life to cut open
cars smashed beyond recognition to rescue motorists and
their passengers.

"A trucker fell asleep at the wheel and veered into oncom-
ing traffic," one of the first-responding officers told Colt
during a briefing.

Colt had suspected something like that. The semi now
sat on its side in the middle of the highway. The driver appeared uninjured but was being taken to Sierra General to be
checked out. A couple of kids had been fitted with neck
braces and were being carried by stretchers. Colt threaded his
way through the chaos, trying to keep out of the medics' way.

He didn't recognize any of the victims, but given how
many cars were involved, some had to be local. A little girl
was standing off to the side, unattended, crying, while her
mother was being worked on. Colt went to the child and
picked her up.

"It's okay, sweetheart. Your mom's gonna be fine." The
woman looked alert and was talking, so Colt didn't think it
was too much of a stretch.

The girl wrapped her arms around Colt's neck and hung
on for dear life. He went looking for a firefighter or one of
his officers to see about calling a relative or the girl's father.

"The husband is on his way," one of the paramedics
told him.

He tried to put the girl down but she wouldn't let go. That
was okay. He kept her with him until her father showed up
and gave the man time to check in with his wife, who was
being loaded into one of the ambulances.

His officers, along with Colt's help, eventually got traffic moving through the area again, diverting it to one lane.
Though cars moved at a snail's pace, it was better than

nothing. Someone tooted his horn and Colt looked up to find his brother Josh waving.

"You need any help?" he called from his truck.

"I think we've got it under control. Just waiting for some more tow trucks."

The ambulances had left for the hospital and the crew was in cleanup mode, getting vehicles and strewn debris off the roadway. A crew had already started on moving the semi.

"All right. See you later, then." Josh pulled away.

Colt didn't get back to the station until later in the day, and was starved when he finally did. After scrounging through the staff refrigerator with no luck, he decided to grab something at the Morning Glory diner, which stayed open all day. Deb was waiting tables and led him to a booth in the back. The restaurant looked like a throwback to the 1950s. Red pleather and chrome bar stools, black and white checked floor, and Formica tabletops. The owner, Felix, couldn't keep a cook to save his life, but the tuna melts and olallieberry pie were consistently solid. They must've been Felix's personal recipes. Colt knew the diner's owner mostly from the slopes; he was a champion snowboarder.

"Just you, Chief?" Deb sat on the bench across from him.

"Yep." He ordered an egg salad sandwich and a side of steak fries.

"Were you out at the accident? I heard it was awful."

"Yeah, pretty nasty, but no fatalities." At least not yet. Two people—a driver and his eighty-year-old passenger—were in critical condition.

"Horrible." She scanned the front of the restaurant to make sure no one else had come in and needed seating. It was late in the day, so the place was quiet. "I met your neighbor, the fashion designer, Monday. I didn't think I would like her, but it wound up I did."

"Why didn't you think you'd like her?"

Deb had grown up in Glory Junction and was Hannah's

best friend. Since middle school, she'd had a thing for Win, but as far as Colt could tell, that wasn't going anywhere. Win was too busy playing the field.

"I thought she would be snooty, being a big designer and all. Plus, I wanted to be loyal to you as far as the parking situation. But she's nice . . . not stuck up at all, even though one of her dresses cost more than my car."

Colt had seen Deb's car and that wasn't saying much. Like a lot of people in Glory Junction, she suffered from ski bumitis and had trouble holding down a steady job. Felix, hard up for good servers, let her play hooky so she could get time in on the slopes. In the summer, she spent as many hours on the lake and river as the Garner brothers.

"Thanks for wanting to have my back, Little Debbie." He grinned because she hated when he called her that.

"Lord knows why I do. But she said you guys kissed and made up."

"I wouldn't go that far." Although he'd be lying if he didn't admit that he'd thought about kissing her in her kitchen the other day. She'd had on a long gauzy shirt, a pair of white stretchy pants, and high-heeled sandals. He knew nothing about fashion, but the outfit was incredibly sexy without showing a lot of skin. What red-blooded man wouldn't have wanted to kiss her? "Let's put it this way, we're learning to share."

"I bet you are." She waggled her brows.

"Now, don't go spreading rumors. She's not my type."

"Why's that?"

Because the next time he fell for a woman, she wasn't going to up and leave him for the bright lights of the big city. For fame and fortune and all the other clichés that made for a bad chick flick. This time he was sticking with his own kind: a small-town girl.

"I prefer blondes," he said with a grin. "You think you could get my food? I'm a little hungry here."

"Sure thing, Chief." She saluted him, walked to the order window, and shouted, "Chicken in the hay and a side of Joan of Arc."

After his late lunch, Colt went back to the office, where he spent the rest of the day returning calls, checking over reports, and listening to Carrie Jo espouse the benefits of a new cleanse diet Foster had told her about. Something about the healing qualities of lemon juice and cayenne pepper. It sounded like a load of crap to Colt, which he'd told her, and had tried to persuade her to go running with him again. She'd come up with a hundred and one excuses. "My knee hurts." "It's too hot." And his personal favorite: "Running gives me diarrhea." Colt didn't want to push too hard and have Carrie Jo see him as a tyrant. Her ex had given her enough shit about her weight.

He got home to find Delaney's Tesla on the easement pad and begrudgingly drove to the top of his drive and exercised the pain-in-his-ass three-point turn. Exhausted, he sincerely hoped the next twelve hours would be crime and accident free. Inside, he stripped out of his uniform, put on a pair of basketball shorts, and planted his ass in front of the flat screen with a beer and a bag of chips, otherwise known as dinner, and spent an hour channel surfing.

Colt fell asleep, woke up to the news, turned off the TV, and hauled himself upstairs to bed. As tired as he was, he couldn't fall asleep again, not with the light from Delaney's window shining through his curtains. *What does she have, a freakin' spotlight up there?* He rolled over to the opposite side, away from the window, and pulled the covers over his head. But it was hot as hell. After a half hour of tossing and turning, he got up, put on clothes, and went over to Delaney's. He didn't care that it was close to midnight.

He banged on her door, ready to rip her a new one. But when she answered in skimpy pajama shorts and a thin tank top, his tongue went numb. Or maybe he had swallowed it. *Don't stare*.

"Hi," she said. "Everything okay?"

He pointed to the side of the house at the offending bedroom. "You left your light on. . . . It's shining in my room."

She walked out onto the deck, barefoot—and braless—and craned her neck to look at what he was talking about. "That's my studio. I'm working."

"At midnight?"

"Yes. When I'm designing I don't pay attention to time."

"Well, I've got to be up at the crack of dawn and I can't sleep. Don't you have shades or something you can pull closed?" Then she could work 24/7 for all he cared.

"Don't you?"

"I have drapes, but the light shines right through. It's like you're making a motion picture up there."

She rolled her eyes. "It is not. Maybe you're just hypersensitive." She said it like there was something wrong with him and he should get over it.

Under ordinary circumstances he would've found her challenge amusing, but he was sleep deprived. "Let me see."

She opened the door and led him inside the house, which was hopped up on steroids. The other day, when they'd had a beer in her kitchen, he'd compared. He was pretty sure his entire house could fit in her pantry.

He followed her up the stairs. *Don't look at her ass*. Instead, he kept his eyes pinned on the industrial-looking metal railing, which he actually liked. It reminded him of an auto body shop. At the landing, she took a right down the hallway to a large room that could've been the master suite but was set up as an office. It had a desk, a bank of file cabinets, a wall covered in cork with pictures and drawings of clothing stuck to it. By the window that faced his bedroom sat a huge drafting table and a lamp that shined as bright as a monster quasar. A person could light the entire earth with that much energy.

He walked over to the switch and turned it off.

"Hey!" She flicked it back on.

"You really need it to be this bright while you're working?"

"No, I just keep it on to annoy you," she said dryly.

"I wouldn't be surprised," he muttered, and went to examine the window. "Why don't you have blinds?"

"Because I don't want anything to interfere with the view. Besides, it isn't a standard-sized window."

Nope. It was more like a wall of glass.

He rubbed his hand down his face. "C'mon, Delaney, work with me here."

"Seriously, how bad can it be?"

He motioned for her to follow him downstairs. When he crossed her deck and headed toward his house, she balked.

"Wait. I'm not dressed."

How had that not been a problem at her house? "Put on a robe, then."

She disappeared, only to reappear in a silky kimono thing that hugged her curves as much as the tank had. But it was the slippers that killed him. High heels. Fluffy feathers. Totally impractical. Bordering on ridiculous. So why were they rocking his world?

"All right. Let's go." She let him take the lead.

As they walked through his house and up the stairs he wondered if she thought he was a slob, then wondered why he cared. The last woman inside his bedroom had been Lisa. Since her, he'd made it a point to date and hook up out of town. As far away as San Francisco if possible.

As soon as she stepped over the threshold, he pointed toward the window. "See what I mean?" He shielded his eyes to make his point.

She gazed around the room, lingered on his messy bed,

then focused on the window where the drapes were drawn. "Huh. I never realized how close our houses are."

He wanted to say, *You mean how you encroached on my property when you decided to build Xanadu*, but refrained.

"It's a little bright," she said.

"Are you freaking kidding me? It's like having Eta Carinae two feet away."

She gave him a look. "This is going to be a problem because I work a lot at night. It's when I'm the most creative."

"Okay. Get some blackout shades."

She scrunched up her nose. "Why don't you?"

"Because I don't think it's unreasonable to expect a good neighbor to turn off her klieg lights at midnight."

She sat on the edge of his bed and his instant reaction was to think about sex. With her. Which wasn't good because pretty soon she'd look at the lower half of him and see what he was thinking. *Shouldn't have worn basketball shorts.*

"I guess I don't have a choice then," she said, clearly clueless of his predicament. "They'll have to be custom, due to the size and shape of the window. That could take some time."

It was a miracle he'd heard what she said at all, since he could see that her nipples were hard where the fabric of her robe puckered. *Avert your eyes, asshole.* "I'd, uh, just appreciate you taking care of it."

She let out a breath. "Between the parking and the lights, you're the most high-maintenance neighbor I've ever had. You know that, Garner?"

He laughed at her use of his last name. It was very football coach for a fashion designer who wore pink feathers on her feet. "That's what you get for living next door to a police chief who likes to occasionally sleep."

"I heard about the accident on Highway Eighty-nine . . . pretty bad, huh?"

"Yep, though it could've been worse." By the time Colt had left work, one of the victims had been upgraded from critical to fair condition.

"Awful when something like that happens." She shook her head. "According to the news, the driver who caused it fell asleep."

"That's what he says."

"You don't believe him?"

"Trust but verify," he automatically recited. "Though it's more than likely what happened. There was no evidence of drinking or drugs."

Delaney continued to inspect his room, making no move to leave. His place must've appeared pretty modest compared to all the high-end furnishings she had. Colt put his money into ski equipment and climbing gear, which didn't leave a lot left over for decorating. Her eyes landed on his guitar case, which leaned against the wall. "Hannah says you play."

"I used to." He shrugged. "Don't really have time for it much anymore."

"You miss it?"

He missed the way it used to be. Before Lisa took that part of him with her when she left. "Sometimes. But I've got my hands full."

"I thought Hannah said you performed recently."

"I did, Thursday night. But I don't have anything else planned." Since they were getting quasi personal, he asked, "How's the designing going?"

"Great. Really, really good," she said a little too enthusiastically.

He raised his brows. "Yeah?"

"Actually, no." She scooted up to lean against one of his pillows, dropped the porno slippers on the floor, and tucked those amazing legs under her. The robe parted as she moved, showing a good amount of thigh. "I'm completely blocked.

Every idea I come up with looks like something I've already done."

Despite it being an exceptionally bad idea, he sat on the bed next to her. "What's wrong with that? You've got a style that's well received, why not stick with it?"

"Because you should constantly grow as a designer. And then there's the fact that I don't want my new lines looking exactly like Robert's."

"But Robert's stuff is . . . was . . . your stuff. Everyone knows that, right?"

"Yes. I still need to rebrand myself, however. That's the difficulty of starting over."

He saw the strain around her eyes and recognized that she must be under a lot of pressure. No wonder she worked late at night. "Is that why you're working at midnight?"

"I need investors. In order to get investors, I have to show them something."

"Even with the track record you have?"

"I'll get some on that, I suppose. But it's not just the designs, it's the track record of running a profitable business. And that was all Robert."

At least she gave her ex his due, Colt thought. Lisa never had.

"Maybe you're pushing yourself too hard. Maybe it'll come back to you when you stop focusing on it so much."

"That's what I keep thinking and then . . . nothing. I'm sure something will happen eventually. But if it doesn't, I'll miss fashion week in late September." Colt hitched his shoulders because he didn't know what fashion week was, so she explained. "That's when houses showcase new collections to buyers and the media."

She swung her feet down and sat upright. "I should let you go to bed. Until I get window coverings I'll try not to use the lamp."

"I'd appreciate that." He noticed she wasn't completely

committing, and it was on the tip of his tongue to say *Why don't you use another room?* But like the parking situation, he decided to take one victory at a time.

When they got downstairs and he started to follow her out, she said, "What are you doing?"

"Walking you home."

"Why?" she asked. "I only live next door."

Colt didn't bother to dignify that with an answer. Instead, he saw Delaney to her door. "Good night."

"'Night."

He stood on her front deck for a few minutes, then walked back to his house. By the time he got to his room the light in her studio was out. He was about to crawl into his bed when his cell rang. Five teens had been arrested for vandalizing the high school. Ordinarily, he would've let the graveyard shift handle the kids' irate parents. But knowing that Pond was gunning for him, he decided to deal with it himself.

Two hours later, he sat at his desk in the police station, filling out the last report. The kids had been returned to their parents, but everything had to be documented for the district attorney's office. Because they were juveniles, no charges would be filed. They'd likely just be cited and ultimately ordered to pay a fine and perform community service. Some of the kids involved were self-entitled shit heads and Colt fully expected the parents to complain that little Johnny or Jane wasn't getting a fair shake. That's why he was crossing every *T* and dotting every *I*. Otherwise, he'd have the mayor crawling up his ass again.

Instead of going home, Colt slept on his office couch and was awakened by Carrie Jo, who brought him a steaming cup of coffee.

"No thanks necessary, but a raise would be good."

Colt sat up and took the mug from her. "What time is it?"

"Nine. There's a clean uniform in the closet if you want to shower and dress here."

"Nah, I'm gonna run home. If anyone is looking for me, tell them I had a long night and that I can be reached on my cell."

Colt drove to his house, noted that Delaney's car was gone, and snagged the parking space, not planning to stay long. After a hot shower, he headed back to town, stopping at Garner Adventure to check in. He hadn't seen his parents in a few days. There was a new receptionist at the front desk and TJ was showing her how to use the computer system.

"What's up?" TJ asked, preoccupied. "Heard the high school got trashed."

"Yeah. Kids. Where's Mom and Dad?"

"Dad's waterskiing with a group of seniors and Mom's in her office. Meet Darcy, Colt."

"Hi, Darcy."

Darcy smiled shyly. She was cute in a librarian kind of way, but sort of intense, chewing her bottom lip and jotting down everything TJ said on a steno pad.

"Hey." Win came into the reception area and shoulder checked him. "I thought I heard your voice. Want to grab coffee?"

Colt's stomach rumbled. "I could do that. TJ?"

"Sure. Let me finish up with Darcy."

"I'll go say hello to Mom quick," Colt said. "See if Josh wants to go too?"

He was headed to his mother's office when his cell rang with a call from the mayor. Gritting his teeth, he ground out, "What now?"

Chapter Six

With a few recommendations from Hannah, Delaney found someone to come to the house to measure for motorized blackout shades. At least during the day, the shades would be hidden, letting her still take advantage of the view. Colt was a real contradiction—thoughtful and attentive one minute, demanding and obnoxious the next.

Despite how aggravating he could be, she was attracted to him, which surprised her. After Robert's ultimatum she'd wanted nothing to do with men. Or sex, for that matter. But the other night, sitting on Colt's bed, taking in his rumpled sheets, she'd entertained a few naughty fantasies. Colt hadn't exactly helped the situation. She'd caught him checking out her breasts and legs a number of times. But that was a man for you. It didn't necessarily mean he was interested. Delaney had no idea what his relationship status was, and if she were smart she'd stay away from him. Nothing good could come from it. Although a short, meaningless affair might be just what she needed to get her motor running again. Perhaps it would give her back some of her self-confidence. Or maybe she was just looking for an excuse to do it with Chief Hottie from Hell.

Through the window, she saw Hannah's car pull up and raced down the stairs to meet her.

"Did he come?" Hannah asked, carrying a white box.

"He did and I ordered them. What do you have there?"

"Fliers and posters for the annual End-of-Summer festivities. I have to bring them over to Colt's house before we leave so he can pass them around the police department and city hall. It'll only take a second."

"No problem. Let me just grab my keys and purse."

"I'll drive," Hannah said. "God forbid I should block Colt from parking in his favorite spot."

They both walked over to Colt's and Hannah unlocked the door and ducked inside to put the box on his kitchen counter. Delaney waited on the porch.

"You have a key?" she asked, curious about the Garner family dynamic.

All the brothers seemed close, from what she could tell. She'd often see two, three, or all four of them together at a restaurant or at Old Glory. Being an only child, she thought it was nice.

"We all have each other's keys. Colt works so much that sometimes I bring him a home-cooked meal. They all love my late aunt's pecan pie, so I try to surprise him with it every once in a while."

On their way back to Hannah's car, Delaney checked her mail. An envelope with the return address of Robert's law firm immediately caught her eye. She quickly stuffed it in her purse, along with the rest of the mail, planning to look at it later.

"Everything okay?" Hannah asked.

She pasted a smile on her face. "Yep. Everything's fine."

When they got to Old Glory, Deb and Foster flagged them over to a table in the corner. Every inch of the bar was covered in American flags. Even the bathrooms had stars and stripes wallpaper. Patrons could help themselves to peanuts in big oak barrels and throw their shells on the sticky, hardwood floor. A row of pool tables stood off to the side and a rather elaborate stage setup with lighting and a sound board took up the back of the hall. Definitely different from the fashionable restaurants in LA that she and Robert had regularly frequented.

She'd yet to attend one of the open mic nights or any of Old Glory's live shows. Delaney hadn't wanted to come alone. But she was working on making friends.

"What took you so long?" Deb asked as they sat down.

"I had to pick up the posters and fliers for the annual End-of-Summer festivities at the copy shop and drop a box off at Colt's. Can you hang a poster and put a stack of fliers in your shop, Foster?"

"Sure," he said. "Are you competing in the kayak races, Deb?"

"Hell yeah! I'm on Team Morning Glory and this year we're going to crush Garner Adventure."

"Delusional much?" Foster rolled his eyes, then turned to Delaney. "The Garners win it every year. I don't know why they continue to hold the damn thing; it's not even a competition."

"Sweet Stems ought to enter, Foster. It's great marketing," Hannah said, adding that the kayakers all wore funny costumes representing their respective businesses.

"Foster doesn't need it." Deb chuckled. "Words out among the bridezillas that he does the best bouquets and centerpieces in Nevada County."

Hannah turned to Delaney. "Since Foster bought Sweet Stems two years ago, he's doubled business."

Foster waved his hand at Hannah. "It's not like it was hard, okay? The last owner's idea of a good floral arrangement involved gas station flowers. She didn't even try to go after the ski resorts. Crazy dumb because they pay my rent."

He tried to get the attention of one of the servers to take their orders.

"I'd love to come by the shop." Delaney had never been there before. Maybe it would give her some inspiration.

"Anytime. I'll put you to work. With your design talents, I bet you'd make killer arrangements."

"I don't know about that. I'm sort of in a slump these days."

"What exactly does a slump for you mean?" Deb asked.

Delaney pondered how honest she wanted to be and decided to go with the entire truth. "I haven't designed anything since my divorce. Like nothing. Nada. Zip."

"How long ago was the divorce? Wait. Hold that answer." Frustrated with the slow service, Foster got up, went to the bar, and returned a few minutes later. "Maureen decided to take a break. Boden is sending over one of the new waitresses. So, how long since the divorce?"

"A year." She grimaced.

"Holy shit, you haven't been able to design anything in a year?"

"Nope. Most days I sit, staring at my sketch pad. On the good days, I draw something and realize it's a piece from one of my earlier collections."

"Has this ever happened to you before?" Deb grabbed a handful of peanuts from the basket at the center of the table.

"Nope."

"It's the aftermath of the divorce," Hannah chimed in. "After a relationship dissolves you go through a period of being shell shocked."

Delaney knew that Hannah had been married to someone else before Josh but was sketchy on the details.

The waitress finally came over and they gave her their orders.

After she left, Delaney said, "I don't know. I'm worried

that I'm tapped out, that my creative juices died with my marriage."

"I doubt it," Foster said. "You're just going through a phase. We all do at one point or another."

She hoped that's all it was. Otherwise she'd have to find a new vocation.

The door swung open and Colt and two other men came into the bar. Colt immediately spotted them and approached the table to say hi, bussing Hannah on the cheek.

"What about me?" Deb protested.

"I thought you were only interested in Win's kisses." Colt winked.

She gave him the middle finger and he laughed all the way back to his party, which had grabbed a booth at the front of the restaurant.

Hannah gazed over at the three men and back to their table. "I bet they're having a meeting about Pond."

"The mayor?" Delaney asked. The creep had once tried to hit on her at a city council meeting right in front of Robert while they were trying to get a variance to build their house larger than city code allowed for their lot size.

"Mm-hmm. He's making poor Colt's life a living hell," Hannah whispered.

"Why?" Foster asked. "He's the best chief we've ever had."

Hannah shrugged. "According to Josh, he doesn't like Colt. Thinks he's too tight with the residents and doesn't kiss up enough to tourists."

"The guy's a dick," Deb said, and they all turned to stare at her. "Not Colt, Pond Scum. I know everyone thinks he's the second coming of Christ. Handsome, rich, and charming. But I think he's unctuous. Why don't the Garners get him recalled? They've got the clout."

"I don't think so," Hannah said. "Carter Pond won by a landslide. He's very pro tourism and all the members of the Glory Junction Chamber of Commerce are counting on him to turn the town into an Aspen or Jackson. At the last chamber meeting he read a *Bloomberg Businessweek* article to us that said ski towns are the richest small towns in America."

"We've already become one of those towns," Deb said. "Six years ago you couldn't have carried Delaney's clothes in your store. No one here could afford them. But now they sell like hotcakes."

"I guess Pond thinks we can do better and the chamber is definitely drinking his Kool-Aid."

"What's Colt planning to do?" Foster asked.

The server brought their food and Hannah waited until she left to respond. "What can he do? The mayor's his boss."

Delaney had had no idea that Colt was experiencing work problems. All the evidence appeared to suggest the opposite. He was well liked. And ridiculously dedicated. Whether it was late at night or the wee hours of the morning, she often heard him speeding down their easement road to deal with a police matter. Now she felt guilty for giving him crap about the parking space.

"You think the mayor will try to edge him out?" Delaney asked.

Hannah snuck another peek at Colt's booth. "I don't know. Josh thinks he's trying. But the Garners aren't a family to mess with. They stand up for each other, and Garner Adventure is partly what put this town on the map. People won't easily forget that."

They ate while Deb told them of her latest dating fiasco—a weekender who'd lied about being single. One of his buddies had slipped by letting Deb know that not only was he married but he had two kids.

"What a troll," Deb said.

"I wish you and Win would get together all ready and save

us from these tragic stories." Hannah glanced over at Foster, who nodded his head.

"Were you two an item?" It was the first Delaney had heard of it other than Colt's earlier quip.

Foster chortled. "She wishes."

"Deb has been in love with Win since the beginning of time." Hannah took a bite of her sandwich. "Unfortunately, Win is an idiot."

Delaney had only crossed paths with Win a few times, so she couldn't attest to whether he was an idiot or not. Deb, however, was gorgeous and seemed to be the life of the party. Delaney couldn't imagine a man not being interested in her. But there was no accounting for chemistry. You either felt it or you didn't.

"What about Colt? Is he single?" As soon as the words left Delaney's mouth she felt three pairs of eyes on her. "For Deb of course. Or Foster. Are you single, Foster?" She'd assumed he was gay. Foster, not Colt.

"I am," Foster said. "But I'm not Colt's type."

"What's his type?" She couldn't help herself.

They all three said "Lisa" at the same time.

Aha, Colt did have a significant other. Delaney knew it. "Who's Lisa?"

"A viper who left him. Not only did she take his heart but she took his—"

"Foster," Hannah admonished, "we shouldn't be talking about this." She turned to Delaney. "Colt is very private when it comes to that part of his life."

"It's not like most of the town doesn't know the sordid story already." Deb came to Foster's defense. "But fine, we won't gossip about your brother-in-law."

"Thank you. I'm sure Colt would appreciate it," Hannah said.

As Delaney watched Colt and his two cohorts finish their

lunch and pay their bill, she wondered what the "sordid story" was with the ex. Lisa. She was merely curious was all.

Colt left Old Glory anticipating another bad meeting with the mayor. When Pond had called earlier that morning, he'd been out of town. But he'd been furious over something Colt had done. Instead of just telling him what it was, Pond wanted to drag it out and make Colt wait until they could meet in person.

Ben headed for city hall and Jack had an errand to run, leaving Colt to walk back to the station by himself. Glancing at his watch, he picked up the pace. He'd like to make the mayor wait, but why borrow extra trouble?

At least Ben had made the lawsuit situation with the drunk couple go away. He'd not-so-casually mentioned to the pair that Colt was thinking of countersuing for being punched in the stomach, reminding them that there had been a sidewalk full of witnesses. The couple promptly took back their threats. Colt didn't think he could've tolerated apologizing to the man. As much as he loved his job, he had to draw the line somewhere.

He figured today's infraction would be about the way he'd handled the parents of the kids who'd vandalized the high school. There was no telling how much Pond would bend over to appease voters. The teens had caused a good deal of damage. No way would a slap on the wrist be enough. Granted they were only kids, but the punishment needed to fit the crime. He and his brothers used to run wild through these mountains as boys. When they screwed up, Gray and Mary Garner made them take responsibility for their actions. They didn't like it at the time, but Colt knew those consequences had played an important role in shaping the type of men they became.

Screw Pond! If the mayor wanted to fire him, fine. But

Colt wasn't about to be Pond's bitch or run the department with the sole purpose of getting him reelected.

Needing to lower his blood pressure before he reached the station, he turned his thoughts to Delaney. She'd looked good at Old Glory. Her hair had been up in a messy kind of style that was sexy as hell and he'd liked her dress. Classy but clingy. So, she and Hannah had become buds. It didn't surprise him. They were both into clothes and stylish things.

He was glad he hadn't made a move on her the other night in his bedroom. He'd gotten the sense that she wouldn't have been opposed to a little fooling around. But it'd be just his luck that she'd become a disgruntled lover and start leveling complaints against him. Not a good idea given the kind of scrutiny he was under from the mayor. He and Delaney barely tolerated each other as it was. And they had zip in common. He liked outdoorsy women who could hold their own on the slopes or a sheer rock face, anything with a degree of danger. And according to his brother, Delaney didn't even ski.

He'd just gotten in the building when his phone buzzed with a call from TJ. Ducking into a corner, he answered. "This an emergency? Because I don't have time to talk."

"Can you do a cave tour tomorrow night? Josh has to go to San Francisco for a doctor's appointment about his leg." He had a couple of specialists there who were trying to decide whether he needed another surgery.

Colt pinched the bridge of his nose. "Let me see if Jack can be on call. I'll let you know later." He hung up, put his phone on silent, and made a beeline for his office, wanting to be at his desk before Pond showed up.

"Cutting it kind of close," Carrie Jo said as they passed each other on her way to the kitchen. "His secretary called; he's on his way over."

"Great," Colt said with the enthusiasm of a dead man.

"Just don't get fired," she shot back. "The town needs you."

He went inside his office. Pond showed up a few minutes later, dressed in khaki shorts and a polo shirt. He looked like he'd just gotten off the links rather than coming from city hall. Probably playing golf all day. Other than hobnobbing with the town's elite, the mayor wasn't from the hard workers. At least Colt's parents hadn't been sucked in by Pond's phoniness. They'd voted for the other candidate.

"What can I do for you, Mr. Mayor?" He really had to learn to curb his sarcasm. Then again, he'd never been good with authority.

One look at Pond and Colt could tell he was fuming. Mottled red face and a jaw clenched tighter than a sealed lid. Pond took a seat, pulled a laptop from his briefcase, fiddled around with it for a second, and shoved it in front of Colt.

One look at the screen and Colt knew he was toast. It was the picture of him with the topless bachelorette party chicks. A lot of bare breasts and nipples filled the shot. One of the girls had posted it on her Facebook page and had tagged Glory Junction, meaning the picture had automatically shown up on the wall of the city's page. Not good. Not good at all.

"It was my day off," Colt said, and then wanted to shoot himself for acting so cavalier. But anyone familiar with his work ethic would know that he'd never do anything intentionally to embarrass the town.

"I don't care if you were on vacation in the Bahamas. This reflects piss poorly on Glory Junction, the police department . . . the uniform." He pointed at Colt's blue police shirt to make his point. "Are these girls even legal?"

"Of course they are." At least he hoped they were. "It was a bachelorette party. I was their white-water rafting guide. After the trip, they goofed around for the picture. It's not like we were having an orgy." The raft, the river, and all their equipment sat in plain view in the background. Hardly a site for a wild sex party.

"Well, that's what it looks like here." Pond turned the computer so he could examine the picture closer. He stared at it so hard Colt wondered if the mayor was trying to memorize the women's cup sizes. "How am I supposed to explain this to the council?"

Most of the council members had known Colt since he was a kid. They knew what kind of man he was. Cavorting publicly with naked women was Win's MO, not Colt's.

"If you want, I'll go to tomorrow night's council meeting and explain the situation," Colt said.

"I think you should resign."

I bet you do, asshole. Colt sucked in a breath. "If the council wants me to resign, I'll resign." *Over a stupid picture on his day off.*

Pond deliberated, clearly infuriated that Colt wouldn't tender his resignation right here, right now. The mayor had the power to remove him as chief, but Colt knew he didn't want to make a misstep. The Garners had a lot of friends in this town and it wouldn't pay to alienate them. No, the mayor would rather Colt go voluntarily or that the council fire him, which Pond knew they wouldn't do.

Pond got to his feet. "I won't tolerate you staining the reputation of this town. Be there tomorrow night, but remember that the ultimate decision lies with me."

Colt didn't say anything, just watched as the mayor stomped out. As soon as he left the building, Carrie Jo burst in.

"Girls gone wild, huh?"

"You saw the picture?"

"Oh yeah. The minute Pond Scum got here the phone started ringing. You're quite the celebrity on Facebook."

Colt frowned. "Glory Junction's page, huh?"

"Yep, and the police department's page. Last I looked, it had two-thousand likes."

"Shit."

His cell vibrated in his pocket. He looked at the display and rolled his eyes, then answered. "What?"

"Looking good there, lover boy," Win said, and he heard his other brothers laughing in the background. Great. They had the call on speaker.

"I'm glad you're all enjoying it. TJ, I can't do the cave tour tomorrow night because I have to go to the council meeting and apologize. But I may soon have a lot of free time on my hands."

"What are you talking about?" TJ's voice came over the line. "The council won't fire you."

"No, but the mayor might. He made sure to let me know that he'd have the final say."

"That's bullshit," Josh said.

"I shouldn't be talking about this here." He glared at Carrie Jo, who'd stuck around to eavesdrop.

"Meet us for drinks at Old Glory after work," TJ said.

"All right. See you later."

Carrie Jo sat in the seat the mayor had vacated. "Pond Scum really said that? He wants to fire you over one silly picture? It wasn't like *you* were naked."

"The man's looking for any excuse."

Colt spent the rest of the day working on reports, fielding e-mails, and setting up an emergency response training for a couple of the rookies. When he finally got around to glancing at the clock, it was nearly seven. His brothers would be waiting for him at Old Glory. He changed into a pair of jeans and a Henley.

Carrie Jo was gone for the day, so he locked up his office and drove to the bar. Boden, the owner, greeted him. About the same age as Colt, he'd bought the bar a few years ago and had added thirty local microbrews to the tap. The guy was really into craft beer and knew a lot about it.

"Hey, Chief. How you doing?" He wiped the bar down and filled Colt a pint glass of an IPA. "Try this and tell me what you think."

Colt took a drink. "Nice. Herbal and citrusy."

"Yup, exactly. That one's on the house. So, when you gonna play for us again? Good crowd we got last time."

If Colt survived Bachelorettegate, he suspected it would be best to lie low for a while. "I got a lot going on right now, Boden. Maybe sometime this fall I can schedule something. You see my brothers?"

"They're over at the pool tables."

"Thanks. And thanks for the beer."

It was packed for a Wednesday night and he had to squeeze through the crowd to get to them. When he finally did, Josh and TJ were playing a game of eight ball and Win and Deb a game of darts.

"Hey," Josh said. "You just get off work?"

"Yeah." Colt grabbed a chair at his brothers' table. Boden may as well put a Garner plaque on it, they sat at it so much. "What's going on at GA?"

"Nothing. But your picture is making the rounds. Dad thought it was hysterical."

"It's been great for business," TJ chimed in. "We got a couple of bookings today with guys wanting to sign up for the topless white-water trips."

"Glad everyone is amused. Pond wants me to resign over it."

Josh and TJ stopped their game and came over to the table. Win and Deb wandered over too.

"I thought you were kidding earlier," TJ said. "He can't be serious. It was a couple of women screwing around. How did that hurt anyone?"

"It's not exactly a good image for the Glory Junction

Police Department. Please tell me, TJ, that the girls were all legal."

"Of course they were. We get parental consent for anyone under eighteen. We have photocopies of their licenses if you need to show them to Pond."

"I may have to show them to the council."

Win pulled a face. "That's messed up, man. Everyone in this town knows you wouldn't do anything to hurt Glory Junction's reputation. The girls were just having fun. It's no different than Rita's calendar, for God's sake."

Deb gave Colt a hug. "Screw Pond Scum. Everyone knows he's a carpetbagger."

That wasn't the point, but Colt appreciated the sentiment anyway. "I'm sure it'll be fine," he said, not necessarily believing it. There was no question the mayor wanted a more malleable chief, someone who wouldn't stand up to him the way Colt did. This was exactly the kind of excuse Pond could use to jettison him.

Hannah showed up and they wound up ordering food. He played a game of pool, whupped Win's ass at darts, and went home, feeling grateful for his family and friends standing by him. The easement parking space was open, so he nabbed it. As he walked to his kitchen door, he spied Delaney on her deck, pacing back and forth with her cell pressed to her ear. He couldn't hear what she was saying, but could tell the conversation was heated.

He started to let himself inside, quickly darted another glance over at Delaney's deck, and saw her crying. His instincts shouted for him to go over to make sure she was okay, but he fought them. Colt didn't have much room to screw up with Pond watching his every move, and as far as Delaney was concerned, he wasn't sure he wouldn't.

Chapter Seven

"Why are you being so incredibly unfair about this? If anything, Robert, I'm the one who should be out for blood in this divorce. I'm not the one who became bored and dissatisfied with our marriage and changed the rules."

After lunch she'd opened the envelope from her ex's lawyer. It was a cease and desist letter, demanding her to stop selling her shoes and handbags under the Delaney Scott name. Her attorney was trying to reach Robert's lawyer. Despite being advised not to contact Robert herself, she'd hoped that he'd see reason if she made a personal appeal.

Big mistake, because he was sticking to his guns and being damned abusive about it.

"*I* became bored and dissatisfied?" he scoffed. "You rarely had sex with me anymore, Delaney. And when you did your mind was elsewhere."

She couldn't argue with that. Obviously their marriage had needed work, but his answer to saving it had been out of the question.

"And this is how you get even? This is the way you punish me for not going along with your warped plan to infuse new life into our relationship? You steal my company and cut off my income stream?"

"It wasn't your company, Delaney. It was our company. Both of us know that I was the one who built it to what it is today. Yes, the designs were yours. But without me, we never would've become a global brand with the kind of retail reach Delaney Scott has. You're an artist, Delaney, I'll give you that. But your head for business . . . well, it's nonexistent."

Her eyes filled with tears because he was right. That's why their partnership had been perfect. At least the professional part of it. And now she wasn't even an artist. Her well of creativity had gone dry.

"Do you realize how much it will hurt my bottom line to do what you want?" she asked in a choked whisper.

"Don't make it sound like this is me doing something underhanded to you. This is what the court found equitable, Delaney. What about my bottom line? In essence, we're both starting over."

No, they weren't. He still owned the name—her name. The Delaney Scott brand was famous. All he had to do was maintain the quality and integrity of the company. She, on the other hand, had to completely invent a new brand, introduce it to the world, and hope like hell it would sell.

"My lawyer says the judge's ruling did not include me taking the Delaney Scott name off preexisting merchandise. And I'll go back to court if I have to for clarification."

"You'll lose in the end, Delaney. And it'll wind up costing both of us a lot of money. It would behoove you to—"

She hung up on him before he could finish the thought. Liz had warned her about calling him and Delaney should've listened. Yet, there'd been a time when he'd been reasonable and she'd hoped to appeal to the old Robert.

"Everything okay?"

She jerked, surprised to see Colt standing a few feet from her deck.

"Yes. Of course." She wiped her eyes with the back of her hands, trying to hide the evidence of her tears.

He came closer. She noted he wasn't in his uniform. Perhaps he'd gone out after work or had put in a few hours at Garner Adventure. The clothes were nothing special, just a faded pair of jeans and a long-sleeve T-shirt. But he wore them better than any man she knew.

"You looked upset," he said, and gave her a long perusal. "I just wanted to make sure there's not a problem."

No problem, she almost said, and sniffled, realizing she wasn't kidding anyone. "I just got off the phone with my ex. He wants me to stop using the Delaney Scott label on my handbags and shoes—the ones already manufactured."

"I thought he got the name in the divorce."

"He did. But according to my lawyer's interpretation, the decision isn't retroactive to include merchandise made before the ruling."

"Ah." Colt nodded his head. "What if it is?"

She let out a sigh. "It's going to cost me a lot of money."

"I'm sorry," he said.

"Me too. Would you like to come in for a glass of wine . . . or some of that beer you brought over?" The invitation had just sort of popped out of her mouth, and from the way his eyes had shifted toward his house, she fully expected him to decline the offer.

"Yeah, okay. But I've got an early day tomorrow." He came up the stairs and followed her inside.

Suddenly she felt awkward, like she might've given him the wrong impression. Of course, he'd asked her into his bedroom the other night, but that had been to see how bright the light in her studio was. Still, there'd been this weird sexual tension and she didn't want him to think that she was hitting on him, which he probably got a lot of.

She led him through the front room into the kitchen and he took a stool at the breakfast bar while she went to the cupboard. "Wine or beer?"

"Beer, please."

He sized up the open floor plan like she'd noticed he'd done the last time, taking it all in. "You keep it neat, don't you?"

"I have a housekeeper." She reached for a bowl on tiptoes and she felt him come up behind her. "I've got it."

He pulled the dish down anyway, pressing against her back in the process. He was big and solid and she liked the feel of him. But he moved away all too soon.

The last man she'd been with had been Robert and he was definitely an ectomorph, thin with long legs. Colt was a mesomorph, classic athletic build. Muscular and strong. Mesomorphs had the most problems finding the perfect fit because of their V shape—wide shoulders, small waist. But she'd have no trouble fitting Colt.

"You didn't come from work, did you?" she asked, and filled the bowl with pretzels.

"I went to Old Glory when I got off duty."

"Again?"

He chuckled, clearly remembering that they'd seen each other there at lunch. "Yeah. I should probably branch out, but there's no other place to play pool and the beer's good. Since Boden bought it, he's vastly improved what's on tap."

"Did you meet someone there?" Delaney hoped the question sounded innocent enough. Admittedly, she was nosy about whom he dated. A guy like him must be spoiled for choice.

"My brothers, Deb, and Hannah. I'm guessing you don't play much pool . . . or darts." He said it like she was too snobbish to hang out in pool halls and dive bars. At least that's the way Delaney took it and it miffed her. He didn't know anything about her.

"I never had much of an opportunity to learn. Maybe I will while I'm here."

He looked at her like *yeah, right*, which only made her

want to prove him wrong. "How's the designing coming along?"

She inwardly groaned. "Not good. I've been working day and night—and nothing. I did order shades for my studio, though." That's about all she'd accomplished this week, besides fighting with Robert.

"Why do you think that's happening?"

"I just keep hitting a wall. It's as if I have brain freeze." She poured them each a beer and slid his down the bar.

He nodded as if he knew exactly what she was talking about. "Maybe you need a change in scenery. What about taking a day off to go river rafting?"

Right now, time was her enemy. Taking a day off would only make her anxious. "What would that accomplish?"

"Sometimes I find being outdoors, communing with nature, or partaking in a little adventure frees me up."

Freed him up from what? she wondered. The stress of being police chief? His music? But she got the sense his music was just a hobby. "I don't know. It's different for me. I usually find my inspiration in big cities, watching people, seeing the way they dress."

He sat back down and took a slug of his beer. "It's just a thought. If you change your mind, I'll take you out. You said you've always wanted to go."

Was he asking her on a date? She didn't think so, but he was being awfully generous. And given the fact that up until recently their relationship had been less than friendly, she wasn't about to look a gift horse in the mouth.

"I suppose it couldn't hurt. And if you're willing to be my guide . . . I have always wanted to try it."

"Sure. Sunday's my day off; we could do it then."

"We won't do anything crazy, right? Remember, I'm a beginner."

He chuckled. "Nothing crazy, I promise."

Colt's phone chimed and he quickly reached into his pocket for it.

"Are you getting called out to a crime scene?"

"Nope," he said, scanning the display on his cell and stuffing it back in his pocket. "I'm good."

He looked up and their eyes locked. Something in his gaze made her catch her breath, then look away.

She took her beer and sat at the short end of the L-shaped bar, facing him. "Did you have a good day at work?"

"Not particularly." He seemed to consider his words and then forged ahead. "I guess you don't look at Facebook."

"Not often, no. Why?"

"I took a bachelorette party out white-water rafting last weekend. We took a group picture. At the last second, they flashed the camera and posted the photo on Facebook. Needless to say, the mayor isn't too happy about it."

And according to Hannah, the mayor wasn't too happy with Colt in general.

Delaney grabbed her phone off the counter and launched the Facebook app. She found the picture in under five seconds. There was Colt standing in the center of a group of women lifting their bikini tops. It wasn't like he was fondling any of them or doing anything offensive. Just a silly photograph of women having a good time. It was clear from his expression that he was an unwitting participant. Jeez, you could find more suggestive poses in a fashion magazine.

"The mayor's bent out of shape over this?"

He hitched his shoulders. "It's pretty unprofessional."

"Definitely if you were in uniform. But clearly you weren't on duty when this photograph was taken. He must know you moonlight for your family's adventure company, so what's the big deal?"

His mouth curved up in a crooked smile. Damn. If she

could find a way to bottle that smile and sell it, she'd be filthy rich.

"Hopefully the city council agrees with you," he said.

Her jaw dropped open. "You have to go before the council?"

"It's either that or Pond gets me to resign." He took another drink of his beer.

She couldn't believe that something this innocent had gotten him into such hot water. It was beyond ridiculous. "Pond's a jackass."

He smirked, then quickly went neutral. "You said it, not me."

"He's also a sleazeball. When Robert and I were trying to get a variance to build this house, he hit on me, like a quid pro quo could be arranged. Can you believe that?"

"Yeah," he said without hesitation. "Pond's got a reputation as a womanizer. Regardless, I imagine a lot of men hit on you."

She did a double take. "Why would you think that?"

"Seriously?" When she didn't answer, he gave her a hard look. "You're not kidding, are you?" He chuckled and held up his hands as if in surrender. "I'm in enough trouble. . . . I can't go there. So did your ex have words with Pond?"

She shook her head. "I don't think Robert noticed." Or cared.

He raised his brows but didn't say anything. She got the impression that unlike Robert, Colt might be territorial, which sent a small shiver down her spine.

"In any event, the incident left a bad taste in my mouth. I know a lot of people are in Pond's camp, but not me. I can't fathom that you would lose your job over this." She indicated the picture still on her phone.

"Yeah, I hope not." He acted nonchalant about it, but Delaney sensed he was anything but. His job—being the police chief—was important to him, she could tell.

"You want something to eat besides pretzels?" She'd noticed he'd made good work of the bowl.

"Nah, I ate at Old Glory. But I'm probably holding you up from dinner." He got up and took his empty glass to the sink. "Thanks for the beer, Delaney."

She'd enjoyed talking to him and didn't want him to leave, but she also didn't want to seem desperate for company. Ordinarily she was fine being by herself. But he was easy to tell things to—at least when they weren't fighting. And the way he looked at her made her feel attractive again. But he wanted to go, and asking him to stay . . . Well, she wasn't going to put herself out there. She already felt like a spectacular failure.

Much to Pond's disappointment, the city council had been unconcerned over Colt's so-called lapse of judgment. Rita Tucker had even publicly laughed about the Facebook post, now referred to simply as the "Girls Gone Wild" picture.

Of course she was one to talk. There'd been a lot of eyebrows raised over her calendar, which got racier every year. Last year, Colt as Mr. July had flat-out refused to wear a stars and stripes jock sock, telling Rita they wouldn't find one big enough. But Win, Mr. December, had posed in nothing but a mistletoe loincloth. They were still giving him shit about it.

Much of the town had turned out for the meeting, and Colt suspected that his father had had something to do with that. Gray Garner usually didn't get involved in town politics unless someone abused his or her power. Then he got very involved.

"So much for Pond Scum's shock and awe show." Win sailed a dart from the toe line and made a bull's-eye. "No one gave a rat's ass. Too bad Josh missed the meeting. He could've been bored out of his skull like the rest of us."

TJ had managed to find a sub to take a group on the cave

tour and had attended the meeting with the rest of the Garners. He and Deb were engaged in a pretty heated game of one-pocket. Hannah had gone with Josh to his appointment in San Francisco.

Boden sauntered over, put two pitchers down on the table, and sidled up to Colt and Win. "A couple of new microbrews from Tahoe I wanted you to try. Sorry I missed the meeting. It got busy in here around six and never let up. Rita says you're good."

"Yep." Colt bobbed his head.

"Saw the picture." Boden lifted his shoulders. "Don't know why the mayor got his drawers in a twist over it. He comes in here and ogles every nice rack in the place, isn't even discreet about it. Girls half his age."

"The dude's a tool," Win said.

"Hey, guys, could we tone it down?" Colt had made no secret of his dislike for Pond, but he'd done it to the mayor's face. Doing it behind his back . . . not cool.

"Sorry, man." Colt watched Boden do a visual lap around the bar to make sure his staff had the place covered. A band was setting up on stage and soon the place would get rowdy. "Hey, I almost forgot, I had a cancellation for the End-of-Summer party. A band from Sacramento. I know you said you were jammed, but any chance you'd take the slot? It's a big night not to have live music."

Old Glory would be packed. Tourists as well as locals.

"Yeah, maybe." Now that the heat was off him, Colt figured why not? "I have to see if the rest of the guys can do it. Can I let you know in the next couple of days?"

"Sounds good to me. I better get back to the bar." Boden cut across the room, getting waylaid two or three times by various women. Since buying Old Glory, the scruffy, tattooed barkeeper had made a big impression on the ladies.

Colt stayed another hour and then decided to call it a

night. Everyone had work in the morning, including Deb, who had a breakfast shift at the diner.

At home, Colt found a folded piece of paper taped to his door and opened it.

Watched the meeting on local cable access. Seemed like the photo was a nonissue and that you still have a job. Congratulations!
                                        Cheers,
                                        Delaney

He glanced over at her house. The lights were out. Probably for the best, otherwise he might've strolled over.

Between their two schedules, he didn't wind up seeing her until Sunday morning. One look at her eager face as she came down her front porch and he kicked himself for inviting her river rafting. It had been a damned stupid idea and he fervently hoped she didn't think it was a date. Because it wasn't.

"Is this all right?" she asked as he loaded his truck with PFDs and other equipment they'd need.

"Hmm?" He glanced up to see what she was talking about.

"What I'm wearing? Is it okay?"

Clingy little exercise shorts and a matching top. Hell yeah, it was okay. "You got a pair of old tennis shoes you don't mind getting wet?"

"I think so. Let me go check." She went skipping off and Colt took a couple of minutes to stare at her ass.

Better to get it out of his system now, he told himself. She came back twenty minutes later.

"What, did you wind up making them?"

"I had to dig through my closet."

He glanced down at her feet but not before taking a leisurely trip down her long, shapely legs. Yep, definitely an idiotic idea.

"Those will work. I've got a jacket and a floatation device for you in the truck. We better get moving."

She hopped up into his cab and they got the rest of what they needed, including the boat, at Garner Adventure. And being the lucky SOB that he was, his entire family was there when he showed up with Delaney. He would've been blind not to have noticed the pointed glances exchanged between his nosy-as-hell brothers.

Ignore them, he told himself. They could think what they wanted but there was nothing going on here. He wouldn't make the same mistake twice. And just to hit it home, Lisa and the damn song came on the radio as they headed for the river. Colt turned it off.

"You don't like country music?" Delaney asked.

"I like it. I just thought we could go over how this'll work."

"Oh, okay."

He gave her the safety-tip spiel and what to expect. Because it was only the two of them, he'd taken a much smaller raft than he had the last time. Colt figured he'd be doing most of the oar work and just wanted her to enjoy herself.

When they got to the spot where they'd put in their raft, he helped her with her PFD and helmet and made sure she slathered on plenty of sunscreen.

"You ready to do this?"

"I . . . uh . . . think so," she said.

"Don't worry." Colt winked. "I won't let anything happen to you."

It might've been his imagination, but he thought she blushed. Twenty minutes later, whatever he'd seen was replaced with sheer fear when they encountered their first rapids.

"What if we capsize?" she shouted over the roar of the water.

"We won't. But if we do, remember what I told you."

She nodded, then let out a small shriek each time they hit heavy water. After a while, she appeared to relax. He turned around a few times to make sure she was okay and found her beaming. With the wind whipping through her hair, excitement sparkling in her eyes, and the sun lighting her face, he felt his chest squeeze and everything in him constrict.

"This is fun," she called.

"Yep." He couldn't stop staring at her and smiling.

He paddled them toward calmer waters so he could collect himself, afraid if he didn't, he'd lose control of the boat. Considering these were Class II+ rapids, intended for novices, he'd never hear the end of it.

"Those were pretty big, huh?"

"Not bad. There are more up ahead. Let me know when you're ready." He'd never gotten so much pleasure from another person's enjoyment. It made him yearn for more. To watch her light up like that . . . well, it was everything.

"Okay." She stuck her hand in to feel the water. "It's cold."

"It's worse in winter. You ever go out in the lake?"

She shook her head. "We were going to get a boat but . . ."

Not for the first time, Colt wondered about Robert. What kind of guy let another man make a pass at his wife? Colt wanted to ask why they'd broken up, but he didn't know her well enough to get that personal. Besides, it didn't pay to become too involved. She was here to restart her company. As soon as that happened, she'd leave.

Chapter Eight

The day was perfect. Sunny and warm with a soft breeze coming off the river. Delaney had never been to this particular spot on the water but it was gorgeous. Tall pines for as far as the eye could see. Cattails and grasses of various species, heights, and colors covered the riverbanks. And everything smelled so fresh and green.

Exhilarating is how she would describe riding in the raft with Colt. He navigated with wicked dexterity that seemed effortless and made her feel extremely safe. She knew he'd been rafting and leading tours since a teenager. Delaney had never been outdoorsy or athletic, or even the slightest bit adventurous, but the outing had been so much fun she'd be tempted to try other activities. Especially with Colt as her guide.

"You enjoy that?" Colt helped her out of the raft, got her onto dry land, then dragged the boat in.

"Amazing." She couldn't stop grinning.

He gave her a quick inspection. "I should've told you to bring a set of dry clothes."

"That's okay. I'll be fine in the sun." She'd read on the Internet not to wear cotton because it took too long to dry.

The only thing she had that was even remotely appropriate was exercise clothes.

"Well, I need to change." Colt grabbed a bag from the truck and headed for a tree. "I'll be right back to load everything up. Don't try to look."

He said it so dryly that at first Delaney didn't realize he was joking. Colt was sort of an enigma. It was difficult to tell when he was being playful or flippant. He returned a few minutes later in a T-shirt and a pair of worn, faded cargo shorts. They'd definitely seen better days, but on him . . . yum.

"So, you get any design inspiration from the trip?" Colt asked, and she forced her face up to meet his eyes, instead of his chest, its own kind of inspiration.

"Uh, I don't know yet." She didn't think so. Still, it had been a wonderful respite from sitting in her studio, frustrated.

"I'm pretty optimistic something will come from it," he said with a touch of arrogance. Men always thought they could fix everything. Yet, Delaney wasn't annoyed. His heart was in the right place and it had been so sweet of him to take her out on his day off.

"I can't believe it took me this long to try river rafting," she told him. "Had I known how much fun it is, I would've done it a long time ago."

"Next up, waterskiing."

She tilted her head back to look up at him and see if he was teasing. "You want to go waterskiing today?"

"Nah. But we could go next Sunday."

"Uh, I don't think I'm quite ready for that." Although the idea of spending another day with him appealed to her. "What else you got?"

He thought about it for a few seconds. "Maybe just a hike."

She could do that. "Nothing too strenuous, right?"

"Nope. We could just do something scenic. Maybe bring your sketch pad."

"You do realize I'm a fashion designer, not a pleinairist, right?"

He slung his wet clothes over the opened driver's door, dragged the raft closer, and hefted it into the bed of his truck. She helped him gather up the paddles and load the rest of the equipment. Then they both sat on Colt's tailgate in the sun, silently listening to the birds sing and the river flow. The sounds were peaceful, and she found their lack of conversation oddly companionable for two people who hardly knew each other. As time lapsed, Colt's stomach growled.

"Hungry?" she asked.

"Yeah, you?"

Delaney wished she'd thought to pack a picnic lunch. "A little bit."

He eyed her still wet clothes. "Want to go home and change and then grab something?"

"Sounds good." She wanted to take him somewhere nice as a thank-you. One thing she knew about Colt from the short time they'd lived next to each other was that he didn't get many days off. It had been mighty generous of him to give up his Sunday to her.

They got in his truck and he took the winding road back to the highway. She managed to get in and out of her house in under thirty minutes—just enough time to change and put on a little makeup. He still had on the cargo shorts and tee when she found him sitting on his porch, talking on the phone. Something about a gig at Old Glory.

"You're planning to play?" she asked when he hung up.

He nonchalantly lifted his shoulders. "Boden needed someone to fill in. You look pretty."

"Thanks." The compliment delighted her. Compared to him, she was overdressed in a white fit-and-flare dress from her summer Every Day collection. In LA, she could eat a hotdog at Pink's in the dress and not stand out. In Glory

Junction, it looked like she was trying too hard. But she'd wanted to be—and feel—attractive. For Colt. For herself.

He stood up and wiped the back of his shorts with his hands. "So, where do you want to go?"

"I want to take you somewhere nice . . . a token of appreciation for taking me rafting. Any suggestions?"

He thought about it a little. "The Four Seasons has a good restaurant."

"Perfect," she said, and expected him to go inside to change.

Instead, he led the way to his truck and helped her in to the passenger seat. It made no difference to her. While the shorts had seen better days, Colt wore them better than most men did designer suits.

He drove them up the mountain, passing two of the smaller resorts. "I heard somewhere that you don't ski. That true?"

"Yep." She laughed at the look he gave her. She knew that most people moved here for the skiing.

"Hannah doesn't ski either."

Delaney hadn't known that about her friend. "But Josh does, right?" With his injured leg she didn't know if he could.

"All Garners do, have since we were old enough to walk. How come you don't?"

"It wasn't something my family did. Too expensive, I guess. And when I got older and could afford it . . ." She trailed off because she realized she didn't know why she'd never learned. "I suppose I never had the time."

"You should add it to your list of new things to try." He pulled in to the ornate gated entrance of Winter Bowl and followed the signs to the hotel.

"I hope we can get in without a reservation."

"It won't be a problem." He pulled up to the entryway of the mammoth lodge, which looked more like expensive apartments than a hotel, helped her out, and tossed his keys to one of the valets, saying something she couldn't hear. It appeared as if they knew each other.

He put his hand at the small of her back and guided her inside the lobby to the restaurant. She'd eaten here a few times before with Robert, yet the views out the huge picture windows never ceased to amaze her. The sun shimmered off the blue green waters of Lake Paiute, thousands of towering pines stacked up the mountainside, and the lush peaks of the Sierra Nevada rolled out like a life-size mural. The snow-less ski runs now played host to daredevil mountain bikers, who took the lifts up and traversed down the rugged trails.

"Good afternoon, Chief," the maître d' greeted them. "Will you be dining with us this afternoon?"

Colt nodded. "Could we have a window table?"

The maître d' scanned the half-full restaurant, grabbed two menus, and showed them to their seats, a spot with one of the best views in the house. In the distance, Delaney could see a group of paddleboarders on the lake—another thing she'd never tried—and boats of various sizes. She thought about the town's motto: "Welcome to Glory Junction, where life is always glorious." Sitting across from a man who was as outrageously sublime as the great outdoors, she'd have to agree.

"This okay?" he asked.

"Are you kidding? It's better than okay. You come here a lot?" He seemed to be more than familiar with the hotel and she doubted he got a lot of police calls here.

"My family does a fair amount of business with the resort. We refer them and they refer us. It works out well for every-one."

It had never occurred to her before, but an adventure company offered luxury experiences the same way the Four Seasons did. The same way she did with her clothing.

"How about you? You come here a lot?"

"Not a lot, but I've been a few times before. We used to stay here when we were building the house."

"They say a construction project can kill a marriage." He let the sentence hang, but it was evident he was fishing for the reason she and Robert had broken up.

"It wasn't what killed ours."

"No?" He raised his brows in question.

She'd never told anyone about her ex's unacceptable proposal and she wasn't about to tell Colt Garner. "We grew apart." A hundred percent true. Robert had accused her of losing interest in him and she hadn't been able to refute his charges. They'd become more business partners than soul mates. "What about you? Were you ever married?"

"Nope. Never got there."

"Do you date?"

The corner of his mouth curved up. "Why? You interested?" He was teasing, of course, but it didn't stop her face from heating.

"Just curious, since you seem to work constantly."

"There's that," he said. "And it's a little difficult given the nature of my job."

"Why?" Was he afraid he'd date someone who turned out to be a criminal and then have to lock her up?

"Like with that Facebook photo, my private life is up for public scrutiny. It's easier to see women outside town."

Reading between the lines, it sounded like the police chief was only interested in hookups. "So you're a serial dater," she asked. The notion that he was a player disappointed her. Why did men have a problem with monogamy? Or was she being sensitive because of Robert?

Before he could answer, a server came to take their drink orders. Delaney got an iced tea and Colt a beer. He seemed to know a lot about local craft brews.

When the server left, he said, "I'm not a serial dater. How about you?"

"Me?" The question caught her off guard. "I'm not a dater at all."

"Still not over Robert?"

That's the thing. She was totally over Robert, but he'd left her wounded and unsure of herself. "It's more that I'm overwhelmed trying to get a new collection off the ground." *Trying to start completely from scratch.*

"You'll do it," he said with confidence.

That took her aback. "Why are you so sure?"

His eyes moved over her dress, the action so intimate it felt like a caress. "You make that?"

"Yes."

"I don't pay a lot of attention to women's clothing, to any clothing for that matter. But that dress . . . well, let's just say you could enslave the entire male population with it. Maybe that wasn't your intention when you designed it, but you're good. Incredibly talented."

She'd had the top fashion critics in the world praise her designs, but none of their reviews thrilled her the way Colt's just had. "Thank you."

"It's just the truth. Of course, you're what makes the dress." His eyes lit on her again and suddenly her tongue became tied like a pretzel. When had grouchy, demanding Colt gotten so deft at giving compliments?

Luckily, the waiter came with their drinks and took their orders, relieving her of having to respond. Because there were no words for how good he'd made her feel.

"What's going on with the mayor?" she asked when it got too quiet at the table.

"Last I checked, he was still an asshole." He quickly scanned the room. "I shouldn't have said that. Totally unprofessional."

"Hey, it's just the two of us. And I already thought he was an asshole."

"It must be nice not having a boss," he said, amused. "As

far as Pond and me, the city council put him in his place. I doubt he'll give me any more problems."

"I'm glad," she said. "You're a good chief."

"Thanks."

The server brought their meals, they ate, talked, and when it came time to pay the bill, Colt grabbed it.

"I wouldn't have suggested going out if I'd known you were going to pay. Come on, Colt, let me get this. It's the least I can do."

Despite her protests, he handed his credit card to the waiter.

"Are you one of those guys who can't let a woman pay for him?"

"Nope. Are you one of those women who can't let a man pay for her?"

She narrowed her eyes at him, trying to decide if he was just playing with her. "Fine," she said. "But next time it's my turn." And she hoped there would be a next time because maybe she enjoyed outdoor activities after all. Or maybe she just enjoyed her neighbor.

Colt drove them home, and when he left her at her door she again was sad to lose his company. He'd been attentive and funny and unbelievably sweet.

She trudged upstairs, changed into a baggy pair of shorts and T-shirt, and entered her studio, hoping to summon some of those creative juices Colt said she would get from her day communing with nature. He had funny ideas about inspiration. But at this point she was willing to try anything.

She sat down to draw and checked her voice mail instead. Two furious messages from Robert. Apparently, he hadn't gotten the memo that she was no longer talking to him. That's what she paid her lawyer to do, since calling him herself had accomplished nothing other than to raise her blood pressure.

She erased both messages and began to doodle on her sketch pad to see where it would take her. The other day, she'd visualized a dress that she hadn't been able to put to paper. She tried drawing it. The first attempt she balled up and threw in the trash.

Focus, you need to focus.

Her second attempt was only slightly better. That too went in the garbage. She got up, walked to the window, and stared out at Colt's house. His police cruiser was still parked on the easement road and his truck sat at the top of his steep driveway. She wondered what he was doing, then forced herself to go back to her drafting table, where over the next ninety minutes she drew a house and two stick figures. A shrink would have a heyday with that one.

She thumbed through a few fashion magazines, read a profile on Olivia Lowell that made her want to puke, and grabbed a bottle of water from the minifridge. For the next twenty minutes, she traced the bottom of the bottle, drawing dozens of circles like a crazy person.

Enough! You're not leaving this room until you have at least one good design, she told herself.

Pencil to paper, she began sketching. First a woman's body, then she gave her a flirty little dress with a fitted bodice and flared skirt. She added patterns, nipped in the waist, and embellished the flounce at the bottom. She emphasized the lines in black ink and shaded the folds using marker in a bold apricot. She filled in the pattern with colored pencils, holding her breath.

Finally, everything was working.

By the time she finished, the dress was sexy, fun, and had that indefinable special quality that put it above the rest. Perhaps Colt's nature theory had actually unlocked her inhibitions, because the design was awesome. She'd done it.

"Will you look at that," she said proudly, holding the drawing to the light for a closer inspection. Phenomenal . . . and a complete replica of what she'd worn to the restaurant with Colt. The only difference was the color and pattern.

Crap, crap, crap!

She laid her head on the drafting table and pounded her fists on the laminate surface. What the hell was wrong with her? She turned to the window, wanting to jump out. Unfortunately, the second story wasn't high enough to do anything besides break her legs.

Not leaving this room. One original design.

Delaney got up and paced. Just one original design, she repeated over and over again.

She sat back down and absently drew her croquis. A man with broad shoulders, wide chest, muscled arms, flat belly, and narrow hips. *Hmm, I wonder who that looks like?* Clearly, her thoughts were on Colt, not design. But okay, she'd go with it. She'd designed plenty of men's clothing in the past.

For the next couple of hours, she let her mind take her wherever it wanted. She didn't question herself or even stop to think about what she was doing. She just sketched. Half the time she didn't even look at the drawing. Her hand moved of its own volition, sweeping across the page in bold strokes. Shading here, outlining there, and letting her pencil mark the final touches. At long last, she looked down at the pad to see what she'd accomplished.

A fairly good likeness of Colt's face, complete with Ray-Bans, stared back at her. That, and a pair of cargo shorts. *Cargo shorts*. Wouldn't her instructors at Parsons be proud? It turned out that nature hadn't been her muse today, but Colt had.

She studied the drawing for a while and all she could do was laugh. Cargo shorts, for the love of God. She'd been designing couture since her eighteenth birthday. At least she now could officially leave her studio, having met the goal of one original design. Even if it was a dopey pair of cargo shorts.

Just about to go downstairs for a snack, she changed direction and on a lark headed to the room's walk-in closet and sifted through her fabric samples. A cotton-synthetic blend in a navy blue cried out to her. The material would dry quicker than pure cotton and still be rugged enough to stand up to a beating. She played with it between her fingers, tugging it this way and that, liking the way the fabric gave. There was just enough yardage, too.

She tilted her head back and stared up at the ceiling. "I can't believe I'm doing this."

Tossing the fabric onto her cutting table, Delaney went to the computer. Normally, she'd send the hand sketch, a technical sketch, and a measurement chart to one of her pattern makers. But for this project she was just screwing around.

A couple of hours later, using professional software, she had what she needed. She could only guess Colt's measurements. But having been in the business as long as she had, Delaney had a good eye. And frankly, she'd spent enough time looking at Colt to get it close to perfect.

She cut and sewed well into the night, using low lighting so Colt wouldn't complain about the glare. It had been so long since she'd actually sat at a sewing machine that she feared she'd forgotten how to thread one. But like riding a bike, her memory took over and she got lost in the work.

By bedtime she had a pair of shorts that were light enough for wicking water, tough enough for weathering a rough rock climb, and as handsome as the man who would be wearing them. She hoped.

Chapter Nine

Colt nearly knocked Delaney down. She'd been at his door, poised to knock, when he rushed out. Due to good reflexes, he caught her before she hit the ground.

"Sorry." He kept his hands on her arms, reluctant to take them off. Not because he thought she was still in danger of falling but because she felt good. Soft and womanly. She smelled good too.

"You have an emergency?" she asked.

"No." He was just running late as usual. "What's up?"

"I made you something."

That's when he noticed the girly gift bag she held in her right hand. "You did? Why?"

She waved her free hand in the air. "It's a long story. Just consider it a thank-you for yesterday. . . . It was lovely." She handed him the bag, then waited expectantly.

Colt presumed she wanted him to open it in front of her. He untied the ribbon, felt into the bag, and pulled out some sort of a garment. Shorts. Navy blue ones that looked similar to all his others. But newer and lighter.

The last time someone had given him a gift, besides his parents, was his secret Santa at the annual Garner Adventure Christmas party. It'd been a ten-dollar Starbucks travel mug.

He wasn't quite sure how to react to Delaney's present. She was a world famous designer. The shorts were probably worth at least three figures.

"Try them on," she said, and practically pushed him back inside the house.

He didn't really have time, but under the circumstances how could he say no? Taking the shorts to his bedroom, he got out of his uniform pants and slipped them on.

Whoa! What was he thinking? These were nothing like his other shorts. These were freaking unbelievable. First off, they fit him like they'd been custom made to his body. Secondly, they were incredibly comfortable while being . . . Hell, he didn't know anything about fashion. But these seemed deluxe, plenty of pockets, and a cut that wasn't so bulky and long that they made him look distorted.

He knew cargo shorts had a bad rap. A dozen women had told him so. Still, there was a reason why they were the uniform for adventure tour guides everywhere. How else could they store gear on a long hike or a climb or a sport fishing trip? Backpacks were great but not always easy to get to when you needed bear spray in a split second.

He checked them out in the mirror. Yeah, the shorts were unbelievable, all right.

"Well?" Delaney called. "Come out so I can see them."

He walked out of his room. "Can you make me more?"

She zoomed in on him, made him turn a few times, and pulled a pin cushion out of her purse. "Stand still. They're too long and a little too full in the hips."

"What are you talking about? They're perfect."

"Not quite, but they will be when I alter them."

"You're going to take them?" He felt a sudden, irrational possessiveness over the shorts.

She had her hands all over his waist, hips, thighs, even his ass. If it weren't for her jabbing the pins a little too close to his package, he would've gotten a hard-on.

"Only for the day. Then I'll return them. Promise."

"Jeez, Delaney, you could make a fortune with these shorts."

"I'm glad you like them, but a fortune? Highly doubtful. I hate to break it to you, but cargo shorts are not so much in style."

"These could be. You could singlehandedly bring 'em back."

"I think I'll pass. They do look great on you, however."

"Yeah?" He looked down where she was putting the last pins in the hems.

When she finished and looked up, they locked eyes and he was a goner. If he stood there any longer he was going to kiss her and that would be . . . a stunningly bad idea.

"I've got to get to work," he said, but didn't want to move.

"Okay." Was it his imagination or did her voice sound huskier than usual? "Just be careful of the pins when you take off the shorts."

"I will." He told his legs to move, but she was so close. Right there by his crotch. *Ah, Jesus.* "Uh . . . thanks . . . Delaney. Best gift ever."

"I doubt it, but I'm glad you like them. I'll make the alterations and have them back to you by this evening."

He wanted to ask her to dinner, which was stupid on so many levels. Ultimately, he didn't because he couldn't predict his hours. In the long run it was better that way. He could fall for a woman like Delaney Scott. But he'd already done that with Lisa, and look at what a train wreck that had been. Why couldn't he just fall for a nice, safe, local girl?

He made it to work thirty minutes late.

Carrie Jo glanced at the clock on the wall as he passed by her desk. "Oversleep?"

He stopped and eyed her bowl of cottage cheese. "I thought you were on that cleanse."

"I signed up for Weight Watchers." She pointed at her meal. "This is only four points and the fruit is free."

He had no idea what she was talking about. "Is that good?"

"I get forty-four a day, so yeah."

"Did you exercise?"

"If you count walking to my car."

He shook his head. "Well, at least that's healthier than those vile juice drinks. Anything going on I should know about?"

"So far it's been quiet. Haven't heard a peep out of Pond Scum."

"Don't call him that, Carrie Jo." Even though the name suited the mayor, he didn't want his staff to use it. "I'll be in my office."

"Want coffee?"

"Why? You planning to get me a cup?"

"I figured if you were getting yourself one, you could get me one too. But not the swill here." Jack made a pot every morning and it tasted like a cross between sludge and burned tires. "I was thinking you could get it at Tart Me Up. I'm slaving away here for you."

He rolled his eyes. "Give me ten minutes to get caught up." The fact was he wanted breakfast anyway.

In his office, Carrie Jo had already booted up his computer and he quickly scrolled through his e-mails. Nothing important. He made a few calls, then popped into Jack's office.

"You want anything from Tart Me Up?"

"Nah, I'm good," Jack said. "You hear anything from Pond Scum?"

Jeez, that name was going to get them all in trouble. "Not since the city council meeting. Hopefully that'll keep him off our asses for a while."

Jack made a face. "Doubtful, but I'm keeping my fingers crossed."

Colt walked the short block to Tart Me Up. The door jingled when he went inside. A good crowd—all waiting for their numbers to be called—called out a chorus of "Hi, Chief." Rachel Johnson came out from the back, her apron covered in white powder.

"You have a fight with a flour sack?"

"Something like that." Rachel's eyes sparkled, and not for the first time Colt noticed how pretty she was.

She'd moved to Glory Junction three years ago from San Francisco, where she'd been a corporate lawyer. Following her dream of being a baker, she'd quit her law job, gone to culinary school, and bought the old Glory Junction Bakery, which had been floundering ever since Starbucks and Peet's had come to town. For months after opening, she'd given away free samples of her delicious pastries, delivered her mouthwatering sandwiches to local businesses, and had been active with the Chamber of Commerce, which had paid off. Judging by the lines of people that started early in the morning and didn't let up until well after lunch, Rachel was killing it.

A few times she'd subtly hinted to Colt that she was interested. He'd never acted on it, using his chief position as an excuse when really he'd never felt that zing. Who could say why? Rachel was smart, successful, gorgeous, a damned good skier, and here in Glory Junction for good. Maybe if he gave her half a chance something would develop. But that was the thing about being a public official—you couldn't take every attractive single woman in town on a test drive.

She filled him a large cup of coffee. "What else can I get for you, Chief?"

His number hadn't been called yet. "Why don't I wait until my turn?"

"If you say so. I only figured that your time would be

better spent keeping our streets safe. But I certainly enjoy your company." She smiled at him. "How's life treating you?"

"Not bad. You?"

"Good. We're planning to compete this year in the End-of-Summer kayak races and to kick Garner Adventure's butt."

Colt scrutinized the three kids working behind the counter. One he'd known since grade school: the boy had more piercings than brains. Another looked as if she hadn't seen sunlight in three years, and the third was having trouble operating the espresso machine. "I wouldn't get too cocky."

"Don't underestimate us," she warned good-heartedly.

"I would never do that, Rachel." He grinned back at her, hoping that if he flirted . . . tried hard enough . . . he might feel the same pull of attraction he did with Delaney. But nothing. Not so much as a twitch south of his belt.

When it got to his turn, he ordered a ham and cheese croissant and two coffees to go. "See you, Rachel."

Back at the office, he ate his sandwich and fielded calls. There was a domestic up on McClatchy Ridge. Those could get hairy, so he sent two of his most seasoned officers. Then TJ called to see if he could teach a beginning rock-climbing class on Sunday.

"Come on. I thought you were looking for more people to hire."

"I'm working on it. But with school starting . . ." A lot of their guides were college kids who moved to Glory Junction just for the summer. Some literally camped at the state park for three months and used the showers at GA.

"I'll look at my schedule," he told TJ. "In the meantime, see if you can find someone else."

"I'll do my best, but no one teaches that class better than you."

Colt groaned. "Nice try, but flattery will get you nowhere." He hung up.

It turned out to be a peaceful day, despite his late start. Colt was even thinking of taking off on time for once when his private line lit up. Usually Carrie Jo intercepted those calls but she'd already gone for the day.

He picked up. "Garner."

"Please stay on the line for Mayor Pond," said his honor's secretary, who then whispered, "Sorry, Colt, he makes me say that."

Jesus Christ, you would think the guy was the POTUS. "No problem, Josephine." Colt waited, listening to the god-awful Muzak in the background.

"Colt"—the mayor's voice finally came over the line—"I wanted to talk to you about the End-of-Summer kayak races."

"What about them?"

"I want you to head up Glory Junction PD's team."

"We don't have a team." In the past, the city had always represented all its municipal offices in the races and Colt had been on the Garner Adventure team. "We don't even have kayaks."

"I have one on order for you."

The city had voted against new Kevlar vests for the department, but it could afford a kayak? Pretty shitty prioritizing if you asked Colt. But no one was.

"All right," Colt said with reluctance. He had nothing against representing the police department. It was his department after all. It's just that he'd always kayaked for GA and he got the distinct feeling that Pond Scum wanted to cause division between Colt and his family. A little payback, perhaps, for the Garner show of solidarity at the city council meeting.

"I expect a victory, Colt." And with that the mayor hung up.

Colt couldn't be sure if the mayor had just made a veiled

threat: win or else. The guy was enough of a dick that Colt wouldn't be surprised.

He packed up and headed out before the mayor called to bother him again. On his way home, Colt contemplated dinner. He didn't have anything in his fridge. His brothers had eaten the last of his chips and bean dip. After changing out of his uniform maybe he'd go to the Indian place for some tandoori. If Delaney happened to be available, maybe they could go together.

Ah, Jesus, he was so screwed.

When he pulled onto their easement road there was a car in the coveted space. A Mercedes Roadster, not Delaney's Tesla. His stomach sank. She probably had a date. At the top of his driveway, Colt took the time to turn the cruiser around in case he got called out, then walked down the steep grade.

Halfway to the kitchen door, he heard raised voices coming from Delaney's house. He took a detour across the lawn to get a better look. She was on her deck with Robert and they appeared to be having an argument. It didn't look physical and he mulled over whether to intervene or not. It was clearly a postdivorce thing, probably having to do with their business and the use of her name. Unfortunately, he'd seen domestic arguments turn to violence on a dime, not that he expected it in this case. But for Delaney's sake, he wanted to break it up. He supposed he could say they were disrupting the peace, even though in reality the only peace they were disrupting was his.

Ah, the hell with it. He couldn't leave her without backup and continued across the easement.

"Excuse me, is there a problem here?" he asked loud enough to be heard over their dispute.

Delaney froze and turned a dozen shades of red. "Uh . . . no."

"Hell yes, there's a problem." Robert's face was also red

but from anger. Colt thought he was a few seconds away from erupting.

He climbed the deck stairs and put himself between Delaney and her ex. "How about we take it down a notch?"

"How about you mind your own goddamn business?"

"Robert!" Delaney's eyes widened. "What's the matter with you?"

"What's the matter with me? What's the matter with you? You've been ordered by a court of law to stop using the Delaney Scott name, yet you keep using it."

Delaney started to say something in response, but Colt held up his hand. "I suggest you go through your respective attorneys on this. What you can't do is stand out here and disturb the neighborhood."

"Fine." Robert pushed his way past Colt. "We'll go inside. No law says we can't."

Colt looked at Delaney for guidance. It was up to her. If she wanted to let her ex into her house, there was nothing Colt could do about it. But under the circumstances, he didn't think it was wise.

"I don't want you in my house, Robert."

Good girl.

"I built this goddamn house," Robert shouted, and tried to force his way in.

"Delaney said no, Robert. I'm going to have to ask you to leave."

Robert turned and glared at Colt. "Fine. But this is going to cost you, Delaney. Mark my words. You'll regret it."

Robert walked off in a huff and that's when Colt noticed the jacked-up suit he had on. Ankle-length pants—they looked like they had shrunken in the dryer—with a jacket, wingtips, and no socks.

"What's wrong with him?" Colt asked as Robert peeled off in his Mercedes.

"Besides the fact that he's from Assholia?"

"No, his clothes. Did he borrow them from a twelve-year-old?"

"Hey, I designed that suit," she said, obviously peeved by his comment. "I'll have you know it's the height of fashion."

Colt made a face. "If you say so. But if I were you I'd stick to cargo shorts."

"Oh, be quiet."

One side of his mouth kicked up and then he turned serious. "I'm sorry he gave you a hard time."

"He's a moron. Thanks for stepping in. I was holding my own but I appreciate you having my back. You don't think any of the neighbors heard, do you?"

"Nah," he said. "I wouldn't worry about it. He won't come back later to harass you, will he?"

"I don't think so. Before you'd gotten here I'd made my position clear. Without clarification from the court, I'm not doing anything. It would be too big a hit for my new company." She opened the door. "Come inside and try on your shorts."

"Okay, but I should get out of my uniform first." He motioned to his gun, which he needed to lock in his safe.

He crossed over to his house, took a quick shower, and returned to Delaney's a short time later. She had him come up to her studio and handed him the shorts.

"You can try them on behind the screen or in the bathroom."

He opted for the bathroom and came out when he had them on.

"Stand up there." She pointed to a little stage in front of a three-way mirror. She was bossy but he did what she said, feeling a little foolish.

"They fit great," he said as she examined him with a discerning eye.

She stuck her fingers between the waistband of the shorts

and his hips. Her hand felt good on his skin and he sucked in a breath.

"Yep, they do. I suppose if the designer thing doesn't work out for me, I could make it as a tailor."

"What are you talking about? These are the best damn shorts I ever had. Can you make me pants like these?"

She pretended to shudder. "I could. The question is why would I want to?"

"Because I'm a great neighbor and as soon as I change back into my jeans I'm taking you to dinner. The Indian place."

"For most of the time I've lived here, you've been a lousy neighbor . . . whining incessantly about parking . . . bitching about my light," she teased. "But I do like Indian food, so there may be a pair of pants in it for you."

Colt enjoyed their banter. She didn't shy away from giving him hell, which he liked. He sat in the chair next to her drafting table. "How long had Robert been here before I came over?"

"About twenty minutes. He's probably still here . . . somewhere. He drove up from LA."

"Seems like a long way to come for a fight. Why not let the lawyers deal with it?"

"One of the reasons Robert's a successful businessman is because he doesn't take no for an answer. He wants the Delaney Scott name off merchandise that belongs to me . . . a clean break for his company. It's confusing to consumers, especially since he has a new designer who will want to set a different tone for the house and put her mark on things."

"It seemed pretty heated to me. He wouldn't raise a hand to you, would he?"

"No. Never. We had our problems but never that."

"You grew apart, right?" He figured there had to be more to it than that.

"Mm-hmm. So do we need a reservation at this Indian place?"

Nice subject change. "Nah. You've never been before?"

"I have; I just couldn't remember whether you needed a reservation or not."

He supposed that was his cue to get moving. "Let me put on my jeans."

"I'll meet you downstairs," she called to him. "I want to change too."

He got into his pants and beat her to the living room, where he snooped around until she came down. She had a lot of nice things and way too many throw pillows. He could tell a lot of time had been put in to decorating the place whereas his idea of decorating was putting in a sixty-five-inch flat screen.

"You ready?" She came down the stairs in another one of her killer dresses and, man, did the woman have a pair of legs.

He didn't want to stare, so he held the shorts up in front of his face. "I just want to drop these off at my house. I'll pick you up so you don't have to walk up my driveway in your shoes."

She had on high heels. He didn't usually go in for stilettos, preferring a woman in a pair of hiking boots. But the ones Delaney had on—red, strappy things—would fuel enough erotic fantasies to last him a lifetime.

"Too much?" she asked, and looked down at her feet. "They go with the dress."

"They don't exactly scream Glory Junction, but they're sexy as hell. Did you design them?"

"I did," she said, and beamed proudly.

"They're a hell of a lot better than Robert's Pee-wee Herman suit," he said.

She laughed but added, "What you know about fashion could fit in a thimble."

"I'll concede to that." It was fun messing with her. She gave as good as she got, just like his three brothers.

He dropped the shorts off at his house, got his truck out of the garage, and stopped in front of Delaney's house to pick her up. By the time they got to the restaurant he was starved. Luckily, one of the owners showed them to a table almost immediately. He ordered a plate of naan to hold them over.

"You hungry?" he asked Delaney.

"I am." She toed her purse under the table and Colt was momentarily distracted by her red shoe and one very shapely ankle.

They got their flat bread, ordered, and watched as a steady trickle of people flowed in. They'd been fortunate to get to the restaurant before it had filled up. TJ came through the door, spotted Colt, and made a beeline for their table.

"Shit," Colt muttered under his breath. He didn't want his brother giving him crap over Delaney, especially because this was the second time TJ had caught them together. His family was great, but they had an annoying habit of getting in each other's business.

"Hey." TJ came over wearing a grin the size of the Grand Canyon. Colt wanted to wipe it off his face. "What are you two up to?"

"Gee, we're in a restaurant. Perhaps we're getting a bite to eat," Colt said, which only made TJ's grin widen.

"Me too. Pickup."

Good, Colt thought. The sooner his brother got it, the sooner he'd leave.

TJ grabbed the chair next to Delaney. "You have a good time white-water rafting with Colt the other day?"

"It was wonderful," she said. "Initially I was nervous about it, but Colt made it seem effortless."

TJ smirked. "Yup, you were in good hands." He turned to Colt, who wanted to sock him. "We're having a brief meeting tomorrow morning to talk about the races. Can you come?"

Colt shook his head. "Pond wants me to lead the police department's team."

"The police department doesn't have a team."

"We do now." Anything Pond could do to get under Colt's skin.

"Ah, Jesus." TJ broke off a piece of naan and ate it. "He's really trying to screw with you, isn't he?"

Colt shrugged. Sure, it would break with Garner tradition to have him compete against his own family, but it was far from the end of the world. "It's an amateur race. No big deal."

"Don't let Dad hear you say that." Their father had founded the annual contest and to him it was a source of pride that GA won every year.

"He'll get over it," Colt said.

One of the owners came out of the kitchen with a sack for TJ.

"I better get going. Nice seeing you, Delaney." TJ paid at the register and took off with his bag of takeout.

Delaney turned to Colt. "What do you think the mayor is up to? Is it possible he's just getting into the spirit of the races and wants the city to be more involved?"

"The city has always been involved, just not the police department. I think TJ's right; his intention is to mess with me. He knows I'm part of Team Garner every year. It's a vindictive maneuver to get back at my family for rallying the town to support me over the picture on Facebook. It's petty and stupid, but it's easier for me to go along than fight it. And frankly, the police department should be involved. It's a nice way for us to interact more with the community."

"You're a better man than I. As far as I'm concerned the mayor is a creep and I look to avoid him every chance I can."

Their food came and Colt waited until the server left.

"I know you said he made a move on you a while back. He hasn't continued to pressure you, has he?"

"No. Once I made it clear I wasn't interested, he acted like nothing had ever happened. What's his deal, anyway? Has he ever been married?"

"Divorced twice, according to Carrie Jo. That's all I know about his personal life other than the fact that he's wealthy, or so he says."

"You don't believe him?"

Colt thought Pond had money, just not as much as he wanted everyone to believe he had. "I think he did well when he sold his startup. As far as how much he has in the bank, I don't have any idea." He didn't really care, either, unless he was intentionally misleading the good people of Glory Junction.

They dug into their dinner. "Mmm. This is delicious," Delaney said.

"I think TJ eats here four times a week."

"What about your other brothers?"

"Win's always training for a triathlon or some other competition, and eats accordingly . . . a lot of protein shakes and complex carbs. Josh eats Hannah's food. She's a great cook."

"What about you?"

"I usually grab takeout or go to my parents' house." He knew that sounded lame for a grown man. "And you?"

"I buy a lot of prepared meals at the market. I know how to cook some but am usually too busy."

"You having any luck with the designing?"

"Nope." She shook her head. "Absolutely nothing is working."

"I wouldn't say that. The shorts are amazing, Delaney." He locked gazes with her, staring into her blue eyes, and the song "Galway Girl" went off in his head again.

"The shorts are basic," she said. "Nothing too exciting as far as design."

"Maybe not runway exciting, but they're original. I've been wearing cargo shorts most of my life and your design is superior. The fit is better, the pockets more accessible without the bulkiness and boxiness, and the cut is more comfortable."

"That's because they were custom made to your body." As soon as she said "body" her face turned pomegranate red. The color matched her hot shoes.

He wondered if she thought about his body as much as he'd been thinking about hers. She'd certainly gotten his size right. The shorts had fit him to a T even before she'd made the alterations.

"Even so, they're damned fine shorts."

"Thanks." She blushed again.

"Just giving credit where credit is due," he said, and continued to stuff his mouth full of tandoori chicken to keep from asking her back to his place. Best not to wind up like the guy in the song. By himself with a busted heart.

Chapter Ten

Delaney wanted to invite Colt in after dinner, but he seemed to be in a rush to get home. He was tough to read. Flirty one minute, almost standoffish the next. But she could tell he really had loved her gift, even if it was just silly shorts. He didn't strike her as the type to make a big fuss over something if he wasn't impressed.

She peeked out the window and the lights in his house came on. It was too early to go to bed, so she wandered up to her studio. The shades were coming on Friday, but as long as Colt was up she figured she could work a few hours. Before she knew it, she was cutting out a pair of pants similar to the shorts. He'd asked for them, so why not? It wasn't as if she had any other ideas. And she'd quite enjoyed fitting him, touching all those hard-as-granite muscles. A lot of male models spent countless hours in the gym and still couldn't attain a physique like Colt's. She would bet he got his build from outdoor sports rather than working out in a fitness center. Doubtful he had room in his busy life.

Because she'd gotten the preliminary work done on the shorts, the pants took half the time. Before Delaney knew it, she'd finished the last row of stitches. She turned on the iron and carefully pressed her seams. It felt good to be working again, even if it was just for fun. Besides, Colt deserved her gratitude for coming to her defense and chasing Robert off the way he had. Not that Delaney couldn't have done it herself. She wasn't afraid of her ex or even remotely intimidated by him. Still, it was nice to have someone in her corner. Plus, having her handsome neighbor rush in like that in front of Robert had been good for her ego.

She put the last touches on the pants, playing around with the pockets to get them just right and reinforcing some of the seams. Rugged pants for a rugged guy. A guy she had nothing in common with. The list of their differences was a mile long.

She was an urbanite, while Colt obviously reveled in his small-town roots. He gravitated toward anything adventurous while her idea of daring was testing a new restaurant. She'd always aspired to be a famous designer and move to a glamorous city while he seemed perfectly content with being the chief of a small police department. Pretty wide gulf between them.

Still, she was a little fixated on him. She chalked it up to postdivorce infatuation, nothing more.

Holding the pants up, she liked what she saw. They were even better than the shorts. A nice silhouette. Slim through the hips and tight enough through the seat to showcase a fabulous backside. Excited, she grabbed the pants, went downstairs, dashed outside, and crossed over to Colt's house.

It took a while but he finally opened the door in his boxer shorts and a heavy dose of sleep in his voice. That's when it hit her that all his lights had been out.

"Everything okay?" he asked.

No shirt, just his Gerard Butler chest staring her in the face. And his hair sticking up on end should've been the opposite of hot. But somehow it worked for him and the temperature rose twenty degrees.

She took one look at his sexy, sleepy self, then at her

watch, and flushed with embarrassment. Here she was on his doorstep at two a.m. in the same dress she wore to dinner. This could only look like one thing.

"Sorry," she stammered, and started to go.

"Delaney."

She turned around to face him and that's when he kissed her. Soft and slow at first, then exploring her mouth with his tongue. Delaney leaned in, reveling in the taste and feel of him—so good—realizing that if she let this go any further, they'd wind up doing a whole lot more than kissing. But as he took the kiss further, tangling his hands in her hair and holding her head so he could go deeper, she let him. Then, somewhere at the back of her mind, good sense told her to stop, even though her body told her something entirely different.

She must've froze, because he stopped and dragged his hand through his hair, visibly confused. "You want to come in?" That's when he spied the pants she awkwardly held in her hands. "Ah, jeez. Did I misinterpret what was going on here . . . you coming over here like this?"

"No . . . yes . . . I got caught up making these and lost track of the time." She shoved the pants at him and covered her face, mortified.

"Hey." He gently pried her hands away. "No worries, just a small misunderstanding. We're all good." Colt tugged her inside and maneuvered her toward the couch in the living room. "Take a seat."

"Just for a minute. Just long enough to apologize."

He glanced at the pants, surprised. "You made these after we got home from dinner?"

She nodded. "I hope the light didn't disturb you." The light? How about her banging on his door at two in the morning? "Sometimes I get so immersed in what I'm doing it's like a trance."

He got up and walked into his kitchen, which was right off the living room. The house wasn't overly large. She didn't know if she was supposed to follow him but eventually did, interested to know what he was doing. He had the refrigerator door open and was drinking milk out of the carton.

When Colt saw her watching him, he said, "You want some?"

"Uh . . . no, thanks. I should go."

"You don't want me to try on the pants?" He motioned toward the kitchen table where he'd put them down.

"You can do it later, when you're fully up." Oh God, had she just said that? "I mean . . . uh, after you get home from work."

He checked the clock over his stove. "I'm awake now. May as well do it. Did you bring your pins?"

She hadn't, which made it look even more like a booty call. "Really, Colt, let's do this another time. I don't know what I was thinking."

"You sure?" He was trying to smooth over the situation, which wasn't working.

"Look," she said, deciding to be up-front, "I'd be lying if I said I wasn't attracted to you. But I really did lose track of time and came over to bring you the pants, not to fool around. I swear."

His glance dropped to her lips. "Clearly the attraction is mutual, but us . . . this"—he waved his hand between them—"I don't like to get involved with local women. As the police chief it's too complicated."

"Exactly," she said, but secretly wondered what was so complicated about it, and got up to go.

"I'll walk you." He followed her to the door and she turned and pointedly looked at his state of undress. *Hello, you're practically naked*.

He grabbed the new pants off the kitchen table, put them

on and closed the zipper, leaving the top button undone. "They feel great."

They looked even better, but she kept that thought to herself. He crossed the easement road with her, waited for her to get inside, then went back home. She climbed the stairs, shut off the light in her studio, and headed for bed. But not before gazing out the window at Colt's bedroom.

Colt didn't know if he could fall asleep again. Delaney had him worked up pretty good. When she'd first shown up, he'd thought it was a dream. Her standing in his doorway, backlit by the full moon, so freaking beautiful it made his chest hurt. And when he'd kissed her . . . Well, it had been a while since he'd lost his head over a woman. Maybe never.

It was for the best that they'd stopped it when they had, he told himself. He wasn't interested in being her rebound guy until she moved back to Los Angeles. And while Colt wasn't opposed to no-strings-attached sex, doing that sort of thing in Glory Junction was out of the question. Especially with a woman he could fall for.

At seven his damned alarm went off. Even though he wouldn't be part of Team Garner at the races, he decided to go to the family meeting anyway. There would be pastries and coffee that didn't suck. He also decided to wear plain clothes today, instead of his uniform. Pond wouldn't like it, so it was Colt's little F-you to the mayor.

Delaney's pants were sitting on the top of his dresser. After his shower, he dragged them on with a polo shirt. The cargos really were fantastic. Lightweight but durable and as comfortable as tactical pants. He strapped on his gun belt and clipped on his badge. On the way to his cruiser, he checked out Delaney's house for any signs of life. He couldn't tell for sure, but it appeared that she was still asleep.

He tried to block a vision of her in bed, flushed and tousled.

The image didn't help his state of mind, which was still in the gutter after her early morning visit.

He drove to Garner Adventure and parked in front. Darcy, the new girl, was laying out the Danish in the conference room when he got in. He snagged a bear claw before the rest of his family arrived and poured himself a cup of coffee.

"How you liking the job so far?" he asked Darcy.

The question seemed to throw her, because she waited a while to respond and finally said, "It's good," then turned beet red.

Win came through the door and put his stuff down on the long burl wood table. Gray Garner had had it specially made for the room. He'd known a guy. . . .

"Hey, Darce," Win said.

This time, the receptionist looked as if all the blood in her body had rushed to her cheeks. She was either incredibly shy or had it bad for Win, which wouldn't surprise Colt. Ninety-nine percent of Glory Junction's female population had it bad for Win. The rest were six feet under at the Glory Junction Cemetery.

Colt figured his little brother would eventually settle down with Deb. Poor Deb had been pining for him forever.

TJ showed up next. "I thought you weren't coming," he said to Colt.

Colt held up his Danish. "Food."

"Did you take the only bear claw?"

"Yes I did." He licked the whole thing, like they used to do when they were kids to claim dibs.

"What's up with you and Delaney Scott? I thought you didn't like her."

"I never said I didn't like her."

"Weren't you feuding over parking?"

"We've worked it out."

TJ raised his brows. "And now you're having dinner with her?"

"Yeah, so what's the big deal? We live next door to each other and were both hungry."

"And you took her river rafting. Seems like there's something going on there." TJ looked at him for confirmation.

"Absolutely nothing going on." If you didn't count the kiss, which Colt wasn't. It was a one-time deal. No harm, no foul.

"Too bad. She seems nice and it's high time you got over Lisa."

"I'm over Lisa." Just not what she'd done to him . . . what she'd taken.

TJ did the eyebrow thing again. Luckily, Josh came in, distracting everyone.

"Where are the bear claws?" Josh asked, perusing the assortment of pastries.

"In Colt's stomach," TJ replied. "He ate the only one."

"Asshole," Josh called across the conference room. "I'm the one going under the knife next week."

"I heard."

Josh's doctors wanted to do another operation on his leg. There was a chance that the surgery would significantly improve his mobility. Colt knew that even more than the pain, the limp bothered Josh the most. No one thought less of him—his brother was a war hero, for God's sake—but to Josh it was akin to losing his manhood.

"But I didn't realize the surgery was next week," Colt said.

"They want to move quickly while there is still some elasticity left in my muscles."

"It's good, right?"

"If it goes as well as my doctor thinks it will, it'll be better than good."

"What'll be good?" His mother walked in at the tail end of Josh's sentence and kissed Colt on the cheek. "I haven't seen you in a while."

"Been up to my neck in alligators," he said.

Mary turned. "Josh?"

"I was just telling Colt about the surgery next week."

Her expression lit up. "Isn't it wonderful how fast they want to do it?" They'd all been devastated by Josh's injury.

"Yep," Colt said, a little choked up.

"And what's this I hear about the mayor saying you can't be part of our team for the kayak races?" Mary asked.

"He wants me to race a kayak for the police department. You'll have to live without me this year."

Since he was the best kayaker in the Garner family, it would be a big loss. The good news was he couldn't beat his brothers with Jack as his teammate. Jack was an amazing skier but he couldn't paddle worth a damn.

"I never liked that man Mr. Pond and voted for Ken Jenner," Mary said.

"Pond is who we're stuck with, so for now I'm playing by his rules," Colt said. "Where's Dad?"

"He's taking a group parasailing, and because I've got a pile of work on my desk, I'm going to duck out and let you boys run the meeting," Mary said.

"Okay, Mom." He kissed the top of her head.

"And you don't be a stranger. I get to see your brothers at work every day, but I'm missing my eldest. Come by the house one of these nights, Colt, and I'll fix you dinner."

"Will do."

As she sailed out of the room, she called, "Don't fight."

Win looked over the pastries while drinking his green smoothie. He was addicted to the repulsive drinks. "We ready to do this? I've got a mountain bike group I'm taking out in an hour."

"Yeah," TJ said. "Let's get started. But maybe Colt should leave if he's competing against us. I wouldn't want him to know our strategy."

Colt gave his brother the middle finger. "I invented your

strategy." He reached across the table, grabbed a second Danish, and refilled his mug with coffee.

"Nice pants." TJ gave them an assessing look. "Where'd you get 'em?"

"Delaney."

"No kidding?"

Win came over to his end of the room to check them out, and let out a whistle. "I never saw those in Hannah's shop, just dresses and handbags."

"She was playing around with prototypes," Colt lied.

"I thought she was high fashion," TJ said. "She's doing sports and athletic wear now?"

"I think she was experimenting. She made a pair of shorts first. I liked them so much I asked her for pants."

TJ choked on his coffee. "You asked her for pants? You ever see what her stuff sells for? Even the off-the-rack clothes go for big bucks. It would be like one of our clients asking if we could get Jonny Moseley to give ski lessons. Something's going on with you two."

"Nah, she's in a creative slump." Colt doubted Delaney wanted anyone to know that, but his brothers wouldn't spread it around. "I think she was just messing around."

"Hannah said she's having a tough time with her ex, who got to keep her brand," Josh said.

"Well, I'd be interested in carrying those pants"—TJ cocked his head at Colt's legs—"and the shorts at Garner Adventure."

Everyone turned to stare at TJ, and Win asked, "We're doing retail now?" They barely had enough staff to handle the adventure tours.

"There's good money in merch. People have a great experience, they want to commemorate it with a T-shirt . . . or a pair of cargo pants. Maybe we even put our logo somewhere on the pocket and have our guides wear the clothes to market them."

"Who's going to run this shop of yours?" Josh asked the question they were all thinking. TJ liked to think big, but that often meant stretching the rest of the family and the staff to their limits.

"Since Hannah's the retail expert, I was thinking she could help with the ordering and any kid could work the cash register. Hell, Darcy could do it."

"My wife has her hands full with her own business and Darcy has enough to do with keeping the reservations straight. You're doing it again, TJ. I appreciate that you want to grow the business, I really do. But we're not robots."

TJ started to argue and Colt put his hands up to keep the peace. "It's a good idea, TJ. As far as Delaney designing clothes for Garner Adventure—not gonna happen. But I like the idea of T-shirts, sweatshirts, rash guards, whatever. Draw up a business plan, map out who'll run the enterprise—not Hannah—list the kind of manpower we'll need, and we'll take it from there."

That seemed to appease everyone.

Colt, who had lost track of time, glanced at his watch. "I've got to get to work," he told his brothers. "I'll leave you three to strategize."

On his way out he said good-bye to his mother and to Darcy, who barely looked up from her computer monitor. When he got into the office, Jack was hanging around Carrie Jo's desk.

"Something going on I should know about?" Colt asked.

"Pond Scum just delivered our kayak," Jack said. "I'm not much of a kayaker but even I can tell it's a piece of shit."

It's not like they had a chance of winning anyway. The mayor just wanted to mess with Colt.

"Where is it?"

"The garage. Maybe you and I should go out a few times, get a feel for it."

When was Colt supposed to do that? "If I can carve out some time, yeah, sure."

"Nice pants," Carrie Jo said, and fingered the fabric. "They look new."

"Delaney Scott made them."

"You're kidding. Doesn't she make ball gowns and obscenely expensive purses?"

"And pants and shorts especially for me." Colt flashed her an arrogant grin.

"Something going on there?" Carrie Jo asked, and scrutinized Colt's face. "Oh my God, there is. You're finally over Lisa. Hallelujah!"

"There's nothing going on. We're neighbors, that's all."

"Then how come you're blushing?"

"I'm not blushing. Guys don't blush."

Jack asked, "What about you, Carrie Jo? Who you seeing these days?"

"I'm off men for the foreseeable future." She went on to list all the reasons why men sucked, which Colt had no interest in hearing. Strangely enough, Jack continued to loiter at her desk and listen to her bitch.

Colt shut the office door behind him so he could get some work done. Later, he planned to go down to the garage and have a look at the kayak Pond had delivered. While he was pissed that the mayor was trying to separate him from his family, he didn't want to go down in flames at the races. He had a reputation to uphold.

Midway through the day, he strolled over to Old Glory to grab a burger and finalize plans for his gig the night of the End-of-Summer festivities. It was slow and Boden hosed down the back of the bar. Colt grabbed a stool.

"You want to try this new stout we just got in?" Boden asked.

"Not while I'm on duty."

Boden leaned over the bar. "You're out of uniform."

"Not completely." Colt stood up so Boden could see his badge and gun belt. "No beer, but I'll have the Old Glory special."

"Coming right up." Boden called the order in to the kitchen. "How goes it?"

"It goes."

"The mayor still up your ass?"

"Not so much since the city council meeting." Colt didn't bother going into the kayak races. Who knows? Maybe Pond had good intentions.

"You all set for your show?"

"Yep. The band's looking forward to it."

The band was a ragtag collection of musicians from the area who all had day jobs. Lisa had been the only member who'd been a pro. Since she'd left fifteen months ago, they hadn't played too many shows. For a long time, Colt just couldn't bear to do it. Then life got in the way. But he'd like to start picking up a few gigs here and there again. Music had always been a big part of who he was and it was a shame he'd let Lisa ruin it for him.

In fact, later, when he got home from work, he picked up his acoustic guitar, sat on the porch, and strummed a few chords. Before he knew it, he was running through one of the band's favorite set lists. When it came time for "Crazy about You" he stopped, never wanting to hear the song again. Instead, he played "Galway Girl" and stared across the way to Delaney's house. Usually this time of the evening she was out on her deck watering the flowers or drinking a glass of wine. She was home; her car was parked at the top of her driveway. He hoped she wasn't avoiding him.

As if he'd willed it, she stepped outside with her watering can. He whistled and she turned and waved.

"Want a glass of wine?" He'd stopped at the market on his way home and got a bottle just in case someone dropped by. Ah, jeez, who was he kidding?

She called back, "No, thanks. I'm working."

Then why was she watering her flowers? It sounded like bullshit to him. He put his guitar down and crossed the road.

"We're not going to be weird, right?" he asked.

Her lips turned up in a wry smile. "I hope not, but first I have to get over my mortification."

"Ah, come on, nothing to be mortified by. I wore the pants today." He'd changed into old jeans as soon as he'd gotten home.

"You did?" This seemed to cheer her.

"Yep. TJ wants to sell them at Garner Adventure."

"Really?"

"Really." God, she was pretty. "He's always had delusions of grandeur."

"I don't know, at the rate I'm going . . . Not that it wouldn't be an honor."

"Good save," he said. "Seriously, they were a big hit. Even Carrie Jo noticed them."

She glanced over at his porch. "Were you practicing?"

"Nah, just screwing around. You sure you don't have time for one glass of wine? A thank-you for the pants." He told himself that it was only a let's-get-back-on-even-footing drink.

"I suppose I could have one glass."

"Come over, we'll have it on my porch." He hoped he had two glasses that matched.

"Let me put on a pair of shoes." She was barefoot, her toenails painted fire-engine red.

Hot as hell. The little dress, too. Casual, but it hugged every one of her curves.

He rushed back to his house to grab the wine out of the fridge and hoped she liked sauvignon blanc. He preferred red but a lot of women he knew drank white. He set everything out on a small table on his porch and pulled two chairs up.

His stuff wasn't that great, weathered and kind of beaten up, but it would have to do.

She came over a few minutes later, carrying a small platter with cheese and crackers. "I had it and figured what the heck."

"I could grill something if you're hungry," he said, and took the platter from her.

"This should be fine, but don't let me stop you from making something for yourself."

"I'm good with what you brought." He poured them each a glass of wine. "How'd your day go?"

She made the so-so gesture with her hand. "I got frustrated with the designing and worked on costumes for the junior theater."

Somewhere he'd heard that Rita had hit her up. "I wouldn't put too much work into it." Even for junior theater it was pretty second rate.

"I went to Reno and scoured some thrift stores and came up with a bunch of stuff I can repurpose."

"That's good. Robert didn't come by to give you more trouble, did he?"

"Nope. I haven't heard from him since yesterday and assume he went back to LA today, since he actually has a business to run."

"You'll have a business to run soon too." And then she would leave.

"Let's hope, or I'll have to resort to making cargo shorts and pants for Garner Adventure."

"Go ahead and laugh. But I probably don't have to tell you that athletic wear is big business. The stuff I wear as a guide may not be stylish, but I pay big bucks for functionality. We all do. Not just the cargo pants and shorts. Ski and snow-boarding gear and swimwear. Some of the women around here pay as much for their après-ski clothes as they do for their cars."

"I wasn't knocking it; it's just not what I do."

"I get that. But the shorts and pants you made for me are better than anything on the market. I can say that with confidence and I'm not just blowing smoke."

She reached over and touched his arm. "Thank you, Colt. You're good for my confidence."

He didn't know if she was good for his. Not after the way she'd pulled back from him last night. They'd been hot and heavy and then boom. But it was better that way, he told himself. Being friends was actually perfect. Because Lord knew he didn't have enough friends. Only half the town.

"Only being honest," he said.

"Anything new on the kayak races? Is the mayor still expecting you to represent the police department?"

"Yep. He brought our kayak over today. A piece of crap he probably got at a bargain."

"Does the equipment matter that much?"

"Let's put it this way: What kind of sewing machine do you use in your line of work? Something from Walmart or an industrial machine with all the bells and whistles?"

"Okay, I get your point."

"Now, I'm not expecting him to spend city funds on some fancy, super expensive kayak, but at least consult with me if I'm the guy racing the damn thing."

"You want to win, don't you?" She was laughing at him.

"I'm a competitive guy—nothing wrong with that."

"Nope. But somehow I get the feeling that you and your brothers are over the top in that area."

His mouth tipped up. "I'd say you're right. It comes with the territory. We were raised in a family of daredevils."

She shook her head with those sparkling blue eyes of hers as if to say, *you're nuts, you're all nuts.* God, she lit him up. He couldn't help himself and just stared, noticing for the first time the length of her lashes and how they were as dark as her hair. And her lips. Man, he loved her lips. It took everything he had not to kiss her.

"You want more wine?" He tore his gaze away and topped off her glass just to keep his hands busy.

"Uh, not too much. I'm a lightweight. A couple of glasses of wine and, well, you don't want to know."

Hell yeah, he wanted to know. "Here"—he held the platter in front of her—"have more cheese and crackers. It'll line your stomach, unless you want to get drunk."

"No. I made enough of a fool of myself last night."

"You really didn't, Delaney. You had a rough confrontation with Robert, you worked on the pants to distract you from it, and lost track of the time. I've been there."

"Because of an ex?"

That's not what he had meant, but yeah. "Sure. You make pants, I skydive or BASE jump or parachute ski."

"That bad, huh?"

"Pretty bad." He didn't usually talk about it, but he supposed if anyone could identify with a bad breakup, she could. "It's been fifteen months, though. I've moved on . . . she's moved on. We're all good."

"Is that why you don't date women in Glory Junction?"

"Let's just say it was a very public breakup and I'm a very private person. But in general it's really not a good idea. I already have so many ties to this town that everyone is up in my business. I'd like to keep my romantic life under wraps, until I'm in a serious relationship."

"I gather she . . . the public breakup one . . . was serious."

"I thought it was. She had different ideas." Like taking the first plane out of here to Nashville.

"I'm sorry, Colt. I know how much that hurts."

"So it was Robert's idea to leave?" If so, the dude was a first-class idiot.

"Ultimately, I left him. But he was unhappy. In hindsight, I was too. By the end, we were little more than business partners."

"You think you'll try to reconcile?"

"No. Neither of us is interested in a reconciliation. It was over even before it was over. I wish things weren't so contentious now, but I suppose that's what happens when so much of our personal and professional lives are intertwined. What did this ex of yours do? Was she in law enforcement?"

That would've been so much easier. "She's a singer. When her career hit the skids she came here to be a ski instructor with plans to quit the music business. We played around town, some shows in Tahoe, but it was for fun. With Josh in the army we needed someone at Garner Adventure to head up the ski program. She was planning to take the job. . . ."

"And?"

Colt paused, then said, "An indie film that no one expected to do anything suddenly became a box office hit. The movie's score was hers, including the theme song, which got huge airplay. Her music career was resurrected overnight and she decided she wanted that more than she wanted . . . It worked out for the best," especially now that he knew what kind of person she was.

"Are you talking about Lisa Laredo, the country-western artist?"

There was no reason for Colt to keep it a secret. The whole town knew. "Yeah."

"Wow." Delaney did a double take. "I'm not a country music fan, but she's a household name. I had no idea she'd lived in Glory Junction, but I read a story somewhere about her and her songs for the film, about how it catapulted her to the top."

He nodded. The story had become part of her legacy. "She lived here for two years." And was supposed to stay permanently. They'd even begun to search for a bigger house.

"You couldn't make it work? I mean, I know she probably has to go out on the road a lot, but couldn't Glory Junction have been her home base?"

It could've been. But after what she'd done, what she'd stolen, he hadn't wanted any part of her. Clearly being a big star meant more to her than the life they could've had together.

"Nashville is home to the industry," he said. "That's where she wanted to be. I'm over it, Delaney."

He could tell she didn't know how to respond, so they drank their wine in silence as the sun set over the Sierra. It felt comfortable, just the two of them. Too comfortable. He didn't realize how much having someone to talk to at the end of the day was missing from his life, and how much he enjoyed it. And that's what worried him. He was enjoying it a little too much.

Chapter Eleven

It sounded like there was more to the story than Colt was telling her, but Delaney was surprised that he'd confided as much as he had. It didn't take a rocket scientist to deduce that Colt wasn't much of a talker. No touchy feely there. She'd say he was even more reticent than most guys.

Lisa Laredo. Wow.

Delaney had seen the singer on television a few times. Gorgeous, and a body that wouldn't quit, all of it real. Delaney had dressed enough celebrities to know. Colt could say he was over her all he wanted, but Delaney didn't think so. There was a rawness to his voice when he talked about her, like she'd left a festering wound in his heart. To see that kind of sadness in someone was difficult, but even more so when it was a strapping, stoic, alpha male like Colt. That kind of vulnerability . . .

"I should probably go," she said. "I was hoping to actually design something tonight or at least attempt to."

She helped gather up the glasses and take them to the kitchen.

"I've got it, Delaney. I'll wash your platter too."

"Don't worry about it. I'll take it home and stick it in the dishwasher." She took the opportunity to look around. The two times inside, she hadn't paid much attention to the living area. "This is a cute house, by the way. Though it could use some accessories." Other than a family picture over the mantel, the walls were bare. "How long have you had it?"

He seemed to be calculating the years in his head. "I got it about a year after I moved back to Glory Junction from the city, maybe five years ago. I added the deck but haven't had much time to do anything else."

"I like the old-time trim." She walked into the living room to examine the crown moldings. With a fresh coat of glossy white paint and maybe the walls in a dove gray, the place would really pop. Everything was a dull off-white. Sort of dingy. "The hardwood floors are nice too."

"Thanks. The place suits me okay, except for the driveway, which sucks."

She suspected that it was a reminder that he needed the easement parking pad for his police car. "Perhaps someday we could go in together and have a carport put in, using land from both our yards."

"I'd be down with that. In the snow, it's a real hassle getting down that steep grade. But something like what you're talking about won't be cheap."

"I could get a couple of bids," she said.

"Nah, let me. My family's got contacts." Colt chuckled as if he was sharing a joke.

"What's so funny?" She didn't get it.

"My dad is the king of wheeling and dealing, always has someone who can undercut the competition. When anyone in our family is looking to contract work, we have a joke: 'Dad knows a guy.'" When she didn't respond, he said, "It's kind of a Garner thing."

"Your family is a tight-knit clan, isn't it?"

"Yup. They're part of the reason I came back to Glory Junction."

"You never wanted to take a bigger role at Garner Adventure?" She'd always been curious about that. He was the only member of the family who had an outside job.

"I guess Josh and I had a strong urge to serve the public. Being a local cop allows me to do both, though it's killing my social life. What about your family? You close?"

"I'm an only child," she said. "But I'm close with my parents, even though they live in Michigan and I live here. They've always been supportive of my work, though they don't understand why anyone would pay so much money for clothes." Or why she would leave her working-class roots for a life in the fast lane.

He smiled—his teeth so white against his tan skin—and her insides did a little flip-flop. The memory of his kiss, the way his body felt so warm and hard, flashed through her head. The strength of his arms around her, the sensuous pull of his mouth, and the gentleness of his hands had made her feel safe—and incredibly aroused. Then the things Robert had said and wanted had come floating back and she'd frozen.

It was really time to go. She'd stayed longer than she'd planned. Work awaited. She should at least finish the *Grease* costumes, which would take the rest of the night. "Oh, and FYI, my shades come on Friday."

"I appreciate that, Delaney."

He walked her the short distance home. She went up to her room, changed into yoga pants and a lightweight hoodie, and got to work in her studio, careful to leave the drafting light off. By midnight, she'd finished most of the costumes but her sketch pad was bare.

The next morning, she heard from her lawyer.

"Do you want to get a restraining order?" Liz asked.

"That seems excessive, not to mention excellent fodder for the gossip sheets."

Delaney had been lucky so far. The news hadn't paid much attention to her and Robert's divorce. Of course they weren't of the celebrity status that someone like Lisa Laredo was. But Delaney was well known and had made guest appearances on *Project Runway* and *America's Next Top Model* as well as on talk shows.

"I don't expect him to bother me anymore," she continued.

"All right. But if he shows up again I want to know about it. If he wants you to take the Delaney Scott name off your existing merchandise, his lawyers will have to get the court clarification. As far as I'm concerned, the ruling was perfectly clear. You can't use it for new merchandise, but what's done is done. So we'll just carry on."

"Sounds good to me. Thank you, Liz." Her phone beeped. "I have to go; I'm getting another call."

Delaney switched over to the other line. "Hello."

"Hi, Delaney, this is TJ Garner. Did I catch you at a bad time?"

"No." Though she couldn't imagine why Colt's brother was calling her. While she'd met him a few times through Hannah and at the Indian restaurant with Colt, they'd never said more than a few words to each other. "What's up?"

"I was hoping I could take you to lunch. You hungry?"

It was noon and she'd only had a piece of toast and coffee for breakfast. "I could eat," she said, curious. It couldn't possibly be romantic, or at least she hoped it wasn't. The only Garner brother she had eyes for was Colt.

"I could swing by, get you, and we could have lunch at the Morning Glory."

"How about I meet you there?"

"That works too. How soon?"

"Give me twenty minutes." He'd certainly piqued her interest.

Rushing upstairs, she put on something more appropriate for town than her exercise clothes, swiped on some mascara and lip gloss, and combed her hair. She made it to the diner with a few minutes to spare. The restaurant was crowded and she had to put her name on a list for a table. Deb came out of the kitchen and waved hello. When TJ walked in she escorted both of them to a back booth and rushed off to get another patron coffee.

"How did you do that?" she asked TJ. "The hostess told me it would be at least a ten-minute wait."

"I called ahead. They don't really take reservations, but I know people." He winked.

Unlike Colt's dark brown eyes, TJ's were blue and his hair was a little lighter. He was about the same height as Colt, but leaner with a runner's body. There was no mistaking the family resemblance, but in Delaney's opinion, Colt was handsomer.

Deb came back to the table to take their orders. Delaney got a tuna sandwich with fries and TJ got biscuits and gravy.

"The place is swamped today," Deb said. "I haven't stopped running since I got here. Sorry I can't talk."

She trotted over to the cook's window and yelled, "Heart attack on rack and tuna down." A few minutes later, she brought their drinks and dashed off again.

"I wonder why it's so crowded," Delaney said. The diner did a brisk business but she'd never seen it like this.

"The *San Francisco Call* featured it in Sunday's paper. Said it was one of the most authentic diners in northern California. Now everyone's hiking up the mountain to eat patty melts. We've even gotten some business out of it. Just today, a group of walk-ins signed up for white-water rafting."

"That's great." Delaney took a long drink. The walk to downtown had been hot and dry.

"Can't complain. You see my brother this morning?"

"No. Why?"

He lifted his shoulders, trying to seem nonchalant. "No reason. I just thought you two were hanging out."

If TJ was trying to find out where his brother and Delaney stood, she wasn't taking the bait. "So to what do I owe the pleasure of your company?" She wanted him to get to the point of this lunch. And why he was asking questions about her and Colt.

"I saw the pants you made Colt. He says you made shorts too, which I haven't seen, but if they're anything like the pants . . . Anyway, I'm interested in selling them at Garner Adventure."

She'd thought Colt had been joking when he'd mentioned it the other night. "Ah, TJ, I don't really do that. Even my ready-to-wear is, uh, higher concept."

"I know," he said, but she could tell he wasn't ready to give up. "But what if we bought the design from you and had our people make them and sew in our own labels?"

"Under ordinary circumstances I might consider it, but I'm trying to reestablish myself and don't think it's a good idea. I wouldn't want people to find out that I was secretly designing for you and think that's the direction I'm moving in." Besides, her goal was to reestablish herself, not design in anonymity.

"Why? They're great pants."

"Because I don't do athletic wear. My brand is high fashion."

"But you just said you're reestablishing your brand."

He was starting to wear her down, and she said, "You're starting to remind me of my ex."

"Uh-oh, that can't be good." His mouth curved into a mischievous smile and she could see how women would find him incredibly appealing.

"He's relentless and a very good businessman," she said.

Their food came and it gave her a moment's reprieve. She suspected that TJ wasn't finished making his pitch. She bit into her sandwich as Deb talked about the upcoming kayak races. She was on the Morning Glory's tandem team.

"So Colt's racing for Glory Junction PD," Deb said.

"Yep. It's Josh and me for GA this year."

"What about Win?"

"Win sucks at paddling."

"The way I see it, without Colt racing for you guys, the contest is wide open."

"You're delusional, Deb. We'll win it like we do every year. But if you'd like to wager a little bet on it, I'm game."

She considered it for a few seconds. "I'll think about it. I want to know who's partnering with Colt first."

Delaney was coming to the conclusion that this supposedly friendly end of the summer race was even more competitive than she'd originally thought.

"Jack," TJ responded.

"Deb," Felix, the owner, bellowed, "no time for chitchat." He pointed to the line that had formed outside on the sidewalk.

"Gotta go." Deb took off to take orders from the other tables.

TJ cut into his biscuits and gravy, and Delaney wondered how he could eat that way and stay so trim.

"What if besides buying the design, we gave you a cut of the profits?" he asked in between bites. "My idea is to eventually do an online store. We could be talking big money."

"I'll think about it, TJ." Which she would. "But it would be a big change from what I do and I have to be certain that it won't hurt my commercial image."

He nodded in understanding. "Still, it seems a shame to let such a good design go to waste. With a few modifications, they could be the Rolls-Royce of cargo pants."

Not that she wanted to be known for creating the "Rolls-Royce" of cargo pants, but she was inquisitive about the modifications. At the same time, she didn't want to encourage TJ.

"So are you and my brother seeing each other?" he asked.

"No." The man certainly cut to the chase. "We're just neighbors."

"Really? I got the impression the other night that maybe you two might be dating. Ever since . . . uh, he doesn't get out much."

"Ever since Lisa?"

TJ just about spit his coffee out. "He told you about her?"

"Yes. I didn't realize it was a secret."

"It's not. The whole damn town saw what she did to him. He's the one who never talks about it. What did he say?"

"I suppose if he wanted you to know, he would've told you."

TJ smiled. "You're all right, Delaney Scott."

After lunch Delaney popped into Glorious Gifts and browsed while Hannah helped a customer. Hannah had a lot of beautiful items in the store. Delaney checked the handbag inventory to make sure Hannah had gotten the new order.

"I can't keep them in the shop," Hannah said. "I've already sold half of the new shipment." She finished ringing up the shopper and afterward came over to Delaney. "You here to check inventory or are you shopping?"

"I just had lunch with TJ."

Hannah gave her a quizzical look and Delaney explained about his idea to sell the cargo pants.

"You made pants for Colt? That was awfully nice. I thought you two were like cat and dog."

"We've called a truce." *And now we kiss.*

"Are you thinking of doing the pants, then?"

"I told TJ I would consider it, but it's not really the direction I want to go." But if the court made her take the Delaney Scott name off her existing shoes and handbags, she might have to find a new revenue stream. "What do you think of Garner Adventure selling merchandise?"

"Josh thinks they're stretched too thin as it is. But honestly, I think it's a brilliant idea, especially if they open an online store. They'll probably have to hire someone with retail expertise and that won't be me. I know retail but nothing about adventure wear and sporting equipment."

Delaney nodded. "Same here."

They chatted for a while and then the store got busy again. Delaney said good-bye and decided to stroll down Main Street. For a Wednesday, the boardwalk was busy, full of bicyclists and pedestrians, taking advantage of the last days of summer before school started. She splurged on a piece of chocolate at Oh Fudge! and got a loaf of bread at Tart Me Up. As she passed Old Glory, she noticed a poster promoting Colt's band. He was playing the night of the End-of-Summer races. The show must've been what he'd been talking about on the phone the other day. She made a mental note to put it on her calendar.

"You going?"

She looked up from the picture of Colt on the poster to see him in the flesh.

"I was thinking I might," she said. "Where are you off to?"

"To pick up a late lunch at the Morning Glory and take it back to my office."

"I was just there with your brother."

She saw something flicker in those brown eyes of his but couldn't quite identify it. Whatever it was, he hadn't looked happy.

"Win?"

"No, TJ. He wanted to talk to me about the cargo pants and shorts I made you and an idea for selling merchandise."

Colt seemed to relax. "I told him you wouldn't be interested. But TJ is pushy that way."

"I was flattered. I told him I'd think about it."

"But you're not, right?"

She shrugged. "He's so enthusiastic about it that I hate to say no. There may be a way to work something out. I'd have to talk to my people first."

"It's up to you. But TJ will understand if you're not interested. Garner Adventure is small-time compared to the retailers you sell your stuff to. The design is great, though. I'd hate to see it go to waste, especially when you could make a mint from the pants."

"TJ seemed to think it needed a few modifications." That had sort of peeved her, which of course was her pride. She certainly wasn't an expert in adventure wear.

"Did he now?" He took her arm and headed toward the diner. "Walk with me."

"Do you think they need modifications?"

He pondered it for a bit. "The fit and weight are great, but there are a few things you could do with the pockets that would make them more user-friendly for guides, something more akin to tactical pants."

"What are tactical pants?"

"They're close to cargo pants and originally worn by mountain climbers. Cops, soldiers, and firefighters wear them because they're made specifically to hold their gear, including a heavy gun belt, knives, and cuffs."

"So more pockets?"

"Maybe not more but configured differently. The pants should have side zips at the bottom of the legs so you can put them on over your crampons and boots."

"What are crampons?"

"A metal plate with spikes that you put on your boots to walk on ice or rock climb. I'd also include a gusseted crotch for freedom of movement and a little more stretch in the fabric, especially for rock climbers operating in the snow."

"I never realized how much performance was required

from adventure wear. What brands come close to doing all of this?" She'd like to check them out just for the sake of it.

He rattled off a short list. Most of the brands were familiar but she didn't own anything from the companies.

"It's a whole different objective than what I do, which is to be fashion forward and flatter the human figure."

He nodded, then let his eyes roam over her body. His inspection gave her goose bumps.

"You design that?"

She looked down at her white pencil pants and cropped linen jacket. "I did."

"Then I'd say it's working, especially the figure part."

"Was that a compliment on my work or are you flirting with me?"

"I guess both." The corner of his mouth ticked up.

"Then why did you make such a big point of telling me that you had a hands-off policy when it comes to local women?" She said it with a smile, but he was sending mixed signals.

"Last I looked, I didn't have my hands on you."

"You know what I mean."

He nodded solemnly. "You're right. My bad, and I apologize." Colt pointed to the entrance of the Morning Glory. "This is where I get off."

She went her separate way, wondering what game he was playing. He certainly acted interested for a man who so much as said he wasn't. Whatever, she told herself. He clearly found her attractive, and if nothing else his compliments gave her a nice boost.

When she got home she went on the Internet to search the brands of pants Colt had told her about. She really should've worked on her own stuff but looking at other people's designs was better than failing at her own. Blowing up a couple of the pictures, she saw what Colt was talking about. The clothes appeared highly functional but definitely lacked in the aesthetics department. Dull colors, boxy fit, and plain old unimaginative. No reason why someone couldn't be fashionable while climbing the side of a mountain as long as the clothing performed. She got out the pattern she'd used for Colt's shorts and pants and started to improvise.

Before she knew it, it was dark outside and she had a new pair of pants she thought were better than the first. Only one way to find out. Delaney didn't want to make the same mistake twice by traipsing over to Colt's. This time she searched her phone for his number and gave him a jingle.

"Everything okay?" he answered.

"Yes, why wouldn't it be?"

"I don't think you've ever called me before." No, she just showed up in the wee hours of the morning, making a fool of herself.

"I made another pair of pants, incorporating some of the elements we talked about." She waited for him to say something but he didn't. "I wanted to see what you think."

"I'm at my parents' right now for dinner."

"Oh, I'm sorry. I'll let you go."

She was just about to disconnect when he said, "I'll be home in about an hour. You want me to stop by?"

"You don't have to. I can just leave them on your doorstep and when you get a chance you can let me know what you think."

"Okay. Delaney, why are you doing this?"

She wondered if he meant why was she bothering him. "Doing what?"

"Trying to perfect a pair of pants you don't want to make in the first place."

She let out a breath and shut her eyes. "Because right now it seems to be the only thing I'm good at."

There was quiet on the other end of the line, then he said, "All right. Talk to you later."

She gave the pants another good pressing, wrapped them

in tissue, stuck them in a bag, crossed the driveway to Colt's, and left the package where she said she would. When she returned home her answering machine was blinking. Delaney wondered if it was Liz with bad news. Her lawyer often called at odd hours because she was in court most of the day. She pressed the button, holding her breath.

"Hi, Delaney, it's Karen. Call me as soon as you can. I'll be up until eleven."

She rang Karen's number, wondering what was up. It wasn't like her ex-office manager to call this late.

Karen picked up almost immediately, as if she were waiting for Delaney. "She's driving us crazy."

"Who is?"

"Olivia, the wicked bitch of the West. She's demanding, moody, and mean. I almost quit today."

"Oh no." As much as Delaney felt competitive with Olivia, she didn't want her former employees to be unhappy. "Don't do that."

"Why? She's impossible to work with."

"Because it's a good job and Robert will talk to her." Delaney was angry with him but Robert was a good employer. He wouldn't want discord in the ranks.

"Robert bends to her every wish. It's pathetic, Delaney. This thing with him wanting you to take your name off the existing shoes and handbags—that's Olivia. She's threatening to leave over it."

Delaney wasn't surprised. She'd suspected Olivia of pulling Robert's strings. Olivia wanted to be the face of the new Delaney Scott and couldn't do that if Delaney's merchandise still carried the name.

"Give her a chance to assimilate. It's got to be tough walking into a new house and filling the shoes of the designer who founded it."

"I understand that, Delaney, I really do. But I'm done giving her more chances. I've given her too many already. I want to come work for you."

There was nothing Delaney would like better. Bringing in Karen would solve her staffing problem. Karen had been with Delaney Scott for years and had the skill sets to oversee the entire operation from manufacturing to sales. While Delaney's warehouse supervisor had been a saint to take on the extra responsibilities, the job called for someone like Karen.

"I would love to have you, Karen, but for all intents and purposes I'm starting from scratch. There's no guarantee that my new company will thrive the way Delaney Scott does. After all these years, you deserve job security."

"I'll risk it."

Delaney admired Karen's loyalty. Still, it wouldn't be fair to take her on if Karen didn't know what she was getting herself into.

"Karen, do you know what I've been spending my days doing?" When Karen didn't answer, she said, "I've been perfecting a design for cargo pants."

Karen laughed as if it were a joke.

"My neighbor and his family own an adventure tour company. They want to sell my cargo pants. The reason I'm even entertaining the idea is because I can't design anything else. I'm stuck, completely blocked. For all I know I'll never be able to design again."

"I thought your neighbor was the police chief of that little town and you couldn't stand him."

"He is, but we've buried the hatchet." If Karen only knew. "Are you listening to me? I haven't been able to put anything on paper since the divorce. A full year."

"You'll get it back," Karen said, sounding so confident that Delaney almost believed her. "You've been under enormous stress. Not just with you and Robert breaking up, but with the settlement hearing. Losing a big chunk of everything you built has to be devastating, Delaney. Cut yourself some slack. Make cargo pants for a while. It can't hurt."

Delaney found it hard to believe, but she actually enjoyed creating the cargo pants. Or maybe she was just enjoying having Colt as a muse. If only she could visualize him in an evening gown.

"Can I come work for you?"

Delaney thought about it. There was nothing in the settlement that said she couldn't employ former personnel from Robert's company.

"If you want to take the chance, I'd love to have you."

"Yay! I'll give my two weeks and start with you in September if that works."

"I could actually use your organizational skills at the warehouse."

"When are you coming back to Los Angeles?" Karen asked.

"Not until I have a collection to show to investors. If I feel pressured now, could you imagine how bad it would be in LA?"

"You'll come up with something fantastic and show up the wicked bitch of the West."

Delaney appreciated the pep talk, but the thought of competing with Olivia made her stomach churn. What if she was done? Over? She hung up with Karen and proceeded to have a panic attack.

Chapter Twelve

The call came just as Colt was leaving his parents' house. By the time he got to Old Glory, a man was being taken out of the bar on a stretcher. Another was being checked out by a paramedic. Broken bottles and shattered glassware littered the floor, and a couple of stools had been knocked over. Boden stood behind the bar looking angrier than Colt had ever seen him.

Two of Colt's officers acknowledged him with nods and resumed interviewing their witnesses. Colt didn't recognize either of the culprits, which probably meant they were out-of-towners.

"What happened?" he asked Boden.

"Destination wedding up at one of the resorts. The groom and best man decided to get their drink on early. Turns out the best man's been boffing the bride-to-be and decides after three Jacks it's time to confess. At least that's my interpretation of what went down. I only caught snippets before the shit began to fly."

"Who went out on the stretcher?"

"I believe that would be the best man."

Colt glanced around, taking better stock of the damage. "You got insurance?"

"I do, but there's a heavy deductible, which I expect the wedding assholes to pay."

"We'll see what we can do." He walked over to Dutch, who'd been on patrol with Glory Junction PD since Colt had been a boy, and pulled him aside. "Boden says it was a groom and best-man situation. Is that consistent with what you're getting?"

"Yeah," Dutch said, and snickered. "Apparently the wedding's off."

Colt stayed a while to make sure everything was done by the book. Weddings were the resorts' bread and butter in the off-season. The last thing he needed was the mayor giving him hell about how the department handled a bar room brawl. He told Dutch and Bobby George, another veteran officer, to have their reports on his desk by morning in case Pond Scum tried to second-guess him, and then went home.

He found Delaney's package on the doorstep. It was too late to knock on her door, especially since her lights were out. Colt took the bag inside and headed for the shower to wash off the day's grime. Afterward, he unwrapped Delaney's pants and examined the modifications closely before trying them on. Perfect, he thought to himself. If he thought the first pair was superior to anything on the market, these were even better. The woman had mad skills, that's for sure.

Brains and beauty. Delaney Scott was the full package. And totally out of reach.

He didn't get a chance the next morning to call and tell her how much he liked the new version of the cargo pants. TJ needed a substitute guide to take a group on a sunrise hike. The seventy-two-year-old former park ranger who usually conducted the nature walks for GA was having a hip replaced and wouldn't be back until next summer. TJ hadn't found a sub yet, so Colt was stuck filling in.

"You've got to be freaking kidding me," he barked at TJ over his Bluetooth as he drove to the trailhead. "Why can't

Win or Josh do it? You do know that I have a full-time job, right?"

"Sorry," TJ said, but didn't sound sorry at all. "It was an emergency."

"Didn't Greta tell you about her hip replacement a month ago? A month's notice is not an emergency; it's bad planning. Besides, a nature hike? A freaking nature hike? Give me a break, TJ."

"What? It's a nice Zen way to start your day. You know, stopping to smell the roses."

"I'm saluting you right now with my middle finger." Colt hung up.

By the time he made it into the office he was thirty minutes late and in desperate need of a shower.

"Look what the cat dragged in," Carrie Jo said as he came in the door.

"Don't start with me." He scowled.

"Heard about the fight at Old Glory. What do you think the bride's doing today?"

"Don't know, don't care. Any messages?"

"Nope. You want coffee?"

"I'm not going to Tart Me Up, Carrie Jo!"

"My, my, aren't we testy today?" She stood up and kissed him on the cheek, then wrinkled her nose. "Eww, you need a bath. I'll go to Tart Me Up. I suggest you head to the locker room. You have an extra uniform in your office?"

"I'll get it." He grabbed the dry-cleaning bag from his closet and marched to the shower.

Twenty minutes later, he emerged feeling human again. Colt fired up his computer and quickly scanned Dutch's and Bobby's reports.

Carrie Jo came in his office, carrying a large cup of coffee. "Rachel Johnson was soooooo disappointed that it was me instead of you. Why don't you ask that lovely woman out on a date? Oh yeah, I forgot. You're too busy not dating Delaney Scott."

"Thanks for the coffee, Carrie Jo. Now go away."

She sat in the chair next to his desk and peeked at his computer. "What are you doing?"

"Police work. What are you doing, besides bothering me?" He looked up from his computer and she stuck her tongue out at him. "Real mature."

"What's got you in such a foul mood today? Could it be that you haven't gotten laid since Lisa left?"

"Boundaries, Carrie Jo. Boundaries."

"Oh my God, you haven't, have you?"

"What do you think?" He cocked his brows as if daring her to argue with him. Of course he'd gotten laid, just not as often as he would have liked given his self-imposed twenty-mile rule or the fact that he liked his sex to be more meaningful than a quick roll in the hay. "TJ coerced me into taking a group of senior citizens on a sunrise hike in the state park before coming to work. As if I don't have enough to do."

"At least it was good exercise, right?"

He shot her a look. "If you consider a forty-minute mile in the hot sun exercise. Two of the participants had walkers."

She giggled. "Oops. Well, it must've been nice getting out in nature."

"No, it robbed me of my morning run, which you and I should be doing together."

"Uh-uh. You're too hard on me. I have to do it at my own pace."

Colt didn't want to push it, otherwise she would accuse him of thinking she was fat. Which he didn't. He thought she was great the way she was.

Jack knocked and let himself in. "Heard about the bar brawl. Those yahoos planning to pay Boden restitution?"

"Sounds like it," Colt said. "I was hoping for a quiet summer."

"Good thing summer's almost over." Not really. In northern

California summer bled into September—and sometimes even October—weather-wise. The tourists would at least go home and Glory Junction wouldn't get its next wave of them until the first snow. "Speaking of, you think we should take the new kayak out for a test run, see if the thing even holds water. Get it? Holds water?"

Jack was the only one who laughed at his own stupid pun. Colt didn't miss the fact that Jack seemed to ham it up around Carrie Jo. He didn't think Miss Former Homecoming Queen would look twice at Jack, which was a shame. Jack might not be the slickest or the handsomest, but he was one of the best men Colt knew. Steady and solid. The kind of guy you'd want at your side in a bad situation. Besides, they'd both been burned by love. Carrie Jo's husband had been catting around on her for years, and Jack's longtime girlfriend had dumped him right around the time Lisa had left town.

The police station had not been a fun place during those dark days.

"Yup," Colt responded. "Let's try for lunch if all stays quiet."

"You want to come, Carrie Jo?" Jack asked.

"Nope, I'm going to CrossFit with Foster."

Colt doubted that would last but wanted to stay supportive.

"I'll do CrossFit with you guys," Jack said. "Is it every Thursday?"

"And Tuesday. But don't try to show me up, Jack." Carrie Jo smiled at him and Jack turned red.

"I won't."

Colt wanted to tell him to get a grip. "Are you going to CrossFit or are we taking the kayak out?"

"We'll take the kayak out and I'll go to CrossFit on Tuesday," Jack said.

"All right. Let's hope the next few hours are noneventful."

Jack and Carrie Jo left his office and Colt tried to get

some work done. At around ten, he figured it was late enough to call Delaney. He got her voice mail and left a message.

Carrie Jo buzzed in. "Your mother is on line two."

Why she didn't call his cell, he'd never know. "Hey, Mom."

"Hannah says Sunday is the best night to hold the dinner for Josh. Monday they're heading to San Francisco so they'll have a day before the surgery."

"Okay. You want me to bring anything?"

"TJ says you're seeing your next-door neighbor. Why don't you bring her?"

I'm going to kill you, TJ. "TJ doesn't know what he's talking about. We're neighbors . . . friends. That's all."

"Well, you could still bring her if you'd like. Deb and Foster are coming too, and if Jack and Carrie Jo want to come there's always room at the table."

"You sure Josh wants such a big crowd?" Mary Garner could get carried away. She liked to entertain, but maybe they should wait until after Josh's operation to start celebrating.

"If Josh wasn't okay with it, Hannah wouldn't have invited Deb and Foster. It'll be fine, dear. Come around five."

"All right. I'll bring beer."

He signed off and texted TJ. "Hey, asshole, quit meddling in my business." Colt found an emoji of a giant middle finger, tacked that onto the message, and hit the send button.

That's when Win barged into his office. "Carrie Jo said you weren't busy."

Carrie Jo is about to get fired. "You don't even knock?"

"Why? Were you having a little special time with your right hand?"

Colt looked up at the ceiling and counted to ten before he throttled his brother. "What do you need, Win?"

"How do you know I didn't come over to spend some quality time with my big brother, huh?" He sat on the love seat, stretched out, and made himself right at home.

"What do you need, Win?"

"Can you fill in for me Sunday? I've got a white-water rafting group but want to go to Tahoe for the day."

"What's in Tahoe?"

"A lake."

Colt picked up an old baseball cap on his desk and sailed it across the room to land on a hook on the wall. "We've got a lake here."

Win nodded. "Can you take my group?"

Colt guessed there was a girl involved. When it came to Win there was always a girl involved. "Do you guys not get that I have a full-time job? Do you not get that I have only one day off a week?"

"Isn't that illegal?" Win got up, took the hat off the hook, and put it on his head.

"Aren't you going to Josh's dinner?"

"I'll be back in time."

"Get TJ to take your group. He needs to get out of the office and remember what it's like to do some actual work for a change." The truth was no one worked harder than TJ. Colt's brother was a certified workaholic.

"He can't do it. I already asked him. You're my last resort."

"What about Dad? Maybe Chip could use some extra cash. He's still sober, right?"

"Yeah, Josh would love that." Chip was Hannah's first husband and Josh's ex best friend. "Come on, Colt. Can't you help me out? I'll return the favor, I promise."

"You planning to fill in as police chief? Because in case you forgot, that's my real job."

"Sure, I'll fill in as police chief," Win said. "Seriously, I'm desperate here."

"Fine. But you owe me big-time."

"I'm good for it." Win lay long ways on the couch, hanging his feet off the end. "TJ says you and your neighbor are an item now."

"TJ's wrong."

"According to him, you told her about Lisa."

Colt clenched his fists. Why the hell had Delaney told TJ that? "So? The whole town knows about Lisa."

"Did you tell Delaney what Lisa did?"

"We're not talking about that, Win. We're never talking about that."

"Then I gather you didn't tell her."

"If you still want me to take your group out on Sunday, you better drop it."

Win sat up. "Relax. Is Delaney going to let us carry her cargo pants and shorts?"

"I doubt it. It would be a pretty big step down, don't you think?"

"I don't know about that." Win shrugged. "She'd just be branching out into a new market."

"If she wanted to branch out into adventure wear, she could sell to REI or make a deal with Patagonia or North Face, not a small tour company that doesn't even have a retail division."

"I don't know," Win said. "I think TJ is on to something."

Yeah, his brother was on to a lot of things, including being a big mouth and a shit stirrer.

Colt flicked his chin at Win. "You thinking of leaving anytime soon so I can get some work done?"

"All right, I can take a hint. Thanks for Sunday." He got to his feet.

"Win, whatever you're doing in Tahoe, don't lose track of the time and miss Josh's dinner." It would be just like his irresponsible brother to screw up. "It's important that we're all there . . . for Josh."

"I won't miss it. Catch you later."

With Win gone, Colt settled in and worked steadily until lunchtime, when he and Jack took the kayak out on the river.

The boat was a recreational kayak as opposed to a downriver kayak used for racing. It was too broad for fast and nimble maneuvering and lousy for traveling in a straight line. Racing kayaks were typically long and skinny with a bow shaped like a narrow V for speed.

Unfortunately, they were stuck with what they had and would have to make the best of it.

"We're not going to win this, are we?" Jack said. Like Colt, Jack was competitive.

"Not unless Josh and TJ come down with a stomach flu."

Josh's doctors had said he could race after the surgery, since kayaking required mostly upper body strength, which Colt's brother had in spades.

Jack scratched his chin. "I guess it wouldn't be right to wish that upon them."

"I'm not above it. With this piece of crap, I don't know if we can even beat Deb. Don't underestimate her, she's a damn good kayaker. I'm pretty sure we can take Rachel and her crew, even in this. So at least we won't come in dead last."

"That's little consolation."

Yup, they were screwed.

Colt finished out his day, went home, and managed to get a run in to make up for his lost morning. Three miles. Afterward he got in a shower and ate cereal for supper, staring out the window. Delaney's Tesla was nowhere in sight. He washed his bowl, went upstairs to get his guitar, came back down, and ran through a few songs. It was slow going at first because he was rusty as hell. Eventually, though, he fell into a comfortable groove, playing a number of the band's standards. With Colt's schedule there wouldn't be time for the band to practice before the show. In the past, they'd always been able to pick up where they'd left off without much rehearsing.

Since Lisa had left, he and the rhythm guitarist traded off on lead vocals. While he didn't consider himself much of a singer, he got the job done. It had been more than a year since he'd written a song. He didn't know if he'd ever be able to do it again. These days, his only inspiration was his black-haired, blue-eyed neighbor. No way could he do better than Steve Earle's "Galway Girl."

Colt strummed the chorus and belted out the lyrics, thinking of Delaney. Pretty Delaney.

Halfway through the tune, he heard her drive up the easement. He peered through his window and saw her get out of the car with a load of packages.

Setting down his guitar, he went to the back door and called, "You need help?"

"Sure."

He slipped on a pair of huarache sandals, hiked up her driveway, and grabbed an armful of bags from her car.

"Did you buy out a store?"

"It's more stuff for the *Grease* costumes."

He helped her haul the bags into her house, carried them upstairs, and left them in her studio.

"You get my call?" he asked.

"I did. I tried to call you back around lunchtime, but there was no answer. I figured you must be busy."

He hadn't checked his cell. "Jack and I took the department's new kayak out for a test run."

"How was it?"

He shrugged. "Not the best. You go to Reno?"

"Yep. While I was there I went to a sporting goods store and checked out some of the pants you told me about. I could only get so much detail from the pictures on the Internet, so I bought a couple of pairs."

He stood back and scrutinized her. "Are you serious about this . . . about making adventure clothes?"

"You mean as part of my collection? No. But once I get a bee in my bonnet to perfect something, I don't give up. Plus, I might be willing to design a prototype for Garner

Adventure. I still have to talk to my people but haven't ruled anything out."

"Really?" She was singing a different tune than she had before, and Colt wondered at the sudden change. "Why's that? Not that TJ won't be into it."

"Crazy, but I'm having fun making them. I guess they've given me purpose, which I haven't had since the divorce."

"If you're having fun, then by all means do it. But don't feel like you have to do my brother a favor. And as far as I'm concerned, you've already perfected the pants. The ones you sent over last night rock the house. And I think I can speak with authority when I say that, because I've tried them all."

"Seriously?" Her face glowed from the praise. "You're not just saying that to make me feel good?"

"Delaney, if all I wanted to do was make you feel good, I could do that with my hands and my mouth and my . . ."

"You're flirting again," she said. But from the way her nipples puckered through her top, it was plain that he'd turned her on. Either that or she was cold in eighty-degree weather.

Regardless, the woman knew how to work a simple cotton T-shirt, that was for sure. Jeans . . . yeah, those too.

"You want a glass of beer? I got some of that fancy stuff you like," Delaney offered.

"You did?" *Fancy. That was funny.*

"You know, to return the favor of the other night. The wine we had on your porch."

"Sure," he said, even though he knew it wasn't prudent to stay.

She moved into the kitchen and he followed her like Mary's little lamb. *You're pitiful, Garner. Absolutely pitiful.*

"So other than taking the kayak out, how was your day?"

"Well, it started with me taking eight geriatrics on a nature hike and went downhill from there."

"Really? The hike sounds nice."

"Perhaps not as bad as having terminal cancer. My family doesn't seem to understand that I have a full-time job. They're constantly hitting me up to sub in, which I wouldn't mind occasionally. But it's become a regular thing. I only get one day off a week."

"Why is that?" she asked while pouring his beer into a chilled pilsner glass.

"We're short staffed and I'm a control freak."

She bent over to hand him his beer and he could see down her shirt. Nice lacy bra. God, he was such a dick.

"Can't you hire more people?"

"Thanks to the mayor, I don't have the budget. But Jack and I have written a proposal and plan to bring it up at the next city council meeting." Which was sure to piss off old Pond Scum.

"I would hope so. Working six days a week and being on call all hours of the night is crazy. You need help, Colt."

"Want to sit on the deck?" Maybe the mountain breeze would cool his ardor, because he was seriously thinking about carrying her into the nearest bedroom. Ever since that kiss, he'd been hot to sleep with her, despite his misgivings.

"Sounds great. I'll just throw together some nibbles."

He took her arm. "We don't need nibbles."

"Okay. Let me at least pour myself a glass of wine."

He watched her reach up into the cupboard for a goblet and nearly lost his mind as her shirt inched up in the back, showing an expanse of creamy skin. For a second he fantasized about what it would feel like to press his lips there.

"You ready?" With glass in hand, she led the way.

It was definitely a few degrees cooler outside, but it wasn't helping. Colt waited for Delaney to choose a seat among the wrought-iron patio furniture and took one as far away as he could without being conspicuous about it. He had to get a grip.

"You close to finishing the costumes?" he asked, for the sake of something to say.

"I am. Just needed to come up with a few things for some of the minor characters, but Danny's and Sandy's are all set."

"It was nice of you to take it on."

"I actually enjoyed it and it was easy. The 1950s don't require much. Shakespeare would've required more of a challenge."

"Rita will be happy. I don't know why she doesn't run for mayor; she does everything else in this town."

"Hopefully, I'll still be here to see the performance."

He froze. "It's the last week in October. You planning to leave before then?"

"The plan was for me to stay long enough to get a collection going and to buy a new place in Los Angeles. I do have a business to run and it's there, not here."

"Right." He'd known that from the get-go, so why was he suddenly surprised? "You don't have a house there anymore?"

"I've listed mine, which I got in the divorce. I don't need all that house and I'll need capital to run my new company. I'll probably get a condo in Santa Monica or Venice."

"You like the ocean, huh?"

"And the mountains too." She gazed around the house. "This place was Robert's idea, but I've come to love it—and the town."

"Yep, Glory Junction's something." Lisa had called it quaint, which he'd found insulting. Quaint wasn't the way you described home. And for him this was home—everything he loved. Family, friends, and the people he'd known his entire life, who had shaped him into the man he was today.

"What if you don't have a collection?" He wasn't quite sure what defined a collection, but he knew she hadn't been able to design anything of substance lately.

She thought about it. "I'll go to Los Angeles and try to design there. Maybe the change in scenery will spark something. I came here to lie low while Robert and I hashed out the details of our divorce. I guess you could call it running away."

Colt watched her for a moment. "What were you afraid of?"

"Failure mostly. I was the talent, but Robert was the business. Without his urging, I'd probably still be working for another designer and never would have had the confidence to go out on my own."

"So what really happened between you two?" he asked.

The question seemed to startle her. "Like I said, we grew apart."

"Call it a cop's intuition, but I'd say there's more to it."

"You don't believe people can grow apart?"

"Sure. But from what I've seen there's usually something that happens, like an affair or a life-changing situation, to make two people realize that they don't belong together." For Chip and Hannah, it had been Chip's newfound sobriety.

She was quiet for a long time, then finally said, "Yes, but it's too personal to talk about."

"Okay. Should we change the subject?"

She took a few sips of her wine. "I think we should delve into *your* personal life."

"I'm an open book. What do you want to know?"

She snorted. "You're closed tighter than a vault."

"No, I'm not. To prove it, you want to know what I'm thinking right now?"

"What?"

"That despite all the reasons it would be a colossally bad idea, I want to sleep with you."

She leaned toward him. "And why would it be a colossally bad idea?"

"Never a good idea to sleep with your neighbor, for one."

"And two?" Her eyes sparkled with laughter.

"You already know two. I don't mess with local women, not unless it's serious."

"How can you know if it's serious if you don't get involved in the first place?"

"Because you're leaving to go back to Los Angeles. Therefore, it definitely won't be serious." He drained the rest of his beer.

"Most guys would like that. Sex with no commitment requirements." She raised her brows in challenge.

"I'm not most guys."

His phone buzzed and he fetched it out of his shorts' pocket. "Shit, I've got to get this." It was the office.

Colt got up, walked to the other side of the deck, and took the call. Lately, it had been one emergency after another. No rest for the weary, he told himself.

After he signed off with Jack, who was technically on call tonight, he took his glass into the kitchen. Delaney followed him in.

"What's going on?"

"A little boy got separated from his family during an evening hike. They've been searching for him for the last couple of hours and finally decided to call in the authorities."

"It'll be dark in another twenty minutes," she said.

"Yep. They should've called as soon as they noticed him missing but figured he couldn't have gone far. It was a mistake." Hopefully not a critical one. "I've gotta go."

"Is there anything I can do?"

"Not at this point. We've got the volunteer search and rescue team coming in and a few dogs. We should be okay, but thanks for the offer."

He wanted to kiss her but left, showing a great deal of restraint.

Chapter Thirteen

The next morning, Delaney got out of bed, padded across the hallway to her studio, and checked the window for Colt's cruiser. It wasn't there. The poor man never caught a break.

She planned to check the online version of the paper to see if they'd found the little boy. But the shade installers were coming and she didn't want them to catch her in her nightgown.

She quickly got ready, went downstairs, and put on a pot of coffee. While waiting for it to brew, she fired up her laptop and searched for the story. According to the news, they'd found the boy at five a.m., huddled under a tree about three miles from where his parents had lost him. He appeared to be fine but was transported to a local hospital to be evaluated. Thank goodness it was summer. In winter, he would've frozen to death.

It had certainly been a long night for Colt. She thought about what he'd said, how he wanted to sleep with her. Never before had she been as physically attracted to a man as she was to Colt. But they were both tender from their last relationships. Not a good time to get involved, especially because she'd be leaving soon.

The doorbell rang, pulling Delaney from her thoughts.

The shade installers. While the men worked upstairs she ate her breakfast and kept one ear open for Colt's car. At around ten Hannah called.

"You want to meet the gang for lunch at Old Glory?"

Delaney wasn't exactly sure who the gang was. Probably Deb and Foster. She agreed immediately, hoping that the installers would be done by noon. She changed into a long, flowy skirt, a ruched crossover top, and a pair of sandals, then accessorized with an assortment of sterling silver bangles on one arm. What the hell, she thought, and even put on a full face of makeup. Staring at her reflection in the mirror, she looked like the woman she'd been in LA, before everything went to hell with Robert.

Happy and confident.

She supposed some of it was due to Colt's attraction to her and, bizarrely, also due to the cargo pants. It felt marvelous to finally complete a project from beginning to end and to actually be proud of the results, even if they weren't the couture designs that had made her famous.

She went to check on the progress of the workers and found that they had finished and were cleaning up. One of the installers demonstrated how to open and close the shades with the remote control. Nice and easy, and now she'd be able to work into the night with her drafting light on.

She waited for them to leave and walked into town, enjoying the last days of summer. The temperature hovered in the midseventies, and even from a few blocks away Delaney could see the edges of Lake Paiute, the wide expanse of the Sierra Nevada range, as well as the chairlifts going up and down the mountainsides. That's how clear it was.

She'd miss this in Los Angeles, where the air felt thick and dirty and hung over the city like a dark film. When she arrived at Old Glory, Hannah, Deb, and Foster had already gotten a table and a large plate of pub fries.

"Hey," Hannah greeted her. "Check it out." She stood up

and modeled a black and white color-block dress that had been part of Delaney's Every-Day summer collection from last year. Delaney could objectively say the dress was stunning, and on Hannah, amazing.

"Wow," Delaney said. "You could've been my runway model. The dress is fantastic on you." And here she was getting excited over a pair of silly cargo pants.

"Thanks. I bought it last year when I first got it in the store, and thank goodness I did, because I'm dropping the line now that you're no longer the designer."

"I appreciate the loyalty, but you should still carry Delaney Scott if it sells well." Even if they'd be Olivia's designs.

"What's this I hear about you making kick-ass cargo pants?" Deb asked. "I want a pair."

"You do?" With Deb's gorgeous figure she could make a gunnysack look good. Just the same, Delaney couldn't understand why she'd want to wear something as shapeless as cargo pants. "Come over and let me take your measurements." Perhaps she could make a pair that would accentuate a woman's curves as opposed to hiding them.

"Seriously? I was being presumptuous, but I do really want a pair."

"Then come over and you'll get a pair."

Deb clapped her hands together like it was Christmas.

"Win alert at twelve o'clock," Foster said. Deb tried to act uninterested, but Delaney caught her sneaking a peek.

"He's seeing a blackjack dealer in Tahoe," she said. "Whatever. I'm so over him."

Delaney didn't think so, not the way Deb followed him with hungry eyes. He'd come in with a few men Delaney had never seen before. Guys about Win's age, late twenties, early thirties, some wearing Glory Junction Search and Rescue T-shirts.

"Did you hear about the little boy who got lost?" Hannah asked.

"Colt was at my house when he got the call about it."

Three pairs of eyes examined her as if she'd been holding out on them.

"What's going on with you two?" Hannah asked. "Colt seems to be hanging out with you a lot."

"We're neighbors. Occasionally, we'll have a drink together on one of our decks. No big deal."

"Yeah, it sort of is. Except for hanging out with his brothers, Jack, and Boden—because they both like craft beer—Colt's a lone wolf." Hannah reached for a fry. "And other than Carrie Jo, who's like his sister, he doesn't get involved with the women of Glory Junction. Not that the single women around here don't throw themselves at him. Rachel Johnson has been after him for a year and the woman's a major catch."

"The owner of Tart Me Up?" They all nodded. Delaney hadn't known that Rachel was interested in Colt, but of course she would be. Look at him. "I don't know what to tell you." She gazed over at Win to keep from having to look Hannah in the eye.

Boden came to take their orders and Delaney noticed that he paid special attention to Deb, even taking the chair next to hers so he could tell her about the specials. Deb was too busy watching Win to notice. They resumed their conversation about the missing boy and Boden added what he'd heard.

"The dogs lost his scent at the river and searchers feared he'd drowned. But Colt was able to track him into the forest. He found him curled up in a ball, crying. The mayor's holding a big press conference in time for the six o'clock news. Bet you didn't see that coming," he mocked.

"How'd you hear all this?" Deb asked, impressed. "It wasn't in the paper this morning."

"I saw Gray over at Tart Me Up. He's on Search and Rescue and told me what happened. Colt's been at the hospital with the kid's parents."

"The boy's okay, isn't he?" Delaney asked.

"That's what I heard, thank God." Boden got up. "I'll get this stuff out to you as soon as I can."

As soon as he was out of earshot, Foster told Deb, "Boden's hot. You ought to focus on him, instead of Win."

So, Delaney hadn't been the only one to notice Boden's interest.

"Win's dead to me." Deb dipped a fry in the catsup, sucked on the tip, and followed Boden with her eyes as he called out their order to the kitchen. "He is kind of hot, isn't he?"

"This just in?" Hannah also turned to take a second look. "Haven't you noticed the female clientele shoving their boobs in his face?"

"It's nice to know that the Garner brothers have some competition," Deb said. "I for one am sick of them. . . . Well, not Colt. Colt's the good brother."

"Hey, Josh is a good brother," Hannah insisted.

Conversation evolved into the End-of-Summer events and, of course, the kayak races. Delaney asked if any of them were going to Colt's show. They all said yes, and she made plans to sit with them. She wanted to ask more about Lisa but didn't want to be obvious about her interest in Colt's past. They were already on to the fact that she and Colt spent time together; no need to stoke the gossip fires.

It was a nice lunch and she couldn't remember the last time she'd felt so comfortable with a group of people. In LA, most of her lunches had been to network and wheel and deal. The fashion industry was filled with ambitious phonies and cutthroats. She didn't miss that part of the business. Here, people were more laid back and genuine.

After they finished eating, Deb made plans to come over that evening and get her measurements taken. Delaney started for home, first stopping at Tart Me Up to pick up bread and a few pastries to have on hand. At least that was the excuse she gave herself. In all the times visiting the bakery, she hadn't paid much attention to its proprietor. Rachel Johnson seemed to spend most of her time in the back, baking, while her staff worked the counter.

Today, though, Rachel worked the cash register and graced Delaney with a big smile. She really was lovely. Blond, big brown eyes, and flawless skin. Delaney wanted to hate her but the baker exuded such warmth that she made it impossible.

"Hi, Delaney. What can I get you?"

Delaney didn't think they'd said two words to each other, yet Rachel greeted her like she was a regular.

"How about the Dutch crunch and an assortment of turnovers."

"Sure thing." Rachel put the bread in a bag and grabbed a pink box for the Danish. "How's it going?"

Delaney sighed. "I've been dabbling with designing adventure wear."

"What a great idea. A Glory Junction line for the adventurer in all of us." Rachel waved her hand in the air. "Don't mind me. I'm taking a marketing class at the junior college. Back in the old days I used to wear some of your suits. Loved them."

"The old days?"

"Yup. I was lead counsel for Del Monte in San Francisco."

"The food company?" Delaney had no idea.

"Uh-huh. I traded it in for this." Rachel waved her hand around the bakery. "Best move I ever made."

"Impressive." Delaney thought the baker certainly appeared happy. Even covered in flour and pastry cream, she seemed so positive, so comfortable in her own skin. Good for her.

Rachel rang Delaney up and handed her the pink box and bread. "Good luck with the adventure line. Can't wait to see it in stores."

Delaney didn't bother telling her she was just playing until she got her mojo back. Taking a detour, she went to Sweet Stems and had Foster create an arrangement for her. The house could use some fresh flowers and it just so happened that his shop was next door to the police station. A coincidence, Delaney told herself.

"How you going to carry that all home?" Foster asked while Delaney explored the store, which had so many pretty things, she didn't know where to look first.

"Good question. I hadn't thought of that."

He went to the back of the shop and returned with a market basket.

"Thank you, Foster. I'll return it on my next trip into town."

"No worries. I've got plenty."

They both turned to stare out the storefront window when they heard engines outside and watched a few satellite news trucks jockey for position in front of Glory Junction PD.

"They must be here for the press conference," Foster said.

She craned her neck, hoping to see Colt in the gathering crowd of reporters, but there was no sign of him. It was too early, she supposed.

Delaney rushed home so she could put everything away and get some work done in time to watch the conference on television. Instead of sketching, she wound up playing with her new shades, repeatedly making them go up and down.

At six, before Deb got there, she turned on a local station. The press conference was at the top of the newscast. In front of the police station Colt and a line of city officials stood behind the mayor. Pond told the cameras that the little boy was home safe with his parents and doing well. Then he launched into a gratuitous speech about "his" town and how it pulled together in times of crises.

"Could you be any more smarmy?" Delaney muttered at her flat screen.

He thanked the Glory Junction Volunteer Search and Rescue team, praising it to the moon, and glossed over the role Colt and the police department had played in finding the boy. According to Boden, it had been Colt who'd actually rescued the child. Delaney wanted him to get the credit.

She waited for Colt to speak, but the mayor never called him to the podium, hogging the spotlight until the press conference was over and the newscast moved on to footage of a wildfire on the Central Coast.

Delaney flipped through the channels, catching the tail end of the conference on other networks. Same thing: Pond's smug face filled the screen. A knock came at the door and she got up to get it.

Deb carried two bottles of wine in. "Sustenance," she said, and peered past the foyer into the great room. "Wow. Fabulous place."

"Thanks. Let me turn off the TV." She took the bottles from Deb, dropped them off in the kitchen, and proceeded to the entertainment center.

"The press conference?" Deb continued to take in the house, stopping in front of Delaney's favorite painting—a Jared Javitz oil she'd paid a pretty penny for.

"Yeah. The mayor seems to have left out the part that Colt was the one who found and rescued the boy."

"I'm not surprised. The man's an egomaniac." She turned and assessed Delaney. "You're interested in Colt, aren't you?"

"Me?" Delaney stuttered. "Why would you think that?"

"All signs point that way. I can't blame you—something about those Garner men." Her lips pulled up on one side but she still looked sad.

"Nope," Delaney lied. "We're just friends."

Deb continued to measure her, then sighed. "You're better off. Colt never got over Lisa."

Delaney suspected that she was right.

* * *

That had certainly been interesting. If Colt hadn't known better, he would've thought Pond had run the entire search and rescue operation on his own.

"What a nut sack," Jack whispered as the two of them walked inside the building together.

"Hey, at least the boy's safe and sound. Let Pond get his rocks off talking to a bunch of reporters. Anyone with a lick of sense knows how these rescues work. I'm just happy he gave credit to the volunteers."

"Who was that guy with him?"

Colt had never seen the man before, though he had all the telltale signs of a cop. The posture, the aviator sunglasses, and the Marlboro Man mustache. He'd shown up with the mayor at the press conference and had stood on the sidelines, observing the crowd, his right hand resting near his hip, where he would've carried his duty weapon. Call him paranoid, but Colt had a sneaking suspicion the guy was here interviewing to be his replacement. Pond was probably putting him up for the weekend so he could check out the town.

"Don't know. Possibly your new boss."

"Nah," Jack said. "Pond talks a good game but he'd never fire you."

Colt wasn't so sure about that.

Carrie Jo was sitting at her desk, flipping through the local stations on the office TV. "That was it? Where were you guys? It was like the Pond Scum hour."

Jack chuckled.

"Hey, a little respect." Colt needed them to stop with the Pond Scum crap. It was getting out of hand.

He wasn't in his office five minutes before his phone pinged with a text from Win.

That was bullshit, it said.

TJ called on Colt's cell. "What the hell was that?"

Josh yelled in the background, "The mayor's a douche bag."

"Who cares?" Colt was more concerned with Pond's mystery friend. "The important thing is the kid's all right."

"Still," TJ said, "you're the one who found him. Everyone else thought he'd drowned in the river."

"I don't need a pat on the back for that. It's my job. Besides, finding the kid . . . that's enough."

"Drinks tonight at Old Glory?" TJ asked.

"Yeah. I'll ask Jack and Carrie Jo if they want to come too." Colt would've liked to invite Delaney but needed to cool things down with her. By Halloween she'd be gone, returning to her real life in Los Angeles.

When he got off the phone he went out to the bull pen to talk to Carrie Jo. The mayor and his buddy were wandering through the office, talking in hushed tones. Yep, the guy was Colt's replacement, all right. Carrie Jo thought so too, because she caught Colt's eye and mouthed, "Shit." He signaled for her to keep her lips zipped.

"Colt," the mayor called. "I want you to meet a friend of mine."

Colt walked over to where they were standing. The man wore a cheesy grin and stuck his hand out. Colt took it and introduced himself.

"This is Brian Dooney," the mayor said. "He's a captain at the Fremont Police Department and loves Glory Junction."

"It's a good place," Colt said, trying to sound amiable. "I was raised here."

"Oh yeah?" Brian sounded like he couldn't care less; he was too busy checking out Carrie Jo.

"Colt's family owns a little adventure tour company on Main Street."

Little? It wasn't so little. But Colt didn't correct Pond.

"That must be fun," Brian said.

"Yep. Fun. You up for the weekend or are you looking for a job?" Colt couldn't help himself.

The mayor suddenly looked uncomfortable.

"Up for the weekend, but I wouldn't mind making it permanent if the job was right. Who's the big blonde?"

Colt clenched his fists at his sides, just thankful that Carrie Jo was too far away to hear the conversation. He'd take her with him to Garner Adventure before he'd leave her to this asshole.

"That's Carrie Jo Morgan. She's the department secretary," Pond said.

"Executive assistant," Colt corrected. "How do you know Mayor Pond, Brian?"

"Brian used to work off duty doing security for my startup before I sold it."

Interesting, Colt thought. Captains didn't usually take off-duty jobs, but maybe Brian hadn't been that high up in the ranks back then.

"It was nice meeting you," Colt lied. "Enjoy your stay in Glory Junction."

"Maybe I'll stop by your family's company. I do a little motorcycle racing; you got anything like that?"

"No. Most of our stuff is for the seasoned adventurer. BASE jumping, cave diving, hang gliding, ice climbing, extreme skiing. Probably nothing you'd be interested in." Colt walked away.

"What's going on?" Carrie Jo whispered as he passed her desk.

"Not now." He went inside his office, shut the door, and called his old partner at SFPD.

Even though Colt had been gone a while, he was still tight with the friends he'd made on the force in San Francisco. Still regularly went on ski and camping trips with them and had them up to Glory Junction for GA's special events.

"Yo, Garner, what up?"

"You know a Brian Dooney? He's a captain at Fremont PD."

"Not off the top of my head. Why?"

"He's looking to get hired here and I wanted to know what the off-the-record rap on him is."

"I could ask around. How soon you need the information?"

"Soon."

"Let me see what I can do."

"Thanks, buddy."

As soon as Colt got off the phone Carrie Jo and Jack rushed into his office, their expressions panicked. If Colt's job was at risk so was Jack's. Whoever became chief would want to bring in his own command staff. People loyal to him, not his predecessor. That's just the way it was in any department.

"They're gone," Carrie Jo said. "What the hell, Colt?"

"Your guess is as good as mine."

"No way is he getting rid of you." Jack plopped down on the couch. "The city council won't stand for it."

"Look at the city charter. The mayor has the ultimate say in these situations. If he wants to dump me, he can."

"He doesn't have the balls. The whole town will turn against him."

"I don't know about that. Have you looked around lately? This isn't the same Glory Junction it was ten, fifteen years ago. Lots of new residents. Remember, Pond won by a landslide. People have faith in him."

"That Brian guy gave me the willies." Carrie Jo sat next to Jack. "He thinks he's Thomas Magnum, PI, with that mustache."

"I agree with Carrie Jo," Jack said. "The dude made my skin crawl."

Colt didn't know what to say. He didn't want his people to be unhappy but he had no power over the situation. "Let me talk to Ben, see if Pond has a contractual obligation to keep me on. But, guys, I'm pretty sure I'm an at-will employee." Meaning he could be terminated at any time. "I'm meeting my brothers at Old Glory. You two in?"

"Let me get my purse and lock up."

Jack said he'd meet them at the bar. Since he was on call tonight, he needed to brief the watch commander. Colt and Carrie Jo walked over together. The place was packed, as it usually was on a Friday night. He spotted TJ and Josh at their regular table and went to the bar to get a pitcher of beer.

"Missed you at the press conference," Boden said. "It looked like the Carter Pond hour on my TV."

"No comment."

Colt brought the pitcher back to the table with a couple of pint glasses and put it next to TJ and Josh's half empty one. He started to pour a glass for Carrie Jo but she shook her head.

"Too fattening. I'd rather take my calories in chocolate."

"Suit yourself."

His brothers finished their pitcher and topped their glasses off with his. A few minutes later Jack came in the door with Pond and Brian on his tail.

"Don't look at me," Jack said once he got to their table. "I didn't invite them."

The two men sat at the bar, far enough away that they couldn't hear Colt and the rest of the gang, especially with the music from the jukebox blasting. In a couple of hours, a live band would take the stage. The Racketeers. Colt had seen the poster on the door advertising them, but had never heard of the group before. He probably wouldn't be staying long enough for the band anyway. Tomorrow was a workday.

TJ and Josh played Jack and Carrie Jo in a game of pool. Win eventually showed up and challenged Colt to a game of darts. He kept one eye on the mayor and the Fremont police captain, who was scoping out every woman in the place. Colt was pretty sure he'd seen a ring on Brian's wedding finger.

Boden came over with a fresh pitcher on the house. "Who's the steroid head with the mayor?"

"I'm getting the feeling that he's my successor," Colt replied.

Win immediately turned his head to check out Brian at the bar. "What are you talking about?"

Colt told them about his suspicions.

"No way," Win said. "Pond can't just fire you without cause."

"He can do whatever he wants. All he has to say is he wants to take the department in a new direction and that he and I couldn't come to terms on the mayor's vision for the future. It happens all the time."

Jack and Carrie Jo had obviously filled TJ and Josh in, because the four of them came over to the dartboards. His brothers looked furious.

"That's the guy?" TJ cocked his head at Brian.

"Yup. Try not to be too obvious, people."

"I'm going to talk to Dad about this," TJ said. "Pond is messing with the wrong people."

Colt shrugged. "It is what it is, TJ. The mayor has the right to handpick anyone he wants. The voters put their faith in him."

"The voters didn't know what a jerk off the guy is," Josh said.

Colt's family was a loyal lot and he loved them for it. But sometimes they had an inflated view of their influence in town. A lot had changed since his parents had left the Bay Area to put down roots in Glory Junction, back when it was still a cow town. Since then, a whole crop of wealthy baby boomers and Gen Xers had become residents. To them, Gray and Mary Garner were the old guard.

He stayed for one set of the Racketeers and went home, feeling more dejected than he had in a long time. Being Glory Junction's police chief was a big part of who he was. TJ was the businessman in the family, Josh the war hero, and

Win the charismatic charmer. Law enforcement had given Colt an identity separate from the family business. He supposed he could always apply for a position somewhere else, but this was his town, his home, the place where the people he loved lived.

Turning up the easement, he noted that Delaney was charging her Tesla and parked at the top of his driveway. He got out of his car and checked Delaney's studio windows to see if the lights were on and if she was still up. New shades made it impossible to tell. But as he got closer to her deck, he heard female laughter.

"Hey," she called to him. "Saw you on TV."

He walked closer and saw that his sister-in-law and Deb were there, drinking wine. "Yeah?"

"You looked good," she slurred slightly. Clearly, she'd had a few.

"Thanks. You having a party?" He waved to Hannah and Deb, who waved back.

"Sort of. Deb came over so I could take her measurements for a pair of cargo pants. Hannah decided to come over, too. You want to hang out with us?"

They looked pretty happy to have their girl thing going. He didn't want to intrude. "I'm gonna call it a night, but thanks for the invite."

"Sure. You okay? You look kind of down. Is it because Pond hogged the press conference?"

"Nah," he said. "Just tired."

"Okay. 'Night then."

"Good night." He started back across the road, stopped suddenly, and pulled Delaney aside, out of earshot from the others. "You want to have dinner at my parents' house Sunday?"

She seemed surprised by the invitation. "Me? Why?"

He was a glutton for punishment, that's why.

"Josh is having surgery next week and my mom's having everyone to the house."

"Of course," she said, pleased to have been asked. "I'd love to go."

"Good. Hannah could use the support of her friends." God, he was such a dick.

Chapter Fourteen

On Sunday, Delaney rode over to the Garners' house with Colt. It was easier than taking two cars, but he'd made it plenty clear that this wasn't a date.

Their house, a two-story chalet reminiscent of the older style cabins popular in the area before modern mountain architecture had taken over, was larger and homier than she'd expected. Despite the home once housing five men, there were feminine touches everywhere. A cute wooden welcome wreath on the door and vases of fresh-cut flowers. Big, overstuffed, upholstered couches and chairs anchored the spacious great room, which had a spectacular view of the mountains and lake.

Two Labrador retrievers—Lucy and Ricky—slept on dog beds by the hearth of an enormous stone fireplace. Colt crouched down and scratched the labs behind their ears.

There were family pictures everywhere. Photos of all four brothers at various ages, skiing, snowboarding, rafting, rock climbing. Delaney especially liked the portrait of Colt graduating from the police academy with his parents by his side, and a similar photo of Josh as an army ranger. She stopped to admire a wedding picture of Hannah, gorgeous in her white sheath gown.

Mary came out of the kitchen with her apron on. "Everyone should be here soon. Gray just called to let me know that he dropped off his group and is on his way home. Would you like something to drink, Delaney? A glass of wine or a soda?"

"Wine would be great."

"I'll get it, Mom. You go finish getting ready."

"Thanks, Colt." She kissed him on the top of the head, which she wouldn't have been able to reach if he wasn't on the floor playing with the dogs. For the mother of four very tall boys, she couldn't be more than five-foot-five. And adorable.

"Your parents have a beautiful home," Delaney told Colt as she followed him into the kitchen.

"Tell my mom. It's her pride and joy. We were forever tracking through it, building forts under the dining room table, using her best linens—turning the place into a pigsty."

"It couldn't have been easy with four boys. She was completely outnumbered."

"Yep. Dad wasn't much help either. Before building a workshop, he used to work on his projects in the house. He spent an entire winter crafting a canoe in our living room. That was the year Mom threatened to divorce him."

Delaney laughed and gazed around the kitchen. A big center island, butcher block countertops, and a potbelly stove. It wasn't up to date like her kitchen but it oozed warmth and charm and family.

Colt moved in front of her to get a wineglass from one of the upper cabinets. He had on the most recent version of her cargo pants, the ones she'd made using his recommendations. They rode low on his hips and hugged his perfect backside.

"You want red or white?" he asked, and turned around just in time to catch her ogling his ass.

She quickly flicked her glance away. "Whatever everyone else wants."

"No need to stand on ceremony," he said, impatient the way men get when women are trying to be polite. "There's plenty to go around, just pick one."

"Red then. The pants look good." Let him think she was admiring her own handiwork.

"TJ's going to bug you about them. Feel free to tell him to screw off."

"I'm still thinking about it." She'd worked on Deb's pair all day and was pleased with the progress. Instead of baggy and shapeless, like the other pants on the market, hers were form fitting.

"Whatever floats your boat," he said, and handed her a glass of pinot noir, their hands brushing, sending tiny tremors up Delaney's arm. "But don't do something you're not into."

"I won't."

He looked at her, holding her gaze, like he wanted to kiss her. Then the moment passed and he squeezed by her. "Let's go in the living room." They carried in their drinks and sat together on the couch.

Someone came in the front door and Colt got up to see who it was, returning a few seconds later. "My dad. He went upstairs to shower and change. No one told me we were starting later than planned. Sorry."

"No problem. I'm enjoying myself." She held up her glass of wine. "What did you do today?"

"Took a group river rafting for Win. He had plans in Tahoe." Colt never got a day off and it was starting to show. He seemed on edge, not himself.

"How about you?" he asked.

"Not a lot." She'd spent much of her day trying to figure out how she'd make the deadline for fashion week. By now, she should be planning a runway show.

They sat there quiet for a few minutes until Colt got up and turned on the radio, which reminded her of his upcoming concert.

"You ready to play next weekend at Old Glory?"

"Yep." He sat back down next to her but didn't say anything more. Something was clearly bothering him. Perhaps Josh's upcoming surgery, which had to make the whole family anxious.

She didn't get a chance to ask him about it because Hannah and Josh came in.

"Hey, where is everyone?" Hannah bussed both of their cheeks with kisses.

"Jack has to hold down the fort and Carrie Jo's babysitting her sister's kids. Everyone else is running late," Colt said. "But we're here. You guys want a drink?"

"I'll get it." Hannah started for the kitchen. Delaney began to follow her but Hannah told her to stay put.

Josh sat in the recliner and put the chair back.

"Your leg hurting you?" Colt sounded concerned.

"A little too much exercise today. I'll be fine. I'm looking forward to getting this operation over with. How you doing, Delaney? Thanks for coming."

"Thanks for having me. I'm sorry your leg hurts."

He waved off her sympathy. "It's a hundred times better than it was last winter."

Hannah returned with the drinks. The doorbell rang and Mary jogged down the stairs to get it. Delaney could hear Deb and Foster, who joined them a few minutes later. Gray followed.

"I guess it's too warm to make a fire," he said.

Delaney thought Gray looked a lot like Colt, just an older version. He had to be nearing sixty, yet had stayed in amazing shape. Tall and broad shouldered, like his sons. No middle-age paunch. Not even a receding hairline. Colt came from excellent genes.

"Too warm for what?" TJ came in at the tail end of Gray's

conversation. He looked over at Colt. "How'd the rafting trip go?"

"Fine. Dad was thinking of making a fire."

"Are you kidding me? It's got to be eighty outside." He scanned the group. "Where's Win?"

"Late as usual," Colt said.

Mary announced that dinner would be on the table in ten minutes and brought out a few appetizers. The Garner men dug in like they hadn't eaten in days. Delaney supposed Colt had used a lot of fuel out on the river today.

"How's Sweet Stems doing?" TJ asked Foster. Delaney had noticed that TJ was most comfortable talking shop.

"Business is good. A lot of weddings this time of year. How about Garner Adventure?"

"We're killing it, right, Dad? It would be nice to get some more permanent guides, though. We're getting too big to just hire seasonal."

"You think?" Colt said sharply.

Deb seemed checked out, keeping a constant eye toward the front door. Delaney suspected she was waiting for Win. It appeared she wasn't giving up on him, despite her earlier declaration to the contrary. If he really was seeing a blackjack dealer, Deb was just setting herself up for disappointment. But the heart didn't always listen to reason. Delaney felt bad for Deb, who'd gone all out for dinner, wearing a short dress that showed off her gorgeous legs.

Colt got up to refill everyone's glasses.

"Hey, are those different from the other pair you wore?" TJ cocked his head at Colt's pants. The man had a keen eye, Delaney would give him that.

"Yep. Delaney made some adjustments."

"According to Colt's recommendations," she added.

Both TJ and Gray stood up to take a closer look, fussing over the side zippers on the legs. It was funny having rugged, not-into-fashion men so intent on a simple garment. They were worse than her staff, who discussed every detail of a new design.

Just before the group sat down for dinner, Win showed up and Delaney saw Colt give him a dirty look.

"You're late," he said between clenched teeth. Win returned a sheepish expression and went off to talk to Josh.

At dinner, everyone talked at the same time as they passed dishes around the table. Every time TJ started to steer the conversation to his retail idea for the company, Colt and the others changed the subject, good-heartedly chiding him for talking too much shop.

A couple of times, Delaney witnessed Josh and Hannah laugh over something private one of them had whispered into the other's ear. It was sweet but made Delaney feel a pang of loneliness. Colt must've picked up on it because she caught him watching her, his brown eyes a mite too perceptive. Later, he surprised her by squeezing her knee under the table.

After dinner, she, Hannah, Deb, and Foster went out on the deck to watch the sunset over the lake while Mary and some of the Garner men cleaned up in the kitchen. As guests, they'd been forbidden from helping.

Foster eyed Deb's outfit and smirked. "A little over-dressed?"

Deb flipped him the bird and addressed Hannah. "Why do you think Win was so late?"

She shrugged. "Maybe he was leading a tour."

Delaney decided to keep the knowledge that he'd been in Tahoe to herself. Why upset Deb when Delaney didn't even know what he'd been doing there?

"Deb, you need to move on," Foster said.

"I know. Maybe I'll ask Boden out."

"I like him," Delaney added, though she didn't know much about the bartender other than he was nice looking and always friendly.

Deb nodded halfheartedly.

Foster patted her head. "It wouldn't kill you to at least give someone else a try. Worst that could happen is you wind up friends, or like my crazy client, divorced three times. She begged me to send the last one a floral arrangement of dead roses, spray painted black."

Delaney's eyes rounded. "Did you do it?"

"Hell no. But I told her I'd give her the dead roses so she could do it herself." Foster peered through the French doors into the great room. "We should go back in. But before we do, spill, Delaney. What's up with you and Colt? Is this a date?"

She shook her head. "He invited me for Hannah and Josh . . . to support them."

"Right," Foster said, and rolled his eyes.

Deb slanted her a glance that said, *You're not fooling anyone, honey*, and linked her arm through Delaney's. "Let's return to your nondate."

They joined their hosts and listened while Win regaled them with a story about a rock-climbing expedition he and a couple of his buddies had taken last summer. Delaney could see how Deb would be dazzled by him. Win was boyish and charming. Colt sat next to her on the couch, his leg brushing against hers. Her pulse quickened, making her feel as if she were back in high school, sitting next to the class heartthrob. *Not a date*, she reminded herself.

When Lisa Laredo's hit, "Crazy about You," came over the surround sound, everyone suddenly stopped talking. The silence became so uncomfortable that Colt got to his feet and turned off the radio.

Win started to say something and Colt cut him off. "We're not talking about this."

TJ began to argue and Gray held up his hands. "It's your brother's call."

Deb had been right the other day. Colt was nowhere near over his last relationship. Delaney felt a prick of envy. What would it be like to own Colt Garner's heart the way Lisa Laredo did? She'd never know, which was another good reason not to get involved with him.

The party started breaking up around ten and Colt told Delaney he was ready to go. He had work in the morning.

"You okay?" she asked him on the way home. "You seem a little down. I was wondering if you're nervous about Josh."

He stared at the road for a while, then said, "Josh is tough. The surgery is nothing compared to what he's been through. I'm more concerned about Glory Junction PD. Pond paraded a Fremont police captain around the department Friday. I'm pretty sure he's getting ready to can me."

"No way. You sure?" Delaney refused to believe it. Not with Colt's dedication to the job.

"No doubt in my mind. He wants someone who'll do his bidding, and that ain't me. I at least have Garner Adventure to fall back on, but I'm worried about Jack and Carrie Jo."

"Will you be okay working full time for your family's business?" She got the sense that law enforcement was his calling. Chief Hottie from Hell.

"Playing for a living is not such a bad way to go and it sure the hell beats having Pond for a boss." But it wasn't his dream job. She could tell just from the wariness in his voice.

"You mind if I ask you a question?"

"Go ahead. I seem to tell you more than I tell anyone else."

"Why is that?" she asked, momentarily forgetting her first question.

He shrugged. "I guess I feel comfortable with you. And then there's the fact that I grew up with three brothers. Not exactly an environment for sharing feelings." He said "feelings" like it was syphilis. "Women are easier to talk to, you in particular."

"Thank you." It was a nice compliment, especially because

her ex had called her distant and cold. "You can tell me anything."

He slid her a sideways glance and smirked. "Yeah? Anything? Even if it's X rated?"

She playfully smacked his arm. "Do all men have one-track minds?"

"Yep."

"You do realize that you're flirting again?"

"It seems to be a habit where you're concerned."

"But local women are off limits, right?" she said facetiously. "The question I wanted to ask before has to do with Lisa. You're not over her, are you?"

He was quiet for a long time, which only confirmed to her that she was right. But then he said, "I'm over her, I'm just not over what she did."

"The way you broke up?"

"Yeah," he said, but she didn't think he was being altogether honest with her, or himself.

"How come you don't like to talk about it?" she pressed.

He took his eyes off the road for a second to look at her. "It's the same as you not wanting to talk about what happened with you and your ex."

Nothing he could tell her about Lisa could be more humiliating than what Robert had done. "Perhaps. To new beginnings, then." She mimed a toast.

"You thinking about your new beginning in LA?"

She sighed. "Yep. I've got to sell my house first and find new office space. Right now, the small staff I have is working out of a warehouse."

"How long you think it'll take for a sale?"

"I don't know. The agent assures me the house will go fast, but she'd probably say anything to get the listing. It is a beautiful place, though, and in an excellent location." She crossed her fingers. "Until I get investors, I'll need some of the money to start over."

"So, you're stuck here until then?"

"I wouldn't call it stuck. I love it here, much more than I ever thought I would. Unfortunately, it's not exactly the center of the fashion world."

"Nope."

He turned into the easement road and pulled over. "I'll walk you to your door."

"Colt, I'm fine. If it'll make you feel better, you can sit here until I get inside."

He got out anyway and escorted her onto her deck. As she unlocked her door, he moved closer and leaned in. For a second, she thought he was going to kiss her. It seemed like he wanted to, just like he had in his mother's kitchen. But then he abruptly backed off, shoved his hands in his pockets, and waited for her to get inside.

"Good night," he said. "Thanks for coming with me. I know it meant a lot to Hannah."

Hannah? She bit her tongue.

Before she even shut the door, he turned on his heels and headed back to his truck. A few seconds later, she heard his engine start and the squeak of his garage door opening. A light went on in his house and she let out a sigh. The man was proving to be more temptation than she'd bargained for.

Delaney went upstairs and changed into her pajamas. Too late to work, she stretched out on her bed with a new book. Not five pages into it and her phone rang.

"Hello."

"What are you doing?" Colt asked.

"Reading. Is there a problem?" Maybe she'd left a lamp on somewhere.

"Can't sleep."

"Colt, you've been home all of ten minutes." He couldn't seem to make up his mind about her. She wasn't going to let him play this on-and-off thing he was doing. He needed to fish or cut bait as her father liked to say.

"I know, but I'm not tired."

"You were the one who hurried to leave. We could've had a drink but I'm in my pajamas now."

"Pajamas? What do they look like?"

"Seriously? You're doing the what-are-you-wearing thing now? I'm starting to think you're schizoid."

"Me too," he said, letting out a long, suffering sigh. "Against my better judgment, you make me want to break my own rules."

"No worries. I'm going to do you a favor and save you from yourself," she said as gently as possible, and hung up.

"You make me want to break my own rules," she mimicked. As if it was her fault that he had a split personality.

A little while later she told herself she was thirsty and got out of bed. On the way downstairs, she stopped in her studio, pulled the shade back, and took a peek. Colt's lights were out.

The next morning, Colt got called out on a GTA—grand theft auto. Morris Finkelstein, who was older than dirt, said someone had lifted his Buick right under his nose. This was not the first time he'd reported it stolen. The problem was Mr. Finkelstein had a penchant for leaving his car in places, walking home, and forgetting that he'd driven.

Colt didn't think he had Alzheimer's or any other kind of dementia, he was just absentminded. And stubborn as hell, because no matter how many times Colt suggested that he'd probably lost his car like he had the last time, Mr. Finkelstein insisted that no, it had been parked in his driveway before he went to bed.

Colt finally gave up trying to convince him otherwise, took a report, and put out a BOLO. As had happened in the past, one of his officers would eventually find the Buick in a parking lot or on Main Street, covered in bird shit. Then Colt would have to go and fetch Mr. Finkelstein's car keys and deliver the heap home.

On his way back to the station, Colt swung by Tart Me Up. The morning called for a cherry turnover and coffee that wasn't Jack's sludge. As usual, a long line for breakfast snaked around the bakery and Colt took a number. Rachel must've been in the back because the kids from the Island of Misfit Toys were working the counter. When it came his turn, he got his Danish and a cup of joe and took it to go.

"You get me anything?" Carrie Jo asked when he came in the door and she spied his Tart Me Up bag.

"You're always on a diet."

"I'm starting on Monday."

Colt tilted his head in confusion. "This is Monday."

"I'm giving myself a week's grace period, then I'm going on the Mediterranean diet. Studies say it's the healthiest and, uh, this is California, land of fruits and nuts."

"Okay, I'll split this with you." He pulled out the pastry and started to break it in half.

"Don't worry about it. I'll walk over in a few minutes and get one for me and Jack."

Colt's brows winged up. "Jack, huh?"

"He likes their cheese Danish."

Colt left it alone. He didn't know what was going on between those two but he fervently hoped Jack didn't get hurt. Carrie Jo went for stockbroker, banker types, like her dickhead ex-husband.

"Any calls?" He stood by her desk drinking his coffee and eating his turnover.

"Nope. Any more intel on the creepy guy Pond brought by the other day?"

"My friend from SFPD's supposed to get back to me." He licked cherry filling off his fingers, threw away the bag, and as he started for his office, called over his shoulder, "Let me know if anyone finds old man Finkelstein's Buick."

Colt signed on to his computer while he finished his coffee and then checked his private e-mail. Nothing yet from his former partner. He swung his feet up on the desk, grabbed the phone, and called the city attorney.

"Hey, Ben, happy Monday. I wanted to ask you about the terms of my contract with the city."

"Funny, because you're the second one to call me about that this morning."

Colt sat silent while he absorbed that information. "My contract?"

"Yep. We're friends, otherwise I wouldn't be telling you this, so let's keep it on the down low. Pond called a few minutes before you did and asked me to fax it over to him."

"He's getting ready to fire me, isn't he?"

"He didn't say that, but I'm reading between the lines here."

Colt told him about Brian Dooney. "Do I have any leverage?"

"Let me go over your contract and the city charter. If the mayor asks for my legal opinion I'm going to tell him it's a bad idea. Knowing him, though, he won't. Pond likes to keep his own counsel and he's extremely aware of how popular you are to the residents of Glory Junction. I'm guessing he sees you as a rival."

"I have no political aspirations, but maybe I'll run for mayor to piss him off."

Ben laughed. "I'll be your campaign manager. Hang tight, I'll get back to you on your contract . . . but there may be something else."

"Like what?" How much more could Pond throw at him?

"For legal reasons I really can't talk about it."

Then why bring it up? Colt thought, but then acquiesced and said, "All right." He knew that if there was any way Ben could help without violating his fiduciary duty to the city, he would.

For the rest of the morning Colt holed up in his office to work on the proposal for a new hire. On the slight chance that he still had a job in a month, he wanted two days off a week, like a normal person. As he worked, his mind wandered to Delaney.

She'd hung up on him, which had served him right for running hot and cold. Maybe if they just did it, he'd get over his infatuation with her and could move on. It wasn't as if he had to be on his best behavior anymore. His job was in jeopardy anyway and he hadn't done anything wrong.

Around noon, Jack came in and asked if Colt wanted to go to lunch. They walked over to the Morning Glory for sandwiches. Deb must've been off because they got a new waitress, someone Colt had never seen before. He wondered what Delaney was doing for lunch. Probably sitting up in her studio, working on her designs. He thought again about her hanging up on him and laughed to himself. The woman kept him on his toes, whether it was fighting over a parking space or the light from her studio window.

He never thought she would've fit in around here—well, at least not with the old guard. But she seemed to have won over Hannah and her clique of friends. Even his brothers accepted her as part of the crowd. At dinner last night, she'd been right at home at his parents' house, even though he was pretty sure that in LA she trucked with the jet set.

"Hey." Jack snapped his fingers in Colt's face. "Where'd you go?"

"Nowhere. Tired I guess."

"How was Josh's shindig?"

"Good. He and Hannah left this morning for San Francisco. My parents are going Tuesday so they can wait with Hannah while Josh is in surgery."

"I'm keeping him in my thoughts."

"Thanks, Jack."

Chip came into the restaurant and Colt nodded his head in

greeting. There was a time when they hadn't been so civil to each other, mostly when Colt had to scrape Chip's drunken ass off the floor. No telling how many times he'd been called out on one of Chip's benders and had to arrest him for being drunk and disorderly in public. It had been awkward because Chip had grown up with the Garner brothers. And poor Hannah had been so humiliated.

But Chip had gotten sober and it seemed to be sticking, thank goodness.

"He's doing good," Jack said as they both watched Chip leave with a take-out order. "I'm glad Fish and Wildlife stuck by him." Chip and his new wife both worked for the department, formerly known as Fish and Game. Some of the folks there had staged an intervention and Chip had gone into a residential rehab program.

"Yeah, me too."

"He and Josh talk anymore?"

"It's still pretty strained between those two." Stuff about Hannah, but that wasn't for public consumption, even if Jack was almost family.

Jack nodded like he understood. "You ready for this weekend?"

Colt wasn't sure if Jack meant the kayak race or his show at Old Glory. "You do know that we're getting our asses kicked, right? The sooner you come to terms with that the better you'll feel when we lose."

"Oh ye of little faith," Jack said. "What do you think of me asking Carrie Jo to your concert?"

"Are you asking my permission or whether she'll go? Because I know for a fact she's planning to be there."

"With me. Go with me. Like a date."

Ah, dude. "You think that's a good idea, Jack? You two work together."

"I was wondering about that, but it's not like I'm her boss. Besides, Carrie Jo can hold her own."

"Yep, she sure can. It's up to you."

"You think she'll say yes?"

No. "I never know what's in that woman's head. You prepared if she doesn't?"

Jack hitched his shoulders. "It might be awkward, especially around the station."

"That's why I personally would steer clear of work situations."

"Colt, you steer clear of any romantic situation, period. You can't get much hotter than Rachel Johnson, who has all but screamed her interest in you. Yet . . ." He considered his next words, then just put it out there. "It's time to get over Lisa."

Why did everyone keep telling him that? He was as over her as a man could get without being dead. He just wasn't over what she had done. That continued to be a festering sore, especially when he was forced to hear her on the radio every day.

"I'm interested in someone!" He practically yelled it, and a few diners a couple of booths over turned to stare. "Does that make you feel better?"

"Who?" Jack folded his arms over his chest as if he thought Colt was lying.

"Delaney Scott, that's who." Jesus, why'd he open his mouth? Jack, unlike his brothers, could at least keep a secret.

Jack leaned over the table. "Seriously? You think she might be a little out of your league?"

"I know she's out of my league."

"Shit. What are you going to do?"

"Nothing. That's what I'm going to do."

Carrie Jo came over his radio. "They found Finkelstein's car."

Colt jotted down the address, they finished their lunch and paid the bill. Jack drove Colt to Morris's house to get the car keys, then followed him back to drop the Buick off.

Finkelstein made them wait while he checked the sedan over for damage to report to his insurance company.

Colt didn't bother to tell him that there wasn't anything wrong with the car. That it had sat all night at the Starbucks parking lot, where he'd left it. The life of a country cop. Yet, he wouldn't trade it for all the money in the world.

The rest of the day wound up being uneventful. Before leaving, Colt checked in with Josh to wish him luck the next day. Then he drove home.

He thought about hiking to the lake for a swim and quickly nixed the idea. Nothing wrong with a quiet night at home. The luxury of it was short lived when TJ showed up with a few take-out containers of Indian food.

"Where's your neighbor? I thought we could invite her."

"I don't think she's home," Colt said, and got down plates.

TJ gave him a look. "You guys seemed pretty cozy last night."

"This isn't like with Josh and Hannah." The brothers had spent the winter playing matchmaker. "She's leaving, TJ. She's moving back to LA as soon as she sells her house there and can buy another one. So knock it off."

"LA isn't that far away, you know? From what I can tell, she's nothing like Lisa."

"And you would know this because of all the time you've spent with Delaney? You used to think Lisa was great, which shows what a great judge of character you are."

"I didn't think she was so great. None of us did. But you loved her . . . and we love you. What she did was about as messed up as you can get. But you can't judge every woman by Lisa."

"TJ, why don't you work on your own love life? When was the last time you had a date, huh?"

"Don't make this about me. I watched you last night. You like her." He jerked his head toward Delaney's house. "All that arguing over parking . . . You two were like kids discovering the opposite sex for the first time. Why don't you just freaking go for it and quit depriving yourself of something good for a change?"

"Why don't you shut the hell up?" Colt shoved a piece of naan in TJ's face and abruptly changed the subject. "I'm going to need a full-time job when I get fired. I want my pick of assignments."

"Why should I give you that?"

"Because I'm the oldest and the best."

TJ rolled his eyes. "You won't get fired. Rita and the others will go ballistic."

"I think you overestimate my popularity and importance. Haven't you heard the saying that no one is indispensable?"

"You're good, Colt. Best police chief Glory Junction has ever had. You're tough but fair and Lord knows you're dedicated. What does Jack think?"

"Jack doesn't know what to think. Pond's a prick."

"Yup, Pond's a megaprick."

They ate their Indian food in silence while Colt thought about just how dispensable he'd been. First with Lisa, now as chief. And if he let Delaney get too close, she'd replace him in a Los Angeles minute. When all he wanted was to be a forever kind of guy right here in Glory Junction.

Chapter Fifteen

Other than the crowds, the day was perfect. Mild, bright, and as clear as the eye could see.

Delaney finally found a strip of grass to spread her blanket. The finish line was even more popular than the starting point for Glory Junction's famous End-of-Summer kayak races. She'd promised to save everyone a place on the packed riverbank.

A lot of the attendees had turned the event into a picnic. Ice chests, folding tables, and wicker hampers dotted the landscape as children competed for the best place to view the race from the river's edge.

Because it was Delaney's first End-of-Summer weekend, she planned to take in as many events as possible. Pie-eating contests, horse and carriage rides, and a diving contest at the lake were just a few of the festival's offerings. And of course, live music at Old Glory, including Colt's band.

She hadn't seen him since dinner at his parents. It seemed to her that he was intentionally making himself scarce. Perhaps he was embarrassed about the phone call, but she doubted it. Colt didn't strike her as the self-conscious type. He was just staying true to form: vacillating between flirtation and disinterest, the way he had the entire month of August. Maybe he'd found someone in another town to toy with.

She saw Hannah and Foster wending their way through the crowd, stood up so they would see her, and waved.

"This is great, nice and close to the river." Hannah plopped down on the blanket while Foster went to say hi to someone he knew. "Carrie Jo's coming too. And Win is around here somewhere."

"Have the kayakers started yet?"

"They took off twenty minutes ago. I followed along the bank, and from what I could tell, Josh and TJ were in the lead with Deb and Felix not far behind."

According to what Colt had told her, pro kayak races covered many miles and went for several days. One of the largest was a thousand-mile race in Canada that took more than a week to finish. Glory Junction's was a short course, only four miles on a relatively wide stretch of river without many rapids. Participants were encouraged to give their teams funny names and to wear goofy getups.

"What about Colt?" she asked.

Hannah grimaced. "He and Jack got off to a rocky start. Their kayak seems to have a mind of its own."

Uh-oh. Delaney knew how competitive Colt could be. And who knew whether the mayor kept score? It sounded like he looked for any reason to give Colt a hard time, though she couldn't imagine how the mayor could hold it against Colt if he lost an amateur race involving the whole town. That would be too petty even for him.

"I'm worried about Josh's leg," Hannah said. She and Josh had come back from San Francisco, hailing the surgery as a huge success. "He's really supposed to be resting for a few weeks, and even though he's using mostly his upper body, it seems reckless to race. But you can't talk that man out of anything."

Hannah loved her husband so much that sometimes when

she talked about him Delaney felt a jab of jealousy. Not a pretty side of herself, but she couldn't help it. At one time, she and Robert had adored each other, but they had never shared the kind of powerful love Hannah and Josh had. She suspected that Garner men were intense about everything, including their relationships. Case in point: look how long it was taking Colt to get over Lisa.

"Hopefully TJ will stop him from doing anything that could hurt his recovery."

Hannah snorted. "Yeah, right. The only thing they care about is winning, especially against Colt. They love each other like crazy but, man, are they competitive."

Foster came back with a box of sandwiches and sodas. "A kid from Tart Me Up is selling them. That Rachel is one smart cookie. I wish I would've thought of it myself."

"Thank God, I'm starved." Hannah grabbed one of the sandwiches.

Foster eyed her closely. "You eating for two?"

"Nope. Not yet, anyway." She sounded disappointed. "Josh wants to wait until his leg is better."

"You're not getting any younger, honey." Foster threw Delaney a sandwich.

Carrie Jo and Win spotted them and came trotting over. Win saw the sandwiches and plucked one out of the box while Carrie Jo perused each and every one, studying the ingredients.

"You think any of these are made with whole-grain bread?"

"No," Foster said plainly. "Just eat half of one and you'll be fine."

Carrie Jo seemed to take Foster's word as gospel and unwrapped half a turkey, cranberry, and goat cheese. "Colt and Jack are getting their asses kicked. The only ones doing worse are Rachel and the kid from her shop. I probably would've skipped the giant foam-rubber cupcake costumes."

"It's good for Colt to get creamed every now and again," Win said between bites. He'd already commandeered the other half of Carrie Jo's sandwich. "Builds humility, something Colt is greatly lacking. Besides, it's still early. Anything can happen."

"I saw Pond with some skank wearing booty shorts. Not a good look on a fifty-something with varicose veins." Carrie Jo stuck her finger in her mouth and made gagging noises. "They were watching Colt and Jack and were laughing."

"Yeah?" Win jumped to his feet. "I'll go stand behind him . . . let him know I'm watching."

Carrie Jo grabbed Win's arm to stop him. "Don't make it worse for your brother. The whole race is supposed to be a joke. The Garners are the only ones who take it seriously."

"Carrie Jo is right," Hannah said. "Let it go."

Delaney admired Win's loyalty, but it wouldn't serve any purpose to get in the mayor's face. "When is he up for reelection? Because when he is, you can work for the opposition and make sure he's voted out of office."

"He just got elected," Win said, and sat back down. "He has enough time left in his term to make Colt's life a living hell."

In the distance a kayak bobbed on the water. It was too far away to make out who was in it. Win pulled up the pair of binoculars hanging around his neck and took a long look. Others started to notice and rushed to the water's edge to join the kids. Soon, Delaney couldn't see anything but backs and legs. Win got up and continued to train his field glasses on the lone boat.

"Who is it?" Hannah asked.

"Can't tell yet."

The rest of them stood as well, shielding their eyes from the sun, trying to make out the winner. Delaney thought it would be a while before the kayak got close enough to distinguish whom it belonged to. It didn't stop bystanders from getting excited and yelling words of encouragement.

"Uh-oh, it's Boden and one of his bartenders." Carrie Jo pointed to the shore where the bartender, dressed in lederhosen, and a woman in a St. Pauli Girl outfit walked, carrying an upside-down kayak on their heads, defeat written across their faces.

Win aimed the binoculars at them. "Looks like Oktoberfest bit the dust."

"What do you think happened?" Delaney asked.

"They either got disqualified or sprung a leak. I better give 'em a hand." Win jumped down a small embankment and jogged toward them.

"Why would they have gotten disqualified?" Delaney went up on tiptoes to get a better look.

"If a competitor gets out of his kayak during the race, it's an instant disqualification," Hannah explained.

The crowd cheered Boden and the St. Pauli Girl as they hiked—not paddled—toward the finish line. Mary and some of the other volunteers dragged coolers filled with drinks to the landing area and a couple of kids ran toward Team Old Glory with bottles of water. Win helped hoist their kayak onto the official race trailer and returned to the picnic blanket.

Delaney spied Gray Garner standing there with a stopwatch in his hand, craning his neck to see who paddled the kayak in the lead, a huge smile splitting his face. He was one of the head organizers and, according to Colt, founded the End-of-Summer races.

As the kayak got closer, Delaney saw a logo on the side of the boat but couldn't make out what it said.

"It's them . . . Josh and TJ!" Hannah shouted and pointed. "See the *GA*?"

"Shocker." Foster covered his mouth, feigning surprise. "They win every freaking year."

"This is the first time they won without Colt," Hannah reminded him. "Josh wasn't even here last summer."

"That's true," Foster conceded.

A few feet from the finish line, TJ and Josh began tossing things at the cheering crowd. A kid in front of Delaney caught a Garner Adventure Frisbee. There were T-shirts, ball caps, and headlamps.

"They've got the best swag," she overheard two boys say as people climbed all over each other to catch the prizes.

As Gray announced Garner Adventure as the first-place winner, Delaney took in Josh's and TJ's Hawaiian-print board shorts, rash guards, and helmets with the GA symbol. The fashion designer in her was more interested in the costumes than the actual race.

"Where are they? Where's GJPD's kayak?" Carrie Jo stared out over the horizon.

Delaney did the same and saw two small objects bobbing in the water. From this distance, they could just as easily be tin cans as kayaks. A dozen kids ran up the shore to get a closer look. Win peered out over the water with his binoculars.

"Is it them?" Carrie Jo asked.

Win continued to scan the river. "It's Sasquatch."

"What?" Delaney thought she might've heard him wrong over the noise of the crowd.

"Big Foot." He hung the field glasses around his neck and squinted in the direction of what now was clearly two kayaks racing neck and neck. "And is that a fish?"

"Let me see." Carrie Jo tugged on the binoculars and tried to look through them.

"Hey, you're choking me." Win took them off and handed them to Carrie Jo, who zoomed in on the boat.

Foster narrowed his eyes. "What on earth are they wearing?"

"Not Big Foot, but a bear," Carrie Jo said. "The other one is definitely a fish."

The mystery contestants stood up in their kayak and waved as spectators cheered. Hamming it up, the bear began to dance with the fish but caught his foot in a strap, tipping the boat to one side.

"Uh-oh," Win said. And the rest of them held their breath.

In their zeal to right the vessel, the bear overcompensated and the kayak tipped over, dumping both of them into the river. The fish went down first but managed to hang on to the bottom of the boat. The bear, weighed down by yards of wet fur, began to sink like a stone, flailing his arms just to keep his head above the surface.

"Oh my God!" Hannah cried. "It's Chip."

Two men on shore began to wade out, but the water was deeper and the current stronger than it looked. By the time they reached Chip it would be too late. Out of the corner of her eye Delaney saw someone from the second kayak hold out a paddle and yell something. Encumbered by hairy paws, Chip's hands kept slipping off the oar. And the heaviness of the costume continued to drag him down.

"He's going to drown." Hannah covered her mouth.

"You think he's drunk?" Foster elbowed his way between Delaney and Hannah as they all watched helplessly.

Win had disappeared and Delaney assumed he'd gone to do what he could. But she had no idea what. They were too far away. Even the fish, who was closest, appeared powerless.

That was when the person holding the paddle jumped into the water. As Delaney watched, she realized it was Colt. He swam against the current, his strokes sure and forceful while the spectators roared with approval. When he finally reached Chip, he tugged the bear mask off his face. Able to breathe, Chip shook his head from side to side, like a hair model in a shampoo commercial, and attempted a fist pump for his fans, only to go under again. Colt hoisted him up by his shoulders—no easy feat, given that all that wet fur had to weigh a ton—put him in a lifeguard hold, and towed him toward shore. When they got a few feet from the bank, bystanders rushed in and helped get Chip onto dry land and out of the bulky bear suit. Jack, in the meantime, got the fish to safety.

"It's Valerie," Carrie Jo said as they watched Chip's wife waddle in her fin to her husband. "Get it? Fish and Game."

A couple more good Samaritans helped pulled the kayak out of the water while a crew from the fire station rushed in and took over. The whole rescue lasted less than eight minutes. Yet, the drama of it whipped up the crowd, especially Colt. Undeterred by the time he'd lost, he swam back to his and Jack's kayak and they resumed the race to shouts of encouragement.

"Go! Go! Go!" the crowd chanted, some jumping up and down.

Others chanted for Team Morning Glory. Deb and Felix, wearing menu boards and chef hats from the diner, rounded the clubhouse turn, and the race for second place was on.

Delaney noticed that Colt and Jack had gone all out for the occasion, wearing ratty police department polo shirts and faded tactical shorts. What drew her attention more was Colt's bulging biceps as he furiously paddled to claim the advantage over Team Morning Glory. He was ripped, no doubt about it. Delaney stood on the sidelines, enjoying the view of Colt's muscles bunching every time he rowed. As with his heroic rescue, the man meant business. With his dark hair glinting in the sun, his brows knitted in determination, and the breadth of his chest outlined by his soaking wet T-shirt, he reminded her of a professional athlete. So fit and lithe. So sexy. The picture of outdoorsy ruggedness, which before now had never been her thing. She'd always been drawn to the debonair, well-coiffed type in a designer suit.

Not anymore. Compared to Colt they all looked like dandies. As she glanced around the crowd it occurred to her that so much had changed in the nine months she'd lived full-time in Glory Junction. Here she was in jeans and flats, her hair tied back in a careless ponytail, wearing very little makeup, and no one cared. Not one single person. Here, no one was judging her or expecting her to outdo her last collection, or pressuring her to be someone she didn't want to be. Here, she could just be herself. And that was enough.

The realization was heady and a little bit scary. A person could grow complacent in a small, accepting town like this.

The cheers pulled her back to the race. As the kayaks got closer to the finish line, everyone on the sidelines amped up the cheering, spurring Colt to paddle like crazy.

"Go Colt! You can do it!" she yelled, drawing raised brows from Hannah, Foster, and Carrie Jo. "What?"

"You should've brought your pom-poms, girl," Foster said, then whispered in her ear, "You're totally into him."

"He's my neighbor." But arguing was futile. They were laughing at her.

Colt and Jack crossed the finish line in a dead heat with Deb and Felix. Colt didn't look too thrilled about it, but it didn't stop him from lifting Deb out of her kayak and giving her a big kiss, which as silly as it was, made Delaney jealous.

Hannah rushed down to Josh, who sat on the landing, icing his leg. TJ wore a giant grin while pumping Felix's hand. Some of the crowd started to disperse but most waited for the Tart Me Up crew to paddle in dead last. Rachel and one of the teenagers who worked behind the bakery counter looked ready to pass out. As far as Delaney was concerned, they should win for best costumes. Carrie Jo was wrong about their cupcake suits. Adorable.

The rest of the kayaks were loaded onto the trailer, which was towed by an all-terrain vehicle that could handle the shale and dirt road back to the trailhead. Chip and Valerie, both in one piece but exhausted, caught a ride out with a few of the firefighters. Everyone else hiked, dragging their coolers and gear behind them. Delaney walked with Carrie Jo

and Foster, reluctant to make the first overture to Colt, who'd
hung back with Jack and a couple of other police officers.
Presumably to make sure that the area had been properly
cleared. Carrie Jo and Foster had driven their own cars so at
the lot they all went their separate ways.

Delaney decided that it would be better to drive home and
walk to town for more of the festivities, instead of dealing
with parking. She pulled the Tesla into the garage, went
inside and grabbed a lightweight jacket in case it got cool,
then headed to the boardwalk for the pie-eating contest.
Boden said he would save them a couple of tables for Colt's
show, which had sold out.

People jammed the river walk and Delaney could barely
see the competitors' table. Rita Tucker sidled next to her and
let out a beleaguered huff.

"I told them to hold the pie eating at the VFW hall this
year. More room in there. This is ridiculous."

"It's a little tight," Delaney agreed. "But it's nice to be
outside."

"I suppose," Rita said. "But it would've been better at
the hall or in the theater, which reminds me: how are those
costumes coming?"

A shout went up and Delaney stood on tiptoes to see what
was happening. All five of the contestants were covered in
berry filling. One of them had moved on to his next pie,
causing all the hoopla.

"They're done," she told Rita. "I've been meaning to
deliver them to the theater."

"Done? Wow, you're fast."

No, the costumes had just been a nice distraction from her
real job. "I'll bring them over next week."

"Great," Rita said, and ran off to talk to one of her friends.

"What are you doing?" a familiar voice buzzed in her ear.

It should've seemed obvious. "What everyone else is
doing, watching the pie-eating contest."

"You can't see back here."

Colt took her hand and led her through the crowd. He didn't have to push or shove; people voluntarily separated for him.

"This doesn't seem right," she whispered.

"I figure I may as well use my clout as chief while I still can." He grinned, and she nearly melted in a puddle at his feet. How did he manage to do that, especially when he hadn't talked to her in a week?

"Congratulations."

He fixed her with a what-are-you-talking-about stare. "For what?"

"The kayak race. Second place—a pretty good showing for someone who thought he would lose . . . and stopped to save a life."

"We were disqualified."

She looked at him, dumbfounded. "What do you mean disqualified?"

"You go in the water, you get disqualified."

"But you went into the water for Chip."

He shrugged. "Those are the rules."

"Did you know that before you came in second?"

"Of course I did."

Then why the heck did you kill yourself to get to the finish line? Did she really need to ask?

"Anyway, we only tied for second. Not a good showing— a joke."

"Are you a sore loser, Colt Garner?" She stared up at his rugged face and thought the man was too handsome for his own good. He hadn't shaved and dark bristle covered that square jaw of his. So much masculinity in one package. . . . It woke up parts of her she hadn't remembered having.

"I've gotta get back to work," he said, without answering her question, and started to back away.

She noticed he'd changed out of the polo and shorts he'd

worn for the kayak races into a Glory Junction tee, a pair of jeans, and his gun belt, signifying he was back on duty.

"Tonight?" He did that chin bob thing he was so fond of.

"I'll be there." She couldn't wait to see him perform. Even if it turned out that he wasn't much on the ears, he was easy on the eyes. So easy.

Colt got to Old Glory early. A couple of friends of the bass player had volunteered to set up their equipment and Colt wanted to do a sound check while the bar was relatively quiet. Most of the town was still at the talent show.

"You good to go?" Boden asked as he set up rows of glasses on the back-bar shelves. The night would be busy. It always was for the End-of-Summer.

Colt sat at one of the stools. "I think so. As soon as the guys get here we'll test things out. What happened to you and Ingrid on the river?" For a while he'd been tied with Boden. Then, boom, he looked up and Boden was gone.

"We were taking on water and I couldn't find the leak." Boden lifted his shoulders. "At least we didn't nearly drown."

"Chip." Colt shook his head. "Man, what was he thinking wearing that bear thing? Now, the lederhosen . . ." Colt leaned his head back and laughed his ass off.

Boden had changed into his regular uniform. Jeans and a flannel shirt. Ingrid had kept on her St. Pauli Girl dress, which showed a great deal of cleavage. Colt figured the outfit would ring in a heap of tips.

"You drinking tonight?" Boden grabbed a pint glass from under the bar.

"Yep. Jack's on call."

"But he'll be here, right?" Boden proceeded to fill the glass with a local lager that Colt particularly liked.

"As long as nothing big goes down." He'd have to keep his eye on his phone all night, though. They really needed another person to handle call duty, someone with supervisory experience.

"I reserved the two big tables by the stage for your posse."

"Thanks, Boden."

A couple of members of the band trickled in and Colt went over to the stage to discuss their set list. When the rest of the group showed up they tested their mics and equipment until he was satisfied with the sound quality. Not that a bar band required much.

They sat around shooting the breeze in a small room behind the stage where Boden stored his extra liquor. Colt hadn't seen some of the guys for a while and took the opportunity to catch up before they had to perform. Boden or one of the bar's staff would let them know when it was time to go on. It wouldn't be long. Even with the door closed, Colt could hear the place filling up.

At nine they got the cue. Without a warm-up band, they were scheduled to do four sets. They walked out on stage with the floor packed so tight that Boden had to open all the doors so people could watch from the street. Colt figured it was just a matter of time before the fire marshal showed up.

There was a lot of hooting and hollering and requests for songs. Some the band regularly played, others Colt had never heard of. They launched into a raucous rendition of Credence Clearwater Revival's "Travelin' Band." Before Lisa left, they'd played a lot more often and could rip through a set like it was rote. He'd worried that without much rehearsal they'd be sloppy tonight. But the band felt tight, falling into a familiar rhythm that came with years of playing together.

He scanned the crowd, looking for Delaney, and saw her sitting at one of the reserved tables with Hannah and his brother. A smile played on her lips and he got so caught up looking at her that he stumbled over a chord.

He quickly looked away so he could finish the song. Throughout the night, he continued to sneak peeks at her, taking in the way her hair shimmered in the dusky lights and how her face shined with animation every time he sang a tune.

Since Josh's dinner and his idiotic phone call, he'd been avoiding her. She was too tempting and he only had so much willpower. He was hoping that the whole out-of-sight, out-of-mind thing would work. That's why during the band's first three breaks he went outside with the drummer, who smoked, and circulated among people he hadn't seen for a while.

Evasion wasn't having the desired effect, unfortunately. Because he couldn't stop glancing her way every now and again—or constantly—to see whom she was talking to or what she was doing. God, she was killing him.

For the last set, he climbed the stage, trying to keep his mind on the music. The audience grew even noisier than before—their last chance to yell out requests for favorites that the band hadn't yet played. For the most part, Colt tried to be accommodating, but when the crowd began chanting, "'Crazy about You,'" he felt the blood rush from his face. The rhythm guitarist gave him a pointed look. *Are we doing this?*

Hell, no, they weren't doing it. The room grew louder. More impatient. "'Crazy about You'!" they yelled over and over again, clapping their hands and stomping their feet. "'Crazy about You'!"

Colt stared out at the sea of faces and held TJ's gaze. His brother gave him an emphatic nod, urging him to do the song. The crowd made such a ruckus, Colt couldn't concentrate over the din. For a minute, he stood there paralyzed, then his attention fell on Delaney. Her black hair, her blue eyes, and it hit him like a lightning bolt.

"'Galway Girl,'" he told the band. They'd never played it together before but they muddled through the first quarter. By the second, they were feeling the groove, laying it down like it was one of their standards.

Colt locked eyes with Delaney as he belted out the lyrics and saw the moment when recognition washed over her face. He was singing about her. About how he wanted her . . . a night together.

Red stained her cheeks but she never turned away, holding eye contact with him as he sang the chorus. The words resonated through the hall as if they were the only two people in the bar. And a shot of desire arced through him like shock waves.

At the end of the song, concertgoers jumped to their feet and shouted for an encore, shaking him out of the moment. Their moment.

Boden climbed the stage and yelled, "Last call for alcohol, and according to city ordinance, the music was supposed to end fifteen minutes ago."

A collective, "You suck" went out.

"Don't blame me," Boden said. "I don't make the rules. Take it up with city hall."

"One more song!" the patrons yelled. "One more song!"

Colt laughed. "You want the police chief to break city ordinance?" For fun, he played a riff of "I Fought the Law" on his Stratocaster, then quickly put it down. "Thanks for coming out, everyone. Drive safely, and if you've had one too many, don't drive at all."

Colt started to get off the stage but was ambushed by a combination of old friends and folks he'd never met before who told him and the rest of the band how much they'd enjoyed the show. Jack and Carrie Jo joined the queue. Colt couldn't tell if they'd come together. Dumb-ass Carrie Jo probably didn't even realize that Jack had the hots for her.

He schmoozed while keeping one eye on Delaney, who'd hung back with Josh, Hannah, TJ, Win, and Deb. The six of them were polishing off the last of the beer when Colt finally managed to break away.

"Your adoring fans." TJ lifted an eyebrow and Colt flipped him the bird. "What happened on 'Crazy about You'?"

Colt gave what he hoped was a nonchalant lift of his shoulders. "Didn't feel like doing it."

"Bullshit."

Josh grabbed TJ's arm. "Leave it alone."

"Yeah," TJ said, "let's not rock the boat. We wouldn't want Colt to actually stand up for himself."

"That's enough, TJ," Colt said. "If you can't hold your booze, you shouldn't drink. I'm going home. Thanks for coming," he said to the group, and headed for the stage to collect his guitars and amplifier.

"You think I could get a ride with you?" Delaney came up behind him. "I walked."

"Sure." He'd wondered if she'd need a ride. He certainly didn't want her walking home alone in the dark.

She waited while he packed everything up and helped him carry it to his truck.

"Thanks for coming tonight," Colt said. *For being my inspiration.* "You like the show?"

"You were amazing," she said as he hefted two of the guitar cases into the bed and opened the passenger side door for her. "It wasn't what I expected."

"No? What did you expect?" he asked, after sitting behind the wheel and starting the engine.

Her expression turned sheepish. "Truthfully, a garage band. I thought you'd do a lot of covers. 'Stairway to Heaven,' that sort of thing."

He released the emergency brake. "We did plenty of covers."

"But you did them in your own style . . . and the originals . . . you're extremely talented, Colt. I'm serious. You could be a professional songwriter. That one about the old man who dies of a broken heart made me tear up. Somehow I didn't see you as the ballad type."

"I'm just full of surprises."

"Sarcasm doesn't look good on you, Colt. Now I know that all that gruffness is a big act. You're squishy as a marshmallow. Sentimental too." She paused. "Is music how you met Lisa?"

"Yeah. She saw us play at Old Glory one night. During the break, she came over, complimented the set and mentioned she was a singer. We invited her to do a song with us, not expecting much. Turned out she blew us away."

"You asked her to join the band after that?"

"We're pretty good musicians. Vocals, though, not so much. It made sense. Having her front the band also got us more gigs." Lisa not only rocked a song, she rocked a miniskirt. Sad to say, for some that was enough.

Colt pulled out of the small parking lot behind the bar and nosed onto Main Street. It only took a few minutes to get home, but he didn't want her to leave. He let the engine idle in front of her house and tried to make small talk. Tomorrow was his day off, so even though it was past two in the morning, he didn't need to rush.

"How come you didn't want to play 'Crazy about You'? I don't listen to country music but I know it's Lisa Laredo's big hit."

You'd have to live under a rock not to know that, he nearly responded.

"Did she write it about you, Colt?"

The clock on his dash ticked away while he contemplated how to respond. "Not exactly. It's a little more complicated. I don't talk about it."

"I got that impression."

Then why the hell did you ask? "You got an early morning?"

"It's already morning, but no. Unless I'm making cargo pants, I usually just stare at a blank sheet of my sketch pad."

"It's still not happening, huh?"

"Nope," she said. Like he didn't want to talk about "Crazy about You," she plainly didn't want to talk about designing. "So what was that last song you sang? It sounded like an old Irish folk song, yet vaguely familiar."

Probably because he'd been playing it a lot. Living so close, she might've heard him tinkering with the chords.

"'Galway Girl'?" he said. "It was written by an American, Steve Earle, and released in 2000. You like it?"

"It was my favorite."

Their eyes met and in a low voice, he said, "The girl in the song looks like you."

"She does?"

"Mm-hmm." Unable to resist, he leaned over and kissed her on the lips. Closed mouth and tentative to test the waters. She didn't pull back, so he went in for more, pulling her closer. The gear shift was in the way, making it awkward. And uncomfortable. But he was all about perseverance. And he wanted her to the point of being stupid. In fact, his mind had completely disengaged. Right now, his cock was doing the thinking, and unfortunately he was okay with that.

"She has black hair and blue eyes," he said against her mouth. "Beautiful . . . like you." So beautiful, she made his pulse race. "I've been thinking about this since that first kiss."

She twined her arms around his neck and tugged him in for more. "Aren't you breaking your hometown rule?"

"Yep," he whispered as he nibbled on her earlobe and worked his way down to the nape of her neck. "Colossally bad idea."

"But you're ready to throw caution to the wind?" she asked, as his lips moved over her throat.

"More than likely I'm getting fired anyway. May as well go out with a bang." Probably a bad choice of word. He blindly reached for the ignition and shut off the engine.

"Wow, you really know how to romance a girl." She arched her neck, giving him better access.

He grinned against her soft skin, enjoying the back and forth. She made him work for it, which he usually didn't have to do with women. "Hey, I took you to the Four Seasons and to the Indian place . . . had you over for wine."

"Should we do it in the cab of your truck?" Her hands moved down his arms, making his stomach contract.

"I prefer a bed." He couldn't tell how serious she was, but they were both pretty worked up from the kissing. "Too old for trucks."

"You looked pretty limber this morning at the kayak races."

"If it means that much to you." He played with the front of her blouse, grazing her breasts with his hands. "You sure you're not drunk?"

"I'm sure."

"Good." He fumbled with the buttons. Although they both possessed way more finesse than teenagers, he felt like he was back in high school when everything was new and fresh and so damn exciting that it made his heart stop and his palms sweat.

"Hang on a sec." He restarted the engine and pulled the truck into their disputed parking space. It was a little more private. "Where were we?"

"Here." She launched herself over the gear shift and climbed into his lap, straddling him.

He slipped his hands down the back of her jeans, pressed her against his erection, and resumed kissing her into next Tuesday. "You feel so good."

His hands moved over something silky. Panties, a thong, the tail of her shirt; he wasn't sure. Wanting to get her pants off, he fumbled with her zipper. But it was impossible in such tight quarters. Damn, he used to be better at this. "Delaney, honey, let's take this inside."

"Don't. Want. To. Move." She rocked against him until he thought he would go off like a fire hydrant.

He managed to get his door open and lift her out of the cab. She wrapped her legs around his waist and he practically ran up her deck stairs because her house was closer.

"Keys." He stuck his hand out.

"I left them in my purse in your truck."

"Shit." He ran back with her still in his arms, her giggles loud enough to wake the whole neighborhood. "Shush."

He opened the door, juggling her with one arm as he reached across the seat and grabbed the handbag.

"Wow, you're strong," she said.

She didn't weigh that much and he didn't want to let go of her. Not even for a second.

He threw the purse at her. "Hurry up and find your keys." Otherwise he was going to take her on the hood of his Ford.

"Got 'em." She giggled some more.

He jogged back, turned the key in the lock, carried her over the threshold, and kicked the door closed with his foot. Mounting the stairs, he asked where her bedroom was. He'd only been inside her studio.

"Go left," she said when they got to the landing.

He backed her against the hallway wall and kissed her long and hard. Desperate to get her clothes off . . . to get inside her. "Foreplay next time, okay?"

She moaned something indecipherable. He took it as she was good with him going straight to the main course and got her into the bedroom, where he stripped off her clothes as quickly as he could. His eyes glided over her body, slowly taking her in. Jesus, she was gorgeous. Full, firm breasts, flat belly, curvy hips, and legs that wouldn't quit. As far as he knew he didn't have a foot fetish, but for some bizarre reason her toenails—pink this time—made him harder than a concrete wall. She went for his belt and he pushed her hands away, afraid he'd come before he even got his pants off.

That hadn't happened since Lucy Singleton had let him get to third base behind the pump house at the lake. He'd been fifteen and still couldn't look at her without remembering the humiliation.

"Please," Delaney said, the word coming out in a single breath.

He groped with his buckle, got it undone, and pushed his jeans down, managing to kick them off without tripping over his own legs. Impatient, she got up on the bed on her knees and tugged his shirt over his head. He shucked his shorts and stood over her, naked, his hands itching to touch her breasts. She pulled him down onto her frilly comforter and he mounted her.

Remembering protection, he hung off the edge of the bed and searched the floor for his pants. In the back pocket he found his wallet and a condom. She practically ripped it out of his hand and opened the foil package with her teeth. Before she could put it on him, he tore it away. If she touched him, it would be over before it started. Colt sheathed himself and let his hands wander over her body, wanting to feel every inch of her and weigh her breasts in his palms.

Her skin was soft and smelled like expensive perfume, flowery but not overly sweet, a scent he'd come to know as purely Delaney. She had on fancy underthings, which he planned to pay more attention to later. Right now all he could think about was getting inside her, feeling her supple body underneath his.

She moaned as he kissed the inside of her thighs, spreading open for him. His fingers explored, finding her wet and ready. In one swift motion, he entered her. She adjusted herself so that he could go deeper and he about lost his mind.

"Jesus, Delaney."

"It's been a while."

He slowed his pace and framed her face with his hands. "You okay?" He started to pull out but she stopped him.

"I'm fine. . . . It's so good."

"Good" was a freaking understatement. "I'll go slow for a little while." Colt was happy just to be enveloped in her warmth and to hear her sweet little moans of pleasure.

He kissed her, darting his tongue in her mouth to the rhythm of his strokes. God, she was so responsive, her body arching to accommodate him. He sucked her breasts, licking her nipples, and she shivered.

"Colt?"

"Hmm?"

"Faster now, please."

He quickened the pace, pumping in and out, his hands kneading her firm ass, pulling her closer. She wrapped her heels around his back and he increased the tempo until he felt her clench and shudder, calling his name.

That's when he let himself go, taking his release, which seemed to go on forever. He lay there for a few minutes, trying to catch his breath, trying to figure out what had just happened.

"You still alive?" He peeked under his arm at Delaney, who wasn't moving.

"Just barely," she said, her face flushed and her hair a wild mess. She was so unbelievably beautiful it made his chest hurt.

He rolled off her but she reached for him. "Not yet."

He wrapped her in his arms and cradled her head against his chest. And for a while they lay there silent, alone with their thoughts. He didn't know what had just happened, but it had been better than good. Hell, it had been a tsunami. A volcano. An avalanche.

He let his eyes roam over her breasts, hips, and legs, taking in all he'd missed during their frenzied sex. She quickly tugged the blanket over her in a sudden show of modesty, which he found hilarious. *Too late for that, sweetheart.*

He rolled over and swung his legs over the side of the bed.

"Where are you going?"

He glanced at the clock. "It's closing in on three a.m. Home to get some sleep."

"Oh." One word, but she sounded disappointed.

He sat on the edge of the mattress, feeling guilty. "You want me to stay?"

"You don't have to if you don't want to. I just thought . . ."

"Let me get rid of the condom." He found the master bath, which wasn't hard to miss. It was the size of his old San Francisco apartment. The towels were so fancy he was afraid to dry his hands on them.

He finished up and got back in bed with her. She was still sitting there, propped against the pillows, looking a little shell shocked.

"Delaney, was this a mistake?"

"Not for me. Was it for you?"

Probably. But regretting mind-blowing sex wasn't in his DNA. He reached over and took her hand. "What's on your mind, then?"

"Do you think it was a fluke?"

"What? Us sleeping together?"

"How good it was?"

He cocked his head to the side. "Only one way to find out."

Chapter Sixteen

When Delaney woke up Colt was gone. She looked over at her bedside clock. Ten-thirty and, based on the drizzle of sunshine streaming through the spaces between the drapes, already a scorcher. She grabbed a robe from the back of her closet door and padded into the hallway, hoping to smell fresh coffee brewing. No such luck.

He must've gone home for breakfast, or more sleep, and disappointment kicked her in the chest. *Stop being needy*, she told herself. But the night had been so wondrously perfect that she didn't want it to end. They'd had sex twice more, each time better than the last. Colt Garner knew his way around a woman's body, not to mention that he had the stamina of a bull. She supposed it was all that kayaking, climbing, and skiing. The one criticism she had was that she never knew what he was thinking. He'd been complimentary enough—telling her that she was beautiful or that he liked this or that—but when it came to any real emotions, he was a brick wall. Impenetrable. Frustrating because she couldn't get a read on the guy. Was their morning together just sex or the start of something real?

She went into her studio and peeked behind the shade. His truck was parked where he'd left it and his squad car sat at

the top of his driveway. Unless someone had picked him up
or he'd gone for a run—which she knew he did a lot—he had
to be home. She considered calling him and asking if he
wanted to have coffee on the deck. Too clingy, she decided.

*He's the one who left, therefore it's up to him to make the
next move*, Delaney told herself. She went downstairs, started
a pot of coffee, and showered while it brewed, planning to
spend her day sketching. At least it would keep her mind off
Colt.

She brought a pad with her into the kitchen and doodled
while she waited for her bread to toast. Crazy, but she had an
idea for a fleece turtleneck with thumbholes to keep the
sleeves down and stretch panels on the arms for extra flexi-
bility. She'd seen something similar while researching cargo
pants and thought she could improve the design, make it a
little splashier. Evidently the shirt was for hiking or bouldering, whatever the heck that was.

A weird idea had recently formed in her head—to fill her
creative void with a few adventure wear designs that would at
least keep what few investors she had and the fashion press
at bay. She could say that living in Glory Junction had inspired her to do a fun line of athletic clothing. Hell, if Vera
Wang could do bedsheets, why couldn't she do sports attire?
She could beta test the pieces with Garner Adventure.

By four, she'd finished a few promising drawings and
was just about to work on the patterns when the phone rang.
Her pulse quickened until she saw it was Hannah.

"Hi," she answered, wondering if Hannah knew about her
and Colt, then mentally chiding herself for being ridiculous.
How could she possibly know unless Colt went blabbing,
which was patently absurd. The man was about as close
lipped as an underworld spy.

"Want to meet us at the diner for an early supper?"

"Sure." It would be good to get out of the house, get some
exercise and fresh air. "Do I have time to walk?"

"Absolutely. We'll meet you there at five."

She changed out of her shorts into a pair of leggings and a linen tunic from her summer collection, slipped on a pair of flats, and shoved her sketch pad into one of her oversized Delaney Scott handbags. On her way out, she checked the driveway again. Colt still hadn't moved his truck. Maybe he was catching up on his sleep.

She walked to the restaurant, glad that the festivities from the End-of-Summer events were over and that the tourists were on their way home. The town got a little cramped with all those people, though she supposed it was a boon for local businesses. As she strolled down Main Street, she ran into Boden.

"Good show last night, huh?"

"Fantastic," she said. "You have a lot of cleanup?"

"We got most of it done last night, so not too bad. Is Colt recovered?" He'd evidentially seen them leave the bar together.

"I don't know." Delaney looked away, hoping she hadn't turned red.

"The guy works too hard, needs to let loose every once in a while."

Oh, he'd let pretty loose, all right. "Mm-hmm. I'm meeting friends at the diner so I better get going. Have a good evening."

"See you, Delaney."

She was the first to arrive at the Morning Glory and got a table for four, not sure if Deb and Foster were joining them. Felix, the owner, waved to her from the kitchen window, and for the first time Delaney felt like a bona fide local. She hadn't realized it until now but she'd always seen herself as a vacationer, albeit one who had come to hibernate for the winter and had never left. But somehow she'd become part of the community to the point where people recognized her beyond being "that famous fashion designer." In fact, her professional success had become a footnote instead of her entire identity, which she rather liked.

"Hey, sorry I'm late." Hannah sounded out of breath. "I got a customer who wanted to buy out the store five minutes before closing. I shoved the cash register in the safe, locked up, and ran the half block. Deb and Foster aren't here yet?"

"Just me . . . and now you. So sales are good, huh?"

"End-of-Summer packs 'em in and we made a killing. It starts all over again in November, especially if we get snow. I'm certainly not complaining. What's going on with you? Colt get you home okay?"

Delaney could feel her face flush and she grabbed a glass of water, hoping to extinguish any tell. "Yep. All good." She reached in her bag for her drawings to redirect the conversation. "What do you think of these?" Delaney flipped the pages.

"I want one of these." Deb came up behind Delaney's chair and pointed to the fleece turtleneck. "I love it, especially in stripes. I've never seen a rock-climbing shirt like that. Foster can't come; he's dealing with another bridezilla."

Hannah took the pad and examined Delaney's drawings. "Wow, you're going in a totally different direction."

"Those are just for fun . . . a placeholder until I get my groove back. Besides, lots of designers have a sideline, something different from their usual bag of tricks."

"I like it," Hannah said. "Josh wears this stuff all the time and it's dull as dirt. Yours has pizazz."

"I'm wondering if it's too much. Clearly, the clothes are monochrome and drab for a reason. I just don't know what that reason is."

"The reason is that unimaginative men design them," Deb said. "A little pattern is fun, and I like what you did with the sleeves . . . very practical." She took the pad from Hannah and turned the page to a ski jacket Delaney had designed. "Now this . . . Can I put my name on a list for one of these?"

Thrilled that Deb liked the designs, especially because she was the target consumer, Delaney said, "Really? You're not being nice because I'm your friend?"

"I don't ski or climb anything higher than my stairs and I'd wear all that stuff." Hannah pointed at the sketchbook. "And I'm one-hundred percent positive that my customers would too. But if you want I could show them to Josh. Although now that you and Colt are friends, you could show them to him. He'll tell you the truth. Just don't show TJ or he'll start up again about you working with Garner Adventure."

A waitress came to take their order and she and Deb complained about Felix for a while. They made him out to be quite a taskmaster, but given that the two women whined about him right under his nose, Delaney figured he must be a decent boss. According to the scuttlebutt, he'd been a champion snowboarder, injured himself in the half-pipe event in the 2010 Olympics, and could no longer compete. He'd moved to Glory Junction for the slopes and bought the diner to support himself.

"I was actually thinking of partnering with Garner Adventure to beta test them, perhaps have some of the guides wear the gear and let me know how to improve the design," Delaney said.

"Seriously? That's awesome. But are you sure? No offense to my husband's family's company, but it's got to be small potatoes for someone like you."

"At the risk of sounding extremely corporate, I think it would be good for my brand to work with a small, family-run operation in the middle of adventure paradise. It would make the clothing more authentic, rather than fashion wear made to look sporty, don't you think?"

"When you put it that way, yeah, I do," Hannah said. "It's smart marketing. Hey, why don't you do a big fashion show debuting the line at Garner Adventure? How fun would that be? You could even have the Garner brothers and the other guides model the clothes."

"I don't know. This is just a sideline . . . something to keep me occupied." Although the idea appealed to her and could be the answer to fashion week. She'd need more than the athletic wear, though.

"Keep it in mind," Hannah said. "And I'll help any way I can."

Delaney was still mulling Hannah's suggestion over at the grocery store a few hours later. So much so that she wheeled her cart around as if in a daze, returning to the produce aisle a number of times for salad makings without putting anything in her basket.

That's when she saw Colt over by the cold beverages, pulling a six-pack from one of the refrigerators. She waved and he waved back. After a few minutes of her just standing there he finally came over.

"How you doing?" he asked.

"Good, you?"

"Good."

For God's sake, you'd think they'd just met each other even though only hours ago, they'd been as intimate as two people could be.

"I better get going." He did that head bob thing, and she watched him slip away as stealthily as a cat burglar. Colt Garner was trying to avoid her; she was positive of it.

"You can't just sleep with me and then run away," she muttered, knocking things off shelves with her cart in a mad dash up and down the lanes to hunt him down and give him a piece of her mind. But the man had disappeared. *Poof.* Gone. Clearly he'd left without even buying his damn beer.

And then it occurred to her that she was acting desperate. Worse: pathetic. They'd hooked up, had a one-night stand. He probably had tons of them—badge bunnies, band groupies. He was a walking chick magnet. And here she was chasing after him in the feminine hygiene aisle like a lovesick lunatic. Where was her dignity, her self-respect? She was freaking Delaney Scott, designer to celebrities, rock stars, and British royals.

This was all Robert's fault. If he hadn't told her how frigid and unattractive she'd become, hadn't shocked her with his creepy proposal to spice up their marriage, she wouldn't be throwing herself at a man who would rather go without food than have to face her in the safe confines of a supermarket.

She paid for her groceries, loaded them into the back of her Tesla, and drove home, vowing to kick him out of the easement space if he'd dared to park there.

Colt felt like a heel for ditching her. It hadn't been his intention, but it seemed easier to flee than have the awkward postcoital conversation in a goddamned grocery store.

His stomach growled and his refrigerator was empty. He called Old Glory for takeout and swung by the bar on his way home. A nice quiet evening in—without the mayor chewing his ass or the watch commander getting him out of bed, or his brothers bugging him to take their shifts at GA—was exactly what he had in mind. And if the stars aligned he might actually get it.

"You wouldn't sell me a six-pack, would you?" Colt asked over the noise of the jukebox and a heated game of darts as he waited at the bar for someone to bring out his order.

Boden took a moment to consider it. "I can't sell alcohol to leave the premises. But I can give you a six-pack."

"Nah, that's all right." As the police chief he shouldn't take free stuff, though he wasn't such a stickler when Boden wanted him to taste a new brew on tap. He chalked that up to them both being craft beer buffs.

"You sure?"

"Yeah. I think I have a couple of bottles at home."

"Hey"—Boden pulled him aside, away from prying eyes and ears—"you hearing any weird rumors about Pond?"

"Like what?"

"I don't know exactly, just snatches of conversation from a few council members who were in having lunch on Friday. What got my attention was they stopped talking as soon as they saw me hovering. That doesn't usually happen to bartenders. . . . There's an unspoken privilege. We're lawyers and therapists, rolled into one."

Colt remembered something Ben had alluded to and wondered if it had anything to do with what Boden had heard.

"My sense was that they were looking into something," Boden continued. "I'm speculating that it may have had something to do with you, but I didn't hear your name mentioned. I'll keep my ear to the ground."

Colt didn't say anything. It didn't seem right to tell the local barkeep to spy on city council members, but knowing Boden, he'd have Colt's back regardless. His food came out of the kitchen and he left, tempted to call Rita and do some digging, but rejected the idea. It was unfair to put Rita on the spot and would make him sound paranoid. Screw Pond.

He pulled his truck into the garage. Tomorrow he worked and would be driving the cruiser. Besides, Delaney had taken the easement spot. Again, he felt crappy about his shitty behavior back at the store, though it probably hadn't bothered her. He figured she'd just been scratching an itch with him anyway. What could she possibly want with a small-town cop who was about to lose his job?

He unpacked his burger and fries, found an AleSmith Speedway Stout hiding in the back of his fridge, and ate in front of the TV. A few times he gazed out the window at Delaney's second story and noted the light on in her studio. She had the shade up and the window open. There was nothing good on television, just old movies and a repeat of a Giants game he'd already seen. He threw away his wrappers and went upstairs to get his guitar.

Back in the living room his fingers automatically began strumming "Galway Girl." Halfway through the song his conscience got the better of him. He walked over to Delaney's and rang the bell.

The sun had started to set and reds and blues streaked the clear mountain sky like paintbrush strokes. There was nothing like the Sierra in summer. All puffy clouds, white-capped peaks, and cascading waterfalls from the melted snow. The smell of pine thick in the air and carpets of freshly bloomed Tehachapi tarweed signaling that the season was nearly over.

It took so long for her to answer the door that Colt had started to walk away.

"Hi," she said, leaning against the jam.

He felt a jolt in his chest, like his engine had just been jump-started. "Want to go for a drive . . . look at the wild-flowers?" It would be dark in less than an hour and he sounded like an imbecile.

"Now?"

He lifted his shoulders as if to say why not?

"Okay." She sounded hesitant.

"I'll get my truck." He didn't want to give her a chance to change her mind and took off for his house to get his keys.

By the time he pulled down the driveway, she'd slung a handbag over her shoulder and a light jacket over her arm. He leaned across the truck cab and opened the passenger door. God, he was a masochist. Hadn't he learned from his last mistake?

He headed for the Arbuckle Trail, a meandering country road right out of town where Garner Adventure led nature tours. A viewing point offered sweeping vistas of the Glory River Valley and the surrounding Sierra mountains. He parked in the small lot and shut off the ignition. There was no one else there and for a moment he stared off into the distance.

"I'm sorry about before at the grocery store," he finally said. "I like you, Delaney. But you're leaving and . . ."

"And you don't do long distance."

No, once she left, she wouldn't do small town. There'd be no place for him in her big-city world. "It doesn't work."

"It seems a bit premature in our relationship to be worried about it, don't you think?" she said.

"So we continue to sleep together and hope that by the time you go we're bored with each other, is that what you're proposing?" Because it was a piss-poor idea.

"I'm proposing that we see where it goes," she replied.

He turned to look at her. "I guess I'm a nice distraction."

She reeled back as if he'd slapped her. "Do you know how insulting that is? I'm not Lisa. The woman clearly did a number on you, but Robert did one on me and I'm still willing to try again . . . find the right person."

"What did he do to you that was so terrible?"

"You mean in addition to stealing my name?"

Colt understood the violation of that more than she could imagine. "Lisa stole my song." He couldn't believe he'd just blurted that out.

"What?" She sat there, slack jawed. "What do you mean she stole your song?"

"'Crazy about You.' I wrote it . . . the lyrics, the music. It's my song."

"And she told people she wrote it?"

She'd done more than tell people; she'd given herself songwriter credit on the goddamn record. Colt felt the same sharp metallic taste of bitterness on his tongue as he had the first time he heard the song played on the radio. The DJ had said, "That's Lisa Laredo's newest single." No mention of him at all.

"I think she must've been desperate. She'd just come off

the hit from the movie and her manager and record label expected her to come out with another one. But she hadn't written anything in more than a year. The movie theme had been a fluke."

"My God, Colt. I don't know much about the music industry, but that song is a huge hit. It had to have made her a fortune. Please tell me you're getting royalties."

"Delaney, my name's not on it. All this time, she's passed the song off as her own. She never even asked, just took it, and had it published under her name."

"Do you not have a way to prove that it's your song?"

"The entire town knows I wrote that song. I wrote it about her."

"You need to go to court, Colt. What she did . . . she shouldn't be allowed to get away with it. You're entitled to the proceeds."

He leaned his head against the back of the seat, sorry that he ever brought it up. "I don't give a shit about the money." Colt knew it made him sound like a chump.

She scrutinized him until he felt like he was under a microscope. "You're still in love with her, aren't you?"

"In love with her?" He snorted. "That ship sailed when she stole my song."

"Then why won't you fight her for it?"

"Why? What purpose would it serve? I wrote the song about a woman I thought I knew, who I thought I loved. It turned out she wasn't any of the things I thought she was. I'd never perform the song again, so let her have it. Let her live with the fact that she's a fraud and a thief and that a whole town knows it."

"Then why hasn't anyone said anything?"

"Who should they tell?" TJ had begged to go to the press, but unless Colt hired lawyers and filed a lawsuit, a random accusation would make his brother look like a crazy person, or at the very least someone who wanted fifteen minutes of fame. "I'm over it, Delaney."

"Are you? Because you don't seem like it. It makes me so angry, Colt. You're so amazingly talented and she's getting the credit. I want to . . . punch her."

"I'm over it, Delaney, but thank you for being outraged on my behalf." He pointed outside. "It's too dark now to see the flowers. It's the end of the season, not much time left."

"That's okay," she said, and turned her head to stare out the window. "Next time."

"What are you thinking?"

"That I like you, that I'd like to see where this"—she waved her hand between them—"goes. But you have trust issues. And now I know why."

She was right. "You don't?"

"Have trust issues?" She pondered it for a while. "I have issues but not so much about trust. Robert worked his ass off to make the business a success. He deserves his share. Not necessarily my name, but that was a judge's decision to make."

"Then what kind of issues?" When she clammed up, he said, "I told you mine."

"Someday, maybe, but not tonight."

He figured that her ex-husband had had an affair. He'd probably run off with someone younger and made Delaney question her sex appeal, which was absurd because Colt had never met a sexier woman.

"I should get back to work," she said.

According to his dashboard, it was almost nine. "This late? You must've come up with something."

She didn't answer at first, then said, "A fleece shirt for bouldering, kayaking trunks, and a ski jacket."

"Seriously?"

She gave a long explanation about how the sports stuff was a sideline, just something to keep her busy until she found her inspiration again. But the way her face lit up when she talked about the designs told a different story. He thought she dug it.

"Would you mind looking at my sketches, letting me know what I can improve? I was thinking that I'd make up some samples and let you and your brothers test them for me."

"Yeah, sure. If they're anything like your cargos, TJ's gonna harangue you to sell them out of GA."

"I'm actually considering it. Hannah even suggested I do a fashion show there."

Colt registered surprise. "A fashion show, huh? Yeah, that would be weird."

"Not so weird. Hot models." She lifted her chin and held eye contact with him.

Colt stared back. "No one hotter than you." He reached out to touch her, but she pulled away.

"You're doing it again, saying one thing and doing another. Think about what I said, Colt. I'd like to try this but the ball is in your court. You've got to decide what you want. Either we're going to date and get to know each other or we're not."

Colt wasn't a big fan of ultimatums. But Delaney was right; it wasn't fair to toy with a person's emotions. He knew what he'd wind up doing because at the end of the day he was a weakling. But he still had to sleep on it.

Chapter Seventeen

"How soon can we get these?" With a gleam in his eye, TJ stared down at the samples Delaney had laid on his desk. A dozen different pieces in all.

"Not so fast. First I want you, Colt, Josh, and Win to wear them when you take groups out, see how they work on the job."

"Delaney, it's seventy degrees out." He picked up the ski jacket. "We won't get snow for another month or two."

"You can at least try the rash guards, dry suits, board shorts, and the climbing pants."

"I can already tell you that they're fantastic. We'll sell a bunch."

She'd worked a week making the samples and had even hired a couple of local seamstresses who'd come highly recommended. "Don't get carried away, TJ. I don't have any experience designing adventure wear and I don't want my name on something unless it's perfect."

"What about the fashion show? Hannah says you're down with it being at Garner Adventure." TJ's ambition amused Delaney. He had zero interest in fashion or fashion shows but smelled publicity for his family's company. Frankly, Garner

Adventure was lucky to have him at the helm because he was one hell of a businessman.

"Let's take one thing at a time. First I want to know how the pieces perform. I read somewhere that North Face employs professional athletes to take its products on more than two-dozen trips a year for testing."

TJ nodded. "We know a few guys on their staff. Are you trying to be North Face?"

"No. But I want the clothes to be as functional as they are attractive otherwise what's the point?"

"Absolutely," he said. "We'll start beta testing ASAP."

"And, TJ, we want to keep this hush-hush. I'll determine when and where we do the announcement. Understood?" It felt new to Delaney to be running her own show, but at the same time, good. Empowering.

TJ smiled. "Understood. I suppose you have a publicity team."

Her publicity team had stayed with Delaney Scott and Robert. But the team's expertise was couture and prêt-à-porter, not an outdoor lifestyle brand. She had tasked Karen with interviewing agencies in Los Angeles, San Francisco, and New York. Delaney wanted to make sure the world knew that she wasn't deserting high fashion. The way she wanted to spin it was that in addition to the made-to-measure clothes, the ready-to-wear, the shoes, and the handbags, she was branching out into adventure wear. The right PR firm would know how to sell it. According to her research, outdoor apparel was a four-billion-dollar industry with 143 million Americans participating in adventure activities a year. She wasn't the only high-fashion designer trying to break in to the lucrative market. In fact, she didn't know why Robert hadn't proposed it years ago. She already had her shoe and handbag designers focusing on après-ski boots and accessories.

"I'm working on it," she told TJ. "Don't worry, Garner Adventure will be a big part of the narrative. As soon as we choose a firm I'll need background on GA. I really want to play up that it's a family business and that every piece was designed to the specifications of professional adventure guides. I was even thinking we can name the clothes after each one of you."

"What am I?" Colt stood in the doorway, his hands gripping the top of the frame, his muscles straining under his navy blue uniform shirt. His dark hair was tousled, like he'd run his fingers through it a few too many times.

Delaney hadn't heard him come in. "Which one do you want to be?" she asked lamely, afraid that he would see what his mere presence did to her.

He shrugged.

"The Colten Cargo," TJ offered. "The Win Windbreaker. The Josh Jams."

"The TJ Gives Me a Rash . . . Guard," Colt finished, and TJ threw a Nerf ball at him. He had a collection of them and a dart gun on his desk.

"You guys are good," she said, flustered by Colt's sudden appearance. She hadn't seen him since Sunday night, not since they'd had their so-called heart-to-heart and she'd delivered her conditions. He could've been busy—not a stretch given his intense work schedule—or he could've been avoiding her. With Colt she never knew. But she had missed him.

"I'll get out of your hair now. I'll be back tomorrow with a few more samples for you to test." She gathered up her purse and portfolio.

"I'll walk you out." Colt took the large leather case from her. When they got outside he asked, "Did you come on foot or drive?"

She pointed to her car, which she'd parked on Main Street, a few doors down from Glorious Gifts, and rummaged through her handbag for the keys.

"You have lunch yet?"

"No. Why, you want to get something?"

"The diner or Old Glory?"

"Whichever you want." She didn't know how much time he got for lunch. He was in his uniform, so she assumed he was on duty.

"The diner's good."

They unloaded her portfolio first in the trunk of the Tesla, then walked to the Morning Glory. Deb was waitressing and got them a quiet booth in the back and rushed off to help someone else.

"I guess the summer crowds are gone," Delaney observed. The restaurant was almost deserted.

"September. Everyone goes back to school. But as soon as we get our first dump of snow they'll be back."

"You been busy?" She tried to make it sound casual.

"Yeah. There've been a couple of burglaries. Vacation homes up near the resorts."

"Oh no." Glory Junction had a relatively low crime rate, but like any other place, bad things happened. "You catch the culprits?"

"We're working on it. I can't get into it, but it's kept me busy the last few nights." He glanced across the table at her and she wondered if he was trying to tell her that was why he hadn't come calling. She'd left it up to him.

"I hope you catch whoever did it." She leaned closer and asked in a soft voice, "Anything new with the mayor?"

"Nope." His gaze ran over her, lingering on her low-cut top, male appreciation gleaming in his eyes. "I thought we should clear the air . . . you know, after last week."

"Okay." Delaney waited for him to say more but her cell rang and she pulled it out of her purse to look at the display. Her lawyer. "I have to get this."

She walked outside and leaned against the diner's exterior wall to take the call. "Do you have bad news for me?"

"Robert's attorneys filed a request for a clarification from the court. We could hear something anytime and I wanted you to be prepared."

"What if the judge says that I have to take the Delaney Scott label off my existing merchandise? How do we handle that?"

"We could appeal," Liz said. "But that could cost as much money as removing the name."

Delaney doubted it. Not only would removing the labels be a major expense but the items wouldn't be worth much without them. The best she could hope for was selling them to an off-price store.

"Let's wait for the clarification before we come up with a game plan," Liz said. "I still think we were right all along."

Delaney desperately hoped so.

Another call came in and Delaney checked the ID. "Liz, my real estate agent is on the other line. Let me know if you hear anything." She quickly clicked over before she lost the call. "Hello."

"We've got an offer," the agent trilled in a singsong voice.

"A good one?" If the judge's clarification was in Robert's favor, the proceeds from her house would be a godsend.

"An excellent one. I'm sending you an e-mail with the offer attached. Take a look and call me back. We have forty-eight hours to counter."

"Okay," Delaney said, a bit overwhelmed. She hadn't expected a house listed at four million dollars to have buyers this fast.

She went back in the restaurant. "I just got an offer on my house. And my lawyer called to tell me that Robert's legal team asked for a clarification from the judge on whether I can sell existing merchandise under the Delaney Scott label."

"What happened?"

"The judge hasn't responded yet."

"Is the house offer a good one?" he asked.

"I haven't seen it yet." She scrolled through the phone to

see if her agent's e-mail had come through yet. For some reason she felt funny about Colt knowing the price, even though anyone trolling Beverly Hills real estate listings could find it. It was just so excessive to the point of being vulgar. At least to someone who had come from her humble beginnings. "Here it is."

Deb came to take their orders and she waited to pull up the attachment. Colt ordered a roast beef sandwich and potato salad. She got the Cobb. Customers started to filter in and Deb took off to seat them.

"Well?" Colt asked, craning his neck to see the e-mail on her phone.

She tapped on the document icon and breezed through the fine print until she got to the offer price. "It's pretty close to what I was asking." Delaney would let her agent advise her on whether to counter with something higher, but if the buyer wouldn't come up, she'd take it.

"Good," Colt said, leaning back against the pleather bench. "You gonna go back to LA to buy something else?"

"Eventually. Right now, I want to launch the outdoor line with your family's company. I'm excited about it." She hadn't been this enthusiastic about a line in a long time. Adventure wear—who would've ever thought such a thing would appeal to her high-fashion sensibility? But the challenge of making rugged, functional clothing beautiful filled her with excitement, as did the man sitting across from her.

He was looking at her. A look so sexy, it charged through her like a jolt of electricity. "Then I suppose we'll be working together."

"Why? You thinking of taking over the retail end of the family business?" She didn't see it. Colt had many facets— adventurer, crime solver, musician—but being buried in profit-and-loss statements wasn't one of them.

"You never know." He hitched his shoulders, his gaze darting to her lips.

She assumed Colt was alluding to his problems with the mayor but was having trouble concentrating with him looking at her the way he was.

"You want to go out tonight if I get out early enough?" he asked.

"What are we doing, Colt?" Did he not remember their last conversation?

"Yeah." He scrubbed his hand through his hair and turned somber. "I can't stop thinking about you and I'm tired of fighting it . . . have been for a while. As long as you're living next door, I don't have the resolve to overcome my attraction to you." He waited a beat and continued, "Permanently, though? We're not gonna work, you know that?"

"Not all women are like Lisa," she said in a soft voice. "We've been over this."

"Too many similarities."

"That's offensive. I would never intentionally hurt someone. And I certainly wouldn't steal their work from them."

"That's not what I meant. We want different things out of life. I have no interest in fame or fortune, just want to serve my community."

"You make me out to be shallow when there's nothing wrong with wanting success." She'd dreamed of being a famous designer since making her first Vogue McCall dress on her mother's Singer. "You are trying to pass your trust issues off as reverse snobbery. It's not working."

He snorted. "Baby, if you say so. You're the one moving away. But if you want to try, I'll try. I just ask that we keep any relationship between us quiet. No telling Hannah, my brothers, not anyone, not even when it's over."

Deb came with their order. "One beef-on-wreck and a Cobb," she said, placing the plates down on the table.

The interruption gave Delaney time to think about Colt's parameters. After her spectacular breakup with Robert,

Delaney didn't need to advertise her love life any more than Colt did.

Felix came out of the kitchen and beckoned Deb, who dashed over to do his bidding.

"If that's the way you want to handle it."

"Yep." He nodded with conviction.

Fine with her. It was just a fling, after all. A fling with an expiration date because he'd already decided that once she left they were doomed. Honestly, he was probably right. Relationships even under the best circumstances were difficult. Just look at her and Robert. "Okay," she said.

He scanned the restaurant, presumably to make sure no one could hear them. "You want to go to Tahoe tonight?" Thirty miles from Glory Junction, the likelihood of running into any of their friends there was next to nil.

"All right," she said. "Sounds fun."

Colt got a call from dispatch—a car accident on the outskirts of town—paid their bill, and took the rest of his sandwich to go. She finished her salad, said good-bye to Deb, and drove to the seamstress to get the rest of her samples. The whole way there she thought about her and Colt's date and how his arrival in her life had been so unexpected. Just like the adventure wear she was now designing.

The fabrics she'd chosen for the sports clothes were gorgeous. Forest green florals, winter white checks, electric blue with geometric designs, metallic silver, and pastel paisley. Nothing too loud, but definitely a swish of flair in an otherwise banal market.

She took the garments home to press and spent much of the afternoon preparing for her date with Colt, including applying a beauty mask, taking a long bath, and pawing through her lingerie drawers for maximum frill factor.

At six he called to say he was running late. At seven she heard his police car come up the easement road and watched for him through the window. He went home first. Delaney presumed he wanted to shower and change. Forty-five minutes later, he knocked at her door.

She opened and said, "Hey" when what she should've said was *wow!* He'd put on a crisp white Oxford, a pair of jeans, and cowboy boots, nothing designer, but on him the clothes could've been Ralph Lauren or Ryan Michael.

"Sorry I'm late."

"Was the accident bad?"

He snaked his arm around her waist, pulled her against him, and went in for a kiss. Losing her balance, she grabbed onto his shoulders, feeling his hard chest pressed against her breasts. She took a second to luxuriate in his brawn and sniff his neck, which smelled like aftershave and something distinctly Colt. Despite all his misgivings and rules, he felt inordinately safe. Like no matter what, he had her. She never remembered feeling safe with Robert. Mostly judged, like she constantly had to prove herself.

"What's this for?" she whispered as he devoured her mouth.

"You look hot and I've been wanting you for days."

And here, in the privacy of her home, no one was watching. It didn't bother her, she told herself. Who cared if they weren't out in the open? Discretion was good.

"Thank you, so do you." She closed her eyes and let the kiss take her away for a while, getting more and more aroused. "Are we skipping the date part of the program?"

"Nah." He pulled away but she could tell it was a Herculean effort. "I promised to take you to Tahoe; I don't renege on my promises. Not even for sex." He flashed a crooked smile that never failed to turn her inside out.

She considered forgetting dinner and leading him upstairs but wasn't quite comfortable being the aggressor, which she knew men enjoyed but could never bring herself to do.

"I'll grab my purse."

"And a jacket. It's getting cooler at night."

She found a cashmere wrap in the coat closet and followed him outside.

He eyed her silver Delaney Scott stilettos. "Wait here while I get my truck."

"We can take your police car," she said, kind of liking the idea of fooling around in the backseat of a squad vehicle.

"Against policy." He hopped over her deck railing and climbed the driveway to the garage.

A few minutes later, he drove down the hill and jumped out of the cab to help her in, intentionally grazing her butt with his hand. At this rate, they wouldn't get through a meal. She wanted him. Bad.

He got on the road, turned at the on-ramp to the highway, and headed east. Not for the first time she noted what an excellent driver he was, taking the curves as smoothly as she drove a straight shot on the interstate. He had one hand on her leg while he steered with the other. Ordinarily that would've made her nervous on a dark road. Not with Colt. She wondered if he'd learned his driving skills in the police academy.

"You okay?" he asked as they headed further up the mountain.

"Of course, why wouldn't I be?"

"You seem quiet." He moved his palm higher on her thigh.

"Just enjoying the drive." She put the back of her hand on the passenger-side window. "You were right, it's getting chilly."

"September is usually a nice month in the Sierra, but the temperature drops in the evenings. You want me to turn on the heat?"

"I've got the wrap." Her dress was a sleeveless sheath that matched her shoes. Clingy knit fabric better suited for a warm summer night.

He slid her a sideways glance, which heated at the sight of her. "You have a busy rest of your day?"

"I got the pieces for Garner Adventure from the seamstress and countered on the offer."

"What did the buyers say?"

"Nothing yet. They have twenty-four hours to respond. My agent thinks they'll take it."

He got quiet, mulling over what she'd just told him. "I guess that's good, right? You'll miss ski season, though."

She couldn't tell if he was being flip or a good sport about her eventual departure. "I don't ski, so that won't be a problem."

He shook his head. "I still don't get that. You live in one of the best ski towns in America."

"I like drinking hot toddies in the lodge. Does that count?"

"No." He said it like he still couldn't wrap his head around the fact that she didn't ski. "If you're still around when we get our first snow I'll take you out for a lesson."

"All right, but you have to promise to be gentle. I'm not the most athletic . . . or adventurous."

"You had game when we went kayaking." His hand slipped under the hem of her dress and the skin-to-skin contact made her wet.

"I've always liked the water. Ice and snow, not my favorite."

He surprised her by pulling through the circular driveway of the Ritz-Carlton.

"We're going to the restaurant here?"

"Yeah. That okay?"

Extravagant and not at all what she'd been expecting. "Wonderful. But do you have a reservation?"

He fixed her with a look and left the truck with the valet before escorting her inside. The maître d' asked for their name and led them to a table. Colt glanced around the room as he pulled out her chair. She wondered if he wanted to make sure no one there knew them or was just taking in the dining room.

They sat and Colt perused the menu. "Wine?"

"Yes, please."

"Don't get drunk," he teased. "I have plans for later."

"And what might those be?" She liked this playful side of him.

Before he could answer, a waiter came over and Colt ordered a pricey bottle of Hanzell Vineyards chardonnay. For a man who preferred beer, he knew his wines.

"You like white, right?"

"I like that white in particular," she said.

"Good." He reached across the table and laced his fingers through hers. "Nice dress. One of yours, I presume." When she nodded he asked, "Do you have lacey things under it?"

"That's for me to know and for you to find out." He'd reduced her to a silly fifteen-year-old. *That's for me to know and for you to find out.* She wanted to roll her eyes at herself.

He cocked his brows. "Baby, I'm looking forward to it."

The sommelier came with the wine and started to give a dissertation on it. Colt listened politely but Delaney could tell he was in a rush for the steward to leave. Afterward, the waiter took their orders.

Coq au vin, she told the server because it was the first thing on the menu and she couldn't concentrate. Colt had taken his hand away to order and she wanted it back. When the waiter finally left, he slipped his palm under the table and played with her leg. Careful. If his fingers slid any higher, he'd give her a spontaneous orgasm.

"Colt?"

"Hmm?" His lips slid up.

"What's gotten into you?"

"That first time was like crack."

Yet, he'd run off like a scared little rabbit and then had gone five days without contacting her. "For a guy who's supposedly addicted to me, you've been missing in action."

Colt's expression turned pensive. "I had to do some serious thinking about this . . . about us." He took another visual lap around the room. Delaney thought he was nervous that someone would see them together.

"What changed your mind?"

"The fact that you told me I was being a dick, that I needed to make up my mind. And the truth: I can't seem to stay away. I think it probably started nine months ago, when you and I began fighting over parking. Usually I don't get involved in petty shit like that."

"But?"

"I enjoyed butting heads with you." He grinned. "I kinda became that mean boy in school who's attracted to a girl and doesn't want to admit it. Not even to myself. But I want to keep it light, Delaney, if that's okay with you?"

Light worked. She was getting over a bad marriage, trying to rebuild a business, and had no plans to stay in Glory Junction indefinitely. There had never been an expectation that they'd become an immediate couple. Still, she couldn't help needle him. "It took you five days to decide you just wanted to fool around?"

"Not just fool around," he said, sounding insulted. "I like you, Delaney. I like talking to you, drinking beer or wine together, this." He swept his hand around the restaurant. "I like spending time with you."

He just didn't want to like it too much, she suspected. Not with her life in flux the way it was. Colt was more sensitive than he let on, hence the whole privacy issue. She could understand how he didn't want the town to have a front-row seat to his love life, especially after what Lisa had done to him.

"Plus, we've been doing surveillance in connection with those burglaries I told you about," he continued, putting his finger to his lips. "That's not to be repeated. But that's at least part of the reason I've been MIA. It was either that or come over in the wee hours of the morning. It seemed a little douchie, even for me."

She felt a rash creep up her neck, remembering the time

she'd gone banging on his door to show him a pair of cargo pants and he'd rightfully assumed it was a booty call.

"How's that going . . . the surveillance?"

"Jack's got it tonight, but let's not talk about work." He rubbed the toe of his boot against her calf and she shuddered.

That must've been why he was having a glass of wine, Delaney thought. He wasn't on call tonight, a rarity on a Friday. And how was it that she'd come to know his schedule so well?

"I guess you've got the night free?" she said.

"Yep." He hitched his brows again. "Like I said, I've got plans."

"Do share."

"It'll start with me taking off that dress." He nudged his head at the bodice, making a big production of staring at her chest . . . her puckering nipples.

"Then what?" She pressed her thighs tightly together to stem the tingling between her legs.

"Then I'm going to take my time looking at you." He put his hand under the table again, pried her legs apart, reached up until he touched the layer of ruffles on her panties, and grinned.

"Then what?"

"You know what." He winked.

The waiter arrived with a big tray and took forever putting it on a stand and serving each plate with a flourish, chattering endlessly about the black truffles on Colt's risotto. At this point the only thing she was hungry for was Colt, so she tuned the server out until he left.

Colt tucked into his food like a starving man and when he caught her watching, said, "What? I'm gonna need my strength."

Yes, you are. So sexually worked up she could barely see straight, she tried to eat her chicken. This meal would put a big dent in Colt's wallet and she didn't want to waste it, even though she couldn't wait to get home and have him do all the things he said he would.

"You like it?" he asked.

"Delicious. Would you like to try some?" She held a fork-ful of the coq au vin to his mouth and watched him devour it.

"Mmm, good. You want to try some of this?" He gave her a taste of his creamy risotto, which melted in her mouth.

"Wonderful."

They continued to feed each other across the table, probably annoying the rest of the diners. Away from Glory Junction, Colt was more flagrant with his affection and she was too wrapped up in him to worry about decorum. They were entitled to a romantic night out and it wasn't as if they were sucking each other's toes.

"Delaney?"

"Huh?"

He took a visual stroll over her dress . . . her body, his eyes narrowing. "Hurry up and finish."

Thank the Lord Jesus. "I'm stuffed. We can go anytime."

He flagged over the waiter and asked for the check, not bothering to look at it when it came, just shoving his credit card at the poor man. As soon as the server returned with the receipt, Colt wrote in a tip, signed the bill, and pulled Delaney out of her chair. "Let's go."

They got as far as the lobby door when he suddenly turned around and steered her to the reservation desk.

"What are you doing?" she whispered.

"Getting a room." He whipped out the same card he'd used to pay the bill and slapped it on the counter. "Just give us whatever you've got."

It was a king suite for nine hundred dollars. Delaney gasped.

"This is crazy. Here, put it on mine." She rummaged through her purse for her wallet. When she raised her head with her credit card in hand Colt shot her a look, one that said, *don't you dare*. She quickly put the Visa away.

The reservationist gave them key cards and asked if they needed a bellboy for their luggage. The young woman wasn't the sharpest tool in the shed.

"I've got it." Colt practically shoved Delaney toward the elevator.

When they got inside and the doors shut, she said, "You're insane. Nine hundred dollars!"

He pinned her against the wall and kissed her. "Shush. Don't be a buzz kill."

His mouth and tongue tasted like chardonnay and melted her insides as he licked inside her. She clutched his shirt, trying to hold on and stretch up to his height to take the kiss deeper. Even with her three-inch heels she was a good six inches shorter than him.

The door slid open and they stopped kissing long enough to find their room and jam the key card in the door. They got just inside the threshold when Colt unzipped the back of her dress.

"Very pretty but it's gotta go."

She let it slither down her body and stepped out of it. He leaned against the wall, slowly took her in from head to toe, and let out a low whistle. Then he reached out and yanked her against him while she wrestled with his belt buckle.

"Slow down," he said. "I want to look at you some more." He gazed down her bra and she felt him grow harder against her belly.

"I want your clothes off." She untucked his shirt from his jeans, and he chuckled.

"Demanding, aren't you?"

"Why should I stand here half naked if you're going to stay fully clothed?"

He conceded her point with a bob of his head, then traced the lace on her bra with his finger. "I like this. And this." His hand moved to her matching lace panties and he rimmed the elastic waist with his thumb, dipping in just low enough to tantalize her but not enough to stop the pulsing between her legs.

"Colt?" She let out a moan as he started to slide his hand lower. "Please."

"Please, what? Tell me what you want."

"You know what I want," she said, her words coming out in halted breaths.

"Say it," he whispered in her ear. "Tell me."

She shivered as he continued to touch her. Colt pushed her against the wall, got down on his knees, slid her panties down her legs, nudged her legs apart, and kissed her so deeply she lost her mind. And her balance.

"I've got you, baby." He clasped her hips in his large hands. "Tell me what you want."

She couldn't breathe, let alone talk. What he was doing felt so good. He ran kisses up and down the inside of her thighs, teasing. She tangled her fingers in his hair and guided his head . . . his wonderful mouth . . . to the place that quivered for him.

"This? You want this?" He delved his tongue in deep, making her cry out something nonsensical and slam her hands against the wall for purchase.

"Yes," she said as he tortured her with that clever mouth of his. Sweet, sweet torture. "Colt, Colt."

She felt herself clench and shudder as he brought her to climax. It seemed to go on forever, her entire body shaking, her legs wobbling, and her heart pounding. Colt lifted his head to watch her.

"Good?"

She tilted her head back against the wall, shut her eyes, and tried to catch her breath. "Mm-hmm."

He got to his feet, picked her up, and carried her to the bed, where he gently laid her down. She heard his boots drop to the floor and the swish of his pants followed. Lifting up on her elbows, she watched him undo the first few buttons on his shirt, give up, and drag it over his head. He stood there in nothing but a pair of black boxer briefs that barely contained his arousal. In under a second he shucked the shorts, too. He grabbed a foil packet from his wallet and tossed it onto the side table. And then he was on top of her, kissing and fondling her breasts. The hairs on his chest tickled as he moved over her, touching and licking until she burned and begged.

She felt around for the condom, found it, and ripped it open with her teeth. Impatient, he took it from her and rolled it down his thick length. Then in one fluid motion, he entered her and slipped both hands under her bottom so he could go deeper. She folded her legs up to take all of him and began moving to his rhythm, matching him stroke for stroke.

He pumped harder and faster until all she could do to keep up was wrap her legs around his back and hang on. His mouth clamped onto her nipple through the thin lace of her bra and sucked as he moved in and out of her, the sensation so exquisite she thought she'd died and gone to heaven. Colt switched to her other breast, sucking and laving until she couldn't take it anymore. Her senses spiraled out of control, her muscles contracted, and she found her release.

Colt pumped a few more times, threw his head back, called her name, and shuddered. He lay there for a second, cradled in her arms, then swung his legs over the bed and disappeared inside the bathroom.

Delaney crawled under the covers. Without Colt's body heat the room had turned cold. She noticed that in their sex-driven haste, they'd forgotten to close the drapes. It appeared from what little she could make out in the dark that they had a view of the lake. And the mountains. She still couldn't believe Colt's impetuousness, but it made a smile bloom in her chest. He was spontaneous, generous, and adventurous.

And she'd fallen for him, hard, despite his efforts to shut her out. He'd made her rediscover herself as a woman, made her feel whole again, and safe. She kept coming back to that word. Safe. Safe to be who she was and not something she could never be. Safe to try something new. Safe to fail.

"What are you doing?" Colt came out of the bathroom unabashed in his nakedness. And why shouldn't he be? He was gorgeous.

Thinking about how you've changed me. "Recuperating. Considering enrolling in an exercise class to keep up with you."

"No worries there." He let his eyes wander over her. "You're in excellent shape."

She looked around the room. "We're staying, I presume."

"Hell yeah, we're staying."

"It's beautiful, but I feel bad that you spent all that money."

"Because you're a midwestern girl at heart with simple tastes?" Colt asked facetiously. "Or because you don't think I can afford it?"

"Because we live thirty miles away and nine hundred dollars is a lot of money on a—"

"On a cop's salary?" He stood at the side of the bed, putting on his shorts, which was too bad. She liked looking at him.

"On a whim. But yes, it's a lot of money on any salary." *Sensitive, much?*

"It won't cut into my beer budget." He plopped down on the bed and kissed her. "And for the record, I wouldn't have made it the fifteen miles. You do that to me."

"I do?" She still couldn't believe it.

"Come on, Delaney. You've got to know how beautiful you are, how desirable."

"Robert didn't think so." She stopped, suddenly appalled with herself. "Sorry. I'm not bringing him to bed with us. You're the only person I want to be here with."

He fluffed a pillow, put it behind his head, and stretched out next to her. "He told you you weren't beautiful?"

"No, he told me he wasn't attracted to me, that I was cold and sexless."

Colt snorted. "The guy's a worm and wears shrunken pants."

"Colt, I designed those pants."

"That's okay, you were probably drunk."

She shoved him but he didn't budge.

"Baby, you're smokin' hot. And sexless?" He jerked his head. "What planet does he live on? If what we just did a few minutes ago was sexless . . . maybe we should send him pictures."

Her face must've turned white, because he said, "Delaney, I was kidding." She remained silent. "Delaney, what?"

"He wanted me to sleep with other men." This was what she meant about Colt making her feel safe. She'd never told this to another living soul.

"While you were still married?"

She nodded. "He wanted us both to . . . him with other women."

"Like an open marriage?" Colt asked, and she wondered if the idea appealed to him, to all men.

"More like swingers, I guess. He thought seeing me with other men, and me seeing him with other women, would help him be attracted to me again. Save our marriage."

She remembered the first time Robert had raised the idea, the repulsion that had swirled in her stomach.

"Don't be so judgmental, Delaney. Plenty of couples are in the lifestyle, even people we work with."

She wondered how he knew that. It didn't seem like something anyone would advertise.

"We can start out slow. You could pick someone you're attracted to, have him over to swim in the pool or barbecue, and take it from there."

"You wouldn't be jealous?"

"No, because we would be doing it for each other. Watching another man get you off . . . it would make me happy, Delaney."

"Well, it wouldn't make me happy. In fact, the very idea of it disgusts me."

He looked at her for a long time, his eyes turning sad. "Then I'm no longer interested in being married."

And that was that. The next day, she moved out.

Colt turned on his side so he could look at her. "Did you try it?"

"No." While she wasn't one to denigrate another's lifestyle, sleeping with other men and other couples with her husband's consent was not her idea of a marriage. "He gave me an ultimatum and I chose divorce."

When Colt didn't say anything, she felt exposed. Even though the fashion crowd was known for being experimental, she'd been too embarrassed to tell any of her designer friends for fear that they would judge her. Find her lacking.

"Why?" she finally said, unable to stand the silence. "You think I should've done it to save the marriage?"

Colt sat up and folded his arms over his chest. "Call me old-fashioned, but sharing my woman with another man—never gonna happen. To me, it doesn't sound like a marriage worth saving. And Robert sounds like a prick."

Something in her chest fluttered like a caged bird that had been freed. Until now, she hadn't realized how insecure Robert had made her.

"Don't tell anyone." She sounded like a twelve-year-old.

"Never." He pretended to lock his lips with a key. "But, honey, you don't have anything to be embarrassed about. Any red-blooded man would be attracted to you, and in my opinion Robert was looking for a way to get you to sanction his screwing around without the risk of losing half the business.

This bullshit about strengthening your marriage by sleeping with other people—give me a break."

"Millions of couples share this lifestyle; I looked it up." She didn't know why she was being defensive. The truth was she'd had the same reaction as Colt. It had sounded like Robert wanted a license to cheat.

"I'm not judging." He raised his hands. "If both a husband and wife want to swing, if it's their thing and it makes them happy, that's their business. But for Robert to have told you that it would help him be attracted to you again . . . that's fucking wrong. Personally, I don't see how a man could let another man touch his wife. No way in hell would I."

The possessiveness in his voice sent a shot of warmth through her body. It was exactly how she felt. When you loved somebody, you didn't want them to be with anyone but you.

Chapter Eighteen

"That captain from the Fremont Police Department is back," Jack said in a hushed tone as he stood in the doorway of Colt's office. "He and Pond Scum came through here at about eight this morning."

"Were they looking for me?" Colt had gotten in late after taking Delaney home from the hotel, showering, and changing into his uniform.

"I don't think so. They went into your office, though. When I heard them I came to investigate and made it known that they shouldn't be in here. After that they left."

Colt thought they were probably taking measurements for Brian's new desk. "Thanks, Jack. Why are you here, anyway?"

"I had some reports to finish and thought I'd clean my office. Between the summer hordes and the burglaries, I haven't had time to organize."

Colt sniffed bullshit. Jack was hoping Carrie Jo would come in, which she often did on weekends to catch up. He let it go, though. No reason to embarrass the dude, who clearly had it so bad for their receptionist that he'd waste a perfectly good Saturday off.

"You hear from your friend yet at SFPD?"

"Crickets," Colt said. "I'll bug him again. In the meantime, it might be good to put some feelers out there. The sheriff's department or maybe even Nugget PD might have openings. If Brian comes in, he'll want to select his own assistant chief, someone loyal to him."

"I'm not worried about me, but I don't like the bloody injustice of it. You're an excellent chief, Colt, and you're getting shafted."

"Shit happens." He tried to sound nonchalant about it, but it would hurt. The bottom line: Colt loved his job and would hate to lose it. "I've got a pretty good safety net."

"You'd go full time at Garner Adventure?"

"Sure. It's probably time I shouldered some weight there anyway."

Jack snorted. "You shoulder plenty of weight. If I didn't know better, I'd think there were two of you."

"You're a good friend, Jack."

Jack started to go, then turned around. "If you don't mind me asking, what's going on with you and the fashion babe? She seems to have put a little pep in your step. It's nice."

Colt knew he'd been a downer since Lisa had left. "Don't know." He let out a breath. "I'm probably setting myself up for another heartbreak." Not probably—he was. But he couldn't seem to help himself where Delaney was concerned. He was like a kid who couldn't stop himself from touching a bright flame. The hotter it burned the more it beckoned.

"Why? She not into you?"

"She's into me." At least in bed. "Her business is in LA."

"So? That's not so far. She planning to split her time between both?"

"I don't think she knows yet. But when has the long-distance thing ever worked?" And eventually a wealthy fashion designer was going to get bored playing around with a small-town police chief. He could still see the expression on her face when he'd paid for the room at the Ritz. Yeah, that nine hundred bucks would set him back. But he'd do it again if it meant another night like the one he'd had with her.

"If you like her enough you'll make it work. At least she's being honest about her situation." They both knew he was talking about Lisa, who'd sworn up and down she was done with the music industry, but as soon as the first call came in she was off like a shot. "You trust her?"

He had no reason not to. She'd been a straight shooter from the get-go, but he didn't have any trust left in him. Not since Lisa took off and stole his song. Intellectually, he knew that he couldn't judge all women by her. But emotionally he couldn't seem to let his guard down, which made relationships difficult, if not impossible.

Everyone—everyone being his brothers—said he needed to confront his demons, but he didn't know how. Once bitten, twice shy.

They heard rustling in the bull pen and Jack turned to see what it was. "Carrie Jo's here."

Colt watched his friend light up. Poor son of a gun.

"Hey." She brushed by Jack and made herself comfortable on Colt's couch. "The whole gang's here."

"Pond brought that captain from Fremont back again," Jack told her.

She grimaced and turned to Colt. "Not good, right?"

He shrugged because what was he going to say? *Yeah, I'm getting shit canned.*

"Well, I've got a double whammy for you. 'Crazy about You' just got nominated for a CMA."

He did a double take, his first thought being, *Holy shit, my song is that good?* Then anger set in, swirling in the pit of his stomach like fiery acid. He would've given Lisa the damned song if she'd only asked. There was a time when he would've done anything for her. He told himself that he didn't care, that he didn't personally need acknowledgment—or fame.

Just knowing that the song was nominated was good enough. He could quietly celebrate the honor with a pint at Old Glory.

His cell went off, ringing and pinging all at the same time. He checked caller ID, saw it was Delaney, and picked up.

"Hey."

"Are you sitting down?" she asked.

"Carrie Jo already told me."

"My God, Colt, you're nominated for a CMA!"

"No, Lisa Laredo is."

Silence, then finally, "You have to speak up. Now is the time."

"We've already been over this and I've got company."

"Call me later then. I'm not through trying to talk some sense into you."

"Roger that." He smiled to himself. Lisa wasn't someone he talked about, not even with his brothers. But with Delaney he was getting used to it.

Jack had moved to the sofa with Carrie Jo. Both stared at him, curious.

"Who was that?" Carrie Jo asked. "It didn't sound like one of your brothers. You usually don't have a goofy grin on your face when you talk to one of them."

Colt glanced at his texts. His brothers had sent group messages.

Josh: You hear the news?
TJ: WTF?

Win sent a picture of Lisa with a drawn-on mustache. Classy.

"Colt?" Carrie Jo prodded.

"It was Delaney. Looks like the news is out." He put down his phone to give Carrie Jo his full attention.

"So it's true—you two are dating?"

He didn't know what they were doing, only that he'd

broken his own policy of not engaging in casual relationships with local women. But for the first time he wasn't going to overanalyze it. He was just going to enjoy it while it lasted. Until she left.

"Something like that," he responded. "Why don't the two of you go home and enjoy the rest of the day."

"I just came to get my blender."

"You juicing again?" Jack asked her as they both got up to leave Colt's office.

When they were gone he turned on his computer and searched the Country Music Awards. According to the Web site, the nominations had been announced Friday night and had made the news this morning. He scrolled through various headlines until he came to one about Lisa. She was thrilled and honored, the story said. Blah, blah, blah. How did Lisa look at herself in the mirror every day?

He closed out of the page and tried his former SFPD partner. Voice mail, so he left a message. Any intel Colt gathered wouldn't help him keep his job, but at least he could prepare his staff. He wondered whether Ben had examined his contract yet but didn't want to bother him on a Saturday. Whatever the paperwork said, Colt knew the mayor would find a loophole large enough to walk through. Pond was obviously high on this Brian guy to have him come up twice. Colt suspected the city was footing the bill, which meant the council had to know. Yet no one had said a word. Not even Rita, who'd been friends with his parents since the 1970s.

He spent a few hours doing paperwork, keeping his ear on the police scanner, and ignoring his brothers' constant texts. Thank goodness the three of them were guiding tours today or they'd be here, giving Colt a rash of shit for not calling foul on Lisa. He thought about his night with Delaney—how hot and spontaneous it'd been. For a woman who claimed not to be adventurous, she'd rocked his world. Her ex-husband was a pig. He didn't want to even think about what she'd told him about Robert.

At three he got called out on another burglary. Unlike the others, this involved an eighty-two-year-old woman with dementia, who'd mistaken someone else's house for her own. When the owners came home they found her napping in their bed. Thinking that she'd locked herself out, she'd managed to crawl through an open window. He'd gotten her home to her kids, who'd been ready to call the National Guard. One of the woman's daughters had been so grateful that she'd loaded him up with enough apples from her tree to feed a small country.

That's what it was like being the police chief of a small town. Best job in the world.

At six he went home, exhausted. He and Delaney had only gotten a few hours' sleep, which he wasn't complaining about, but he wanted to lay low and hoped like hell that he didn't get called out on anything. As he rummaged through his fridge, searching for something he could call dinner, someone tapped lightly on the door.

Delaney stood there, her hands full of take-out bags. He took them from her and ushered her in.

"From the Indian place," she said. "I hope you haven't eaten yet."

"Nope." He sniffed the bags. "Smells great. Thanks, I'm starved."

She went to his cupboards and started setting the table and he wondered when they'd gotten so domestic. Most nights he fended for himself or went to Old Glory. On the rare occasion when he had time, he dropped by his parents for a home-cooked meal. But a guy could get used to this.

"What did you do today?" he asked while she flitted around his kitchen, opening cartons and spooning them into what few serving bowls he had.

"I designed a dress." She turned around, leaned against

his tile counter, and beamed. "A gorgeous dress. A dress that will kick off a whole new couture collection. I'm back, Colt! Delaney Scott is back."

Lord, did she rev him up. Seeing her this way . . . so happy. He pinned her against the counter and kissed her. "Welcome back!"

"I think it's the sex. We have to have more tonight because I need to knock out a few more pieces."

"I'm willing to take one for the team . . . you know, if it'll help."

"Thank you. Very magnanimous of you."

"I thought so." His lips did a slow crawl down her neck. She smelled good, like that expensive perfume she always wore. "What about the outdoors stuff?"

"What about it? As soon as you guys test everything and I make whatever adjustments you deem necessary, I'm shipping it off to the manufacturer. Oh my God, Colt, I'll have two lines. *Two* lines. A few weeks ago, I had nothing." She wrapped her arms around his midsection and coaxed him into a little twirl.

"Food's getting cold," he said, and danced her over to the pantry, where he just so happened to have a bottle of wine. "If you want me to keep my energy up . . ."

"Yes, by all means, eat."

But he didn't want to let her go. Holding on, he maneuvered her to the cabinet with the glasses and got two down from the shelf, then balanced them in one hand and her in the other. "You mind getting the corkscrew?" He bobbed his chin at the drawer.

She got the opener out and he moved them toward the table.

"I guess we'll have to let go if we want to eat," he said, and bent down to kiss her nose.

"Okay." But she still had him around the waist, so they stood there for a while, just staring into each other's eyes.

Colt felt like a sap but he couldn't seem to stop. "You go first."

He pulled out a chair for her and gently pushed her down, switching his gaze to all the food she'd brought. Enough for an army. He took his own seat and scooped a little bit of everything onto his plate.

"Thanks. This'll hit the spot."

"I figured we needed to celebrate your nomination." She pierced him with a look.

"It's no big deal, and I'd appreciate it if you'd drop it. I've been harangued enough by my brothers."

"So you don't plan to out her?"

"What would be the point in that?" He felt like a god-damned broken record. "The damage has already been done. And I don't care about the money and I don't care about the fame."

"What about not letting Lisa Laredo get away with taking credit for your work? If someone stole one of my designs—"

Colt put up his hand. "Stop. This is not top on my priority list, Delaney. I've got bigger problems."

Her face dropped. "What? What's going on?"

"Pond waltzed that captain from Fremont PD around the station again. It's looking more and more like my days are numbered there."

"Oh no! Isn't there something you can do?"

"I'm checking my contract, but if he wants to get rid of me . . ."

"I'm sorry, Colt. You're a wonderful chief. The mayor has to know how popular you are. Getting rid of you will turn the whole town against him, and when he's up for reelection, I'll personally head up a group to campaign against him."

He appreciated the sentiment, he really did. "You won't be here, Delaney."

She was over her design slump, over Robert, over the moon about her new collection. Her Los Angeles house had sold and soon she'd need a new one. It didn't take a crack detective to see that her life was falling neatly into place and that there wasn't much in Glory Junction to hold her. Not even him.

She didn't contradict him, dashing any far-fetched hope that he was wrong.

"LA is not so far away," she finally said.

He was getting sick of hearing that. It was 486 miles, to be precise. A whole day by car and a half day by plane if he factored in the drive to the airport, the long security lines, and LA traffic. But more importantly it was a different world—a different galaxy—than the slow pace of Glory Junction. Soon, she'd have no reason to come back, especially when she didn't even ski.

"Nope," he said, and shoveled in a forkful of food. "Just a hop, skip, and a jump."

"What'll you do if you lose your job?"

"Work for Garner Adventure full time, I suppose. What else do you have in mind for this collection of yours?"

She frowned. "We're going to talk fashion now?"

Anything was better than talking about him. "I'm interested."

She gave him a look like she didn't believe him for a minute but launched into her plans anyway. "The concept is elegant mountain living with a little bit of adventure mixed in. I'm even doing cargo trousers. I wonder where I came up with that idea?" She went on to exuberantly describe the pieces she envisioned.

He had no idea what elegant mountain living looked like or if it was even a thing. But he loved hearing her talk, the way her face filled with animation as she described the fabrics and textures and colors she wanted to use. The way her very essence vibrated with excitement. It was the same way she embraced sex. All in. And, man, did it turn him on.

"Your eyes are glazing over," she said.

"No, they're not. I like hearing about what you're working on. And we forgot to toast." He raised his glass of wine. "To your new collection."

She clinked her glass with his. "To your CMA nomination."

Such as it was, he thought to himself.

"Come here." He crooked his finger. "Let's go upstairs."

Chapter Nineteen

"Put your hand there." Colt pointed to one of the grips as he stood on the gym floor, managing the other end of Delaney's rope in case she fell. "Thatta girl. You've got it."

"You sure I'm doing this right?"

"Yep. You're doing great." Especially for a beginner. At this rate, he'd have her on one of the tamer mountains in no time.

"I suppose this is easier than real life."

Colt got a kick out of that. "This is real life."

"You know what I mean. An artificial rock wall, instead of the real thing."

Colt shrugged as he watched her climb. "It's no joke. When my dad put it in, he wasn't messing around." Gray had made sure to overlay the colored grips to create different routes with varying degrees of difficulty. Even the most accomplished rock climber could find a challenging pattern on the Garner wall. "That harness too tight?"

"If it's not supposed to give me a wedgie, then it's too tight."

"Afraid there's no helping the wedgie. Keep your hips tight to the wall and push with your legs instead of pulling with your arms. You use less energy that way."

"Like this?"

"Yep." He nodded. "Pay attention to your route."

"Got it."

He continued to guide her while holding the rope. "Remember, the goal isn't to reach the top; it's to enjoy yourself."

She grimaced. "Reach the top? I'll be happy if I don't fall."

"You won't fall."

In the week since their stay at the Ritz, they'd spent every night together. He'd even managed to carve out time after work to take her on a few dates in Tahoe and Reno. Their new arrangement should've felt smothering but it didn't. It felt too good to be true, which it was. Because the clock was ticking. He knew it. She knew it. They just didn't talk about it, preferring to simply enjoy the time they had together. At least with Delaney, her pending departure wasn't out of left field, like it had been with Lisa.

The trick was preparing for the inevitable without losing his shit when it happened. Otherwise when Delaney went back to LA, he'd head straight to Yosemite's El Capitan and get stupid, free-soloing the sheer granite mountain. But today they were here, climbing with ropes and doing the no-strings-attached relationship thing.

This morning, after an hour of primo sex, Delaney had announced that she wanted to learn to rock climb. Colt suspected her sudden yen for adventure had to do with the athletic clothes she now designed. They'd grabbed breakfast, then wandered over to Garner Adventure to see if the coast was clear. The place had been empty—a rarity for a Sunday. But Colt figured everyone was out, conducting tours.

"Can I come down now?" she called from the center of the wall.

"Anytime you want. This was your idea."

"I know. But it's more exhausting than it looks." She started to make her descent.

"Watch your footing." Sometimes coming down was harder than going up.

He spotted her as she slowly retraced her footholds, getting an excellent view of her ass in the process. Outstanding in the stretchy pants she had on. "You okay?"

"I'm good," she said, out of breath.

When she got all the way down, he unhooked her rope and harness, lifted her in the air, and kissed her. "You're a pro."

She let out a girlish giggle that never failed to kill him. "You want to go up now?" Delaney eyed the wall.

"Nah. I liked watching you. Shower here or at home?" She'd worked up a sweat during their short lesson. He inched his hands up her bouldering shirt, feeling her slick belly and touching the underside of her breasts.

"Mmm." Delaney glanced over his shoulder and searched the gym. "Are we still alone?"

"Yep. Just the two of us. No telling how long that'll last, though."

Her lips turned up in a sneaky grin. "Want to shower with me?"

"Uh . . . at home. No way in hell are we doing it here." All he needed was for TJ or Win to walk in on them. Josh wouldn't be terrible. He was the one person in their family who could keep his mouth shut.

"No?" She bent over, picked up her gym bag, and did one of those model struts to the locker room.

Ah, jeez. He raked his hand through his hair, then followed her. "You're crazy, Delaney."

"A little bit," she said, locking the door behind them and immediately beginning to strip.

"This is a bad idea."

"Should we stop?" She damned well knew the answer. Hell no, they weren't stopping.

He helped her get her exercise bra off. Delaney's breasts were pure poetry and he didn't waste any time touching them, circling her nipples with his thumbs to make them pucker.

"That's good," she moaned, leaning her head against the door of the shower stall and shutting her eyes.

"What about these?" Her yoga pants. He hooked his fingers in the waist and pulled them down.

She walked out of them, leaving her in nothing but a thong. All curves and alabaster skin. God, she made him hot.

"Off with this." She rucked up his T-shirt and helped him drag it over his head, then pushed him back for a long, lingering look. "You have the best chest, Colt."

"Yeah?" He pulled her back into his arms and felt her full breasts press against him. "So do you."

He clamped his mouth over hers and kissed her so thoroughly he felt her knees buckle. He nudged her back against the door for leverage so his hands could wander. "I've got you."

She reached for the buttons on his jeans. "Off, so we can get clean."

He somehow was able to get his pants and shorts off at the same time as maneuvering her into the snug shower stall. She tugged off her thong, threw it over the door, and turned on the water.

"This too hot?"

"Huh?" He pushed her against the tile wall and rocked into her, letting her know what she'd gotten herself into.

"Colt? Condom."

"Uh . . . right." Lifted from his sex fog, he hopped out of the shower.

"Where you going?"

"To find one." He was almost certain there was a stash in the men's locker room.

"You're naked," she called as he unlocked the door and checked the gym to see if they were still alone.

"Be right back." He ran across the fitness center, zig-zagging around the exercise equipment, praying that no one caught him. They—his brothers—would never let him live it down.

Inside the men's showers, he tore the place apart looking for rubbers. Finally, he found two next to a package of old razors in one of the sink drawers and quickly checked the expiration date. Still good, thank God. He raced back to the women's locker room and rushed into the shower stall to find Delaney in hysterics.

"What's so freaking funny?"

"This"—she gestured at his nakedness—"running."

Well, it wasn't funny that he'd lost his hard on, which he planned to rectify. Immediately. "Be quiet and kiss me." He didn't wait, just covered her mouth and stuck his tongue inside.

"Did you relock the door?"

"Shush." He spread her legs apart with his knee. "No more talking until I'm inside you."

She wrapped her arms around his neck and pushed against him. He felt his erection spring back to life. Harder than before, and throbbing.

"You feel good," he said as he trailed kisses down her neck and reached around to hold her ass in the palms of his hands, pressing her tighter.

"You too." She reached down and stroked him and he felt himself jerk.

"Uh-uh. No more. Not yet." He moved her hand away, grabbed one of the condoms off the shampoo ledge, ripped it open, and rolled it down his length. Then he lifted her and slid in, moving in and out in slow motion.

She moaned and tilted her head against the tile as the water sluiced over them.

"Okay?"

"Beyond okay." She wrapped her legs around him and he increased the pace.

He pressed her deeper against the wall so he could pump harder. "This hurting your back?"

"Don't stop" was her only answer.

"I don't want to hurt you, Delaney."

"You won't." She clung to him as he continued to drive into her. "I'm so close."

She moved with him, closing her eyes. He let the rhythm of their pulsing bodies take him away, urging her higher and higher. Her lips dragged across his shoulders as her breath rose.

With the water washing over her body and her dark hair tangled in a wet mess, she looked so damned beautiful he nearly lost his mind. He watched her come apart in his arms and something jackhammered in his chest. Pride that he could fulfill her like this. A fierce possessiveness. Hell, he didn't know what it was . . . whether he even liked it. It made him feel like he was losing control.

As she called out his name, he took his own release. His orgasm was long and powerful, coming in waves that made him shudder and grunt. They just stood there for a while, entangled in each other's arms until finally he shut off the water. The cool air formed tiny bumps on her skin.

"You cold?"

"A little bit. But I like it like this." In his arms.

He picked her up and carried her to some shelves where there were towels, put her down, and wrapped her in terrycloth. "Better?"

"Yes, thank you." Her blue gaze held his. "That was intense."

"Yeah. It always is with us. . . . I mean the sex."

"Right," she said. "The sex."

He didn't want to talk about it, so he kissed her instead. Long and deep, making his heart kick. She laced her hands around his neck and he let the kiss go on and on, partly because he didn't want to let her go and partly because it was easier than exploring a truckload of feelings he didn't want to have. And she tasted good. Like heaven.

"You hear that?" She lifted her head to a voice coming from one of the back offices.

"Shit!" It was either his dad or one of his brothers. "Hurry up and get dressed."

"No one will come in here, right?"

Only his mom but she'd gone to Reno. "No, but we need to get out of here."

She started to laugh again, covering her mouth so no one would hear her. He couldn't help it and laughed too. They huddled together, to keep from collapsing in hysterics.

"Seriously, we need to get dressed," he said.

It took them more than a few minutes to find their clothes and put them on. Colt put his ear to the door, hoping that whoever it was had left. No such luck. By his count at least two people were out there.

"I'll go and distract them while you sneak out the side door," he whispered.

"Don't you think you're being ridiculous? Why don't you just tell them the truth?"

"That we were having sex in the women's locker room?"

"No, of course not. That you were teaching me how to rock climb."

One look at them and his brothers would know instantly what they'd been doing. He eyed the frosted window in the corner and wondered if Delaney could fit through it. That is, if he could manage to pry it open without making a lot of noise. Too tight for him, but she was much smaller.

"Don't even think about it," she said, watching him size her and the window up.

He shrugged. "Just an idea."

She did an eye roll, then wiped the steamed-up mirror with the towel and finger combed her hair, deftly swooping it up and clipping it with one of those barrette things. When she started for the door he grabbed her arm.

"What are you doing?" he asked.

"Going out and saying hi to whoever it is."

"Let me go first. Wait about five minutes, then you come out." It would look pretty bad otherwise.

"Whatever," she said, plainly perturbed.

He made it halfway to the door and turned around. "Come here."

When she didn't move, he went to her and dropped a kiss on her forehead. "Thanks for rocking my world."

He walked to the door, opened it a crack, and peeked out. There was still time to salvage this as long as no one saw him coming from the women's locker room. The gym remained empty and the voices appeared to be coming from the lobby. He quickly darted out and stealthily went in search of whoever was there. At the front desk, he found TJ and Win dicking around on the computer.

"Looking for porn sites?"

TJ jumped. "What the hell? Don't sneak up like that." He gave Colt a sharp perusal, noting his wet hair. "You worked out?"

"Climbed the wall . . . with Delaney."

Win peered around his back. "Where is she?"

"Women's locker room. Showering, I assume."

"I didn't know Delaney climbed," TJ said.

"She wanted to learn so I gave her a lesson."

"I bet you did." Win snickered and Colt had a very real urge to punch him in the face.

"How are the adventure clothes coming along?" At least TJ had a one-track mind. Business. It was always business with him.

"You can ask her when she comes out."

"For two people who aren't seeing each other, you seem to see a lot of each other," Win said.

"We're neighbors."

"Hey." Delaney came strolling into the reception area, carrying her gym bag, looking about as innocent as a three-time felon.

"Heard you did the wall," TJ said.

And me, Colt thought to himself.

"Mm-hmm." Delaney turned pink, probably because her

mind had traveled the same route as his with the "did" comment. "Colt was kind enough to show me the ropes. I figured for the sake of the clothes, I should try some of this stuff."

TJ had the decency not to make an off-color remark, which was huge for him. "It's addictive. Pretty soon, you'll be one of us, an adrenaline junky."

"Highly doubtful, but it was a lot of fun." She adjusted the bag on her shoulder and Colt took it from her and put it on top of the counter.

"Colt's an excellent teacher," Win added with sarcasm, and flashed him a smarmy-ass smile.

"He is."

"Well, we better get going," Colt said, and glanced at his watch. "It's getting late and I've got stuff to do."

He grabbed the gym bag, put his hand at the small of Delaney's back, and guided her to the door.

"See ya," his brothers called in unison. Colt didn't have to look behind him to know that they were high-fiving each other. They were idiots but not stupid.

Chapter Twenty

Delaney spent her days in a creative whirlwind and her nights in Colt's bed. It was the most gratifying time of her life. After she had delivered the last of the samples, the Garner brothers had put the adventure wear through the ringer, wearing her pieces while kayaking, climbing, bouldering, windsurfing, and paddleboarding. They'd come up with a list of tweaks—a pocket here, a gusset there, a dart a half inch over—but nothing major.

Garments for her couture line had gone to the cutter and she was just waiting on samples. She'd begun sketching a second collection for a ready-to-wear line. Once again, she'd let the mountains be her inspiration, using a palette of muted colors. Moss, clay, wood, and winter white. Short, flowy dresses paired with hiking boots; suede skinny pants under long sweaters; cashmere tunics over leather leggings; and body-conscious angora cowl-necks. The pieces were rich and warm and Delaney's hopes soared that the collection would be a hit.

After their lovemaking, she would sit up in bed and show Colt her work. For a man who knew nothing about fashion, he had good instincts. Perhaps it was the musician in him, because he knew what flowed and what didn't, what worked and what tried too hard.

They'd argued more about the CMAs and forcing Lisa to come clean. Adamant, Colt refused to budge. At least the awards weren't until November, time enough for him to put it out of his mind.

While Delaney's career got a second wind, Colt's gasped for breath. It became more and more evident every day that the mayor wanted to replace him. Members of the city council had become surprisingly tight-lipped on the subject. Even the city attorney, who was supposedly Colt's friend, had clammed up, leaving him in an anxious state of limbo. Although he tried to remain blasé, she knew it was killing him. Garner Adventure would welcome him with open arms, but Colt's true calling was law enforcement.

At least she'd managed to distract him with her upcoming fashion show. Given more reflection, she'd decided to showcase all three collections, using GA as her venue. Glory Junction had, after all, inspired her new lines and she hoped that using it as a backdrop would be a marketing tool to entice investors. But there was so much preparation she didn't know where to start first, including coming up with a name for her label.

Colt and his brothers had begun building a set and stage. Karen had been charged with organizing the show. And in the next couple of weeks, Delaney's staff, sound technicians, and lighting crew would descend on Glory Junction. She'd already reserved rooms at two local hotels, including the Four Seasons, and made arrangements with the area's private airport for a chartered jet. The show would cost her an arm and a leg.

She only wished she had more time. But if Delaney wanted to be taken seriously, she had to follow Fashion Week's September schedule. Besides, the show would help secure investors. The sale of her house—the buyers had accepted her counter—would help a little. But she needed some of the proceeds to buy a new place to live. And LA real estate, even a condo, didn't come cheap.

Her phone rang, which it had been doing nonstop these days.

"Hi, Karen." Hiring her had been Delaney's best move yet, though Robert had been furious.

"I still think it's crazy to try to pull this off in two weeks but the models are handled. They're thrilled to be working with you again. Some did London's Fashion Week with Olivia and are still complaining about what a mean bitch she is."

Models, especially the big-name ones, were typically hard to please, regardless of the designer. "They whine, Karen, you know that."

"Well, I didn't, not until I worked for Olivia."

Delaney didn't have time to think about Olivia. She had her hands full with her own company.

"I'm glad you were able to get them." With Fashion Week, models were in high demand, traveling between Milan and Paris. "We have sound and lighting secured?"

"Check. But you haven't even had samples made for the ready-to-wear collection. You sure we're not rushing this?"

"I need investors, Karen. I'll make the deadline, don't you worry. You just keep doing what you do and we'll be fine." She hoped.

She clicked off with Karen and drove downtown to meet the girls and Foster for lunch. Their get-togethers had become a regular thing and Delaney enjoyed them more than she ever could've imagined. She grabbed a jacket from the backseat of her car and walked the half block from her parking space to Old Glory. A blonde sat at the bar, chatting up Boden. He waved to Delaney and pointed to the back of the dining room to where Deb sat.

"I took the liberty of ordering the buffalo wings," she said as Delaney took a seat. "Foster is running late, as usual."

"Where's Hannah?" Her purse and jacket were slung over the chair.

"Bathroom. At least the store is slow right now and she can linger over lunch. How about you? Things must be crazy."

Hannah returned and sat down. "What's crazy?"

"Trying to get this show together in such a short amount of time. My house manager called right before I left to tell me I'm nuts."

"You're not nuts," Hannah said. "Everything's coming together. I went over to bring Josh breakfast this morning and the stage is half done. It's going to look amazing. I've never seen TJ so excited. He thinks the partnership and the fashion show will bring a lot of press."

"I don't know about that." Delaney had been away from the LA fashion scene for a year. And holding the show in Glory Junction could be risky. Her PR people warned her that daring to be different might be misconstrued as a publicity stunt. "Was Colt there this morning?"

"No, he and Jack may have caught someone involved in those burglaries. It's supposed to be hush-hush, so don't say anything." Hannah looked directly at Deb when she threw out the warning, then turned back to Delaney. "You and Colt have certainly gotten cozy."

"He's a good friend." *He's everything.*

"The rumor is that Pond is planning to can him this week," Deb said, and both Delaney and Hannah gaped at her.

"You waited until now to drop that little bomb?" Hannah said.

Boden came over with a pitcher of iced tea and the three of them instantly stopped talking. "Did I interrupt some serious girl talk?"

"We were just discussing Colt," Deb said.

"The gossip that he's getting axed today?"

"We all knew it was only a matter of time," Deb said. "Pond's been introducing that cop from the Bay Area all over the place."

"The guy's a first-class weasel." Boden filled their glasses with tea. "Anyone hear from him . . . Colt, not Pond Scum?"

Everyone looked at Delaney. "Not a word. Should I call him?" She reached for her phone.

Truthfully, she wanted to run over to the station and make sure he was okay. Colt wouldn't like it, though. He was an island when it came to his own problems, remote and self-reliant. Case in point: the situation with Lisa. She and all the Garners agreed that the woman shouldn't be allowed to make millions off his song. But when Colt made his mind up about something he was unyielding.

"Nah," Boden said. "It could be a bad rumor. Why stir shit up?"

Good point, but she still intended to call him when she got home.

Foster rushed in. "Sorry I'm late. I got a last-minute gladiola shipment. I heard 'rumor.' What's going on?"

They told him.

"Yeah, I heard it too, from Rachel. She heard it from a teller at Wells Fargo, who heard from Pond's housekeeper. It doesn't look good. But hey, at least he's nominated for a CMA."

"The one Lisa Laredo, the wonder slut, is gonna get credit for," Deb said. The whole town really did know about Colt's song. "I say someone drops a dime to TMZ."

"Hey," Hannah interrupted, "this is a sore spot for Colt. He's got enough going on in his life right now."

Boden nodded his head as if he agreed. Despite the fact that Colt didn't let many people in, he had good friends. People who had his back. People who knew what a good man he was, honest, fair, and hardworking.

And she was so into him, it stunned her.

After lunch and against her better judgment, she swung by the police department. Carrie Jo sat at her desk, eating cottage cheese. Delaney surmised she was on another diet.

"You here to see the big guy?"

"If he's not too busy."

Carrie Jo got up, went to Colt's office, and popped her head inside. She returned a few minutes later. "Go on in."

Delaney had never been in his office before. Like his house, it was devoid of adornment. A dartboard, a Garner Adventure calendar, a few plaques and trophies, and a photo of Colt in his San Francisco police uniform with another officer. As far as personal items, that was it.

He sat at a metal desk with his feet up. "Hey, everything okay?"

"You tell me."

His expression turned quizzical. "Did I do something wrong?"

"There's a rumor going around that—"

"Yeah, Carrie Jo told me. So far, I'm still gainfully employed, but the day is young."

She tilted her head and looked at him, knowing that the self-deprecation was just a coping mechanism. Or a cover-up of his real feelings. "You don't have to be tough for me, Colt. It has to be awful. I'd like to beat some sense into the mayor."

His mouth curved up. "Unfortunately, I think he could take you. There's no sense getting myself worked up about it. The whole thing is out of my hands. How are the plans for the fashion show coming?"

"Crazy, but good. Hannah says your brothers are halfway done with the stage."

Colt nodded. "That's what I hear. I plan to go over later and help out. Drop by if you're not too busy."

"Okay. Maybe we could get dinner afterward."

"Sure." He got up from behind the desk, walked to the door, closed it, and pulled her in for a kiss. It was long and passionate and made her heart pound.

His phone rang and he eventually pulled away to take the call. She sat on the sofa, trying to assess if the conversation had anything to do with Colt's future on the force. He must've read her mind because he shook his head when she looked at him, her face a giant question mark.

"Hang on a second," he told the caller, muted the sound, and turned to her. "It's about the burglary case. I'll see you tonight?"

"Yep." Hitching her purse over her shoulder, she headed to the door, feeling a domesticity she'd never shared with Robert. And that was the bitch of it.

Chapter Twenty-One

By the following Friday, Colt still couldn't believe he hadn't been sacked. The rumors continued to swirl, each day Carrie Jo reporting the latest gossip twist about his future. No one at SFPD knew Brian, though a few of them continued to reach out for intel. Colt didn't delude himself into thinking that he was out of the woods. Firings tended to happen when you least expected them to.

As a distraction, he'd immersed himself in preparations for Delaney's big fashion show. TJ thought the show would turn Garner Adventure into a Fortune 500 company, which made the rest of them mock him to no end. Needless to say, everyone was excited, most of all Delaney, whose creative streak had come back with a vengeance. Despite putting the finishing touches on her designs, orchestrating a large-scale production, and dealing with potential investors, she still made time for him. They spent every night together and had even taken a Sunday to go on another white-water outing. Fall had arrived and soon the snow would come, not leaving many days left for river rafting.

She hadn't said anything about moving back to LA, but Colt wasn't delusional enough to think she'd settle in Glory Junction or that their relationship was anything more than a fling—her rebound after Robert. At least this time he knew what to expect and braced himself for her departure, never letting himself get too attached. That way when the time came, he'd deal with it like a man, not an adrenaline junkie.

Carrie Jo stuck her head in his office, pulling him from his thoughts. "Benjamin Schuster is here."

He could see fear in her eyes. Looked like the mayor had sent the city attorney to do his dirty work.

"I can tell him you're busy, to come back later."

Why put off the inevitable? "Send him in, Carrie Jo."

"Fine. But I'm quitting in solidarity."

"Don't do that. Let's get you another job first."

While she left to get Ben, Colt sat stiffly, ready to go to his own execution. Jack came in and shut the door.

"Ben can wait a few minutes," he said. Jack, a mostly jovial guy, breathed fire. "I just want you to know that you're the best boss I've ever had and that this whole thing is bullshit. Pond is a jackass and come reelection he won't have my vote. In fact, I'll actively campaign against him for whoever is running."

The words echoed Delaney's, which made Colt feel good. "Don't worry about me, Jack. Just take care of yourself. I'll be fine. The department will be fine." Though it felt as if he were giving his baby to someone else to raise.

Jack looked like he wanted to say more but thought better of it. "Drinks on me at Old Glory after work. I'll cover you tonight so you can get shit-faced."

"Thanks, Jack."

As he left, Jack ushered Ben in, scowling at the poor city attorney, who was just the messenger.

"Hey, Ben, come on in." Colt offered him a seat. "Carrie Jo get you something to drink?"

"I suspect that if I took a drink from Carrie Jo it would be poisoned. You have a loyal staff, Colt, which speaks volumes about your leadership."

Enough with platitudes. Colt wished Ben would just do it already. Rip the Band-Aid off.

"What's up, Ben?"

"I suppose you've heard the rumors." Ben squirmed uncomfortably in his seat.

"What rumors?" Even though Ben was only doing his job, Colt didn't want to make it too easy for him.

"You know what rumors. I'm not here to fire you, Colt. But it's imminent; Pond wanted it done a week ago. I'm stalling him because there's something going on that may save your job."

Colt leaned forward in his chair. "Like what?"

"Something I'm not supposed to talk about, something I've been putting off telling you because it's critical that this doesn't leak out." He had Colt's full attention. "The city council has hired a forensic accountant to look at the mayor's spending habits. It's all very hush-hush, as you could imagine."

Colt jerked his head in surprise. "Embezzlement?"

"Let's just say some numbers don't add up. Rita noticed the discrepancy. The woman might seem flighty with her nutty beef-cake calendars and her hundred and one projects, but she's sharp as a tack—and she's on your side."

Colt had wondered. The council had been so quiet in the last few weeks, he'd thought that they'd sided with Pond. This explained a lot.

"Why didn't you bring the police in?" he asked.

Ben leaned forward. "Given the fact that everyone in town knows Pond wants to fire you, the council thought it would be better to go with an objective outsider. But, Colt, we could be wrong about this. Pond may have an explanation for the inconsistencies."

"What about this Fremont captain Pond wants to hire?"

"You know he used to do security for Pond's company before he sold it?"

"The mayor said something about it. Why do you bring it up?" It wasn't unusual for cops to moonlight.

"If you were stealing from the till, wouldn't you want your own guy in the town's top law-enforcement position?"

Colt hadn't thought of it that way, probably because he wouldn't protect anyone who was breaking the rules. "You think that's what this is about?"

"I don't know and I really shouldn't be talking to you about any of this. I'm depending on you to keep it on the down low. Pond doesn't know we're looking at him and it would be better to keep it that way."

"No problem. How are you stalling him from pulling the trigger on me?"

"I've told him that we have to take various legal steps to protect the city from getting sued, which isn't altogether a lie."

Colt nodded. "Okay. Thanks for giving me a heads-up."

"I'll let you know where we're at when the dust clears." Ben got up, shook Colt's hand, and headed out.

Colt found Jack and a half dozen of his men and women gathered around Carrie Jo's desk, gazing at him with troubled faces.

"Someone die?" he asked.

Carrie Jo was the first to speak. "What happened?"

"I still have a job . . . at least for now . . . so you can all go back to work." Damn, he loved these people.

Carrie Jo launched herself at him with a big hug. "Thank the sweet baby Jesus. I'm still paying off my Nordstrom card."

Colt gave her a squeeze, knowing she would've quit on his behalf. Jack grinned and there was a lot of back slapping. He didn't have the heart to tell them that it wasn't over yet. That if Pond came up clean, Colt would be out of there faster than a bullet train.

That evening he went over to Garner Adventure. His

brothers, Delaney, Hannah, and Deb were gathered around the stage and catwalk they'd finally finished building in the center of the gym. Instead of covering the rock-climbing wall, Delaney wanted it as a backdrop, assuring everyone that with the proper lighting and special effects it would create a mood.

He didn't see it, but assumed she knew what she was talking about. He brushed her waist with his hands, hoping to appear casual. Despite keeping their relationship—or whatever you called it—private, he itched to touch her. Get her in a corner and kiss her blind.

She smiled up at him. "How was your day?"

He wanted to tell them what he'd learned from Ben but couldn't break his promise. The last thing he wanted to do was hurt the investigation.

"I wasn't fired, so there's that."

"I bet Dad knows a guy who could take care of Pond Scum." TJ made a gun with his fingers and pretended to shoot it.

"Not funny," Colt said.

But Josh thought it was and started to laugh. So did Win.

"Enough." Colt slugged Win in the arm because he was closest. "I'm the police chief. You shouldn't be saying shit like that, even in jest."

Someone rang the bell. Darcy must've locked the doors on her way out for the evening.

"That's Boden with the food." TJ crossed the room and let him in. Boden had some kind of catering cart filled with takeout. "Nice! Where'd you get that?"

"I've had it and never use it. Figured it would come in handy tonight."

Boden started unloading to-go boxes. "Dig in, everyone."

Colt grabbed a turkey burger for Delaney. If anyone noticed, they didn't say anything. He took a steak sandwich for himself and sat next to her on one of the lobby couches.

"Who's watching the bar?" he asked Boden between bites.

"I've got people." Boden sat next to Deb.

Colt looked over at Win to see if he'd noticed, but his brother was in his own little world. If he continued to move this slow, Deb was going to fall in love with someone else. Boden wouldn't be a bad choice. Despite his outlaw shtick, he was solid as they come.

They ate and afterward covered the catwalk with some kind of wet-looking vinyl tiles that Delaney had gotten. She'd insisted on hiring a company that specialized in building runways, but he and his brothers had balked at the idea. Their venue, their stage. The chairs were being delivered on Monday. And the special effects people were going to project ski slopes behind the catwalk. Colt had never been to a fashion show but this seemed like a pretty elaborate setup. Delaney appeared pleased with it, because every time he looked up from what he was doing she beamed at him. Her smiles turned him upside down. Everything about her did, and that scared the ever-loving shit out of him.

On the day of the fashion show, Delaney wouldn't let go of Colt's hand. She couldn't remember the last time she'd been this nervous.

"It's gonna be a big success," he told her, squeezing her gently. "Try to relax and enjoy everything you've accomplished."

"I have to go back there now and make sure the models are dressed. Where are you sitting?"

He maneuvered her behind one of the big curtains that hung from the ceiling to separate the audience from the backstage area and then drew her into a hidden corner. People were frantically running between the stage and GA's offices, which had been turned into dressing rooms.

"I'll sit wherever you want me to." He kissed her as the ensuing chaos swirled around them, and her worries temporarily melted away. It was just Colt and his big, broad shoulders, bolstering her, making her feel buoyant, even though only a moment ago she felt the weight of the evening pulling her under, like a drowning woman.

"In the front, so I can see you. Okay?"

"Okay." He lifted her chin. "You've got this. You're Delaney Scott. This is nothing, a walk in the park."

Right? The top fashion writers in the country were here. As soon as word had gotten out that she was unveiling three new collections—in a small resort town in the Sierra no less—the fashion world went on overdrive. London Fashion Week hadn't gone well for Olivia and the Delaney Scott brand. The critics called her ready-to-wear line tired and uninspired and her couture collection immature. There were a lot of comparisons to Delaney's past designs and how Olivia wasn't doing the house justice. The fashion press was a mercurial lot and could just as easily turn on Delaney as it had on Olivia. The worst part was she didn't even have a name for her new label yet. One of the fashion magazines had quipped that she was the artist formerly known as Delaney Scott. Surreal that she could no longer use her own name. But no way was she rushing in to adopt another one without a lot of thought.

Her marketing folks said not to worry about it. That by waiting, they'd get a second wave of press as soon as they announced the new name. In the meantime, they were just calling everything DS, which in her mind sounded too much like DK, Donna Karan. And knowing Robert, he'd probably drag her back to court.

"What if the investors don't like it?"

"How can they not? You're awesome, baby."

She smiled and hugged him tight. "Thank you. I . . . you're the best."

"Go do what you've got to do. If you need me, I'll be up front." He'd worn a pair of Colt Cargos and looked so fine in them her knees went weak.

She ran off to see what bedlam she'd find in the dressing rooms, bumping into Foster on the way. He'd done the arrangements for the event. Huge vases of tree branches and an assortment of white, green, and red flowers that Delaney didn't even know the names of. In Los Angeles, the florist would make a fortune; he was that good.

"One of the models is having a hissy fit. You may want to avoid her right now."

"Oh, Jesus." She took off at a run, ready to give her standard pep talk, which consisted of a lot of brown nosing, a promise of an extra grape with dinner, and finally: "If you screw up my show, you'll never work again."

By the time she got to the dressing room, the problem had been quelled. But one of the other models needed to be pinned. Her ski pants—a size zero—gapped at the waist. Delaney plucked a handful of straight pins from the cushion around her wrist and with a few strategic tacks, the pants fit like a second skin.

A dresser rushed in, trying to compensate for her carelessness. "Let me help with that, Ms. Scott."

"No worries. I've got it." Delaney looked up at the model. "Just don't breathe."

Surprisingly, everything else appeared quite organized. She credited it to her efficient staff, who'd been doing fashion shows with her since her internship at Marc Jacobs. As anxious as she was, being backstage before a runway show with the hiss of hairspray, the smell of cosmetics, and the hum of blow dryers was as familiar to her as the glamorous lifestyle Colt shunned. Yet, here he was. Cheering her on, knowing full well that the show's success would reopen the doors to her old world. A world he wanted no part of. Still, her happiness and victory was of paramount importance to him.

The knowledge of that stirred something in her chest, and that's when she knew. She loved him. Not like she had loved Robert, which had been more about mutual respect and building a business than it had been about passion and selflessness. This was different. This filled her heart to bursting.

"How we doing?" Karen came in, pushing past models in various stages of undress, carrying a clipboard, and wearing a headset to communicate with the stage manager.

"Okay, I think." Delaney took a deep breath. "Lots of big money here tonight." She wasn't sure if it was the press that had gotten them here or the opportunity of a working weekend in one of the most charming towns in California, but she'd take it.

"Good. That's what this is about. Everything looks great, Delaney. The shows going to be a big success."

"I hope so." Out of the side of one eye, she noted one of the dressers struggling with the zippers for the crampons on a pair of cargos. "Not like that, like this." She demonstrated.

TJ knocked on the door. "Everything okay in there?"

"We're good," Delaney called back. "Five minutes to show time."

"I'm gonna take a seat, then. Break a leg. Are you supposed to say that for fashion shows?"

She opened the door just wide enough to wedge her face through. "Sure. Why not? Keep your fingers crossed that this goes off without a hitch." Which would be a miracle, since there was always a hitch.

"Will do," he said, and headed to his chair.

"So all those Garner brothers are single?" Karen asked, staring over Delaney's shoulder to get a peek at TJ's ass.

"Josh is married and Colt . . . he's spoken for."

"But TJ—and what's the youngest one's name?—single?"

"Win. Yep, single."

"I'm getting a place in Glory Junction," Karen said.

The Garner brothers were certainly eye candy and enough to entice even a hard-core city woman to move to Timbuktu. At least on the weekends.

"Let's roll," Delaney announced, and left the dressing room, only to encounter several reporters and photographers milling around the hallway. A few flashes went off and

Delaney immediately slipped into her game face. Big smile, lots of feigned confidence.

"Thanks, Ms. Scott."

"You're welcome, Todd. You all get some food?" She'd had Rachel from Tart Me Up set up a feast in one of the back rooms. Lord knew the models wouldn't eat any of it, just copious amounts of Diet Coke.

A few members of the media nodded and a reporter she recognized from *Vogue* asked, "Will you be available for interviews after the show?"

"Of course." She glanced at her watch. "Time to move out."

Karen relayed the message to the male models' dressing room on her headset. They were starting the show with the adventure line and ending with the couture collection. Delaney followed Karen to the back of the stage where the models began to line up. They'd be able to stay there and watch the show on short-circuit TV while tending to any mishaps, including wardrobe malfunctions.

The director motioned for the lights to go down, except for a single dramatic spotlight that shined on the first model. Delaney could hear a hush fall over the crowd. Then the music went on and shards of colored light strobed across the stage. Pictures of ski slopes, mountains, rivers, and lakes flashed in the background. Even from the back, Delaney could feel the energy in the room. Granted, she'd packed the audience with locals who probably had never been to a high-end fashion show like this. Still, the mood was electrifying. She couldn't see Colt in the audience; the cameras focused on stage. She wished she could see the expression on his face. He'd been so instrumental in the line and helping her reclaim her creativity. In a lot of ways, he'd had more faith in her design ability than she'd had in herself.

"We're moving into the ready-to-wear," Karen whispered in her ear, and suddenly the music switched from Townes Van

Zandt's "My Proud Mountains" to Rascal Flatts's "She'd Be California," signaling the change in program.

"What do you think so far?" she whispered back.

Karen peeked behind the curtain, which Delaney had been too anxious to do. "I think we've got a hit."

They just had to make it through the rest of the show without any snafus. Of course, the press would have the final word. If they liked what they saw—fingers crossed—the money would come pouring in. The next ten minutes went so fast Delaney forgot to breathe. By the time her couture collection strutted up and down the runway, she was ready to hyperventilate. Next thing she knew she was hoisted up on stage to take her bow to a standing ovation. Someone whistled and she looked down to see Colt smiling up at her. His face was so reassuring, so proud, that she considered doing a swan dive right into his arms.

After the lights went on she was inundated by reporters and then VIPs who'd been flown in for the show, losing track of Colt, though her eyes constantly searched for him. It wasn't until the after-party that she saw him again. The entire Garner clan came and she immediately reached for Colt's hand, forgetting herself. He took it, raised her knuckles to his lips, and kissed them.

"You killed it!"

Her heart soared because she really had, and because it was the first time all day she'd had time to spend with him. "I missed you," *and I love you*, she almost started to say.

"Yeah?" He scanned the room and found his family shamelessly staring. "We have an audience."

"Is that so terrible? Don't you think it's time to take us public?"

"I'm going to get us something to eat," he said, and dropped her hand.

Apparently that was as big a commitment as she was going to get. A plate of food from the buffet line. Why couldn't he trust her? Instead of letting it ruin her night, Delaney decided that she'd give him time to see that she wasn't Lisa. That they could have something together, even with her design career.

She planned to talk to him about it when they got home. But that never happened. Her lawyer had been trying to get a hold of her all day with a dire message. The ruling had come in and she needed to do damage control.

Chapter Twenty-Two

It had been three days since Delaney had left for LA and all Colt had received was one lousy text. He got it—she had major problems. But it felt like shades of Lisa all over again. This was the way it started. Girl has career crisis, finds man to latch on to, then dumps him as soon as she resolves her professional problems.

It wasn't like he didn't have his own job issues to focus on. It had been a while since he'd talked to Ben and hadn't heard a word more on the subject. For all he knew Pond had been cleared and Colt's pink slip was in the mail. Still, all he could think about was Delaney.

The judge had issued a clarification, ruling that Delaney had to take "Delaney Scott" off all her existing merchandise, which would cost her a fortune. So much so that it put her company at risk until she could get capital. Luckily, investors had been impressed with her new designs, but she had to stop the bleeding before anyone would commit.

He knew she had a lot of meetings set up and planned to squeeze in house hunting. To his mind that meant she'd move back to Los Angeles. It made sense. She'd been away from the business end of her company for nearly a year. He suspected that this was a wake-up call to return to the mother ship.

"I lost six pounds." Carrie Jo came into his office and he blinked up at her.

"Yeah? Weight Watchers?"

"No diet, really. I cut my portions and have been walking in the evenings."

"You look good, Carrie Jo." She'd always been hot to him with or without the extra pounds.

She sprawled out on his sofa. "You in here feeling sorry for yourself?"

"What makes you think that?"

"Colt, I've known you since before you could drive. And for the record: I don't think Delaney is anything like Lisa."

"Who said she was?"

She snorted. "You're like one of Lisa's bad songs. One woman does you wrong and you think they're all alike."

"You saw that fashion show. Did you happen to notice the Who's Who list of people sitting in the audience? I don't exactly fit in with that crowd."

"No, you don't. And the little I know of Delaney, neither does she. She needs those people for her business, which doesn't necessarily make her one of them. From what I can tell, she fits in to this little town just fine. Her clothes may be better than the rest of ours, but there's nothing about her that's pretentious or snobby."

"Her company is based in Los Angeles."

"So? You'll both have to commute. Have phone sex. Or Skype sex. With technology the possibilities are endless."

He shook his head. "It won't work."

"It'll work if you want it to work, if you make it work, which means letting go of what Lisa did to you."

Colt didn't know if he could do that. She'd just walked away without so much as a phone call, not only taking a piece of his heart with her but eviscerating his trust. How do you let that go?

Josh popped his head into Colt's office. "I looked for your gatekeeper but I see she's in here."

Carrie Jo got up from the couch, squeezed by Josh, and cleared her throat. "Do you have an appointment, sir?"

"I don't need no stinkin' appointment." He came in and took her place on the sofa. The love seat got more use than Colt's couch at home.

"What's up?" Colt asked, noticing that his brother's limp was barely noticeable. That last surgery may have done the trick.

"We missed you for Sunday dinner at Mom's."

"I had stuff to catch up on."

Josh gave him a hard look. "You hear from Delaney?"

Colt hitched his shoulders. "I got a text from her Saturday night." And a missed call Sunday, which he never heard ring. "She's busy."

"I would imagine she is. Hannah says this could cost her millions."

"Yep." Colt nodded his head.

"But you think she's running away, like Lisa did?"

"Ah, jeez. I just got an earful from Carrie Jo. Enough, already. It's not like we were a couple. Whatever she wants to do is fine."

"Ah, that's bullshit, Colt. We can all see that you care about her."

He more than cared about her. This time he didn't know if a rash of cave diving, BASE jumping, and extreme skiing would fix the damage she could do.

"We truck in two different worlds," he said. "I knew that from the get-go, so it's nothing like Lisa. Don't you have a tour to guide, paperwork to do?"

Josh gave him another one of his penetrating army ranger stares. "You can lie to yourself all you want but you're not fooling me. I almost lost Hannah because of stupid pride. If Delaney is important to you, which I know she is, man up and make it happen."

Josh got to his feet and walked out. Good! Colt was tired of everyone telling him how to run his life. The clock on the wall said lunchtime and that's the only advice he had use for. He hauled his ass out of his chair and walked over to Old Glory for a burger.

The usual crowd was there, including Rita, who avoided eye contact with him. That couldn't be good. Colt took a seat at the bar. Boden came out from the kitchen and took his order. At least he had the decency not to ask Colt about Delaney, too caught up with the good-looking brunette filling out a job application.

Halfway through his burger "Crazy about You" came over the sound system. Just what Colt needed. Boden stopped talking to the brunette, opened a panel behind the bar, and the music suddenly changed to a Bruce Springsteen song. A couple of patrons grumbled. Colt bobbed his head at Boden and left without finishing his meal, his mind made up.

After returning to the office, he got on his computer, then went into Jack's office to ask if he'd cover him. Colt needed a few personal days. The next morning, he got in his truck and drove to Portland.

It took ten hours, but he made it in time to get to the Moda Center before the show opened. Tickets were sold out. He wandered to the back of the stadium, hoping to find a roadie or someone who had access to the talent. Eventually, he latched on to a security guard, whom he showed his police badge to. Pretty unethical, but it got him in the door.

He wandered the bowels of the center, looking for someone who seemed important enough to get him where he wanted to go. A couple of gaffers taped cords to the stage and he managed to get their attention.

"You know Gordon Richards?" he asked, and one of them

grunted in the affirmative but kept his eyes on his task. "Can you get him a message for me?" Once again, Colt flashed his badge. That got the guy's attention.

"Gordon's busy." The other one wasn't impressed. "Show starts in an hour, so unless you've got a warrant . . ."

"You want me to pull Lisa Laredo out and make a scene during the show?" he bluffed. "Tell Gordon that Colt Garner is here. That it concerns Ms. Laredo's future."

The stagehand got up and stood in Colt's face. "You know how many whack jobs have used that line in the past? Look, buddy, in ten seconds I'll have you thrown out on your head. Why don't you save yourself the embarrassment?"

"Colt?"

Colt's head jerked up, remembering that voice as if it were yesterday. She looked good, Lisa did. Thinner than he liked, but beautiful.

"You want me to call security?" the stagehand said, showing no surprise that the number-one country act in America was standing next to an empty stage in an empty room in a pair of faded jeans and a college sweatshirt.

"No, he's a friend."

A friend? That was a good one.

"Did you come to see the show?" she asked him, a hesitance in her voice.

"I came to talk to you."

"You could've just called." She shifted her weight from one leg to the other and Colt could tell she was nervous.

"Like I did all those other times when you first left?" She hadn't even had the decency to tell him where he stood.

"Colt . . . there's someone else now."

"Seriously, you think I'm here to get you back?" He laughed. "You want to do this now or in private? Makes no difference to me. I'd like to get on the road before traffic."

She shuffled again, clearly contemplating what to do. It

would be a little strange for her to call security after she'd told the gaffers he was a friend. "Come with me."

He followed her through a private hallway to a dressing room. The cloying smell from all the flowers gave him a headache. And under the good lighting he could see worry lines around Lisa's eyes and brackets around her mouth. Stardom had made her road-weary.

She sat at her dressing table and motioned for him to take one of the chairs. He preferred to stand but sat anyway so as not to tower over her. Someone knocked and she curtly told whoever was on the other side of the door to come back later. She seemed so brittle, like she could snap at any minute, and he wondered if she'd always been that way and he'd failed to see it.

Clearing her throat, she leaned forward in her seat. "How much do you want?"

He jolted at her bluntness, having expected her to play the woe-is-me card. "I want an explanation. I want an apology." Colt had also wanted to ask if she had ever loved him. But oddly, standing here, seeing her now, it didn't matter to him anymore because he felt nothing for her. Not even a stirring of nostalgia.

She glanced at her watch. "My hair and makeup people will be here soon. Name your price, Colt."

"You mean to shut me up? There's no price. Why'd you do it, Lisa? Why'd you steal my song?"

"You gave it to me." She actually had the gall to say it with a straight face.

"I wrote it for you. There's a difference."

A tear ran down the side of her face and she swiped it with the back of her hand. "I was desperate, okay? 'Lonesome Night' went platinum and I was finally a star . . . everything I had worked for. You don't know what that's like, Colt. Arenas filled to capacity with adoring fans. All the music executives, who before wouldn't give me the time of day, kissed my ass. Musicians I idolized wanted to collaborate. The fame—there's nothing like it. But I was going to lose it all, be relegated to a one-hit wonder without another hit. And 'Crazy about You' . . . Well, it was perfect for me."

"Did it ever occur to you that you could've asked me if you could perform it and give me a writer's credit? As the singer, you still would've gotten the glory."

"You were so angry with me, Colt. You would've said no just to spite me."

He was ashamed to admit it, but she was probably right. "So you took it and claimed it was your song?"

More tears ran down her face and a sob escaped her. "It's nominated for a CMA. If you out me now it'll ruin me. I'll never work in Nashville again."

He stared at her, finding it hard to fathom how she could steal from the person who loved her to get adoration from people she didn't even know. People who would drop her like a hot potato if she didn't get enough radio play. He tried to hate her, he really did. But all he could summon for her was pity.

"I'm not going to out you," he finally said, and realized that what he'd needed was to face her. Look her in the eye when she told him what he'd known all along. "You'll have to live with the lie while the people who care for me know the truth. At least give your next royalty earnings to charity."

With that he walked out of her dressing room, out of the arena, into the parking lot, feeling a cool blast of evening air and infinitely lighter than when he'd gotten there.

The condo was a short sale, which meant Delaney could get it for a steal. At least for Venice Beach, where real estate cost a bundle, especially a home set on the beach. It had endless windows of white-water views, twenty-four-hour concierge service, a master closet as large as Hannah's shop, and was less than seventeen miles from her warehouse. Karen had a lead on an office building that could serve as corporate headquarters and studio space only a few minutes away.

Walking through the modern apartment, appreciating the gleaming hardwood floors, she took a moment to exhale. After back-to-back emergency meetings over the last four days it looked as if the publicity from the fashion show may have saved her ass as far as the court's appalling clarification. Her marketing people were confident she could simply change the labels on her Delaney Scott shoes and handbags and still keep the same price points as long as the consumer knew she was the designer. Of course, the labor involved would be a major financial hit. The whole fiasco had convinced her it was time to move into the role of running her business.

Hiding out in Glory Junction, leisurely working on her designs, had been a luxury she simply could no longer afford. It was time to focus. Time to name her company and time to come back to the real world.

"For this price, it won't stay on the market long." The real estate agent's voice echoed across the empty living room.

Delaney nodded, knowing the truth of that statement. "I'd like to at least sleep on it." And call Colt. She needed to tell him what was going on.

When she reached him that afternoon from her hotel room it was on his cell and she could hear road noise in the background. "Where are you?"

"Driving home from Portland."

"Oregon? What were you doing there?"

"Long story," he said. "How's it going in LA? Will you be able to recuperate from the setback?"

"I think so, as long as the investor money comes through. I looked at a condo today."

He was quiet, then finally said, "Yeah, I figured you'd do

that. Are you even coming back?" She heard the tension in his voice, but they'd talked about this. She'd always been upfront about returning to Los Angeles.

"Of course I am," she said.

"Right. I guess I'll see you whenever."

"Colt, you're acting childish. I hoped we could have a real conversation about this, work something out."

He let out a sigh. "You like the condo?"

"It's beautiful." But it wasn't Glory Junction. In the year she'd lived in the little town it had become home. While the condominium was luxurious and conveniently located, it felt like a hotel. And without Colt—not to have him there every day—she would feel an enormous void. A void that would break her heart.

"Does it have good security? What kind of neighborhood is it in?"

"It's safe, Colt. Would you like to see it? I could send you a link."

"I'm driving, but yeah, send me a link."

"You don't want to tell me why you went to Portland? Does it have to do with work?" She assumed it had something to do with a criminal investigation.

He hesitated, then said, "To see Lisa. She had a show there."

Delaney had trouble swallowing as she sucked in that piece of information. A lot of emotions hit her all at once. Jealousy being the predominant one. "Why?"

"I confronted her about the song."

Delaney let out a *whoosh* of relief. It was good that he'd done that, part of the healing process. "Is she going to give you the credit you deserve?"

"I don't care about that, Delaney. I just wanted her to know how I felt about it, what kind of person it made her in my eyes. It's done now. I can move on."

She wondered if moving on included them. Could he trust

her with his heart? Too afraid to ask, she said, "How far are you from home?"

"About an hour away. I took my time, drove down the coast, stopped at Redwood National Park."

"It sounds wonderful." But how had he had the time? Her stomach dropped. "Colt, you didn't lose your job, did you?"

"Nope. Not yet. Jack covered for me. When will you be back?"

"I don't know yet. The business . . . I have to get serious, Colt. I let things go too long. It's time to take the reins."

"Okay." He sounded disappointed but at least he wasn't being unreasonable. "I'll see you when I see you."

"Don't say it like that. It sounds defeatist."

"I say it like I see it, Delaney. I'll call you tonight after I look at your condo link."

He hung up and she suddenly felt lonelier than she ever had before. In a city of nearly four-million people, how was that even possible? But an emptiness spread through her, making her incredibly melancholy. Homesick, she supposed. For Colt Garner.

The front desk called, letting her know that Karen was waiting in the lobby. She took the elevator down and found her smartly dressed house manager on the phone. Karen gave her the one-minute sign and Delaney turned her attention to the small café in the lobby. She hadn't had lunch and only a cup of coffee and half a muffin for breakfast. There hadn't been time.

"That was Fran." Karen dropped her phone in her purse. "She said the reviews from the Glory Junction show continue to dazzle. The press loved all three collections, but the adventure wear . . . they're crazy about it. We're getting calls from buyers who want to stock it, stores that don't even have adventure-wear lines."

Given how much work Delaney had put in to making the pieces functional for outdoor sports enthusiasts, she thought it funny that retailers would sell them strictly as street clothes. Then again, look how fashionable yoga pants had become. Delaney called them the new mom jeans.

"I have to talk to TJ about that. My guess is that Garner Adventure is going to want exclusivity."

Karen shot her a get-real look. "You know how much money we're talking about here?"

"A deal is a deal. Can we eat, Karen? I'm starved."

Karen glanced at her watch. "We've got thirty minutes until our appointment to see the building. In traffic, it'll take forty-five. Your call."

Just the memory of LA traffic gave her hives. "Fine. Afterward, though, we're eating."

"We've got an appointment with your warehouse manager at four and that's clear across town."

She missed being able to walk everywhere. "I guess I'll just starve then."

They walked to the front of the lobby and Karen gave the valet her name. While they waited for the car, Delaney peeked at her phone, hoping that Colt might've had time to look at the link she'd sent him. Maybe the condo and its ocean-front access to world-class surfing would entice him to see the benefits of a long-distance relationship. Of course she didn't know when he'd ever get a chance to come, since he was stretched so thin as it was. And if her days were anything like they'd been this week, she'd be lucky to find the time to e-mail him. The reality was so depressing, she lost all enthusiasm over seeing the building. The building that by all accounts would be perfect and just happened to be available during a commercial real estate shortage.

The valet parked Karen's car at the curb and helped both of them in. As Karen predicted, they barely made their appointment due to the stop and go on the freeway. An agent took them through the building, painstakingly showing them every inch of space. It needed work, especially the front facade and the lobby, which hadn't been updated since the nineties. But it wouldn't take much. Exterior paint and maybe a chic awning with her company's logo. Yeah, she needed to get one of those, along with a name. She'd change the flooring in the reception area from marble to something a little warmer, maybe do a television wall where they could loop video of her various collections. Plenty of room for possibilities, she told herself.

But her heart wasn't in it. It was too busy pining for Colt.

"What do you think?" Karen asked softly.

"It'll definitely work." So why wasn't she more excited? The prospect of finally getting her act together should've been thrilling and not filling her with dread. "Everything's moving so fast, though. Would it be terrible if I took a day or two to think about it?"

"I'd hate for us to lose it," Karen said. "But you need to be sure that this"—she spread her arms wide to encompass the building—"is your vision."

What was she doing? Of course it was her vision. The location was superb; the price was right. *Just bite the bullet*, she told herself.

"You know what? I'm being a wuss. Let's do it, Let's sign the lease and put down a deposit."

"Okay," Karen agreed, and went off to search for the agent.

Delaney wrote a check and the agent said he would send the lease agreement to her lawyer for signing. It was done. And tomorrow she'd make an offer on the condo.

Chapter Twenty-Three

Colt returned to work on Tuesday to find the Nevada County district attorney, a state deputy attorney general, and Ben in his office.

"What did I do now?" he joked.

None of them appeared amused, and for a second, a tremor of apprehension went through him.

"Looks like we've got us a Bell situation," the DA, Mack Goodright, said.

When Colt returned a blank stare, Ben said, "That small city in Los Angeles County where the city manager and six other officials were convicted of graft and corruption for misappropriating funds."

"Only in this case it's just your mayor," Mack said. Colt had known the DA for years and he was a straight shooter.

Colt looked from Ben to the deputy AG, whom he hadn't yet been introduced to but knew by face. "How bad is it?"

"At least a hundred thousand as far as we can tell," Mack said, and Colt let out a low whistle. "Your city manager noticed some discrepancies, told Rita Tucker and Ben. They called in a forensic auditor. Pond's basically been using the city coffers as his own personal bank account, bankrolling work on his ranch, five-star vacations, a fancy country club membership."

Colt didn't have to pretend to be surprised—he was. A hundred thousand bucks! When Ben had initially mentioned it, Colt thought it would be penny-ante stuff. The cost of a hotel room for one of his liaisons, a few unauthorized cab rides, a restaurant receipt that had nothing to do with city business. But this was huge. And bad. Glory Junction might be a wealthy town with its ski resorts, but an elected official ripping off taxpayers . . . the city would be dealing with this for years to come.

"Has he been arrested yet?" Colt figured they would've brought in the sheriff or state police since GJPD was under Pond's purview and prosecutors wouldn't want any appearance of impropriety.

"You don't have anything to do with this," Mack said. "Believe you me, we went over every city worker with a fine-tooth comb. So we'd like you to do the honors."

"I'd be glad to." Because arresting Pond would make his day.

The next few hours passed in the blink of an eye. He and Jack went to city hall, cuffed Pond, and read him his Miranda rights in front of a growing crowd of city workers and council members. A sheriff's deputy carted his ass to Nevada City, where he languished in jail until his attorney bailed him out. News crews from as far away as San Francisco descended on Glory Junction. Pond's ties to Silicon Valley made for an intriguing angle for reporters.

Colt spent lunch regaling his brothers, Carrie Jo, Hannah, Deb, Foster, and Boden with the look on Pond's face when he and Jack told him he was under arrest.

"This means your job is safe," TJ said.

"Hear, hear. Let's drink to that." Boden filled everyone's glasses with the bar's latest microbrew. Colt and Jack were still on duty, so they refrained.

"Yep," Colt said, his thoughts wandering to Delaney, wondering if she'd made an offer on that condo. Swank place, he had to admit. At least according to the pictures. He'd scrolled through them after he'd gotten home from his road trip, tried to call her, but got voice mail instead.

He missed her and had stared out his window at her house much of the night, waiting for that obnoxious bright light in her studio to come on before she pulled down the shade. She'd left her car in the garage, leaving the easement space for him. He hadn't parked in it once, hoping that the damn Tesla would magically appear.

"Ready to go back?" he asked Jack and Carrie Jo. They'd spent enough time yucking it up; there was work to be done.

"Let's go." Jack slapped Colt on the back, happy as hell to know they'd both dodged a bullet. Their jobs were safe.

More than likely Pond would be forced to pay restitution to the city and Glory Junction would get a new mayor, possibly Rita, who was already making noises that she was interested in the position.

It had been a great day and at the end of it Colt quit his job. Gave his notice in a neatly typed letter of resignation and hand delivered it to city hall.

Delaney took a red-eye to Reno and hired Uber to drive her the thirty-five minutes to Glory Junction. It was too late to call Colt. The trip had been impulsive and last minute and all she wanted to do was get home. Home, the best word in the world.

The driver got her carry-on out of the trunk and carried it up to Delaney's deck. She thanked him, waited for the car to drive off, and unlocked her front door. Colt's police car wasn't parked on the pad, so she gazed at the top of his drive-way. Not there either. Perhaps he'd been forced to respond to an emergency as he so often was. They'd been missing each other's phone calls all day, giving Delaney yet another glimpse of life without him in LA. She pushed her suitcase through the entrance and left it in the hallway, too tired to carry it up the stairs.

The only incentive to climb them herself was a pair of comfy pajamas and her king-sized bed. Today had been excruciating, starting with the hour she'd spent in traffic while trying to get from her warehouse to the condo she wanted to buy. By the time she returned to the Biltmore, she craved a stiff martini and Colt. The hotel bar had been happy to accommodate her with the former. She'd been hit on by obnoxious men a dozen times while sitting in the lounge, sipping her drink. And then it struck her: she could go home. Wake up next to Colt in the morning.

Delaney let out a sigh of disappointment and called him again, only to get his voice mail. "Surprise! I'm home but you're not. Don't get all Chief Hottie from Hell on me, but I left the door unlocked for you. Wherever you are, stay safe and come back soon."

She got in the tub, took a long soak, and put on the softest sleepwear she had. Five minutes after hitting her pillow she fell sound asleep. In the wee hours of the morning, something bristly rubbed the side of her cheek.

She swatted at it, murmuring, "Go away." It was probably just a porcupine. The thought filtered through her muzzy head and then she jumped. Porcupine?

"Hey, hey, it's just me," Colt whispered in her ear. "Chief Hottie from Hell?"

She sat up, trying to get her bearings, then giggled, still sleep induced. "That's what I used to call you."

Two dark brows shot up. "Chief Hottie from Hell? That's not a compliment, right?"

"It sort of is." She looked at him to make sure he was in one piece. "Did you get called out on something bad?"

"Nah. Mr. Finkelstein's car got stolen again." Colt rolled his eyes.

"In Glory Junction? Really?"

"It wasn't stolen. He lost it, but that's a story for another day. Why didn't you tell me you were coming back?"

"Last-minute decision. Plus, I couldn't reach you all day. It must've been busy."

"You don't know the half of it." He pulled her back down, kicked off his boots, and cuddled her in his arms. "I arrested Pond Scum on public corruption charges." Colt told her the details.

"A hundred thousand dollars?" She gulped. "Holy cow. Well, good riddance. After what he did to you, the jerk got what he deserved. Thank goodness your job's safe now."

"Yeah, about that . . . I need to talk to you, Delaney."

She turned on her side so she could face him. Running her fingers through his hair, she said, "You don't want to wait until morning?" Truthfully, she was afraid of what he might say.

"Nope." He took her hand away and held it. "I gave the city my resignation today."

"What?" She popped up like a jack-in-the-box. "Why, Colt? You love your job."

"That's the thing, Delaney. I love you more."

"You do?" The words stunned her because he'd never said them before, not even in the throes of intimacy. He didn't even want anyone to know they were seeing each other. "This is a sudden about-face."

"Not really. I think I've loved you since that first night you banged on my door with a pair of cargo pants in your hands." He pulled her back down, tucking her head under his chin. "I'll admit I'm not the best at expressing myself, or at relationships. I have trouble with trust, trouble with opening myself up, and trouble with compromise. But I'm working on it because more than anything in the world I want you and me to be together, and we both know how difficult that will be if we're living clear across the state from each other."

"But, Colt—"

"Let me finish. By leaving the department and working full-time for Garner Adventure I can make my own hours. TJ's swamped with administrative work and this way I can help him, even telecommuting. I'll have to come back to conduct tours, but at least I'll be able to split my time between here and LA. Otherwise we're doomed, Delaney, and I want to fight for this relationship. For us."

A tear leaked from her eye and trickled down her cheek. He wiped it away with his thumb. "Tell me I'm not being presumptuous or making a fool of myself, here."

She put his hand on top of her heart. "Feel that? It's all for you. I love you, Colt. I love everything about you. The way you take care of this town, your family, and me. The way you cheered me on and helped me find my confidence again. But we've got a slight problem."

He went instantly rigid.

"I'm not moving to Los Angeles. It won't work for me."

"Where then?" he asked. "New York will be more difficult but—"

"Glory Junction," she blurted. "I got my deposit back on the office building. I have this crazy idea that maybe I can run the company from here."

He sat up and rested his back against the bed's headboard, and she could see the wheels spinning in his head. "What about your warehouse and your employees?"

"My designers can work anywhere and Karen is willing to move. With the sale of the LA warehouse, I could afford to build one here, if I could find the right property."

"But will it be good for your business?" He sounded dubious. "I don't know, Delaney."

She joined him in an upright position and wound her arms around his neck. "It's going to be good for me and I am the business. LA doesn't feel like home anymore. I hate the traffic, the smog, the crowds. This is where I feel most comfortable. Right here in Glory Junction, especially because it's your home. Home for me is wherever you are."

"I think we should take some time to think about this, not be rash. I don't want your business to suffer because of a bad decision."

She put her fingers on his lips. "Colt, the biggest thing I learned from living here is that happiness is more than a thriving business. I had that with Robert and I wasn't happy. Not like how I am with you."

He lay there for a while, pensive, then finally said, "If it's what you want, we'll make it happen." Then he covered her mouth with his, and whispered against her lips, "I feel the same way about you. You're my home, Delaney. But this Chief Hottie from Hell thing . . . we'll have to talk about that. Later." And then he kissed her.

Epilogue

"What do you think?" Smiling, Delaney stared at the company's new logo on her computer screen.

"You sure you want to go with that name?" Colt gazed over her shoulder as he rubbed her back.

"Of course I am. I picked it." The new brand: Colt and Delaney. It was perfect because they were perfect. And in her heart of hearts, she knew Colt would never take her name.

"Then I think it's great. We'll celebrate tonight, go to the Indian place."

They'd been celebrating every night for weeks and Delaney had never been more secure in a relationship. "That sounds wonderful."

A month ago, she'd found an old John Deere warehouse on the outskirts of Glory Junction and bought the place. With the help of a local architect, she was refurbishing the building and turning it into a combination of executive offices, studio space, and storage for her collections. Karen had found a rental in town and was busy recruiting warehouse workers.

Relocating the company to Glory Junction had been an unintentional PR boon. The media had latched on to the story, lauded Delaney for staying true to her outdoorsy inspired designs by living the country life. In fact, instead of having her garments made overseas, Delaney had vowed to manufacture every piece, including her shoes and handbags, right in the USA. She'd already created a hundred new jobs in Glory Junction.

TJ had set up the retail division of GA and Delaney's adventure wear was blowing off the shelves.

"Honey, you're gonna go blind staring at that logo so long," he said.

"I'm just so happy." She turned around, pulled Colt's face lower, and gave him a kiss. "Aren't you going to be late?"

"Jack and I are meeting with Rita at city hall, so I've got a few minutes." He pulled her out of the chair.

Rita had browbeaten Colt into rescinding his resignation. Colt, being the smart man he was, had recognized his advantage and persuaded her and the rest of the council to approve the budget for a new command-staff position. As soon as they made the hire he'd get two days off a week like a regular person.

"I don't think we have time for what you have in mind," she said.

"Yeah, and what is it that I have in mind?" He looked down the plunging neckline of her nightgown, grabbed her hand, and dragged her out of the studio.

She thought that he would continue to the bedroom and was surprised when he tugged her downstairs. "Where are we going?"

"You'll see."

When he started for the front door, she protested. "We're not dressed." He at least had on a pair of Colt Cargos but was naked from the waist up.

He grabbed a throw blanket off one of the sofas and draped it over her shoulders. "Come with me."

She was too curious not to follow. A blast of cold air hit her as she trailed after him across the deck in her feather mules, and she pulled the blanket tighter. "Colt? What's that in your yard?"

"It's a Bobcat skid-steer loader."

He waltzed her to where the behemoth was parked.

"Why? Why is it in the middle of your yard?" The tractor was an eyesore. "And where did it come from?"

He shrugged, trying to act nonchalant. "My dad knew a guy."

Impatient while she tried to keep up with him in her high-heeled slippers, he picked her up and carried her like a bride.

"This some kind of new adventure thing?" she asked, baffled by what they were doing here.

"Nope." He put her down next to the Bobcat. "I'm planning to clear us a second parking space on the easement road. Pave it in time for winter."

"That's great." They'd talked about it, especially with the snow coming. "Any particular reason you wanted me to get up close and personal with heavy machinery?"

"I just thought we should come out here where it all started."

"What started?"

"Us." He pointed to the parking space where his squad car now sat and dropped to one knee.

Her heart began to race and her palms got clammy. Was he about to . . . ? "Colt?"

"Shush. Let me do this, would you?" He reached into his pants' pocket, hands shaky. "Shit, wrong one."

There were like ten—she'd designed the damn things. Delaney was so filled with anticipation she was about to explode.

He fumbled with one of the snaps, reached inside his right leg pocket, and palmed something, looking supremely proud of himself. Or maybe that was relief she saw in his eyes. Or nerves.

"Hang on a sec." He switched whatever he had to his other

hand and took hers. "Delaney, will you marry me? Will you be my wife? I'll put in that second parking space and even live in your house and let you have mine as extra studio space, whatever you want. Just say yes, because if you say no . . . I love you, Delaney."

Her eyes brimmed with tears and she choked a little with emotion. "The answer is definitely yes."

She didn't wait for him to slip on the ring, just pulled him up and launched herself into his arms. "I love you, Colt Garner."

Dear Reader,

I hope you enjoyed the first full-length novel in my new Garner Brothers series. I love these brothers and I especially love how they have one another's back. I'm the oldest of three siblings and we're as close as close can be, something I'm very thankful for. You know what they say, "blood is thicker than water." Well, that's the Garner brothers.

For Josh and Hannah's story, check out *A Glory Junction Christmas*, in *The Most Wonderful Time*, a Christmas anthology I'm part of with Fern Michaels, Sarah Title, and Shirlee McCoy. If you're familiar with my Nugget Romance series, then you know the fictional town of Glory Junction is only a half hour away from Nugget, in the gorgeous California Sierra Nevada. I suspect from time to time some of Nugget's all-star cast will be wandering into the pages of the Garner Brothers' books.

Next up in the series is TJ's story. I don't want to spoil the plot, so I'm just going to say that I think this story line will surprise you—in a good way, of course. TJ can really use a woman who will help him slow down and enjoy life, instead of spending all his time finagling ways to make Garner Adventure a Forbes 500 company. And I'm aiming to give him one. So stay tuned!

In the meantime, I've been working on a Christmas sequel to *Finding Hope*, the second book in my Nugget series. After unimaginable tragedy, Emily and Clay McCreedy have managed to build a new life together, including having a baby. In *Hope for Christmas* (out this fall), Emily will finally find out what happened to her little girl, who was kidnapped seven years ago. All this time of not knowing has left indelible scars, and the pain is only heightened during the holidays. But she's determined to make this the best Christmas ever for her new family. Then a secret surfaces that changes everything in an instant. . . . Life in Nugget, California, will never be the same.

Want to know when the next book in the Garner Brothers or Nugget series is out? Sign up for the newsletter eepurl.com/bCEHeT. You'll get brief monthly updates on release dates, giveaways, promotions, and exclusive material. Also, follow me on facebook.com/stacyfinzauthor and twitter.com/sfinz, as well as stacyfinz.com/contact.

Cheers,
Stacy

More from Bestselling Author
JANET DAILEY

Calder Storm	0-8217-7543-X	**$7.99US/$10.99CAN**
Close to You	1-4201-1714-9	**$5.99US/$6.99CAN**
Crazy in Love	1-4201-0303-2	**$4.99US/$5.99CAN**
Dance With Me	1-4201-2213-4	**$5.99US/$6.99CAN**
Everything	1-4201-2214-2	**$5.99US/$6.99CAN**
Forever	1-4201-2215-0	**$5.99US/$6.99CAN**
Green Calder Grass	0-8217-7222-8	**$7.99US/$10.99CAN**
Heiress	1-4201-0002-5	**$6.99US/$7.99CAN**
Lone Calder Star	0-8217-7542-1	**$7.99US/$10.99CAN**
Lover Man	1-4201-0666-X	**$4.99US/$5.99CAN**
Masquerade	1-4201-0005-X	**$6.99US/$8.99CAN**
Mistletoe and Molly	1-4201-0041-6	**$6.99US/$9.99CAN**
Rivals	1-4201-0003-3	**$6.99US/$7.99CAN**
Santa in a Stetson	1-4201-0664-3	**$6.99US/$9.99CAN**
Santa in Montana	1-4201-1474-3	**$7.99US/$9.99CAN**
Searching for Santa	1-4201-0306-7	**$6.99US/$9.99CAN**
Something More	0-8217-7544-8	**$7.99US/$9.99CAN**
Stealing Kisses	1-4201-0304-0	**$4.99US/$5.99CAN**
Tangled Vines	1-4201-0004-1	**$6.99US/$8.99CAN**
Texas Kiss	1-4201-0665-1	**$4.99US/$5.99CAN**
That Loving Feeling	1-4201-1713-0	**$5.99US/$6.99CAN**
To Santa With Love	1-4201-2073-5	**$6.99US/$7.99CAN**
When You Kiss Me	1-4201-0667-8	**$4.99US/$5.99CAN**
Yes, I Do	1-4201-0305-9	**$4.99US/$5.99CAN**

Available Wherever Books Are Sold!

Check out our website at **www.kensingtonbooks.com.**